FIRST

"Work, Miss Seldon? *Work?* Is that all you ever do? Is life for you nothing more than the drudgery of a print shop?"

Samarra glared at him. "You know nothing of me, Mr. Holbrooke. At least I don't waste my days translating some worthless piece of literature!"

"So . . . the kitten shows her claws." A lazy grin played upon his mouth. Suddenly he reached out and caught her against him in a viselike grip. "I like holding you, my little hellcat," he whispered.

Before she had a chance to resist, his lips feathered hers, brushing ever so softly against her mouth until she gasped. She felt his elbow brush against her breast, felt his fingertips glide down her throat and around her neck to entangle themselves in her hair. The warmth of his embrace melted her anger. Of its own volition her body pressed closer to his.

"My god, Samarra," he whispered hoarsely. "You don't have any idea what you do to me!"

She responded hungrily to his kiss. It was what she had wanted, what she had dreamed of since the moment he'd walked through her door.

ELIZABETH LEIGH
COUNTERFEIT
CARESS

ZEBRA BOOKS
KENSINGTON PUBLISHING CORP.

For my sister,
Sherri Barr Pearce,
whom I love for many reasons,
for friendship most of all

With warmest regards to Melissa Crockett,
who taught me how much the blind really see,
and to her mother, Bunny,
whose strength of character and unshakable optimism
still amaze me—after all these years

And to Mary Ann and Lenora—
what would I ever do without you?

ZEBRA BOOKS

are published by

Kensington Publishing Corp.
850 Third Avenue
New York. NY 10022

First printing: November, 1991

Printed in the United States of America

10 9 8 7 6 5 4 3 2

Chapter One

Samarra Seldon sat pensively at her desk, her chin resting on her open palm, her other hand absently stroking the long white fur of a large cat curled up in her lap, her golden brown eyes staring blankly at the printer's proof in front of her. Georgiana had outdone herself this time, but it was not the finely detailed image created from her sister's copperplate engraving which claimed the master printer's attention. Beneath Samarra's indifferent scrutiny the intricate scrolls and swirls which composed the border of the theater program undulated in rippling, pulsating waves.

"I don't know what to do, Clementine," she whispered to the cat, who purred contentedly, then stretched its front paws outward, claws splayed, and yawned. "If only Papa were here to counsel me . . ." Samarra's voice trailed off as she lifted her gaze from the proof and allowed it to settle on the cold ashes in the fireplace.

Autumn had arrived in Williamsburg, and with it cool nights and pleasant days. This time of year was Samarra's favorite, for it brought not only more tolerable weather, but one of the Public Times as well. During Williamsburg's sweltering summers and drizzling winters, the town drowsed lazily, its occupants stirring only a bit now and then to weed a garden, cut some firewood, or mend a fence. By contrast, spring and fall were wild, crowded times, for it was during those seasons that the General Assembly and the General Court met in this colonial capital. The great planters and their retinues rode in from Virginia's tidewater estates; lawyers, defendants, and plaintiffs crowded into the taverns; politicians gathered to discuss taxes and tyranny; businessmen assembled to buy and sell, coordinate shipping schedules, and set prices for the year's tobacco crop.

Under normal circumstances, Randolph Seldon conducted much of his business during these times. But these were not normal circumstances.

No, the only thing normal about them had been the departure of summer's heat and humidity and the advent of cooler, drier temperatures coupled with the brisk, vibrant crowds of people pouring into the town, changes which normally invigorated Samarra's spirits in a way nothing else could. In the fall she was a veritable powerhouse of energy, all sixty inches and one hundred pounds of her. Nanna would groan indulgently when Samarra began making her lists of chores and odd jobs she wanted accomplished before winter set in. But the ever-faithful servant, who had, over the years, achieved family status, would cluck her tongue and begin organizing a work force to complete the tasks.

If additional help was required, Samarra would hire it; carpenters, painters, masons, another gardener. Randolph Seldon could easily afford the extra expense, and though he pretended to indulge his daughter's whims, deep down he was proud of her take-charge attitude and her ability to determine what was needed and see to it that everything went smoothly.

But this fall of 1754, the year that marked Samarra's and Georgiana's twenty-fourth, was different. Their father, Randolph, was not in residence, could not, therefore, tease and cajole Samarra about her annual binge. His absence prevented his arrangement, on Samarra's behalf, of suitable escorts to the theater, to a puppet show, or to a goodly number of the many balls held during the Public Times. If he had been home, he would have also assisted her in ridding her professional life of one pesky—and, Samarra thought, potentially dangerous—Sloane O'Quinn. But he was not at home, and this was one problem she would just have to deal with on her own.

A successful merchant, Randolph had made regular trips to London until some six years ago, when he had hired an agent to represent his business interests. "I'm getting too old to continue traipsing all over the world," he had told his daughters, who were not convinced his age had anything to do with the decision. Although he'd never said so, they both knew he had grown concerned about their future, their continued welfare long after his demise. He had devoted the better part of these six years foraging for suitable beaus for one staunchly independent daughter and worrying over the even more uncertain prospects for the other.

But Randolph's agent had quite suddenly resigned, leaving an important business deal in the lurch, and the merchant had been forced to travel to London. He had been gone only a fortnight, but already Samarra missed him terribly. She had become accustomed to having him close by, sharing her problems with him, and bantering with him over his efforts toward seeing her married. The four of them—Samarra, Georgiana, Randolph, and Nanna—were fiercely independent in their own ways, yet they clung to each other in a bond of mutual dependence that enhanced rather than stifled

7

each one's individuality. Randolph's unscheduled absence had forced Samarra to assume his role of mediator and protector, a role which had begun to weigh heavily upon her shoulders.

Despite her concern over her own immediate future, Samarra smiled to herself as bits and pieces of memories flitted through her head, fragmented visions of first one and then another potential suitor her father had found for her. Randolph made a habit of introducing her to proper gentlemen, hoping, she was certain, that the combined virtues and appearance of one of them would satisfy her criteria and he would see her married happily, if not deliriously. "Let's be honest with each other, Papa," she had told him once in her typically straightforward manner. "I am destined for spinsterhood, and you know it as well as I."

"No, I don't," he had rejoined. "Nor do I think you honestly want to remain unmarried all your life, Samarra. Spinsterhood is really not a viable alternative for you. If any woman ever deserved a husband's love and devotion, you do. Spinsterhood is merely something you cling to because you fear the consequences of marriage."

Samarra had gasped in outrage. "Papa! You can't be serious! I've never been afraid of anything in my life! You know the reasons things have to remain this way."

"They aren't reasons, Sam. They're excuses."

Were they merely excuses? she had pondered often since. They seemed so real to her, so much a part of her very existence that she could not imagine exchanging her current obligations for those of wife and mother. Neither could she imagine combining two such diverse life-styles. Yet there were times when she somewhat desperately felt the need of a lifelong male companion, when she yearned for children born of such a union.

But this was territory she had neither the time nor the

inclination at present to explore. She shook her head in an effort to restore a proper perspective.

"Get down," she told Clementine irritably, but her hands gently lifted the heavy feline off her lap, belying the sharpness of her tone. "Go find a mouse or something. You're the laziest being around here. There must be something else you can find to do besides heating up my lap." Ignoring her mistress's command, Clementine sauntered lethargically to the hearth rug, plopped herself upon it, and curled again into a placid ball. "I'll forgive you this time," Samarra said, her voice much softer now, "but only because you're soon to become a mother!"

Despite all her efforts, Samarra found her thoughts refusing the sanctuary of tranquility. *I won't let O'Quinn see that I'm troubled,* she promised herself, stealing another peek at the small clock on her desk. It was almost two. Something to do . . .

Samarra retrieved the program proof from the top of her desk and frowned in concentration, her thoughts centered once more on a possible solution to her present problem.

To an observer less astute than British Army Lieutenant Colonel Clinton Holbrooke—or at least, one not so well informed, the diminutive blonde woman's narrowed eyes and ruffled brow would have indicated her intense displeasure at the appearance of the program sheet. Holbrooke stood outside the front window of her shop, involuntarily wriggling his broad shoulders beneath the unaccustomed feel of a fine lawn shirt and long velvet frock coat, his piercing gaze quickly assessing this young woman whose business he had been ordered to investigate. That she was troubled he harbored no doubt, but he did not believe that her tribulation stemmed from the printed page in her slightly trembling hand.

9

Only the exquisite lines of her profile were visible to him until, seeming to sense that someone watched her, she slowly lifted her eyes and turned her head toward the window. Clint quickly masked the shiver that sluiced through his entire length, which was considerable, by doffing his dark green felt bicorne at her and then taking the three or four steps necessary to reach the street entrance. He stopped in front of the portal, one hand resting on the large brass handle, the other holding the bicorne in front of him while he ordered his racing pulse to return to normal.

Lord, but she was one beautiful woman!

Clint chastised his body for its response to the vision of loveliness before him. If he were to accomplish his mission, he must, he knew, separate himself, both physically and emotionally, from this woman. Only a business relationship was required. The last thing he needed was to have his heart tripping over his good judgment. He had allowed that to happen to him once—and once had been quite enough for a lifetime.

However had he managed to get involved in this investigation? he wondered, knowing he would be unable to deny the governor any reasonable request— nor had he denied him this one. Yet this sort of thing went beyond his usual military duties, went beyond his realm of experience. Had Robert Dinwiddie mistakenly thought him capable?

"No one else holds your reputation for maintaining a calm aloofness in the face of adversity," the governor had told him. "You have a sharp mind and keen wit; in short, a coalition of personality traits which could not constitute a more perfect match for the successful performance of the tasks required. That's why I've personally selected you as chief investigator for this case."

"If you're so certain she's guilty, why don't you just

arrest the woman and be done with it?" Clint had asked.

"Because then I would have only her, and I'm convinced there's a conspiracy involved in this counterfeiting scheme. Her hand may be the master behind the printing press, but she can't possibly be the only one responsible for scattering the currency so widely."

"Do you think, then, that her father is involved as well?"

"Possibly. His extensive worldwide business interests would certainly provide the opportunity." Dinwiddie's eyes had narrowed then and his mouth had pursed momentarily. "I need more evidence, Clint—cold, hard evidence. And a list of her co-conspirators. As you well know, I must devote most of my time and thoughts to the current political unrest—this trouble with the French. It's possible this counterfeiting scheme is somehow connected. Do whatever you have to do, take as much time as you need . . . but get me that evidence!"

Clint had never considered losing his notorious composure as Governor Dinwiddie had outlined the problem at hand. But just looking at the object of this inquest had given his senses a jolt unlike any they had ever experienced. As he pushed open the door, he compelled himself to remember the cause for his visit and its probable consequences.

Samarra smiled pleasantly at the tall, well-groomed stranger, laying the blame for the jolt her own senses had received upon her relief in not knowing this man. She was fully expecting a visit this afternoon from Sloane O'Quinn, and though she, too, had never failed to look adversity squarely in the face, neither could she quell the small comfort derived from its postponement. Yet her customary "How may I help you?" sounded mundane and quite inadequate to the occasion.

11

For a long moment they stood rooted to the planked floor, Samarra's chin lifted expectantly, Clint's lowered in deference to her shorter stature, his opaque hazel eyes boring into her glittering brown orbs. Her eyes reminded him of bottomless topaz. His reminded her of a soft October morning as this one had been.

His lashes were long and thick, their color a rich, satiny black, the ends slightly curled. They were lashes that would stir a monstrous envy in most women, but they served only as a source of fascination to Samarra. She noted the wide set of his eyes, the tiny crinkles at their corners, the thick, russett brows arched now, bespeaking his own amusement.

Her gaze traveled the length of his straight nose downward to settle on the width of his generous mouth. His lips appeared chiseled, the lower one sensuously full, the upper bow-shaped, its valley complimenting the dimple in his chin. She wondered how those lips would feel against her own and longed to place the tip of her forefinger in the indentation in his chin. As her musings suddenly pierced her consciousness, the delicate bones of her cheeks bloomed a becoming rosebud pink. Whatever had made her think such a thing?

The slanting rays of the autumn sun cast their golden glow upon the silken strands of Samarra's honey-colored hair, its skein twisted into a thick knot at her nape; curling wisps had escaped to the refuge of her slender neck, defying the intended severity. Clint found himself wondering how her hair would look loose of its pins, long and flowing down her back. The sun's light illuminated the healthy glow upon the delicate bones of one cheek, casting the other in shadow.

Clint's hazel gaze reluctantly pulled itself from her face—even as his thoughts pulled themselves from the mental picture of her untethered locks—and followed

12

the light all the way to the bare wooden floor, where it puddled around the hem of her skirts. For the briefest of moments, as neither moved nor spoke, it appeared to Clint that the sun had chosen this woman alone upon whom to shed its light, forsaking all others. Then she moved toward him, out of the light, and he stared at it in some dismay when it did not move with her.

Mistaking the cause of his discomfiture, and quite relieved at having been so conveniently presented with a different subject upon which to focus her thoughts, Samarra grinned impishly when her new customer opened his mouth to speak, closed it again, and then cleared his throat. Certain that the blame for his momentary perturbation lay upon the sight of her ink-splotched apron, she had watched in black amusement as his eyes had traveled her length. Despite her excellent professional reputation, the obvious display of stark surprise and barely suppressed skepticism such as this man demonstrated continued to rankle.

But Samarra had learned long ago how to put men at ease when they visited her shop. Her technique began with the impish grin, then she would say sweetly, "Folks are usually startled when they first meet me." She would make a show of wiping her right hand carefully on her apron, even if it was spotless, then extend it warmly, as a man would do. Curtsies never failed to undermine her credibility. The impish grin and sweet voice charmed while the handshake proclaimed her professionalism. It was an unexpected combination that seldom failed to win over new clients, and once they had seen the results of her work, they returned to her shop, eventually forgetting—almost, anyway—that they were dealing with a woman.

She went through the motions by rote, adding as she always did, "I'm Samarra Seldon, but you may call me Sam." Little did she know that her words and manner saved him from an explanation of his behavior, which Clint Holbrooke was hard-pressed to make.

Damn it, Holbrooke! he chided himself. *Start thinking and quit reacting!* In spite of the resolve he had made as he opened the door, her delicate beauty had continued to disarm him, and he attempted to shake off her spell as he resumed his assigned role. His efforts were not wholly effective.

"Pleased to make your acquaintance, I'm sure." His rich, mellow baritone lent more eloquence to the pat response than it deserved. He accepted her proffered hand with some trepidation, for Clint Holbrooke was not accustomed to shaking hands with a woman. Her palm felt pleasantly warm and soft . . . and so very small! . . . against his own large, callused one. The warmth radiated upward, making aspic of his elbow and shoulder joints as it traversed his right appendage before settling somewhere near his throat. When he opened his wide mouth to speak again, his voice squeaked from the constriction. Quickly he harnessed the flush which threatened to stain his cheeks as he cleared his throat.

Although she was careful not to let it show, Samarra was as surprised as he at the unexpected warmth generated by their clasped hands. When dampness began to seep between their palms, she loosened her grip and withdrew her hand. How long had she held his hand? she wondered. Longer than necessary, she reluctantly admitted. Longer than common courtesy required. Never before had she felt so . . . so weak! So devoid of control. And she wasn't at all sure she liked this new feeling.

The businesslike demeanor in his voice broke her preoccupation. "And I am Clint Holbrooke." With his now free right hand, he removed a leatherbound packet from inside his frock coat. "I have a small but rather

14

complicated printing job for you."

His hazel eyes darted about the compact, meticulously kept room, searching for a surface upon which to display the contents of the portfolio. Two long, modestly dressed windows flanked the entrance, their tab curtains pulled back to allow the sun's rays to flood the room. The uncluttered, serviceable oak desk at which he had observed Samarra sitting occupied the space next to a fireplace, in front of which a white cat lay asleep. Jars of ink and stacks of paper were neatly arranged on shelves along the back wall. To his immediate left, a counter jutted out from the wall opposite the fireplace, its length protecting an inside door. Framed printing samples decorated the walls. Neatness reigned, orderliness served, their monotony broken only by a squatty ceramic vase full of bright yellow cushion mums and the sleeping cat. Yet the room exuded a certain warmth for which there existed no readily apparent explanation.

Clint laid the packet upon the counter, next to the mums, and opened it to reveal a collection of rough sketches and scribbled notes. Samarra had joined him there, and when she thought he would explain the task required of her, he surprised her by asking, "You *do* print and bind books here?"

She could not resist allowing the impish grin to claim her small mouth again, turning up its corners even as it ignited a sparkle of gold flecks in her irises. Would she always and forever be forced to deal with skeptical men? It seemed so. Silently Samarra offered a thank-you to the Almighty for blessing her with a sense of humor. "My shingle proclaims this establishment as that of printer and binder, Mr. Holbrooke," she reminded him coolly, her voice devoid of malice. "I have no desire to stand accused as either liar or swindler before a magistrate."

So absorbed was her customer in the delicate timbre of her voice that he paid little heed to her words at first. Then, as they penetrated one by one, his neck stained the color of raspberries, the suffusion traveling slowly upward until he felt it burn upon his cheeks. How dare this . . . this snip of a woman imply his . . . his inability to read! Oh, she would stand before a magistrate, all right, as both liar and swindler! He would see to that. The stocks were too mild for Mistress Samara Seldon. 'Twould be the hangman's noose for her. The lieutenant colonel in him attempted to visualize the kick of her dainty feet as they succumbed to death's throes, and he found himself suddenly and quite involuntarily sickened by the thought.

Clint Holbrooke's voice carried his irritation at her words, at his innate unwillingness to expose her, at Dinwiddie's involving him in the entire affair. "I wish to have a book made," he said through clenched teeth. "Call me a sentimental fool, if you wish"—*God's blood! Why did I say that?*—"but I want to present my mother with a printed and bound collection of her own original poems."

Was this his complicated printing job? Samarra suspected the only complication would arise from his need of it on the morrow. Why did people always wait until the eleventh hour to place a special order? "And I suppose her birthday is tomorrow?"

"No—well, actually her birthday was last week, and I realized too late that this was what I wanted to give her. The book will be for Christmas."

Never before had a lie sat so heavily upon his conscience. Clint Holbrooke was no stranger to subterfuge, but never before had he been forced to involve his deceased mother in his duplicity—or to deal with a woman. Now he wondered whence Dinwiddie had secured the poems, only one of which, in Clint's inexpert opinion, was worthy of being termed poetic. A vision of his somewhat stiff-necked mother blanching at being named their author tickled his fancy. Why, she would turn over in her grave if she knew! He relaxed his jaw and smiled despite himself.

"Good! This job will require a minimum of several weeks' work." As she spoke, Samarra's slim fingers rifled the papers. Clint's hazel gaze pinned itself on their movement. For someone who crafted with ink, her fingers were exceptionally clean, their nails ending in sculpted ovals. The backs of her hands looked enticingly soft, inviting a caress. Without conscious thought, Clint reached to touch them, then came to his senses just in time to pull his own hand away from hers, placing it instead upon the top sheet in the packet, his index finger pointing to the first sketch and accompanying instruction.

"I'm not an artist," he explained, his voice thick again, "and should you not have someone in your employ who can, with more skill than mine, render these illustrations to paper, I will hire someone to do so." A russet eyebrow raised itself to mid-forehead. He felt rather than saw her slightly nod.

"No need for that."

"I trust you can read my handwriting, and that of my, um, mother?"

Samarra glanced through the papers, pausing occasionally to read one of his notes before moving on to the poems. When she had satisfied herself that the penmanship was entirely legible, she nodded her assent. Gathering up the papers, she moved toward her desk. "I do have some questions, though." Her inclined head indicated the opposite side of the fireplace. "Why don't you pull up that chair and make yourself comfortable, Mr. Holbrooke, while I make some notes of my own?"

17

Just as they had settled themselves at the desk and Samarra had dipped a quill in an inkwell, the door flew open, giving passage to both a strong breeze and a tall, slender man with a hawkish nose and penetrating eyes of a blue that was uncommonly pale—eerily so. The man's long black cloak flapped around his stockinged calves and his black tricorne sat low on his forehead, lending him a sinister appearance. A multitude of dry, cracking, slippery elm leaves followed him inside, their reddish-brown corpses swirling around the buckled shoes on his feet before he lifted a hand to shove the heavy portal closed. Clint watched the leaves settle upon the planked floor, heard the sharp hiss of Samarra's indrawn breath at his side.

Had the intruder not been Sloane O'Quinn, Samarra might have associated the color of the leaves with that of Clint's russet hair. But the man *was* Sloane O'Quinn, a man Sam had recently begun to despise—and fear. Slowly she released the air from her lungs, gathering her mettle in preparation for the battle which was certain to ensue.

I haven't changed my mind.

She ran the words through her mind again for good measure, but before she could utter them, O'Quinn barked, "Leave us. I have business with Miss Seldon."

In the blink of an eye, Clint Holbrooke vacated his chair and took three long steps toward the black-caped man, to stand, his long legs spread wide, mere inches from O'Quinn's nose. His hazel eyes flashed defiance but his voice was deceptively smooth and soft. "As do I, and I was here first."

"You can return later."

"So can you. I'm not leaving."

"I have an appointment with Miss Seldon."

"Whatever business you have with her can wait."

Samarra had risen from her chair a split second after

Clint and moved behind the protection of the counter. For once she found herself grateful for her short stature as she reached to the back of the top shelf, her fingers feeling among brown paper-wrapped packages tied with twine which awaited delivery. Although neither man seemed to pay any attention to her, she was careful to watch them. Her petite stature allowed her hand to roam without her having to stoop down, and the bulk of the counter hid her action. Somewhere on this shelf . . .

Her hand closed over the cold steel and she released the breath she had been subconsciously holding. The flintlock pistol was heavier than she remembered, and she used her left hand to grasp its handle as the fingers of her right hand clutched the barrel tightly. Had she checked its priming this morning? she wondered, the trip-tripping of her heart obscuring rational thought. Checking the pistol's priming was as much a part of her early morning ritual as unlocking the door and opening the curtains. Since her father had left for England, she had been doubly sure to inspect her weapon daily.

If Clint Holbrooke was carrying a firearm or any other weapon, he had it well concealed. Nor could she see that O'Quinn sported a weapon, but she did not doubt that he did. The man was utterly ruthless. Her new customer was a fool to argue with O'Quinn, she thought before she dropped her eyes to witness the younger man's clenched fists held tightly against his thighs. Her gaze traveled upward again to Holbrooke's face, where a tick had appeared in his cheek, giving away his barely suppressed ire. Maybe the man was not so great a fool as she had thought. There seemed to be a strength about him that his politeness of speech and manner of dress had effectively camouflaged. In the face of jeopardy he comported himself with the dignity and certain knowledge of superiority one saw in a cougar—

19

sleek and beautiful, yet quietly and innately dangerous.

She stood silently, watching him defy O'Quinn, practically begging the man to throw the first punch; now that some of her fear had subsided, Samarra studied him more closely. With her eyes, she noted the burnished copper gleam of his thick, short-cropped hair, the way its ends curled on the bronze column of his broad neck. Her gaze traveled to the planes of his face, the high cheekbones shadowing hollows above a strong, square jaw. She noted how the rugged masculinity of those features combined so well with the beauty of his eyes, the sensuality of his mouth.

With her heart she saw his confident stance, the inner strength radiating from his very being, collaborating with the thick muscles bulging now beneath the close cut of his garments to create a man who could stand up to a cad like Sloane O'Quinn and live to tell about it.

That one was backing down now, his harsh, gravelly voice apologizing to Clint Holbrooke even as his long, bony fingers pulled the black cloak around his narrow trunk, and his skinny legs began a slinking lope toward the door.

Samarra relaxed, returned the flintlock to its assigned place beneath the counter, stooping now to assure herself that she was putting it well behind the packages, out of the way of Tom's somewhat clumsy grasp. From the corner of her eye she saw Holbrooke turn away from O'Quinn, away from the door, and start walking back to his chair beside her desk. The dry leaves crackled again as the door opened. She released a long breath and closed her eyes, willing the thrumming of her heart to slow its pace. Later, she knew, O'Quinn would return, and she would have to deal with him then. But for now he was gone.

At the same instant, it seemed, she heard the knife whistle through the air, caught the visual white flash of

20

Clementine's body slicing in a wide arc across the room, and tasted fear.

Clint Holbrooke fell.

Clementine yowled.

And the heavy oak portal slammed shut behind Sloane O'Quinn.

Chapter Two

Samarra gasped when she rounded the corner of the counter. One hand flew upward, covering her mouth as the bile rose in her throat; the other clutched and squeezed a fistful of her apron skirt.

Clint Holbrooke lay prone on the planked floor in front of the counter, his body completely still, blood puddling next to his right thigh.

Uncharacteristically, Clementine rubbed her swollen belly against Holbrooke's arm, her soft mews the only sound in the stillness of the room.

Samarra gratefully acknowledged the feline's salvation from harm, though she was startled by Clementine's action. The cat generally took her time warming up to strangers, and her natural reticence was even more pronounced during her pregnancies. But Sam's greater concern, however, was Mr. Holbrooke's immediate care.

"Scoot, Clem," she admonished gently, going down on her knees and applying two fingers to the man's neck. She breathed easier when she felt a strong pulse. Her first instinct was to roll him over, but Samarra quickly discarded the notion. His left side was almost flush with the counter, prohibiting movement in that direction, and she did not think it wise to place any weight on his injured right leg. She was, in all probability, not strong enough to move him anyway. Samarra wished with all her heart that she was.

And that her constitution was stronger, too. The sight of blood turned her stomach inside out, but there was no one else to care for Holbrooke, and Samarra didn't want to leave him unattended. Her limited association with O'Quinn lent her no assurance that he would not return to finish the job. Was O'Quinn a complete fool? she wondered, for he must know she would stand witness against him. The thought only increased her queasiness. Would he indeed return and make her the victim of his wrath as well?

Samarra closed her eyes tightly for a moment and willed her racing heartbeat to decelerate; then slowly she lifted her eyelids. The man had fallen with his left arm outstretched, his right reaching for the nasty gash in his leg, his face turned toward the window. Samarra lifted his hand and folded the lower portion of his arm forward to allow her access to the cut. She forced herself to inspect the wound, fighting the constriction in her throat and chest and the pain in her swelling glands as her fingers pulled the blood-sticky fabric away from the flesh laid bare by O'Quinn's knife. Swallowing the acrid taste of her revulsion, she watched the blood spurt from the ugly gash and determined it to be deeper than she had originally thought.

Staunch the bleeding, she thought immediately.

She stumbled to her feet, stumbled to her desk, fumbled around in the top drawer until she found a pair of scissors. These she used to cut a slit into the hem of her petticoat. When she had torn away a length of cloth, she hurried back to Holbrooke. Folding up several layers from one end, Samarra applied the thickness to the wound and pressed the white linen against the flowing blood. When the bleeding seemed to subside, she wrapped the remainder of the strip around the heavily muscled thigh and tucked in its end.

Holbrooke winced as a searing flame of pain shot through his thigh. By slow degrees, consciousness returned. Through the haze of pain, Clint wondered what had hit him. The grimace that marred his features was as much from the effort of recalling the last few moments before he'd fallen as from the pain in his leg and the burning in his lungs, caused from having the breath knocked out of him. The silvery glimmer of Samarra's pistol as the light had bounced off its barrel pierced his thoughts: had she shot him? Had the governor been right about Samarra Seldon? And who was that skull-faced man? Was he involved in her schemes? Damnation! The pain!

She was trying to help him, he knew, but she was obviously no nurse. Her handling of him was gentle enough, yet awkward. There was much here to be uncovered, but for the moment Holbrooke's suffering superseded his efforts at rational judgment.

Sitting back on her haunches, Samarra stared for a moment at her handiwork, a brief smile of relief touching her lips before the white fabric stained scarlet with a renewed gush of life-giving blood.

Life-taking, too, she thought, a fresh wave of hysteria sweeping through her, but this time the panic was coupled with guilt. The man had been injured, perhaps seriously, on her premises—and by a man she should have ordered away herself. *If only I had been firmer with O'Quinn before today! If only I had interfered when he and Holbrooke were arguing! I had the pistol in my hand! Why didn't I threaten to use it?* But that was wishful thinking, and it would not change her present problem.

She couldn't just allow the man to lie there on her floor and bleed to death. Like it or not, she would have to go for a doctor.

She hadn't heard the back door open, and the sound of Tom's voice startled her.

"Where are you, Miss Samarra?" he called as he came through the connecting door between the workroom and the outer office. "You need me to deliver any of these packages for you?" She could hear the youth rummaging through the contents of the shelves on the opposite side of the counter.

"No, I—" Her voice caught in her throat.

Clint Holbrooke had decided it was time to produce some indication of his consciousness. He moaned and his eyelids fluttered open. He tried to move, lifting his stomach off the floor, then collapsed, letting Samarra think weakness had overcome him. Indeed, his injury was causing him severe pain, but the tiniest essence of a plan was beginning to form in his mind. A bit of playacting now could solidify the half-baked scheme later—nor would its production cause any repercussion should he decide to change tactics later.

"Be still!" Samarra ordered softly but firmly. "Tom, go fetch Dr. Hargrove."

"No! No leech monger!" The words were low but sharp, and distinctively spoken.

"Holy moly, what happened to him?"

Tom's voice came from overhead. Samarra glanced up to see her apprentice leaning over the counter. In her consternation she overlooked his swearing. "Run next door and tell Nanna I need her. Tell her to bring a clean white sheet and something with which to cleanse this man's wound. And, Tom!" she called to his retreating back. *"Hurry!"*

In early June, Tom Wainwright had convinced Samarra to let him work for her during the summer

25

months. "Every printer needs a devil," he had quipped, his boyish grin brightening his face. In truth, she really didn't need any extra help—she had thought. A winsome sixteen-year-old possessing both a capacity for laboring long hours without complaint and a genuine interest in printing, Tom had soon carved his own niche in her business. Now, Samarra wondered at times how she had ever managed without him. When the school session had resumed in September, he had wanted to drop out and continue to work for her fulltime, but Sam had insisted he finish his education. He came every weekday afternoon and all day on Saturday, and next year, when he graduated, he would become her full-time assistant.

Holbrooke had fainted again. Samarra glanced around the room, looking for O'Quinn's knife, and spied it on the floor between her desk and the fireplace, Holbrooke's blood coating its wide blade. While she had no desire to touch the vile weapon, now that she had found it, she could not seem to remove her gaze from its carved ivory hilt. A bit unsteadily she rose to her feet and walked slowly toward the knife. Her hand was almost on its hilt before it occurred to her that she would be tampering with evidence if she removed it. When Tom came back with Nanna, she would send him for the constable—and Dr. Hargrove, too, despite Holbrooke's request.

Why did he not want a doctor? Had he something to hide? She reminded herself that this man was a stranger to her, that she had nothing more than his word that his name was Clint Holbrooke. Samarra gave close scrutiny once more to Holbrooke's appearance. There was nothing criminal looking about him, and yet there was something unusual, something out of the ordinary. But what could a doctor expose that Holbrooke wanted to remain hidden? Perhaps he had merely had an unpleasant experience with a physician. He seemed such a nice man. No criminal would order a book of his mother's poems, would he?

Samarra's reflections were cut short by Nanna's bustling entrance.

"Do na burden me now wi' the tale, lassie." The Scottish woman thrust a neatly folded bed sheet into Samarra's arms. "Just tear that into nice, wide strips for me. Tom, hand me that chair cushion for his head, then come hold his leg up while I clean it with witch hazel and dress it."

Nanna used the scissors to cut a long slit in Holbrooke's fancy knee breeches, then handed the scissors over to Samarra, who collapsed into her desk chair and began snipping and tearing the clean muslin sheet. The harsh sound of the rending cloth mingled with Holbrooke's moans—one particularly loud groan sending a cold shiver snaking down her spine—as Nanna and Tom worked over him. Samarra refused to watch.

"Methinks this mon's in shock," Nanna mumbled to no one in particular. "We have t' get him t' a bed and keep him warm, then I have t' find something t' stop his bleedin'. Ye know anything aboot him, Miss Sam?"

"Nothing more than his name, Nanna. We were . . . interrupted before he could tell me much." Samarra hesitated, thinking again about Holbrooke's unwillingness to summon a doctor, then added, "Tom, when Nanna is finished there, you go find the constable."

"That can come later," Nanna said, her wrinkled features contorted as she pulled the bandage tight. "First, let's get him t' bed. Is that bedchamber upstairs still furnished, Miss Sam?"

Nanna was referring to Jacob McCauley's old quarters. Samarra had not had the heart to dispose of any of the aged printer's possessions following his death seven years before. With the exception of dust sheets, his meagerly furnished rooms had remained exactly as he had left them.

"I'll go on up and make the bed," Samarra replied.

"Call out t' old Zeke on the way. Tom and I have na the strength alone t' move him. This mon is heavy!"

Within minutes, it seemed, Clint Holbrooke lay on Jacob's bed in the attic bedchamber. Tom and Ezekiel, the gardener, had removed the stranger's shoes and stockings, his frock coat, and his waistcoat, so that now he lay half-naked, to Sam's way of thinking, beneath a sheet and lightweight woven blanket. With some reservation as to propriety, Samarra sat next to the bed, bathing his face with tepid water, wondering if this man were not too warm—despite Nanna's insistence that warmth was required—but not daring to remove the blanket.

Lord, but it was just plain hot in these attic rooms! Hot and stuffy! Her removal of the protective sheets had stirred up dust motes to dance and shimmer in the glitter of sunlight pouring in through the room's one window, which Samarra had opened when she felt drops of perspiration forming on her upper lip. She had often wondered how Jacob had tolerated these rooms for so many years.

Nanna had scurried to the toolshed to collect cobwebs with which to pack the wound, and Tom had been dispatched to find Constable Woodcock. This was such a nasty business—the kind of incident that could not help and might very well harm Sam's enterprise. If any good were to come of it, that would be the arrest of Sloane O'Quinn. Should that occur, he couldn't pester her about selling her business to him . . . at least, not for a while.

Clint Holbrooke's complexion glistened like alabaster beneath the sheen of water clinging to his skin, his pallor causing Samarra to shiver in the close heat of the attic bedchamber. She closed her eyes and saw his face with the dark pink stain of raspberries upon it and wondered how it could have paled so much so quickly. Nanna had assured her that the wound was not of the fatal variety, that with proper supervision and care his leg should heal. At the worst, Nanna had insisted, the stranger might be left with a slight limp. And Nanna knew about such things.

But Sam didn't want him to limp, this man who exemplified strength and vitality. As she gently moved the cloth upon his broad forehead, Samarra tried to convince herself that her feelings were strictly platonic. Yet she could not seem to control the stammering of her heart or rid herself of the knot of dread in the pit of her stomach.

Beneath her tender ministrations, the stranger's features relaxed and his eyelids drifted open. "God," he groaned, "that feels good."

"Does your leg hurt?"

The pink tip of his tongue flicked out to moisten his lips before a weak smile touched them. "Abominably."

It was the truth, he knew, yet he used that truth to play his part to the hilt.

His skin felt clammy beneath his fingertips. Or did the clamminess derive from Samarra's palms? The sight of his tongue had unnerved her, affecting her in a way nothing else ever had. And she wasn't at all sure she liked it. Her voice held the sharpness of anger as she asked, "Are you too warm?"

"Yes—no."

Samarra smiled indulgently and consciously molded her tone into a semblance of politeness. "Well, which is it?"

"I—I'm not sure." His lids shuttered those damnable hazel orbs for a moment as a grimace washed over his features, causing Samarra's throat to constrict in an agony greater than that which he pretended.

"What happened?"

Some of the anger crept back into her voice. "You needn't have assumed the role of my protector, Mr. Holbrooke. O'Quinn is a dangerous man. He hurled a knife at you."

Those damnable hazel eyes opened wide at her verbal assault, but he refused to defend himself. "Who is this man O'Quinn?"

"A pest. He wants to buy my business."

"And you don't want to sell?"

"No."

"Why not? His offer not good enough?" When she didn't answer immediately, he added somewhat caustically, "He's not blackmailing you, is he, Miss Seldon?"

"Good heavens, no!" Her response this time was immediate, but her flagrant denial gave him pause. A line from Shakespeare flitted through his head: "The lady doth protest too much, methinks . . ."

His eyes scanned the room. "Where am I?"

"Upstairs, over the print shop. These were the owner's private rooms."

"Were? Don't you live here anymore?"

"I've never lived here, but from the wads of white hair embedded in the dust sheets, I would venture to say these rooms must be Clem's favorites. *She* lives here, in the shop, so you'll have to put up with her, I'm afraid."

"Clem?" His brow furrowed in confusion.

"The cat . . . Clementine. And she's—well, she's in the family way, so she can be a bit cranky at times."

Clint smiled at the obvious discomfort the latter admission caused her and thought again how the rosy blush of her embarrassment blooming upon the crest of her cheeks only heightened her beauty. "But you—you

30

never lived here?" he prodded.

She shook her head. "No. My father bought the house next door when we moved to Williamsburg a dozen or so years ago. Jacob McCauley owned this shop then. He rather adopted me and—" Samarra almost said "Georgiana," but caught herself in the nick of time, "—and, well, he taught me everything I know about printing, then left me this shop when he died."

"How convenient."

The words came out in a snort, his voice derisive. Samarra frowned, uncertain what she could have said or done to warrant such an attitude from him. A commotion on the stairs prevented her from questioning further the venom behind his words.

His voice changed from disdainful to accusing. "I thought I asked you not to summon a doctor." Before she could reply, the door swung open to admit Tom, Constable Woodcock, and—of all people—Sloane O'Quinn!

Samarra dropped the cloth into the porcelain bowl Nanna had set on a small table by the bed and she shot upward from her chair. *"You!"* she spat. "What are *you* doing here? Constable, arrest this man!"

Jeremiah Woodcock's black bushy eyebrows met in a V on his brow. "Arrest him? What crime has he committed, Miss Seldon?"

"He—he—"

O'Quinn had stepped to the side but remained behind the constable. Samarra's eyes raked his black-clad length, her scrutiny settling on the wily smile bending his too-thin lips. The smile dissolved as he addressed the constable. "I think Miss Seldon believes me to be the perpetrator," he explained smoothly, then turning his attention to Samarra, "when in fact, madam, 'twas I who chased the scoundrel who threw the blade—until he disappeared down an alleyway."

31

"So that's your game! I might have known you would concoct some preposterous tale to cover your actions." Samarra's pulse had begun to beat erratically again, but this time it was utter frustration which triggered its thrum.

"Did you actually see who hurled the knife, Miss Seldon?" Woodcock asked, his fingers scraping his chin in some consternation.

"Actually, no, I didn't. But it must have been O'Quinn," she insisted. "No one else was there."

"And you, Mister—"

"Holbrooke," Clint supplied. "Nay, I had turned my back to the door."

"O'Quinn says when he opened the door to leave your shop he encountered a man holding this knife." Woodcock produced the ivory-handled blade, now wiped clean from behind his back. Samarra shuddered.

"Before I could stop him, he threw the knife at Mr. Holbrooke," O'Quinn continued. "I think he was aiming for this man's back, but my presence in the doorway startled him. You should be thanking me, Miss Seldon. Were it not for me, this man might very well be dead."

Samarra remained unconvinced. "And you believe this man's story, Constable?"

"There are no other witnesses, Miss Seldon."

"Except Clementine," she muttered.

"Pardon?"

"My cat."

"I hardly think—" How utterly preposterous! Woodcock shuffled his feet, uncertain how best to treat her revelation, finally choosing to ignore it. "Do you have enemies, Mr. Holbrooke? A rather short man, perhaps in his early thirties, lanky build, brown hair, generally unkempt?"

Clint rolled his head from side to side on the pillow.

32

"This town is littered with men who fit that description, but none I know who would want to kill me."

"Do you have any reason to suspect Mr. O'Quinn of the deed, Mr. Holbrooke?"

"Not unless he throws a knife at everyone who defies his questionable authority." Clint's voice was smooth but carried the slightest hint of scorn.

"Then I see no reason to detain him. Where can I find you, should this man be located?"

Clint's eyes flickered to Samarra, then back to Woodcock. "I'll let you know."

When a smiling O'Quinn followed the constable out the door, Tom lingered for a moment. "Do you want me to go for Dr. Hargrove now, Miss Samarra?" he asked.

"Yes, please, Tom."

The bellowed *"No!"* that erupted from the bed surprised them both. Samarra's eyes mirrored her concern as she swiveled to face Holbrooke. "Nanna is a good nurse," she explained, "but I would feel much relieved if Dr. Hargrove examined your wound."

"I will have no bloodletter attend me. Nanna's care will suffice."

Samarra dropped the argument and took another tack, pursuing a possibility that had gnawed at her since Nanna's decision to move him upstairs. "Is there someone we should send for? Would you like to go home?"

These were questions Clint Holbrooke knew she would ask eventually, questions for which he had hastily prepared responses as she answered his questions about the apartment. "My residence is in a boardinghouse, Miss Seldon, and I have no one to care for me there. Perhaps you know someone who would be willing to see to my needs until I am on my feet again."

What better way, he had reasoned, to spy on this woman than to be housed in her place of business? Clint was almost grateful to whoever had thrown the knife. And that person, he was quite certain, had been Sloane O'Quinn. Clint didn't believe the man's trumped-up tale any more than Samarra did. The question, then, was not who, but why. O'Quinn was no fool. But it was quite obvious that Samarra didn't like him—and perhaps even abhorred him. Clint wanted to know why. He wanted to know everything there was to know about Samarra Seldon. That was his assignment, after all, and he did not believe Robert Dinwiddie would care what methods he employed to uncover the evidence of her wrongdoing. Hadn't the governor given him such leeway?

His wound pained him much less than he had led her to believe. That he was more than likely able to hobble back to his barracks he had little doubt. But for the time being, he would continue to feign weakness and pain. It suited his purposes better than any other scheme he could have devised. The most immediate problem, he decided, was in keeping away visitors. Too many people knew him, and he didn't want one of them stepping through the doorway and exposing him as the spy he surely was. He couldn't recall ever having met a Dr. Hargrove, but neither did he want the man to pronounce him able to walk.

"Very well, Mr. Holbrooke," Samarra said. "Tom will stay here with you until time to close up shop, then either Nanna or I will sit with you."

"I can stay all night, Miss Samarra," Tom suggested. "I'll just need to tell my ma."

Clint seized the opportunity to discover how much information he could pry from this young fellow. "I will be happy to pay you, Tom," he offered.

Tom turned eager eyes to Samarra.

"Very well," she agreed, feeling somewhat deprived instead of relieved. Without conscious direction, her mind had already begun to spin a fantasy in which she, the heroine, nursed the virile Clint Holbrooke back to health. She—Samarra Seldon, whose stomach sickened at the very thought of providing medical attention for anyone, found herself actually wanting to care for this man.

Although Nanna had prepared a delicious meal consisting of roast leg of lamb cooked with potatoes, carrots, onions, and yellow turnips, and served with big, flaky sourdough biscuits, Samarra spent more time moving the food around on her plate than eating it. If propriety had not demanded she avoid the sickroom, her usual aversion to such places would have precluded her presence there. But that was where she wanted to be.

She had volunteered—with the proper degree of nonchalance, she hoped—to deliver the food trays Nanna had prepared for Tom and Clint, but these had already been sent over via Ezekiel. Seeking another reason to go back to the print shop, Sam had declared her absentmindedness: "I forgot to lock the front door!" Her heart sang as she forced herself to walk sedately away from Nanna and Georgiana, who were sharing a pot of tea after supper.

"Tom'll take care o' that," Nanna called. "What's ailing ye, Miss Sam? Ye're as nervous as a fledgling just pushed out o' the nest. Come, have a cup o' tea. It'll do ye good."

Samarra returned to the table, reclaiming her chair, but she politely refused the tea. "Tom doesn't know anything about nursing. Maybe I—we should walk over and check on Mr. Holbrooke. I would never forgive myself if he took a turn for the worse while he was our guest. Someone needs to collect the dirty dishes anyway."

Nanna pinned Sam with a disapproving look, then sighed wearily. "Will there be na rest for ye till ye see that mon?"

Unable to meet Nanna's gaze, Samarra looked down at her hands folded in her lap.

"Well, ye are na going alone, even if Tom is there. I will na have yere reputation spoiled."

Samarra's chin jerked up. "My reputation? You mean the reputation I have for engaging in a man's profession, for owning a business I didn't inherit from a husband? For being the town prude?"

"Samarra Eileen Seldon!"

It was Georgiana who issued the reprimand. Sam's visage immediately displayed her contrition, but Georgiana couldn't see it. Tea splashed from Georgiana's saucer onto the sparkling white linen cloth as her hand set down the porcelain saucer a bit too quickly. Sam reached forward to cover her twin's shaking hand with her own.

"I'm sorry, George . . . I just lose patience with society sometimes. Even that man Holbrooke talked to me as though he had little confidence in my abilities."

"But it was our shop he brought his business to, Sam," Georgiana countered, her eyes—once so much like Samarra's lustrous brown ones—searching instinctively for her sister's position. Sam winced as she watched the jittery movement of George's white-glazed irises.

Her voice carried her current irritation with the world. "I'm beginning to wonder why I even try anymore. Maybe I *should* sell . . ."

"Ye sound as though ye have an interested buyer, lassie," Nanna observed quietly.

Samarra had not shared with Nanna and Georgiana her problems with Sloane O'Quinn, nor did she intend to. All her adult life she had sheltered her twin sister from the outside world—from the innate cruelty and crudeness of the masses. And although Nanna knew everything about caring for a household, she was ignorant of the workings of the business world, of scheming men and veiled threats. As much as Sam needed, desperately needed, to unburden herself, she would not do so with these two women. She could not bear to worry them unnecessarily, and she could not envision any sage advice on this matter coming from either of them.

So she shook her head in resignation and pasted a smile upon her lips, ensuring that her voice smiled, too, before she spoke. "Whatever would we do, George, you and I, without the print shop? Of course, I'm not going to sell it." *Nor am I going to allow either of you to think I want to see Mr. Holbrooke again, even if I do.* "Of a sudden I'm very tired, Nanna. Perhaps you would collect the dishes and see whether Tom needs anything before we retire. I think I will have a cup of tea with George after all and tell her about our new project."

Chapter Three

A cool night breeze fluttered in through the open window, its erratic breath alternately billowing out the sheer muslin curtains and then retracting them, leaving their diaphanous fabric hanging limply against the sill until the breeze teased them into motion again. Their movements were marked by the flickering silver light from a three-quarter moon hanging suspended in a clear, midnight-blue sky.

Clint Holbrooke sat propped up in Jacob McCauley's bed, his wounded leg resting on two fluffy goosedown pillows. Nanna had brought a flask of brandy—"for medicinal purposes only"—when she'd come to collect the supper trays, repack his wound with a wad of cobwebs, and replace the dressing. It hadn't taken much coaxing later to get young Tom to imbibe.

Getting information from the boy had proved more difficult than Clint had anticipated. Tom seemed determined to guard whatever knowledge he possessed of Samarra Seldon and the operation of her business, an attitude which further convinced Holbrooke that something was amiss. But the brandy was beginning to work its magic, loosening Tom's tongue even as it muddled his brain. Clint hoped that the boy's brain wouldn't become too muddled too quickly.

Tom's pale eyes watched the flight of a beetle as the insect sailed through the open window and landed on the clear glass chimney sheltering the candle flame from the draft. Clint's jaw tightened in frustration as he watched the lad watch the beetle. Tom's eyes were beginning to glaze as the liquor worked its wiles upon him.

His tongue was thickening as well. "What was that you said, Misser Holbrooke?"

"The house next door seems enormous for only two women. Who else did you say lives there besides Miss Seldon and Nanna?"

"Did I say?" Tom scrunched up his face as he attempted to recall the remnants of their conversation. "Oh, yes, there's Miss Samarra's father, but he had to go to London on business. He's a merchant, you know. *Ver-r-ry* wealthy. Miss Samarra doesn't have to work. She runs this print shop 'cause she likes doing it. Mighty good at it, too. Why, she's taught me more 'bout settin' type and runnin' a press than I ever 'spected to learn. Good head for business, too. Always has made a profit, I think. Knows how to invest her money. And she's a lady, always, no matter what."

This track had been the way of it all night. Clint would ask a question, couching it in innocence to avoid arousing Tom's suspicion. Tom would answer it—partially, anyway—and then head off on some tangent, usually some paean lauding his employer. The result: Clint knew very little beyond what he'd known when he'd walked through the door that afternoon.

He tried again. "So there's just Miss Samarra, Nanna, and Randolph Seldon. No one else lives with them? Have they no other family?"

Tom dragged on the flask, then wiped his mouth with the back of his hand. "Oh, sure, there's—they have relatives somewhere. Prob'ly. And Ole Zeke, the gardener, he lives above the stables. But the maid lives with her own family, jes' comes in days. Now that maid! Lor', but she's a purty thing . . ."

Clint cut him off at the pass. "I suppose, with all their wealth and that huge house, they entertain often, especially during the Public Times."

Tom shook his head. "Not really. I think Miss Samarra's 'specting some comp'ny next week, a couple she knows who live on the frontier, comin' in to sell their tobacco. But the Seldons're quiet, hardworking folks who live quiet lives."

"This couple you mentioned . . . ever met them before?"

"Nawsir. Can't even 'member their names. I been workin' for Miss Samarra now for four, five months, and I don't recollect her having no other comp'ny afore."

"You ever met Sloane O'Quinn before this afternoon?"

"Nawsir. Don't b'lieve I have."

The more Tom drank, the more his grammar and diction disintegrated. Clint reached for the flask, gently disengaging it from Tom's loose grasp and drawing a deep swig of its contents. One long pull was all that was left. Small wonder Tom's head was lolling against the back of his chair! Clint felt some remorse for allowing the lad to become intoxicated; but he felt sorrier for the paucity of information that intoxication had gained him. He had not been able to discern whether Tom was just protecting his employer or whether the lad was really ignorant of her felonious activities.

Clint reached for the lamp, extinguished the candle, and settled back against the pillows, his eyes wide open and his mind continuing to stir at the mere dustmotes of information he had collected. His analytical mind first set about reviewing the avenues of motivation and gain which could possibly be derived from the commission of the crime he had been sent to investigate.

Someone was counterfeiting colonial currency at a time when such paper money was practically worthless. Great Britain had yet to issue currency, although a number of European banks had been printing paper banknotes for over a century. These were issued to persons who either had money on deposit or had borrowed money from the bank. In 1685 the French had printed currency on playing cards to be used in their Canadian colonies until more money arrived from France, but these had become so popular they were still being used. Paper money had first been printed in the coin-scarce colonies in the latter part of the previous century, when the colonial government had needed money to pay the cost of military attacks against Canadian colonists. Now, over fifty years later, the colonies had much more paper money than they had gold or silver to exchange it for. Merchants would not accept these notes at face value. A purchaser might, therefore, have to pay several times the price of an item if he purchased it with paper money instead of coin. Monetary gain had thus been eliminated as an incentive in this scheme, yet no other motive made sense.

Govenor Dinwiddie clung tenaciously to a premise which named political sabotage as the motivating culprit behind the scheme, yet even he could not explain what damage might be wrought by such plan. What the governor did know—and know with certainty—was that some person or persons (and he listed toward the plural) had flooded the colony of Virginia with fake currency which was so expertly printed as to defy detection except by one who had been trained to note the minute differences.

Clint had suggested to Dinwiddie that perhaps one of his enemies sought to discredit the governor and thus oust him from his post. If that was the case, the governor had argued—and it was a possibility he had certainly considered—the counterfeiters had failed miserably. Dinwiddie had made the Crown aware of the problem as soon as he himself had learned of it. The response from England had clearly indicated not only support of a full investigation but also complete confidence in Dinwiddie's abilities. Although Dinwiddie sought to keep a lid on this particular felonious activity, fearing a panic of public outrage and fear if much were ever made of it, he had publicized the Crown's continued confidence in his governorship. Such publicity should have alerted the counterfeiters to the failure of their plan and squelched any further print runs. It hadn't.

In his mind, that left only the political unrest with the French as a possible avenue of motivation. But if that was the cause, why were other colonies not beset with a similar problem? And how would counterfeiting something that was practically worthless benefit anyone? The only intention, then, was harm, for the increased production of counterfeit Virginia currency drove down what little value the real article possessed. Why would anyone want to do that?

While the motivation could not be ignored, neither could it be explained. With typical efficiency, Dinwiddie had refocused his attention, settling it on opportunity. Whoever was responsible for printing the money had to have a press and the skill to use it. There were less than a half-dozen master printers in Williamsburg, fewer still scattered throughout the rest of Virginia. Of them all, Samarra Seldon was the only woman, but more important, the only one who led a

42

very private life ... the only one connected to a wealthy and much-traveled merchant who could aid her in dispersing the currency. These facts had pointed the finger of suspicion at her; bits and pieces of information, which by themselves meant nothing, had collectively nurtured that suspicion until the governor *knew* she was one of the guilty parties. But he also knew he had to prove it, not because the Crown required any more evidence than he had compiled, but because he, Robert Dinwiddie, had to know beyond a shadow of a doubt he was right.

In the meantime, Dinwiddie had taken upon himself the responsibility of redeeming the almost valueless money, personally repaying the banks for their losses even as he solicited their cooperative silence on the matter. Thus far, it had cost him little, for paper money was seldom deposited. Instead, it was recirculated over and over. And he was safe from major financial loss, for all that would be required to end his self-imposed responsibility was his public announcement of the counterfeited money that was being circulated and the banks' refusal to accept it on deposit.

A sudden heavy fall of feet bounding up the stairs interrupted Clint's reflections, arresting his attention. The sounds halted at the second-floor landing. He needed a weapon, damn it! His hand snaked out to grasp the glass chimney and remove it from the saucer holding the candle. Moonlight flooded the room, allowing him clear vision of the open doorway connecting the sitting room and bedchamber. With bated breath he waited, holding the chimney near the bedpost, against which he intended to break it, if need be. If the intruder was now crossing the sitting room, he employed far more discretion than he had coming up the stairs, for no sound issued forth from that quarter.

As startling as the initial heavy footfalls had been,

even more startling was the streak of white fur which suddenly leaped across the floor and vaulted onto the bed. In reaction, Clint's hand crashed the fragile glass against the bedpost before he could fully assimilate the identity and relative harmlessness of his late-night visitor.

"Damn you, cat!" he hissed.

Clementine purred loudly and settled her bulk against his wounded leg.

"Watch out! You'll cut yourself!" With one arm he lifted the heavy cat aside and pulled her under the covers, while with the other he gently shook the broken glass onto the floor. A syncopated snore served as the only indication that Tom's sleep had been disturbed.

"Okay, girl," Clint's voice came soothingly now, "I'll let you sleep with me. Though I can't say that I'd mind you being some other female—one with a bit more to offer a man."

His sigh was pensive as he settled himself into a comfortable position, his right hand gliding in long strokes down Clementine's soft back as his eyes focused on the moonlight pouring in through the window. Its silvery glow reminded him of silken strands of golden hair. The soft breath of night danced sensuously upon the gauzy curtains, the rhythm of their billowy pulsing matching that of the throb in Clint's loins.

He groaned, pulled the blanket up under his armpits, and closed his eyes tight, but his efforts won him nothing. Even behind the dark veils of his eyelids and the arm he had thrown over them, the vision of a gossamer-draped figure swayed seductively in an undulating rhythm, her honey hair pale, glistening with moonglow; her slender arms beckoning to him, promising surcease.

*   *   *

The inviting aroma of fresh coffee and sweet rolls summoned Samarra from sleep. For a moment the hollow feeling in her stomach battled with the extreme heaviness of her eyelids. Her stomach emerged the winner.

Still it was with effort that she pushed back the covers and dragged her slender, sleep-heavy legs off the mattress. In bare feet she padded quietly to the dresser, where she poured water from an ewer into a large porcelain bowl and began her morning ablutions. The cool water soothed and revived her spirits, and she held the damp cloth she had used to wash her face against her swollen eyelids until their weighted puffiness subsided.

A warm ache settled itself deep within her abdomen, an ache unlike any other Samarra had felt before. No, she had experienced this same feeling once, she decided; she just couldn't quite place the memory.

The stuff of which dreams are made flitted through her memory much as the play of sunshine and shadow dappled the plush rug beneath her bare feet. The stark reality of those dreams grew in direct proportion to her varying degrees of wakefulness, until with sudden and startling acknowledgment their subject's face stopped wavering before her eyes and Samarra recognized it as that of Clint Holbrooke.

And with that realization came a ravishing wave of memory. The ache had accompanied those dreams, had haunted her sleep and deprived her of necessary rest. Samarra felt the blush of that realization creep up her neck and into her cheeks even as gooseflesh prickled her bare arms. For a moment she folded her arms under her bosom and rubbed her palms against the gooseflesh. But as she considered its source, an intense anger weaseled its way through her, its burn eradicating the shiver of desire. How had she allowed herself to be swayed by something so base . . . so

45

primal? Gradually cold, hard reason replaced the anger. Clint Holbrooke was just a man, bones and muscle and flesh—nothing more, nothing less.

When she appeared at the breakfast table a quarter of an hour later, her blonde hair was neatly bound in a chignon and her gold eyes sparkled with the challenge of a new day. Her entire being had, through concentrated effort, been scrubbed clean of the vestiges of her dreams.

Or so she thought.

She was able to enjoy the cup of coffee she poured for herself, but the first bite of caramelized roll stuck in her throat. With disgust—at the betrayal of her body, not at the delicious roll—she slammed the bun down on her plate and set out for the print shop.

There was only one way to deal with her problem, and that was to send Mr. Clint Holbrooke home! She was not a nursemaid, did not have time to take care of the man. A small voice reminded her he had been injured in her shop, but her resolve argued that she had fulfilled any obligation she owed the man. It was not her fault, after all, that a doctor had not been summoned . . . what if Holbrooke's leg became gangrenous and required amputation? He might very well try to hold her responsible. No, he must go . . . and go immediately.

As she climbed the stairs to Jacob's old quarters, her mind conjured an image of an extremely ill, possibly dying Holbrooke. Tom would be standing by the bed, wringing his hands, and she would send him scurrying to the livery to hire a suitable conveyance. Dr. Hargrove would come, too, shaking his head as the men from the livery, their biceps bulging at the weight of Holbrooke's body, carried the stranger outside and whisked him away. Next Wednesday, when she opened her copy of the *Virginia Gazette*, she would see his

46

obituary and know he had not survived the knife wound.

The scenario had so effectively played itself out in her imagination that she fully expected to open the door upon such a scene. Thus, without the preamble of a knock, she pushed open the door separating the sitting room from the bedchamber, then took one step backward and discovered her feet would retreat no farther.

Clint Holbrooke stood in the center of the room, his right leg propped upon a straight chair, his naked body limned by shafts of the bright yellow sunlight that poured through the thin batiste curtain. A bowl of water had been placed on the seat of the chair, and his left hand dipped a cloth into the bowl. He stood half facing the bed, so that his back and buttocks and a goodly portion of his right side were exposed to Samarra's view.

The angle of his propped leg pulled his right buttock tight; Samarra noted its firmness, compared it to the relaxed left one, and found that it, too, seemed fit. The substantial breadth of his shoulders tapered to a narrow waist, and the muscles in his thighs and calves appeared sculpted, so prominent were they. A dark furring of reddish-brown hair trailed its way down his legs, ending at his ankles and then sprinkling itself across the tops of his toes. The foot upon which he stood exhibited a high arch and narrow heel. Samarra's eyes traversed the length of leg upward until they reached the junction of his thighs. In some horror, she realized that the propped leg obscured her vision from a portion of his exquisite anatomy better left to eternal obscurity.

"Just put my breakfast over there." He motioned toward the table by the bed with a jerk of his head. "And thanks for collecting it for me, Tom. I'll see you this afternoon."

Samarra stood frozen in the open doorway, her mouth as firmly set as her feet. Droplets of water glistened in his russet hair and trickled down his neck, and the wet cloth deposited more droplets as it continued down his furred chest and over the taut muscles of his stomach.

"If my nakedness offends your sensibilities, you may wait in the sitting room. I don't think I can walk that far to retrieve the tray, but I'll be—"

Clint's head had twisted around as he spoke, and at the sight of Samarra standing there he halted in mid-phrase. His wide mouth twisted in a devilish grin and his hazel eyes glinted mischievously. Samarra felt a telltale blush of embarrassment, but she could not seem to drag her eyes from the magnificence of him. For a long moment they stood staring at each other, neither moving nor speaking, until Samarra finally regained use of her feet and turned and beat a hasty retreat down the stairs. As she crossed the workroom, Tom opened the back door.

"Good morning," she called brightly, wondering if Tom had seen her descend the stairs as he passed the back window. She was certain her complexion still wore the pink stain of embarrassment, and she hoped Holbrooke possessed enough couth to keep her blunder a secret. She held the portal open as Tom picked up the tray from the stoop and carried it in.

Tom was not himself this morning. He seemed unsteady on his feet—more so than usual, for his bones had outgrown his muscles, making him a bit clumsy. He also seemed as unwilling to face Samarra as she was to face him.

"You didn't sleep well in that chair, did you, Tom?" she asked solicitously, feeling contrite for allowing the youngster to stay the night. From the looks of things upstairs, Clint Holbrooke hadn't required tending.

"No, ma'am, but I'll get over it." Tom's voice was hoarse.

"Have you had breakfast?"

"Nanna is serving me up a plate now." Tom was on his way upstairs. "I have to hurry, Miss Samarra," he called, "or I'll be late for school."

Samarra wandered into the outer office, her hands performing early morning chores while her active mind tortured her with fragmented images of the man upstairs. She opened the curtains, turned the sign in the window around so that it read "Open" instead of "Closed," and unlocked the front door. Samarra noted with gratification that someone had cleaned up the blood, but it had left a rust-colored stain on the floor, a permanent reminder of the horrifying events of the previous afternoon. She checked the flintlock's priming, set kindling alight in the fireplace, added a few sticks of wood to ward off the chill, then sat at her desk to plan her day.

There, scattered on the oak surface, were the papers from Holbrooke's leather portfolio. Samarra sighed heavily, took an ink-stained but still usable piece of paper from a drawer, and began to make a list of items that needed clarification. This meant, of course, that she would have to discuss these points with him. The very prospect of being near him again, though, annoyed her even as it pleased her. Could she see him again without blushing, without recalling vividly how splendid he had looked in the altogether? Was he gentleman enough to keep mum about the matter, or would he tease her about charging through the door and catching him at his bath?

Oh, what an absolutely idiotic thing to do! she chastised herself. But the milk was already spilled, and nothing could undo that fact.

Despite all that had happened, Samarra thought she

was going to enjoy this printing job. Most of her work involved political and scientific writing, usually in pamphlet form; social announcements and invitations; business forms, advertisements, programs, menus, and the like. Printing a book of poetry, then, should prove not only a diversion but also a challenge. It needed to be a pretty book, Samarra thought, a feminine book. She picked up Holbrooke's notes, found that he agreed with her.

Samarra worked at her desk for an hour, the man in Jacob's room momentarily forgotten, the only sounds in this room lending much-needed tranquility to her overwrought nerves: a crackling fire, Clementine's purr, and the soft scratching of her quill.

It was a tranquility that proved short-lived.

At nine o'clock, as she did every morning, Nanna brought Samarra a fresh cup of coffee, then went upstairs to change Clint's dressing and remove his breakfast tray. "He wants t' see ye," Nanna announced when she returned. "I'll mind the store."

"You're actually going to allow me a few moments alone with him? What about my reputation?" Samarra teased lightly.

"Oh, poohie! This is business. Besides, who's t' know except me? This time ye do na have t' cross the yard t' see him."

He must have kept silent, or Nanna could never have been so flippant. Samarra breathed her silent gratitude to him, gathered her notes and Clint's papers, shoved them into the leather pouch, took her quill and a bottle of ink, and resignedly ascended the stairs. This time she was careful to knock.

"I'm decent now," he called, a deep chuckle erupting from his throat when she opened the door.

"Hush!" she whispered, almost hissing in her displeasure. So: he was not going to let it lie. No gentleman, this one. "Do you want Nanna to hear you?"

The devilish grin she'd witnessed earlier graced his mouth again as he braced his weight on his elbows and wriggled his buttocks backward on the bed. "Do you think you could adjust these confounded pillows?"

"Lord, give me strength!" Samarra mumbled, depositing the packet, quill, and ink on a table and moving to the bedside.

"Come on, now," he teased. "Granted, you aren't very big, but a few pillows can't be that heavy."

"I wasn't referring to the pillows!" With more muster than she had intended, she savagely punched the pillows into a backrest as he leaned forward.

"Sweet Jesus, lady! I hope you never decide to throw one of those jabs at me!"

She overlooked that remark, trying to ignore his nearness, the smell of him so close to her nose. It was a heady fragrance, a pungent combination of lye soap, tobacco, and the primrose salve Nanna had applied to his wound. On any other man, the sweet-smelling salve might have seemed feminine, but Samarra knew there was nothing effeminate about Clint Holbrooke.

"You could have come in this morning, you know."

His words, so casually spoken, brought her head up. "What?" she barked, giving the pillow under his right knee one more vicious poke with her tightly balled fist.

Clint shrugged lightly against the pillows, the grin playing at the corners of his too-perfect mouth. "You've never seen a nude man before, have you?"

"What an impertinent question!"

"I'm an impertinent man."

She didn't know quite what to think about his complete and unabashed honesty. "If you're planning to continue in this vein, I'm going back to work," she threatened, defensive now.

51

His arms flew up in mock surrender, elbows wide, palms open. "You win! I promise to behave."

Mollified, Samarra pulled the room's only straight chair—the same one, she realized too late, he had used this morning as a support for his leg—around to the table and began to unpack the leather pouch.

"How old are you?"

She pursed her mouth in consternation. "I hardly see what bearing that has on the matter."

"It makes one wonder . . ."

"If I wanted to be married, *Mr. Holbrooke*, I would be."

"It never pays, *Sam*, to attempt to read another's thoughts. I wondered only because you profess to great expertise at your trade." He grinned broadly. "Tell you what . . . you tell me your age, and I'll tell you mine. Deal?"

She winced at his calling her Sam, though he was but following her instructions. Attempting to ignore his banter, she forced a confidence she did not feel into her voice. "I have a business to operate, Mr. Holbrooke, a business I have been operating for seven years, since I was seventeen."

His hazel eyes twinkled at her subtlety, but he played along with her game, pursing his lips and counting silently on his fingers. "Aha! So you're twenty-four. That means I had reached the precocious age of nine when you were born."

She tapped the pointed end of the quill against the tabletop, thinking to herself that he had yet to outgrow his precociousness. "Do you think you could answer a few simple questions for me—strictly impersonal ones—so that I can return to my work?"

He shrugged again, his hazel eyes twinkling ominously. He made it difficult to keep their conversation on a purely professional level, and it took almost twice

52

as long as she had expected to extract the necessary information from him. Samarra was preparing to leave when he stopped her.

"You haven't asked why I wanted to see you this morning." Convinced that the best way to carry out his investigation was to stay as close to Samarra as possible, Clint had spent a goodly portion of the night plotting a way to stay in these rooms for several days, or even weeks. He couldn't carry on the charade of his infirmity too long. That his plotting had been strongly influenced by the sensuous swaying of the curtains in the moonlight he refused to acknowledge.

The delicate arch of her raised eyebrows silently indicated her lack of understanding while that selfsame confusion momentarily obliterated her firm intention to send him packing. "Are you not comfortable here, Mr. Holbrooke?"

"Oh, quite comfortable. As a matter of fact, more comfortable than I have been in some time. Which brings me to the matter I wished to discuss with you." His hazel gaze, which had warmed to a soft gold, raked her petite figure. "Perhaps you had best sit down again, Miss Seldon."

She complied, sitting primly with her hands folded over the materials in her lap, her thoughts running amok. His demeanor had subtly changed from light-hearted and frivolous to reflective and sober. What could he possibly have on his mind?

His answer to her unspoken question shocked her to her toes.

"I should like to rent these rooms from you, Miss Seldon."

She was so dumbfounded all she could manage was an echo of his request. "Rent these rooms?"

"Yes." Clint Holbrooke found himself fighting for control over the self-determination of his twitching lips

53

and glimmering eyes.

"I thought you had a room at a boardinghouse," she pointed out.

"I do, but my work requires isolation. The boardinghouse is an extremely noisy place sometimes."

"And what is your profession, Mr. Holbrooke?"

"I'm a writer . . . a translator, actually. At present I'm working on a translation of a French noblewoman's correspondence with her daughter. Replete with my own comments, of course, it will be published abroad as an epistolary novel."

"Of course." *And how ludicrous.* This man, who made a mockery of gentility, thought himself capable of analyzing a woman's personal letters? "And there is a market for such material?"

"Not so much here as in England. But that is rather beside the point, is it not? What say you to my proposal?"

"I—I don't know what to say . . . I've never even considered letting these rooms. With the print shop downstairs, and—and—" she floundered, trying to call up any excuse. "The print shop can be very noisy when we're operating the press, and what would you do about your meals? And your laundry? I couldn't be responsible for either of those."

"Then you will rent these rooms to me?"

"Yes—no! You're purposely confusing me, Mr. Holbrooke! I was merely thinking aloud, sorting out possibilities, that's all. I—I'll have to think about it." She rose to leave again, but turned around when she reached the door. "You're welcome to stay, of course, until you've convalesced. I'll try to have an answer for you tomorrow."

Samarra slowly descended the stairs, pondering her sudden and quite unexplainable change of attitude toward Clint Holbrooke. She couldn't let him have the

54

rooms; his continued presence might prove dangerous. Why had she led him to believe otherwise? She ought to climb the stairs and tell him now, insist that he return to his boardinghouse without further delay. After all, he could rest just as easily there as here. Let him change his own dressing, for heaven's sake! Or hire a physician to do it for him. He was taking unfair advantage of her hospitality.

By the time her slippered foot touched the last tread, she had worked herself into a mild rage. Had she not heard Nanna's frantic pleas, she'd have left her materials in the printing room and mounted her offensive back upstairs. Instead, she scurried across the wide hall and into the front room, her heart racing as a loud crash and another pleading cry from Nanna assailed her ears.

Chapter Four

Samarra didn't quite know what to think about the sight that greeted her.

A sea of red coats had washed into her print shop—and Nanna, short, grizzled little Nanna, stood her ground in a ridiculously defiant pose, her chin thrust out obstinately, her fists resting on her hips. "If ye'll just employ some patience, Captain Reed," she ground out, "I'm sure Miss Sam will be here in a moment."

"There she is now."

Samarra recognized the tall, lean officer as one to whom her father had introduced her more than a year past. "Is it captain, now? I seem to recall that you were a lieutenant when last we met."

She walked sedately toward him as she spoke, depositing her notes on her desk and extending her right hand in a warmer greeting than she felt, her smile not reaching her taffy-colored eyes. Her heart pounded in trepidation. Suddenly she wished she knew more about Clint Holbrooke, for it was surely his presence upstairs which had brought this detachment of soldiers to her shop.

Reed's long fingers quickly moved his doffed tricorne from his right hand to his left before he accepted her proffered hand in a businesslike grasp. "You have an excellent memory, Miss Seldon. As I recall, we shared a box at the theater last fall with your father and some charming folks from the frontier. *The Merchant of Venice* was the play, I believe. Nasty business about that actor who played Shylock—Jarvis Whitfield. Who'd have ever thought him a murderer? He jumped ship just off the coast of Cornwall, I believe. Still at large, I understand. And yes, I have received a recent promotion, ma'am."

From behind her back, Sam's left hand motioned Nanna away, but the older woman retreated no farther than behind the counter. She wasn't about to leave her charge—Nanna would always think of Sam as her responsibility—unprotected.

"And how may I help you today, Captain Reed? Does the British Army require my services?"

A snicker from near the door brought MacKenzie Reed's head sharply around. When he turned his face to Sam again, she couldn't help smiling at the flush staining his cheeks.

"No, ma'am." He seemed reluctant to continue.

"Then why are you here?"

"There seems to be a small matter involving your business, Miss Seldon, an incident that occurred yesterday which I have been instructed to investigate." He paused, clearing his throat uncomfortably, the vivid blue of his eyes focusing on some point above her head. She watched his Adam's apple bob in his throat, his discomfiture obviously as great as her own.

"Would this small matter also involve one of my customers, captain? A certain Mr. Clint Holbrooke?"

Relief bathed Reed's features. "Yes, ma'am, it would. Do you know where I might find him?"

Samarra tossed her head toward the inside door.

57

"We moved him upstairs yesterday, into the vacant rooms." Her gaze raked the score of uniforms filling the room. "I do not think the chamber is large enough to accommodate all of you, however. Nor do I think our guest would appreciate such an intrusion. Perhaps you could have your men wait in my backyard?"

Captain Reed's eyebrows rose slightly at her suggestion. Then, understanding her reasoning, he ordered his men to move accordingly. The presence of twenty British soldiers, either on the sidewalk or inside her shop, could not fail to arouse suspicion—if their entrance therewith had not already done so.

"Come . . . I will show you the way."

When all the men but two had filed out the back door, Sam paused at the foot of the narrow staircase, her brow furrowed in some consternation as she considered the unorthodox presence of a presentation of the militia. "Constable Woodcock was here yesterday, Captain Reed. Surely this is a civilian matter."

"You are most probably correct, Miss Seldon." He sidled past her small frame, his next words summarily dismissing her. "I shall attempt to make this inquiry brief."

The two remaining soldiers moved into guard position at the bottom of the staircase. Was she housing a criminal after all? she wondered. Or perhaps a soldier who was absent without leave? Why ever would Captain Reed require so very many soldiers as backup? And to think she had allowed herself private company with the felon! Well, let the captain take him . . . that would be an easy enough way to rid herself of his pesky presence.

But was that what she truly wanted?

Somewhat at a loss, Samarra retraced her steps to the front office, moving immediately to one of the windows where Nanna stood on a chair, attempting to replace the heavy wooden curtain rod upon its mountings. Sam held up one end while Nanna secured the other, then moved aside to allow Nanna to finish the task.

"Too many men in here at once," Nanna explained as she worked. "One of the fools backed into the window."

"That explains the crash I heard."

"What's this all about, anyway?"

Sam shook her head, confusion evident in her voice. "I—I'm not sure, Nanna." She crossed to her desk, taking up the notes she had dropped there moments before. Frustration coupled with supreme irritation colored her voice as she added, "And I really don't care—so long as those men are off my property in short order." When Nanna appeared reluctant to take her leave, Samarra added, "I suppose my reputation remains untarnished?"

"I did na tell them ye were upstairs, if that's what ye mean. Would ye like me t' stay a while?"

"No—no, thanks." Her hand reached for paper and quill. "But you can send Ezekiel with this note to Eliza Garrett."

Nanna accepted the missive, her watery eyes searching Samarra's troubled countenance. "Are ye certain ye do no want me t' send Old Zeke over here instead?"

A half smile graced Sam's delicate mouth. "If it will make you feel better, do send him over to get the note. But I really cannot envision any harm coming to me. What this might do to my business, on the other hand—"

Nanna patted Sam's shoulder affectionately, although perhaps a bit patronizingly as well. "Ye have proved yereself to this town, Miss Sam. Ye can na shape nor alter the attitudes of those who refuse t' accept ye as the fine printer that ye be."

"You're right, of course." A sigh of resignation escaped Samarra's lips. "Those who insist upon narrow-mindedness are beyond my ken, as are those whose suspicions flare at every minor incident."

Little did Samarra Seldon realize at that moment just how narrow-minded and suspicious she herself could become.

"Damn! It's good to see you!" Clint greeted Mac Reed, accepting his fellow officer's hand in a firm clasp.

"When you hadn't returned to the barracks this morning, I wondered whether you'd decided to desert the army!" Mac teased, then sobered as his gaze raked Clint's bandaged thigh. "I came fully prepared to storm the premises, if need be. What happened?"

Clint supplied the necessary details, assuring his friend that all was now well. "But I do need your help," he concluded. "I had to manufacture a reason to rent these rooms from Miss Seldon, and I had to have an excuse to remain here almost constantly. I told her I was a translator who needed peace and quiet."

The captain quirked an eyebrow in amusement. "And what did you tell her you were translating?"

"A French noblewoman's letters to her daughter."

Mac rolled his eyes and groaned. "Was that the best you could do? Can you even read French, Clint?"

"Not very well."

"I didn't think so."

"I need for you to get me some French documents. Oh, and Mac, make sure they're very unofficial-looking."

"That you can't translate? Aren't you concerned you'll be exposed as the charlatan you surely are?"

"I doubt Miss Seldon reads French. And even if she

does, she'll never get close enough to my work to know the difference. It's all strictly for appearance sake. In the meantime, I wouldn't mind having a change of clothing and my razor. Can you send one of your men for those things?"

"Of course. And I'll send over the French 'letters' as soon as I can secure them."

"No—don't do that. Leave them with the presiding officer at the governor's office and I'll pick them up later—assuming Miss Seldon agrees to rent these rooms to me. If she doesn't and I end up back at the barracks, I won't need them anyway. But let's not risk any deliveries to me here just yet."

It was some time later when Samarra heard the sharp staccato of Captain Reed's bootsteps upon her wooden floor and turned from working at her desk to bid him good day. She was surprised to find him alone.

"I trust you have successfully concluded your business with Mr. Holbrooke?" she asked innocently, her wide-eyed gaze traveling the length of the workroom and seeing there no other militia.

"For the present, ma'am. My apologies for the intrusion." He bowed then and turned to take his leave.

"For the present?"

Her question brought him back around. "There are complications to this incident, Miss Seldon, which I am not at liberty to discuss. The need may arise for further questioning of Mr. Holbrooke."

"Have you no questions for me?"

"Not now. Lieu—um—my lieutenant may return later with questions for you, but for now Mr. Holbrooke has provided sufficient information for my report."

"But . . . your men—"

"I sent them through your back gate. I understand

61

your wish to allay suspicion."

So now my backdoor neighbors know, too! she thought. But the deed was done. She supposed it had been kind of him to care, even if his caring had increased her distress. Her other questions—questions which, despite all her efforts to sweep them away, had piled themselves like so much dust upon her consciousness as she had awaited Reed's return—were stalled by the bustling entrance of Eliza Garrett. Even without the interruption, Sam reasoned, Reed would most likely have avoided specific answers.

"My sincere gratitude, ma'am, for your assistance," the British captain intoned, his head nodding briefly at Eliza. "Good day."

Samarra found herself suddenly grateful for his penchant for ambiguous speech as she greeted Eliza, who seemed to have paid no attention to Reed at all.

In her typically straightforward manner, Eliza asked, "You have a job for me, Sam?"

"Yes—a delightful one, too."

As Samarra described the watercolor illustrations she needed Eliza to paint for Holbrooke's book of poems, she could not help thinking yet again how ludicrous it seemed for someone so rawboned as Eliza to perform such delicate artistry with a paintbrush. *No more ludicrous,* an inner voice admonished her, *than a mere slip of a woman working as a printer.*

"And you may do the calligraphy as well, Eliza," Sam concluded. "I'm quite busy with the press right now." That morning Samarra had learned from Holbrooke that he required only one copy of the volume, thus negating the need for either engravings or typesetting. In such cases an artist was commissioned for the illustrations while Sam, if her schedule permitted it, rendered the copy in her own exquisite handwriting on the parchment pages. This time, that task would fall to the rawboned artist. When Eliza's work was finished, Sam would bind the book and deliver it to her newest customer. Would he ever require her services again? she wondered, the very thought of never seeing Clint Holbrooke again striking a dissonant chord deep within her breast.

They settled on a deadline for rough copy, for which Sam would enlist Holbrooke's approval before the final details were added, and Eliza Garrett bustled out with much the same efficiency of movement she had employed bustling in. As Samarra watched the door close behind her, she found herself wondering what Clint Holbrooke would think if he knew how many women she had in her employ—and to what ends their specialties contributed to her professional reputation. What, indeed, would most of her customers think if they knew that the majority of her engravings were created by her blind sister? They might be able to accept the fact of Georgiana's gender, but never would they accept her handicap.

Her thoughts shifted to the man upstairs, as they did so often lately. Maybe he would tell her why a certain British Army captain had come calling that morning. Someone owed her an explanation, and Sam was determined to get one.

She locked the front door, turned the "Open" sign around to "Closed," and mounted the staircase.

The object of her thoughts sat upright in bed, his long legs encased in biscuit-colored breeches, his eyelids closed, his face in complete repose. There was something different about him. Perhaps, Samarra reasoned, it was the look of total peace upon his sleeping face. Her questions would have to wait.

She had turned on her heel and begun her retreat when she heard him call out to her.

"I didn't mean to disturb you."

Oh, you disturb me all right, little lady! "I wasn't asleep."

"I can come back later."

"But you're here now."

The shock of his penetrating green gaze unnerved her, drew her closer, until she was standing within arm's reach of him. She felt as though she was drowning in the deep green pool of his scrutiny. Samarra swallowed convulsively, gasping for air, willing herself to say something, anything. "I came to tell you I've spoken to the artist."

"And my book will be ready before Christmas?"

"Most assuredly."

Samarra cast her eyes downward, no longer able to meet his burning green gaze, which seemed to bore right through her apron and dress—all the way to her chemise and petticoats, and perhaps beyond. To her chagrin, she felt a warm blush suffuse her cheeks. A long pause ensued during which Sam grappled with her lack of composure.

"Was there something else you wished to discuss with me?" Clint hoped she had decided to allow him to stay, though he knew instinctively not to push her.

"Yes, well . . . I could not help wondering why Captain Reed needed to speak with you this morning." There! She had said it!

"It was nothing, a mere misunderstanding, actually— nothing to concern yourself with."

Despite his piercing scrutiny, Samarra forced herself to maintain eye contact as he spoke. If he lied, he did so adroitly. Well, he wouldn't get away with it. Had he forgotten he was on *her* property, and at her invitation? Her voice carried the bluntness of disbelief. "Nothing to concern myself with? Just a score of redcoats littering my yard and alerting my neighbors, who are quite capable of assuming the worst."

"People will do that anyway, whether or not they are given cause. One cannot go through life basing honor on the narrow-minded opinions of others."

"That's philosophical hogwash!"

"Is it?" A shrug of nonchalance touched his shoulders.

She allowed her disdainful gaze to travel his person again. Suddenly she knew what was different about him. "Your shirt and breeches—"

A russet eyebrow rose sardonically. "Yes?"

"They're fresh."

He allowed his gaze to traverse the length of his legs before returning to her face. "So they are."

The man was prefectly exasperating! "But how?"

"Captain Reed was kind enough to send one of his men to fetch my things from the, uh, boardinghouse."

"I could have sent Ezekiel—or Tom, when he arrives."

"I saw no need to trouble you or those in your employ. The good captain was most obliging."

This conversation was gaining her nothing, but her exasperation with him was far better, she concluded, than self-induced embarrassment. At least their conversation now centered on a safe topic, one that had effectively erased her blush. "Did he bring your materials as well?"

A slight frown creased his wide brow. "My materials?"

"Yes. Your writing materials. Do you need quill and ink? Or some paper, perhaps? You *are* above a print shop, you know. I'm sure I have whatever you may require."

"Oh, yes, ma'am, you certainly do." He pursed his lips in a low whistle and his eyes sparkled as he continued to regard her in a way she felt could only be termed lewd. Whatever had she said to turn the tables again? Before she could figure it out, his look softened somewhat, and he continued, "No—no, thank you . . . I don't feel much like working today."

He regarded her with some degree of bemusement then, the green of his irises darkening to a mossy hue, his eyelids lowering themselves to half-mast. "Do you ever let down your hair, Miss Seldon?"

His impetuous question ambushed her senses and sent her pulse racing. "Well—yes, of course I do," she stammered, feeling the blood rushing upward again, mottling her creamy complexion with pink blotches.

His grin was immediate, lazy, and indulgent. Damn, but he enjoyed making her blush—and witnessing the flattering results. "To comb and wash it, naturally. That was not the intent of my question."

Her raw-honey-colored eyebrows, several shades darker than her hair, lifted slightly. Her instinctive response was just that—instinctive, spoken without prior consideration to her words. "Then what *was* your intent?"

She immediately wished she could retract it.

"Do you ever *wear* it down, socially, not just within the confines of your bedchamber?"

"I am at work, Mr. Holbrooke."

"Is that all you ever do, Miss Seldon? Work? Do you never venture outside these walls or those of your grand house next door for any other purpose than visiting the apothecary or milliner? Do you know how to relax, to let your hair down figuratively? Is life for you nothing more than the drudgery of running a print shop?"

She hurled her harsh words at him with the force and resultant sting of darts being thrown at a bull's-eye. "You know nothing about me, Mr. Holbrooke! Nothing at all. How dare you malign my livelihood! At least I perform a worthwhile deed which for me is not drudgery, while you—you waste countless hours translating some insignificant piece of erstwhile literature, pretending to understand the most private writings of a French noblewoman." She paused, drawing deep gulps of air into her lungs, blissfully unaware of the effect her heaving bosom was having on her target.

"So . . . the kitten shows her claws." The lazy grin played upon his mouth still. She found his attitude positively infuriating.

"Were you more secure in your manhood, you might be able to accept me for what I am."

"Just how *do* you perceive yourself, Miss Seldon? Do be so kind as to enlighten me."

"As a person, first and foremost, Mr. Holbrooke—a person forced into a woman's body, assigned by society to menial tasks which the men of this world have precipitated upon women since the dawn of time. A woman who has defied society's edict to pursue a career thought best left to a man. A woman in rebellion, I suppose. A woman who has attained some measure of success despite the whims of man. A woman who *is* secure with herself."

"And a woman who has sacrificed her femininity and the resultant joys that accompany it in order to gain that small measure of security," he finished for her.

She whirled around then, intending to depart from his hateful presence with all due haste. "I do not have to stand here and endure this—this assault!"

Samarra had taken only one step away from his bedside when she felt her right wrist enclosed in his grip. For a moment she struggled against his steel fingers, but he refused to let go. The more she pulled against him, the more her arm hurt. The rational part of her acknowledged that if she did not cease her defiance, he would jerk her arm from her shoulder socket. But her heart dictated her labors, and her heart screamed, "Resist!"

Amazed at such a degree of strength from one so small—and a woman at that—Clint held her wrist even more firmly than before.

"You have effectively demonstrated your superior strength," she hissed through clenched teeth. But when he ignored her, when a deep chuckle erupted from his throat and she felt the hot trail of a crooked finger singe the tender skin of her lower arm, her ire blossomed into fiery wrath. "Unhand me, you brute!" she railed.

In contrast, his words fell coolly, almost soothingly, upon her ears, like a summer shower after a long drought. "I like holding you, you little hellcat. Your skin is as soft as a newborn kitten's fur, but underneath you're as bristly as a disgruntled polecat."

With one swift movement, ignoring the sharp pain from the wound in his thigh, he swung her around and pulled her torso across his lap, his left hand still encircling her right wrist, his right hand reaching upward to cup her thrusting chin in what was, for the moment, a far cry from a caress. In response, she bared her teeth, her golden eyes flashing sparks.

"What lovely teeth you have, my dear."

"The better to eat you with, my dear," she mimicked, gnashing the pearly white luster of her teeth even as his hand drew her chin inexorably toward his open-mouthed astonishment at her riposte.

"So 'tis the part of wolf you'll play to my Red Riding Hood," he whispered against her lips. "Devour me, if you will. I offer no resistance."

His lips feathered hers, brushing ever so softly against the firm hold of her mouth until she gasped, as much from anger as from surprise. As he moved his mouth upon hers, she felt her chin go involuntarily

68

slack, felt his elbow brush against her breast, felt his fingertips glide down her throat and around her neck to entangle themselves in the knotted skein of soft hair at her nape. The warmth of his embrace, an embrace she had secretly yearned for, melted her anger. Of its own volition, her body pressed closer to his. She feasted upon the very essence of him—the feel of his hard-muscled chest against the softness of her breasts, the spicy, almost musky smell of him, the slight raspiness of his jaw beneath her palm as her free hand lay upon his face. It was what she had wanted, what she had dreamed of since the moment he had walked through her door.

He released her wrist then, his open hand sliding over the fabric of her long sleeve, its journey eliciting a shudder across her shoulders as it joined its mate in her hair. Her heart had ceased its cry of resistance and now urged her forward into a chasm darker and deeper than any she had ever known.

The intensity of their kiss, which he had intended as the summit of insult, startled Clint. *Damn the little hellcat, anyway!* His mouth slanted across hers, his lips molding themselves to the softness and pliancy of hers, alternately puckering against hers and then plucking them in small bits between his own.

When her now free right hand took his other cheek, he groaned, giving full rein to his own physical response, his fingers working frantically to remove the tortoiseshell combs holding her hair. As he'd imagined, the heavy skein fell in a rhapsody of golden splendor over her shoulders and down her back. For the briefest moment he removed his lips from hers to bury his face in the fragrant depths of her mane, his hands at her nape pulling her with him to lie prone upon the counterpane. Then his mouth staked its claim upon hers again, his tongue flickering out to rake her small teeth and ravage her gums.

That he was far more experienced than she in the art of lovemaking Samarra had no doubt. Her own limited realm of sensual experience had in no way prepared her for this onslaught of sensation and sexual awareness. His hands were like kindling, his tongue a torch setting a slow fire to burn deep within her being. Her hands answered his, her fingers forging a hot trail along his prominent cheekbones and tracing the shell of his ears.

He rolled her over onto her back, taking his mouth from hers long enough to scald a feverish track of hot, moist kisses from one corner of her mouth to the sensitive hollow at the base of her neck and then returning. When his lips touched hers again, she parted them instinctively, allowing his probing tongue to touch hers. His kiss deepened, his tongue beckoning hers to join his in a dance fraught with desire. His broad hands seemed to touch her all over at once.

Samarra had lost all capacity to reason. Her body responded in wanton disregard of her upbringing, her back arching, her stomach muscles tightening, her nipples growing hard beneath his roving palm, her body writhing beneath his as an ache coiled itself deep within her. The evidence of his own desire grew hard against the tautness of her belly until she felt its hot, burning brand through the stricture of their garments.

"My sweet, sweet Samarra," he moaned, his mouth now near her ear. "God A'mighty! I want you!"

She would wonder later whether it was the fiery rigidity of his response or the love words he breathed in her ear that brought her to her senses.

"No!" she begged. "Please, stop!" She moved her hands from his face to his shoulders and earnestly pushed against him.

He dropped his hands to the bed and pushed himself up, relieving her chest of the weight of his own while crushing his groin more firmly against her lap. She chanced a look into his eyes and witnessed smoldering passion in their dark green depths. Never had she been so frightened of anyone than of him—and never so frightened of anything than of her own awakened passion.

"Can you breathe now, my lovely?"

"Yes, thank you. And I can think more clearly, too."

Samarra watched the blink of his eyelids as the meaning of her words registered. "Oh, Samarra, don't think. *Feel!*"

"I *did* feel—too much," she admitted without rancor.

"What is there to think about, then?"

"I don't know you."

"Forgive me, my dear. I thought we had been properly introduced yesterday. I'm Clint Holbrooke—"

"—translator of obscure foreign literature. That's the sum total of what I know about you."

"Ah—but you know much more than that." His voice and eyes teased her, as did the wiggle of his hips against the juncture of her thighs.

Her body threatened betrayal. She tensed her muscles, willed a stiffness into her limbs. "No, I don't. Now move! Let me up!"

He laughed, a deep, throaty laugh that warmed rather than rankled. "Yes, you do, you little minx. You know what I look like beneath all these clothes."

"That's not enough."

"Isn't it?"

"No. Won't you please move?"

"You must have liked what you saw. You dawdled in the doorway long enough."

She felt the warm color of her embarrassment rise again and knew her face burned with a red as intense as that of a British soldier's coat. With all her might, she

71

pushed against his shoulders, but to no avail. "You—you are a brute! An insensitive brute! Move!"

"Not until I've extracted your promise."

"Promise? What promise?" Her voice and eyes were wary.

"Promise you'll let me stay here."

"No."

His face lowered again to hers, his warm breath tickling the soft down above her upper lip. "Then I'll just have to convince you another way."

When his lips were almost upon hers, she twisted her head around, burying her cheek in his pillow, breathing in the masculine fragrance of him, gasping at the reminder than she was in *his* bed! Clint seemed unperturbed. His mouth nibbled her exposed earlobe, sending ripples of sensation surging through her.

"Stop!" she begged anew, her voice almost wheedling this time, but he ignored her—until a salty tear touched his mouth.

The weight of his body collapsed against her chest, almost knocking the breath from her lungs. "My God, Samarra!" he rasped close to the ear he had so recently caressed with his lips and tongue. "I'm sorry . . . I could never take you by force." He smiled then, and she felt the quick rises and falls of his chest pressed so close to hers. "You don't have any idea what you do to me, do you?"

It was true. She didn't.

But that was the least of her worries just then.

Chapter Five

It was what he did to *her* that bothered Samarra, and it bothered her immensely.

"Are you going to move your considerable weight off me, or do I have to scream?" she snapped.

"You wouldn't do that."

"Why not?"

"For one thing, it's out of character."

"Do you presume to know me so well, Mr. Holbrooke?"

"Ah—so now we're back to formality. I thought we had moved beyond that."

"The only thing that needs to be moved is *you!*"

She watched the play of his facial muscles—watched his jaw tighten, his lips purse and then relax, his ungodly long eyelashes fan his cheeks. When he displayed his magnificent eyes to her again, they sparkled with amusement. Clint compromised then, sliding his body over to lie beside her, but his right arm circled her waist, holding her tightly against him.

"I moved. Does that satisfy you, Samarra?"

"No . . . and don't call me that!"

"Oops! I forgot. I'm supposed to call you Sam, but that has a masculine ring to it. I much prefer Samarra. I wish you would call me Clint. Mr. Holbrooke is far too stiff—and you, *Samarra*, despite your efforts at pretense, are not stiff. No-o-o, ma'am." He squeezed her middle. "You are definitely not stiff."

"Nor am I a bully."

"And I am?"

"Aren't you?"

His eyes pinned her gaze, held her in some sort of magical spell, caressed her in a way that sent a delicious shiver down her spine. She watched his eyes darken with his passion—and knew hers responded in kind. If she didn't leave soon, she would lose all control.

"I have to go back to work, and you, Mr. Holbrooke, need to rest."

Suddenly she remembered why he was in Jacob McCauley's old bed. How could she have forgotten? Not once had she witnessed even the slightest grimace of pain cross his face. A tinge of anger replaced the tinge of desire his smoldering gaze had effectively rekindled.

But her words had reminded him, too, and he winced.

"It's too late, Mr. Holbrooke."

"What is?"

"You can stop pretending. Your leg isn't really bothering you at all, is it?"

"Of course, it is—*now*."

"I don't believe you."

He shrugged. "It isn't *your* leg."

"I want you off my property immediately!"

"Why? Because you find my presence too exciting? Because what we just did offends your code of ethics? Because you're afraid of releasing your own passion? Tell me honestly—didn't you enjoy it?"

Her golden eyes flashed. "Because I find your presence offensive. Because you have no code of ethics.

Because you're a liar and a cheat—"

His russet eyebrows shot upward at her accusations. "If you were a man, I would call you out for that."

"Do you deny it?"

"I deny nothing, nor can you shame me into an apology. And I will gladly pay you for the use of these rooms, if you will just allow me to."

"These rooms are not now, nor have they ever been, for rent, to you or anyone else."

"But I've already sent word to the boardinghouse that I was vacating my room there. Where shall I go?"

"They probably still have your room available. And it's not my fault if they don't. How dare you *assume* you could just move in here?"

He threw back his head, and his laughter resounded in the confines of the small attic room.

She rethought her remark and found no humor there. "Whatever is it you find so entertaining?"

"A sage bit of advice someone gave me years ago."

She waited patiently for him to explain, and when he didn't, she asked, "And that piece of advice was?"

"You won't like it."

"Try me."

"First, you must picture the word in your head. Are you doing that?" She nodded, watching the dimple in his chin move when he continued. "Whenever you *assume,* you make an ass of you and me."

"An *ass* of me?" she railed, raising herself up on one elbow so she could look down at him. His arm held her tighter. "The only *ass* in this room is *you, Mis-ter Holbrooke!*"

He chuckled. "I warned you."

"And I'm warning you. Let me up—*now.*"

Clint released her so suddenly she fell back against the pillow. Quickly recovering, she rolled away from him and off the bed, but when her feet hit the floor, she found her legs did not want to support her. Her head spun and glimmers of prismatic color flashed before her eyes for a moment as she fought for control over her reeling senses.

His voice was husky but solicitous. "Are you all right, Samarra?"

Her voice was soft but contemptuous. "You needn't concern yourself with my welfare, Mr. Holbrooke."

And with all the dignity she could muster, she turned and strode out of the room.

Later—much later, when the gleam of the waxing moon glistened off the crystal facets of her bedside lamp, Samarra lay awake, her mind a jumble of errant thoughts.

Her bedchamber was one of several in a wing that elled from the back of the house, its large leaded windows overlooking the walled rear garden. As was her custom, Sam had parted her drapes and opened the windows just before retiring. Even in the dead of winter, she required fresh air. From her bed, she could see out the windows, could see the twinkle of stars and mentally record the ever-changing shape of the moon.

But that also meant she could see the upstairs window in her shop next door. That window had remained dark for almost seven years—until last night. And it should have been dark tonight. How would she manage to evict the brute? Should she discuss his proposition with Georgiana? The building was, after all, half hers. And now, during the Public Times, Samarra had to admit that the continued availability of Clint's old room was unlikely. Could she turn him out onto the street, with nowhere to go? Even without the injury to consider, she knew she was incapable of such coldness.

Clint's window was open, too. His limping shadow behind the lightweight curtain moved around in his room, and Samarra noted how he favored the injured leg. A stab of remorse gripped her chest for a minute. Had she done him an injustice, insisting he vacate the rooms? Was she not as responsible as he for what had happened between them that afternoon? If she was entirely truthful with herself, wasn't it his animal magnetism she feared far more than what he might eventually discover about her family and her business?

He hadn't known how close he'd come to the truth when he'd accused her of being afraid of her own passion . . . or had he? It had been easy to assume the role of spinster before yesterday, before she had begun to understand that special magic that occurs between two people who are deeply attracted to one another. Of all the men she'd known—of all the men with whom her father had arranged introductions—not one had sent her heart into a tailspin the way Clint Holbrooke had.

She closed her eyes against the moonlight streaming through her windows, against the shadow of him in the window across the yard, against the track her thoughts had taken. Seldom did sleep elude her, but when it did, she played a game, recalling memories of her childhood—when Georgiana could still see. The recollections soothed her troubled spirit and lulled her mind to rest.

She closed her eyes against the present and painted a picture from the past upon the dark curtains of her eyelids. Georgiana was there, and Papa, too. The brilliant green of new grass rolled in waves across low hills dotted with wildflowers. A late March wind billowed the girls' skirts and snatched Papa's cap off his head, sending it flying up into the clear blue of a cloudless sky.

Georgiana laughed, and the breeze carried the merry

77

tinkle hither and yon, just as it carried a yellow kite higher and higher. George held the stick upon which the twine had been wound, and Papa patiently coached her in the finer points of kite-flying as the sailing yellow diamond dipped and swayed against the vivid blue of the sky.

Samarra watched the knotted string tail wiggle and squirm as her twin urged the kite back into a wind current. For a moment, a breeze caught the yellow sail and its limber spine arched against the draft.

"Watch me, Papa," Georgiana called, removing her attention momentarily from the flight of the kite as she sought her father's approval.

Papa's gaze whipped downward from the sky to his daughter. "You're doing fine, sweetheart," he proclaimed, his wide smile dissolving as George's own abruptly disappeared.

The yellow diamond flipped. Its tail went limp, then straightened itself out behind the kite as it nose-dived into an oak tree.

Whatever had caused her subconscious to dredge up this memory?

"I'm not a kite!" Samarra muttered into her pillow as she rolled onto her stomach. "I haven't depended upon the winds of fate to control my life, and I won't let a wind shift alter my course now." *Tomorrow he goes. Even if I have to get Jeremiah Woodcock over here. I don't care what happens to him. Tomorrow he goes.*

He extinguished his lamp and stretched out upon his bed, rolling toward the darkened window and noting an absence of light from the house next door. He reckoned the time to be close to ten and muttered a curse for failing to check his pocketwatch before blowing out the candle.

The spontaneous events of the afternoon had taken him by surprise, muddled his thinking. He had to get back on task. He had to stop allowing his desire to control his thoughts and actions. He had done that once, and it had almost cost him his life. He had to remember that Samarra Seldon was a felon.

Or was she?

Governor Robert Dinwiddie seemed to think so. Could he have been mistaken?

Mac Reed thought her innocent, but Clint suspected the captain's opinion had been prejudiced by the undeniable beauty of the accused. Clint had been much relieved to see a fellow officer earlier that day, for he had begun to wonder how long he could tolerate the growth of his beard and the condition of his garments, which were both dirty and torn, his fine new trousers ruined where Nanna had sliced them with the scissors. Samarra's wrath had saved him—temporarily, he was certain—from an accurate explanation of the reason for MacKenzie Reed's visit.

And, oh, how beautiful she was when she was angry! But there was an innocence about Samarra—not only naïveté, but a certain vulnerability as well. A lack of sophistication—a freshness that bespoke her purity. But was it only a purity of the body, and not one of the spirit? Or had she merely beguiled him into thinking she was inexperienced, and was, therefore, guilty on both counts?

He switched his thoughts toward what his instincts assured him were facts: Samarra Seldon was on the defensive. She was afraid. And she was hiding something.

Clint didn't know how much longer he would be permitted to stay in the attic rooms. Samarra would take only so much of his bullying. He knew better than to count on tomorrow. He would have to make a thorough and careful search of her printshop tonight, but he could not risk detection. In another hour or two, he was relatively certain, he would be able to light a lamp again without fear of discovery. In the meantime, he would rest his leg, which had begun to throb painfully again.

Who had thrown the knife? Who wanted him dead—or maybe just out of commission for a while? He could not blame Samarra for the injury, for it had occurred too soon after he'd met her. She couldn't have known then who he really was and what he was really doing. Even now, a day and a half later and following a rather suspect visit from Mac Reed, her suspicions had not been unduly aroused.

And why not? Every instinct screamed at Clint that she ought to be suspicious. She should have asked more questions, demanded more specific answers. Something was wrong.

Had she used anger as a cover? Had there been a leak? Had someone warned her? Had she hired someone to throw a knife at him—at a time she had known there would be a witness? That skull-faced man—Sloane O'Quinn—had said he had an appointment. O'Quinn's description of a scruffy, brown-haired assailant could fit any number of men in Williamsburg. Suddenly it all seemed terribly contrived.

Damn her! Damn that sneaking, conniving little bitch!

The silvery glow of moonlight danced upon the sweaty flanks of the mammoth gray as it bore its black-clad rider at breakneck speed down the winding ribbon of Ware's Creek Road. A shrill screech pierced the encroaching chill of the night air, causing the gray to balk and snort as the knees of its rider coaxed it into an

80

ebony tunnel created by gnarled and densely entwined tree limbs. For a long moment, darkness engulfed the pair. Each was poised to danger, each sharply aware of every sound, of every tiny movement until they had cleared the cloister of the trees and were once again upon open ground.

A roiling bank of black clouds converged in the western sky, the uppermost fringes alternately obscuring and revealing the broken-plate moon. The black capelet of the rider's cloak settled about his shoulders as he reined in the gray and set his gaze upon the open field to his right.

He could hear the rushing of the creek water now as it flowed over the dam, a certain indication that the deserted mill stood nearby. His eyes searched the countryside for some discernment of a building, but the inky darkness effectively cloaked the weather-stained boards. He had heeled the gray into action again when the clouds released their hold upon night's lamp, allowing its shimmering paleness to illuminate his surroundings briefly before moving to extinguish it once more.

Ware's Creek Mill sat nestled among a stand of young water oaks whose spreading limbs decreed their determination to reclaim land cleared decades earlier. The elements had accomplished their proportionate share of reclaiming the mill itself and the dam beside which it had been built. In the cold light of day, one could easily witness the large, gaping holes in the wood-shingled roof of the mill, could see the rotting timbers of the dam which continued to hold the bulk of the creek water at bay. But in the still shelter of night's swarthy web, the dark structure stood sentinel beside the stardusted waterfall of Ware's Creek, and its state of disrepair went virtually unnoticed.

Some said the ghosts of two lovers haunted the mill.

The rider didn't believe in spirits, but he had to admit there was something almost sinister about the dark structure, with moonlight playing upon its weathered boards and the eerie sound of the water spilling over the dam into the creek behind it.

The man turned the gray off the road and into the close underbrush, slowing the stallion's pace, guiding the gray into the stand of oaks before dismounting. He heard the soft whinnies of at least two other horses nearby. When the gray's reins had been securely looped and tied around one of the slender trunks, the man stood for several minutes within the shelter of the trees, his eyes watching the road. Finally convinced that he had not been followed, he turned toward the mill and made his way stealthily to the diagonal bracings which identified the Dutch door.

The rusty hinges groaned in resistance, and then he felt his upper arm encased in a steel-like grip as he was pulled unceremoniously into the dark confines of the mill.

"It's me—let go!" he hissed.

"Ye're late."

The fetid stench of rotting teeth assailed him, and he fought the shudder of revulsion which threatened to erupt from deep within him. "And you botched the job. Could we have a light?" he asked irritably.

As the door of a ship's lantern opened, the man stepped backward until his spine came to rest against the closed portal, a precaution which not only put him closest to the exit but allowed his visage the advantage of shadow as well. The sputtering candle lent its small light to the cavernous room, disclosing two rough-looking men and casting huge shadows into the far corners. Anyone could be lurking there.

"Who's he?"

"Insurance."

82

His dark gaze swept the duo, noted their own menacing glares staring back at him, their eyes haunted with the misery of their lives. The sourness of their unwashed bodies and filthy garments filled his nostrils, but this time the steel trap of his mind successfully blocked the foul odors, and he focused his thoughts upon the matter at hand.

"I wounded him fer ye, and I want me bread."

"You'll not be paid until the terms of the contract have been met," the man said firmly. "Holbrooke was but mildly injured. Your aim was off—way off."

In all honesty, things would probably work out better this way. He had given the matter a great deal of thought and wished his original plan had incorporated what he wanted this hired assassin to believe had been a serious error. The blame for the deed was supposed to have been placed on O'Quinn, which would have removed him from the picture. Perhaps the odious, skull-faced man could be used in some other way. In the meantime, the possibility of Holbrooke's discovering any incriminating evidence against Samarra Seldon was slight, and the course of his investigation could take weeks—weeks in which even more counterfeit money could be placed into circulation, weeks in which even more damage could be wreaked upon those this tall man sought to punish.

"The forty hogs you offered is but a pittance of what killing that man be worth."

The man blinked in some confusion, pulling his thoughts abruptly back to the conversation at hand. "Hogs?"

"Ye know—shillings."

"Of course."

"And ye want I should keep my trap shut. Ye're askin' fer a whole lot, mister."

Understanding began to dawn. "You winged him on

purpose, didn't you? You never intended to kill him."

A sinister frown wrinkled the scoundrel's forehead. "No one calls me a cheat, mister. I lost a good knife—"

"—that I supplied."

"That don't matter. Ye give it to *me*. Fact is, ye didn't tell me this Holbrooke feller's a redcoat. I don't like not being told the truth. Now, who's the cheat?"

"Look—are you going to finish the job, or do you want out?"

"It's going to cost you a sight more'n our original agreement. It'll be harder now. Little Miss Printer's been fawning over him, let him have the spare room over her shop."

"I'm willing to pay more—within reason, of course. He'll have to wander outside eventually. You just keep him staked out, and the opportunity will present itself."

"Pay me my forty hogs first. Then we'll talk about the rest."

Madam Marceaux ran the most prestigious house of prostitution in all of Virginia, perhaps in all the American colonies. Her clients hailed from the best and richest families, and for their pleasure she provided the cleanest, most discreet, and prettiest of girls. From an exterior view of her place of business, one would never guess what dens of delight had been created within.

Mac Reed marveled once again over the French madam's exquisite taste as he mounted the wide brick steps leading to the front stoop of the Georgian edifice. The delicate, haunting pinging of a harpsichord as it drifted out into the dark night blended with soft laughter from within to create a warm, inviting ambience. He smiled to himself as he pulled the braided silk cord by the door and listened for the jingling bell to add its lambent tones to those of the instrument.

A tiny black maid dressed in a black serge gown and a sparkling white bibbed apron answered the summons, then quietly led Mac to Madam Marceaux's private office.

"Come in, come in, *mon cher,*" the buxom Frenchwoman beckoned in her deep, raspy, heavily accented voice, a flabby arm extending itself to indicate a maroon velvet chair opposite her small Florentine desk. "I've been expecting you all evening!" Her heavily painted face screwed itself into a scowl intended to reprimand. "You have kept me in much suspense, *mon cher,* since I received your note this afternoon. What favor do you need from me that my girls cannot provide?"

Mac grinned in apology as he accepted the proffered seat. "Letters, Madam Marceaux," he explained. "Letters written in your native language such as an aristocratic woman might have written to her daughter, say, a century or so ago."

She regarded him silently for a moment, watching him squirm while she pretended to consider his request. "How many?" she finally asked.

"A dozen or so ought to be enough."

"When do you need them?"

"Within the next few days."

Her thin, kohl-darkened eyebrows shot upward. "You ask for much from a busy woman."

"You will be paid well."

"Of course. For my discretion as well as for the letters?"

Mac breathed easier, although deep down he had known she would cooperate, and he nodded in agreement.

"Come see me again in three days, *mon cher,* and I will have your letters for you. Now!" she exclaimed, smiling and waving a bejeweled hand toward her office door. "Go on out there and enjoy yourself. Tonight is on the house."

And he did just that.

His search had proved a vain effort—and had deprived him of sorely needed rest.

Irritated, frustrated, and outdone, Clint Holbrooke returned to his rooms over the print shop with the intention of going to bed. But his nerves were stretched too taut to allow immediate relaxation, so he set his candle on a table in the sitting room, filled his pipe with tobacco, located the bottle of brandy Nanna had provided, and deposited himself in a comfortable though slightly ratty chair.

An hour later, he was sitting there still, his long legs extended before him, his stockinged feet propped upon the soft velvet plumpness of a hassock, his ankles casually crossed, Clementine asleep upon his lap. He swished the brandy—his third snifter—before taking a sip, then relit his pipe.

The more he thought about it, the more certain he became that someone had tipped his hand. Someone had warned Miss Samarra Seldon in time for her to remove all the evidence. Where had she stashed the plates? Were they, perhaps, as close as next door, or had one of her accomplices taken them? How many people was she working with—besides her father? Or was it just the two of them?

Mentally he listed possible answers to all his questions with attendant measures that would be required to expose the facts.

Assuming she was working with co-conspirators, she had to have a foolproof way of getting the fruits of her illegal labor out of the print shop and into circulation.

What better way, Clint reasoned, than sending them by Tom as brown-paper-wrapped packages for delivery to alleged customers? Acting on that supposition, Clint had carefully undone each of the parcels behind her counter and combed their contents before rewrapping them. He had found tavern menus, monogrammed stationery, political flyers, playbills, and theater programs—all perfectly legitimate and appropriate. But then, if someone had indeed alerted her to the impending investigation, she'd have seen fit to remove anything damning.

And that left him with nothing—for the moment. He would just have to convince her to let him rent these rooms. In a few days he could discover whether or not she had been forewarned. In the meantime, his continued presence above the print shop could gain him far more intimate knowledge of Miss Seldon's business than his original plan had offered.

Clint smiled as he considered the words his thoughts had selected—and one in particular: *intimate*. Yes, he liked that. An intimate relationship with his primary suspect might gain him more than a month's worth of nightly forays through the contents of her shop. An intimate relationship might gain him access to her house. An intimate relationship might quickly provide him with all the facts he needed to collect, and then he could go back to being the military man he was trained to be.

That an intimate relationship might cost him something Clint refused to consider, even when his heart's voice niggled at him by repeating the name Judith over and over. *Samarra isn't like Judith,* he responded. *Nor is this situation similar. I won't become emotionally involved this time. I won't,* he promised himself. Before, he had treated a doxy as though she were a lady. This time, he would treat Samarra Seldon as though she were a doxy. After all, she was nothing more to him than a suspected felon, and he would maintain that perspective. It would be the best way to accomplish his goal, and if anyone was hurt, it would be Mistress Seldon.

He might be ignorant of the workings of a printing press, but if any man in Williamsburg knew how to charm his way into a woman's life—and into her bed—Clint Holbrooke did. And he knew it.

If Samarra Seldon could counterfeit currency, he could counterfeit love.

Chapter Six

If I had been playing Cupid, Clint Holbrooke thought, *I never would have put those two together.*

That evening Clint had just met the frontier couple Tom had told him would be visiting Samarra. Beth McLaird—whose husband insisted on using her more cumbersome full name, Hepzibeth—sat regally at the banquet-sized table, the pale blonde strands of her hair interwoven with rose colored satin ribbons and piled high upon her head. A mere week before, Clint's appreciative male scrutiny would not have failed to note the luster of her pale blue eyes and almost translucent complexion, her swanlike neck, and the expanse of well-endowed chest exposed by the plunging neckline of her stylish rose satin gown. But his appreciative male scrutiny had quite suddenly diminished to the exclusion of all women save one.

He had, however, noted her poised presence and acknowledged the additional grace she lent Samarra's table. In fact, Clint had no doubt Beth McLaird would just as easily grace any court in Europe. So! They did grow more than tobacco on the Virginia frontier.

Beth's appearance and demeanor had taken Clint

quite by surprise, for he had fully expected a rawboned, gritty woman sadly lacking in the social graces.

And yet, Clint realized, there was an indisputable earthiness about Beth McLaird that kept her from being an ice queen while not relegating her to the gutter. This was a characteristic, he acknowledged with a start, that Beth shared with Samarra; the ability to preserve ladyhood while maintaining a warm sense of humor and refusing to ignore the baser facts of life.

Tom's slightly drunken, though probably quite accurate description of Samarra flitted through his thoughts: "And she's a lady, always, no matter what." Yet, that same lady had not only melted in his arms, but had then called him an ass! None of the English ladies he knew would have dared condescend to either—but none of the English ladies he knew had made his heart do flip-flops as Samarra had.

Beth and her husband Edwin must share a magical attraction for one another, Clint finally concluded after spending most of the evening analyzing these two, who were as different as night and day. Edwin lacked his wife's vivaciousness and her obvious gift of gab. Although Clint was not in the habit of assessing male beauty, Edwin's physical attractiveness paled miserably beside that of his wife. But the most prominent difference between the two was neither Edwin's shyness nor his homeliness, but rather his clumsiness.

Clint smiled to himself as he applied his knife to a piece of succulent veal, recalling Edwin's stumbling over a chair as he had moved from the salon, where the four had gathered briefly before dinner, to the dining room. This recollection was swiftly followed by one in which the tall, long-armed, gangly fellow had knocked over a full glass of water. Before a servant could be summoned either time—which would have only emphasized Edwin's lack of grace—Beth had quietly and unobtrusively righted the chair and mopped up the spilled water, the loving gaze she reserved for her husband never faltering.

Clint would have much preferred to spend the evening observing Samarra instead of her guests, but his position at one end of the long cherry table prevented any close scrutiny of her at the other. He had been taken aback at her choice of the stiffly formal room as the setting for this meal, a choice which prevented any intimacy whatsoever. In fact, he had been caught completely unawares when she had invited him in the first place.

His smile disappeared and his eyes narrowed at the remembrance of her invitation, one which should have warned him of the formality she intended. Until this evening, five days had passed since he had last laid eyes upon her person. In the interim, she had sent her maid—who lived up to Tom's assessment as a "purty thing"—over to clean his rooms thoroughly, and his needs had been attended to by either Nanna or Tom. Nanna brought his meals, dressed his wound, washed his clothes, and swept and dusted his rooms, while Tom handled the heavier chores, such as hauling water up the stairs and emptying the chamberpot. Neither had mentioned Samarra or brought him any message from her until this afternoon, when Tom had handed Clint a folded square of crisp ecru stationery upon which she had penned:

Mr. Holbrooke,
  Nanna has declared you now able to negotiate the stairs. If her assessment is correct, I would appreciate your attendance at dinner this evening

at my house, eight o'clock. You may return your
reply through Tom.

It was signed simply, "*S. Seldon.*"

Despite the coolness of her note, Clint's heart had pounded double-time as he read it. He had been certain, before he opened it, that this was Samarra's way of removing him from the apartment. Over the past few days, he had begun to despair that he would not be allowed to stay. Nor did he believe he would ever be allowed access to the house next door, but at last he had been given an invitation—and a respite from eviction.

During that time, he had told himself repeatedly that his desire to see Samarra Seldon had absolutely nothing to do with the fire her kisses had ignited in his loins. He had assured himself instead that he merely wanted to carry through with his plan for developing an intimate relationship with her, one that would lead, he hoped, to discovery of the evidence Dinwiddie required. This psychological exercise had proved a total waste of mental energy.

From the limited viewpoint of his upstairs window, he had been rewarded with occasional glimpses of that one who was so often the subject of his thoughts. More often he had watched the couple visiting Samarra strolling in the rear garden, and he knew without having to be told that this was the couple from the frontier Tom had mentioned last week.

Clint's self-enforced solitude, with only Clementine for company, had provided time for much reflection, and he had begun to expand his theory concerning how Samarra Seldon managed to disperse the counterfeit currency she printed, now including the elusive couple in his imagined design. Yet his continued nightly forays had uncovered nothing incriminating. He had to hand it to her: she was one smart woman—or at least one who had been well informed.

And one who had secured the loyalty of her employees. He had been able to learn nothing new from Tom or Nanna or the pretty though empty-headed maid. The very ambivalence of their answers to his pointed questions had further increased his confidence in Samarra Seldon's guilt.

As he chewed his veal, Clint allowed his gaze to roam the expanse of the table and then to rest upon the object of his thoughts. She sat as primly as her female guest, her deportment that of a well-bred lady playing hostess. He wished he could see her better, hear her better, but two tall candelabra, a large arrangement of fresh flowers, and the considerable length of the table separated them too much for either.

"You really must take some time off," Beth McLaird was telling Samarra, "to visit us. The Appalachians are always beautiful, but especially in late spring, when the rhododendrons and mountain laurel and an abundance of wildflowers are in bloom. That was when Kane first saw our wild land. We tease him and Glynna about it unmercifully—tell him that it was the countryside he fell in love with first, and then Glynna." Beth sighed lightly, her pale eyes misting while a panoply of emotions gamboled upon her delicate features.

"But love her he does—and with all his heart," Samarra declared, herself almost choking on her own emotion. Clint could not help wondering how she knew this and why the admission of it stirred her so. Beth's invitation had implied that Samarra had never traveled so far west as where the McLairds lived, and the sparse information she had imparted about this couple, Kane and Glynna, made it sound like Glynna was a native of the frontier. Perhaps they had visited Williamsburg recently, too. How had Sam met so

93

many people who lived several days' journey to the west? Were they perhaps relatives of the Seldons? No one seemed eager to enlighten Clint one way or the other.

"And of course, Mr. Holbrooke, you are welcome to visit us as well," Edwin said, but his voice lacked the warmth and enthusiasm of Beth's invitation to Samarra. "Our little community would appear rather staid and unexciting, I'm afraid, in comparison to Williamsburg, but we find the absence of so much activity peaceful."

"The imminence of war, then, has not affected your part of the frontier?" Clint asked with what he hoped was the proper degree of ignorance, his military commission permitting him the privilege of such information.

"Oh, we've prepared ourselves for possible danger," Edwin conceded.

Clint raised his eyebrows. "I had not heard of any fortifications being erected this side of the Appalachians."

"No fort, sir." Edwin smiled indulgently. "Just the construction of a gristmill and the addition of a general store to the tavern."

"Which constitute conveniences more than readiness, surely," Clint argued.

"Conveniences, yes—but they keep our citizenry from the necessity of extensive travel, which may become dangerous. It is obvious, Mr. Holbrooke, that you know little of life on our frontier." Edwin's voice carried no animosity, yet his jaw clenched as he struggled to maintain self-control.

Knowing he had to be careful lest his casual remarks reveal the full extent of his secondhand knowledge, Clint nodded in deference to Edwin's observation. Before he could phrase a suitable reply, Samarra deftly changed the subject. Despite the obvious display of interest his action proclaimed, Clint craned his neck to get a better view of her.

While Clint Holbrooke had failed to acknowledge Beth McLaird's beauty, his appreciation of one particular female's anatomy had been duly enhanced. This evening had offered him his first opportunity to see Samarra Seldon attired formally, and the vision was breathtaking. Of a richer, more vibrant hue than Beth's almost platinum mane, Samarra's blonde locks appeared thicker and more difficult to control. Recalcitrant wisps curled at her temples, earlobes, and nape, while the mass of her honey-colored tresses had been dressed in a simple coil on her crown, the rebellious waves held in place by two unadorned ivory combs. Her dark blue gown, too, was of a plainer design than Beth's, yet no less elegant—and not quite so revealing.

Clint grudgingly admitted his approval of the latter difference, but refused to recognize his own possessiveness as the cause. No matter that Edwin McLaird was a married man—a happily married man. He was still a man, and Clint preferred his women to adhere to modesty in the presence of other men.

Reluctantly he returned his attention to the conversation, which had reverted to a discussion of the couple Beth had mentioned earlier. He had no interest in the birth of their child or a visit from Kane's parents, but when an actor named Whitfield was mentioned, Clint's ears perked up.

"Captain Reed told me just last week that the scoundrel had jumped ship off the coast of Cornwall," Samarra said evenly, but the liquid in the goblet she held trembled slightly, betraying her trepidation.

Beth's shudder was more apparent. "So we'd heard. And I suppose they've never found him?"

Samarra shook her head.

"Let's just hope he stays in England," Edwin said. "A

blacker heart I've never known—except, perhaps, that of the Reverend Samuel Mitchell."

No one appeared eager to provide details. "Your life on the frontier doesn't sound so peaceful, Edwin," Clint observed, attempting to sound a bit miffed about being left out of the conversation.

His ploy worked. During the rest of the meal, the three regaled him with the tale of Glynna and Kane Rafferty. Though he enjoyed it immensely and gained the answers to the questions he had mentally posed earlier, he could find nothing in the story to tie Samarra's alleged felonious acts to her friends from the frontier.

Why had Mac Reed not told him about these people? The captain obviously knew of their association or he would not have mentioned Whitfield to Samarra. The only answer Clint could construe was that their activities were not suspect.

As the men retired to the salon for bowl and brandy, Clint reflected upon the tale he'd just been told. All that was decent in him cried out to the wrongs that had been perpetrated against Glynna O'Rourke Rafferty: orphaned at age three, torn from her homeland and reared on the fringes of civilization, abducted by a demented man of the cloth, deceived by her beloved, and finally caught on the threshold of death at the hands of a confessed serial killer. It was no longer a mystery to Clint why Samarra's throat had thickened when Glynna's name was mentioned! Her own small role in helping Kane and Edwin search for the young woman by printing handbills advertising Glynna's abduction had been related as part of the tale, thus clearing up the uncertainty of the relationship of these five people in Clint's mind.

And presenting him with still another dead end.

*   *   *

96

Samarra wasn't the least bit sure why she had quite suddenly decided she must invite Clint Holbrooke to dinner. The more the evening wore on, the more she wished she hadn't.

Had she not enjoyed the coziness of the previous evening meal, with Nanna and Georgiana in attendance? It had been such a casual, companionable evening, the five of them sitting around the oak table in the kitchen, laughing and talking as they satisfied their appetites with large servings of red flannel hash and spoonbread.

Samarra had first met Edwin when he had traveled to Williamsburg with Kane Rafferty over a year ago—when the two had been looking for Glynna. Then, several months later, Edwin had returned with his tobacco crop, bringing with him his new wife, Beth, and their friend Glynna. Having received word that his father was very ill, Kane was in Ireland at the time. Edwin had written to Sam in advance of the trip, asking her to secure theater tickets for the three of them. Randolph Seldon had acquired twice that number, including himself and Samarra as well as MacKenzie Reed in the purchase. The six had thoroughly enjoyed themselves at the theater, and Samarra had not been surprised to hear by post from Edwin and Beth when they had planned their journey to Williamsburg this year. She had responded with her desire to have them as her houseguests, apprising them of Georgiana's handicap—the McLairds had not even known Sam had a sister—and of Randolph's absence from his home.

The couple had arrived late in the afternoon the day before, tired, hungry, and soiled from the four-day ordeal of their trip. The casual meal in the kitchen had been most welcome.

Sam had expected Clint Holbrooke to be gone before the McLairds arrived, but such had not been the case. She had not found the heart—or the courage, she admonished herself—to make him leave. Nor had she discussed with Georgiana his possible permanent occupation of the rooms.

Her secondary plan had called for ignoring his presence in Jacob's quarters next door. This she managed outwardly, but she could not seem to still the thrumming of her heart or the shivers along her flesh whenever his name was mentioned, and quite often when it was not.

When Nanna had carried Clint's supper over the evening before, Sam found herself telling Beth and Edwin all about the man and the sequence of events which had led to his occupation of the rooms. Then, today, she had quite suddenly decided to do something she seldom did—host a formal dinner. And that decision required another: finding a fourth party, a second man, to round out the evening. There were any number of men, she knew, who would have willingly accepted her invitation—even one so impetuously offered.

Why, then, had she chosen Clint Holbrooke?

For five days she had avoided him. For five days she had made excuses, buried herself in work, prepared her house and larder for the McLairds' visit—and missed Clint Holbrooke something awful.

For five days she had felt the firm yet surprisingly soft touch of his lips feathering hers, plucking hers, devouring hers. For five days she had felt the brand of his lean fingers as they tangled in her hair, cupping her head. For five days she had heard his deep, resonant voice murmuring, "My sweet, sweet Samarra."

For five days she had fought valiantly—and lost.

You'll be safe if the two of you are in the company of others, her heart promised.

Now she wondered if wanting to see him had not

prompted her decision to make dinner a formal affair, and not vice versa, as she had been trying to convince herself. A part of her felt guilty, too, for planning an occasion which would from its very design exclude Georgiana.

The whole affair surrounding Georgiana's voluntary seclusion from society was a complicated, sordid mess which had begun with a visit from a self-righteous do-gooder shortly after her complete and absolute blindness had set in. Never would Sam—or her father or Nanna or, most importantly, Georgiana herself—forget the pompous and self-important Mrs. Robinson, nor would they forget the stinging barbs she had so viciously hurled.

Inviting the McLairds to stay with her had proved a difficult decision for Samarra. Georgiana's own penchant for privacy had kept her a virtual prisoner in her own home for almost a decade. It was a penchant Samarra and Randolph had thoroughly and understandably indulged. Sam had only recently begun to consider how much emotional damage they might have allowed George to inflict upon herself with this attitude. Sam had come into contact with enough people since the incident with Mrs. Robinson to know that not everyone would be repelled by Georgiana's appearance. With the seeds of doubt beginning to take root, Samarra had taken it upon herself to finally expose Georgiana—and her handicap—to someone besides her immediate family and their trusted employees. What little she knew of the McLairds convinced her they were not cut from the same cloth as the odious Mrs. Robinson.

When she had written to Beth and Edwin about Georgiana, she had explained to them how much more handicapped a blind person felt when treated like a blind person. Understanding this, the members of the

Seldon household had, since Georgiana's onset of blindness, been careful to ignore her handicap as much as possible. It would have been easy for them to insist upon helping Georgiana move about the house, to assist her as she dressed herself, fed herself, bathed herself. If they had applied any wisdom to George's situation, it lay in their attitude not only to allow but also to encourage her independence. Because they had not patronized her, she was as capable of caring for herself as most sighted people.

The McLairds, having been instructed thus, had applied the same attitude toward Georgiana. Nor had they shown any outward signs of repugnance at her appearance.

But Samarra was not ready to introduce George to Clint, was not certain how he would react to her handicap, let alone to Georgiana's involvement in Samarra's printing business.

"Oh, I don't mind, Sam, really I don't," Georgiana had insisted when Samarra had divulged her plans for the evening. "I had wanted to retire early anyway, and I'll just have supper with Nanna in the kitchen. You need to entertain occasionally, to have some other interests besides me and the print shop. Go on out to the garden now and pick some lovely flowers for the table and I'll arrange them for you."

Georgiana's talents—her ability to "see" beautiful things in her mind and then translate those visions into tangible creations—never ceased to amaze Samarra. But even more amazing to her was Georgiana's acceptance of her absolute blindness. Had her twin been born sightless, had she never known visual beauty, Sam might have been able to understand her sister's lack of rebellion. Georgiana's blindness had stolen upon her during the tender years of early adolescence, though. "White eye," Dr. Hargrove had called it, explaining that the disease almost always led to eventual blindness. Randolph Seldon had refused to gloss over the prognosis, had insisted that the physician inform Georgiana of the probable outcome.

At that point, George was experiencing showers of black particles floating in her vision. These were followed by flashes of light and, finally, by an ever-darkening veil. The road to blindness had taken the better part of three years, but had fortunately proved painless. George's only apparent reaction to the entire ordeal had been her almost complete withdrawal from society. It was this withdrawal which had prompted her after-hours visits to Jacob McCauley's print shop workroom, where Jacob patiently taught her to make copperplate engravings, a task which allowed a keen sense of touch to replace that of sight.

On the rare occasions when his verbal descriptions had proved inadequate, Jacob had developed a compensatory system. He had laid a sheet of heavy vellum paper on a soft pad and used a blunt quill to trace the design, thus "engraving" the paper and giving Georgiana something to "see" in her mind as she ran her fingertips over the back of the sheet. Samarra had continued the use of Jacob's system after his death.

And she had respected Georgiana's desire to remain in the background. Even though Sam had also learned the art of engraving from Jacob, as time passed and her business grew, she came to rely more and more on her sister's talents. Georgiana's emotional needs were no different from anyone else's. Making the engravings for Sam provided pride and satisfaction, and the work filled hours that would have otherwise been empty. But not once, Samarra reluctantly admitted, had she ever attempted to draw her twin out of her shell, helping her to fill her need for personal relationships beyond their extended family. She had used George's reticence, fed upon it, labeling her attitude toward her twin "protective." Her selfish decision to play hostess this evening had finally brought to the fore a partial realization of her own blindness where Georgiana was concerned.

It was that realization which had prompted her animosity toward Clint Holbrooke. That there existed neither rhyme nor reason for this attitude never occurred to Samarra. That the ever-growing frustration fostered by her newly awakened sexuality contributed to this attitude did not occur to her either. Throughout dinner and the half hour she had spent alone with Beth afterward as the two had cleared the dining room table, her deliberations had gradually wrapped themselves into a tight coil in her mind, finally striking with a deadly venom when the four regrouped in the front salon for hot cocoa.

Edwin unwittingly provided an opening for Samarra to vent her spleen when he offhandedly asked Clint what business had brought him to Williamsburg.

Before Clint could form a reply, she sneered, "You can *ask,* Edwin, but don't expect a succinct response. Mr. Holbrooke has mastered the art of verbal duplicity."

Clint's brow folded upward at the challenge in her words, and his hazel eyes snapped brightly in irritation. "Pardon me, Miss Seldon, but do please tell me how you managed to arrive at that conclusion."

Beth and Edwin shared an *I-know-what's-going-on-between-these-two* look and sat back to enjoy both the cocoa and the performance.

"What business *did* bring you to our fair city, Mr. Holbrooke?" She turned to her guests then, directing her words to them, yet seeing neither them nor the humor radiating from their eyes and twitching lips. "This man professes to be a translator of French literature, but you tell me why he would feel the need to

102

leave his homeland and travel thousands of miles to establish residence in our colonial city in order to execute those translations." She paused only long enough to gulp air, then hastened to provide her own response. "Surely one who performed such a task would find himself better served by a large European city as his principal residence. There is no logic there—none that my poor, befuddled feminine mind can perceive. Mr. Holbrooke must think me some kind of dolt to believe such hogwash."

"Would you believe I had grown tired of the hustle and bustle of London?" Clint asked through clenched teeth.

"Yes, I could believe that," Samarra acquiesced, "but if it was nothing other than a more leisurely pace you desired, you could always have moved to the country. England *does* encompass more than London, does it not? I seem to recall that England includes a great deal of countryside. I *did* spend my childhood there, Mr. Holbrooke."

"Do you possess no spirit of adventure, Miss Seldon, no desire to break loose from the bonds that have held you since childhood and test your wings elsewhere? What was it that brought your father to this land? Is his own business, perhaps, circumspect?"

"My father's business has nothing to do with this. And I have broken loose from those bonds, tested my wings, and found that I can fly rather well. I am perfectly content with who I am, what I am, and where I am."

"Oh, yes! Excuse my wretched memory, please. I had forgotten having heard a similar statement from you before. Not everyone shares your contentment, Miss Seldon."

"So now you're asking me to believe that a man of your education, your physique, and your adventur-

103

some spirit is actually a translator? Come, Mr. Holbrooke, don't mince words—tell us the truth. What sort of criminal *are* you? What sort of vile deed are you running from?"

Although her words angered him, Clint found himself more concerned with the near truth of them. If he allowed her to continue on this track, she might very well succeed in exposing him for the spy he was. Quickly, he thought back to what she had just said, and his mind grasped a word which could successfully turn the tables on her. He grinned wickedly, and his words flowed like warm honey from a crystal pitcher. "My physique? Your thoughts seemed determined to dwell on that aspect of my person, don't they?" Later, he realized he should have stopped right there, but instead his anger plowed ahead into seas better left unsailed. "Shall we enlighten your guests? Tell them just *how* you came to know my physique so well?"

It was a mean, contemptible, underhanded thing to say—one which bespoke a boorishness Samarra had not expected of him, nor did she stop to consider how ill-bred her own words had been. She blanched, bolted from her chair, and took two quick steps toward him, raising her right arm and displaying her open palm as her petite stature bore down upon him.

It would have been no mean feat for Clint to reach up and grasp her wrist, thus preventing the loud whack which resounded in the sudden stillness of the room. But he sat perfectly still, his gaze locked on hers, his demeanor saying, "Go ahead, hit me. Show both me and the McLairds what a little spitfire you can be." When she did just that, his eyes continued to hold hers, and he did not even flinch from the sharp sting of her slap.

Samarra backed away as quickly as she had advanced, the fingers of her left hand encircling her right wrist and holding her throbbing hand, palm turned outward, close to her waistline. If Clint's icy gaze had left her face, he would have seen the reddened, quickly swelling flesh of her still open palm.

Samarra winced—as much from the pulsating pain in her right hand as from the stony, unforgiving look in Clint's eyes. The imprint of her splayed fingers gleamed whitely on his tanned left cheek, and though his gaze did not soften, a grin plucked at the corners of his wide mouth.

"Your claws are showing again, kitten," he purred.

And while she stood her ground, her head reeling from both her own unladylike reaction to his crudeness and her worry at how she would ever manage to explain everything to Beth and Edwin, Clint Holbrooke calmly rose from his chair, reached around Samarra to place his cup and saucer on the low butler's table, and smiled sweetly at the McLairds.

"Meeting the two of you was indeed a pleasure. And do, please, accept my apology for spoiling your evening. If you will excuse me now, kind folks, I would like to retire to the peacefulness of my bed—which I traveled *thousands* of miles to find."

Without waiting for a response, but with the turn of a booted heel and a few lengthy strides, Clint Holbrooke took his departure.

Chapter Seven

The remainder of the week passed and a new one began without another invitation from Samarra.

Clint was disappointed—but not surprised.

Why had she attacked him so viciously? And why had he fallen into her trap, returning her challenge with words meant to wound, and wound deeply? How could he have strayed, even momentarily, from his plan? Surely he could have found some other way to extricate himself from the situation in which she had placed him. If he was to uncover enough factual information to indict her, he needed to stay on her good side. Damn it! He was supposed to woo her, not antagonize her!

But the more he thought about Samarra, the more he observed her, the better he came to know her, the more convinced he became that Dinwiddie was barking up the wrong tree.

From his lofty position in Jacob McCauley's attic rooms, Clint watched the house next door for two full days—and a goodly portion of the nights—following the disastrous dinner party. Saturday morning, he had watched Samarra exit through the back door of her house, walk across the rear garden, and go through the gate to the backyard of the print shop. Although he'd lost sight of her before she opened the door leading into the workroom, he heard her key turn in the lock and the scraping noise the door made as she pushed it open. Sunday had been quiet, but this morning, Monday, he had watched her come to work again. Watched and listened. If he was very quiet and concentrated very hard, he could hear her slippered footfalls as she crossed the room into the front office. The tinkle of the bell attached to the front door signaled the arrival of a customer to Clint's ears as well as Samarra's. More often now he heard the syncopated *thump-thurump-thump* noise her press made.

At those times, he had braved seeing her, using his need for fresh air and exercise as an excuse for venturing downstairs, then having to traverse the width of the workroom in order to reach the back door. This journey took him directly past the printing press at which she worked. Samarra's eyes avoided his person, thus allowing him to gain close—though, by all appearances, casual—scrutiny of her work. Not once did he see anything even remotely resembling currency.

Damn him! Damn him all to hell!

As much as Samarra abhorred swearing, she found herself guilty of silent swearing more and more lately. Although three days had passed since the dinner party, her face still burned from acute embarrassment. Her first reaction had been to boot him out of her life—now, before she suffered from a repeat performance of their mutual antagonism. But if she did that now, if she forced him to move while Beth and Edwin were still her guests, the action would surely give credence to his coarse insinuations. Although they had seemingly accepted her explanation—she had told them about walking in on him during his bath—Samarra caught them exchanging secretive smiles which said to her, "There's more to this than she will admit."

And, damn it all, there was! At night, when she lay alone in her solitary bed, staring out at the square of light from his window, her body betrayed her. Deep within her being—her soul as much if not more so than her body—a seed had been planted . . . a seed which demanded softly spoken love words and the silken touch of large, callused hands to water and nurture it as it grew to fruition. Every night, she fought the demands of the dogged seed, commanded it to shrivel and die where it had been planted. Every night the hearty seed won the battle.

By day she immersed herself in work, silently cursing him who had initiated her restlessness whenever she saw him, which, she reluctantly admitted, was not nearly often enough.

On the third day, Clint gave up his vigil long enough to walk a few blocks to a livery and hire a horse and gig, which he promptly drove to the Palace Green. The young second lieutenant on duty snapped to attention when he recognized Clint. "How may I help you, Lieutenant Colonel Holbrooke, sir?" he asked, his words formally clipped as bespoke his lower rank.

"I'm here to see Captain Reed," Clint replied, but when the lieutenant seemed loath to respond, he prompted him. "Would you be so kind as to get him for me, Lieutenant—"

The young man found his tongue. "Morris. Sorry, sir, but he isn't here."

"Where is he?" Clint was becoming increasingly exasperated. In fact, he had left the print shop in a less than chipper mood. Samarra's stony silence coupled with his inability to discover any incriminating evidence had begun to sour on his stomach.

"Gone, sir, to Richmond."

"To Richmond? That little hamlet? Why?"

"It's this business with the French in the Ohio Valley. The governor sent him to meet with General Braddock before the general's departure for Fort Duquesne."

And I'd bet I know why, Clint thought, presuming the captain had been sent with a dispatch to Braddock from Dinwiddie.

Following Washington's defeat at Fort Duquesne in July and his resignation afterward, Edward Braddock had been appointed commander-in-chief of the British Army in America. Clint knew Braddock, knew he was brave but aged, wise in the ways of European warfare but unused to the American woods and the dangers that lurked within them. Clint knew Braddock was incapable of doing the job half as well as Washington.

He had had occasion to meet George Washington, to learn, as Dinwiddie already had, what a brilliant military mind the man possessed. Clint had been present the day last winter when Washington had returned from an incredibly dangerous mission, where he had parleyed with hostile French military commanders on the western frontier. Dinwiddie had not wanted Washington to resign his commission in the army, but even as governor he could do nothing about the royal edict reducing the ranks of American officers which had prompted it several months later. Nor could anyone censure the man for desiring to be treated as an equal with British officers.

Clint knew that Dinwiddie was fully aware of Braddock's shortcomings. And he'd be willing to wager any sum that the governor had sent Reed to Braddock in the hopes of convincing the general that he must take a different strategy in America than he would in Europe.

"When do you expect him back?"

"Any day now, sir. Shall I tell him you were here?"

"Yes—no." Although Clint wanted, nay, *needed* to talk to Mac Reed, he didn't think it wise for the captain to visit the print shop again. "Did the captain perhaps leave a package for me?"

"I believe he did, sir." Lieutenant Morris bent to remove a flat, wrapped package from a drawer and handed it over to Clint, who nodded toward a closed door.

"Mind if I use Mac's desk? I'd like to leave him a note." Clint closed the door behind him, then spent several minutes rifling through the papers on top of Mac's desk and inside the drawers, looking for any notes the captain might have made concerning the counterfeiters. There were none to be found. Quickly he penned a short message to MacKenzie Reed, which he folded and sealed with wax. When he handed the note to the lieutenant, he asked if perhaps the governor had left a message for him.

"No, sir, none that I know of," Morris said, flipping through a stack of papers in a rectangular basket on the desk. The lieutenant shook his head. "Nothing else here, sir, with your name on it. The governor's been mighty busy with this trouble with the French, sir. I'm sorry."

"It's not your fault, lieutenant. But make sure Captain Reed gets my message as soon as he returns to duty here."

Clint's preoccupation with the prospect of war, with Reed's absence from Williamsburg, and with the lack of any new information from the governor's office prevented his notice of an ever-darkening sky—and of the stealthy figure following him as he returned the horse and gig to the livery. He had walked about half the distance from the livery back to the print shop when a loud clap of thunder captured his attention. With utmost haste, he pushed the paper-wrapped package in between his waistcoat and frock coat in an effort to protect it, then wrapped his cape closely about his chest and leaned forward, letting his back take the brunt of the storm.

The heavens unleashed their fury with a torrent of rain, the drops hurtling into his cheeks and neck, stinging like dagger points. Although he pulled his tricorne low on his forehead and hitched up the collar of his cape, by the time he reached the shelter of the print shop's front door, the rain had soaked him to the skin.

He barreled through the door, the clanging bell grating on his already overwrought nerves, his mood as black as the sky without. He had slammed his hat onto a peg and was slinging the drizzling cape from his shoulders when Samarra walked into the outer office from the workroom.

"My God, woman!" he bellowed as a chill seized him. "Light a fire on that hearth!"

Samarra gaped at him. "You're dripping all over the floor."

"Damn the floor! It's cold in here."

She scurried to do his bidding, realizing suddenly how chilled she herself felt—and she was dry. When she turned from the fireplace, her eyes widened at the sight which greeted her.

Clint Holbrooke had removed both his frock coat and waistcoat as well as his shoes and was now unfastening his shirt.

"What do you think you're doing?" she gasped.

"What does it look like I'm doing? Getting out of these wet clothes before I catch my death."

"But—but you can't just strip naked right here."

"Why not?" He laughed shortly. "You aren't likely to

111

get much business in this downpour, so who will know?"

"I will."

Her words gave him no pause. Knowing what the sight of a nude man in her shop would do to her business, she scurried to close the tab curtains and lock the door against surprise intrusion.

By this time he had his shirt off and was peeling his damp stockings down his muscled calves. He slung his words at her much the same as he slung the stockings across the room. "It's not as though you've never seen me this way before, Samarra. You can always go back to work."

"You can't reach the stairs without crossing the workroom, Mr. Holbrooke," she reminded him. "And I'm not willing to soak myself by going home right now." Her volume matched that of the pelting rain and booming thunder, but there was anger there as well, lending a sharp edge to her words. He was down to his knee breeches now. "Can't you finish undressing in your room?" she asked.

"There's no fire in my room," he managed through chattering teeth, "and I'm *c-c-cold!* Why don't you be a good girl and run upstairs and get me a blanket? Then you can light the fire in my room while I warm myself beside this one."

"Don't patronize me, Mr. Holbrooke. I'm not your slave." Samarra had no intention of getting him a blanket—until he started to shimmy his breeches over his hipbones. Muttering something about indecency and an incredible lack of manners, she bolted from the room.

Moments later, he heard her call to him from the stairwell. "I'm leaving your blanket here, Mr. Holbrook. Do, *please,* wear it when you come upstairs!"

Clint couldn't avoid a grin so bold it crinkled the skin

around his eyes and almost obliterated the cleft in his chin. His eyes sparkled with devilment even as a chill shook his frame. His knee breeches clung in wet folds to his legs and dripped icy water in cold runnels down his calves. His ploy to remove them in her presence had proved effective, getting her upstairs again, but once he had reached the privacy of the workroom, he did take them off. On his way, he had picked up his other wet clothes—and the package Mac had left him. When he had settled the blanket around his shoulders and securely tied his damp cravat around his waistline, he draped the remaining wet garments over one arm and slipped quietly up the stairs, his bare feet making only soft swishing noises on the treads, his thoughts centered on Samarra.

Somehow he had to regain control of his emotions. It was not in his nature to be belligerent, to taunt without mercy, to treat anyone as abominably as he treated her.

That one sat hunkered before the hearth in his bedchamber, nervously striking flint against steel, mumbling in irritation at her inability to start the fire. Who did he think he was, anyway, to treat her so subserviently? Hadn't he done his best to embarrass her in front of Beth and Edwin? Never before had she completely lost her composure. Not once in her life had she slapped anyone—until now.

But, damn it, if anyone had ever deserved it, Clint Holbrooke did!

Samarra wasn't sorry she had slapped him. She was only sorry there had been witnesses.

The low, almost husky timbre of his voice right at her ear shocked her, and she dropped the flintstone.

"Here"—he pulled her gently to her feet and laid his wet clothes on her outstretched arm—"hang these to dry and I'll start the fire."

Without argument she passed him the piece of steel, her eyes glittering with anger. When she had safely moved past him, she dragged the quilt frame from its place against the far wall over to the wide brick hearth and busied herself with draping Clint's dripping clothes over its dowels.

"I suggest, Mr. Holbrooke," she said, as she pulled the wrinkles out of the last piece of clothing and straightened it over the rack, "you get into bed immediately."

She heard the rope frame creak as he settled his length upon the moss-filled mattress. Satisfied that he would now behave himself, she made her way down the darkened staircase to the workroom and set about heating water over a spirit lamp. Seldom did she make tea at the shop, since Nanna generally brought coffee over from next door. But in expectation of occasional inclement weather, Samarra kept the makings for tea stored in a cabinet in the workroom.

While the tea steeped, she set about lighting the lamps on the stairs and in the two ground-floor rooms. If possible, the storm had worsened in its severity, hurling great torrents of water so forcefully against the panes that Samarra wondered how the fragile glass could withstand the onslaught. The wind wailed around the eaves and, coupled with the force of the rain, twisted the fruit trees in the garden into limber bows arching against a tarnished silver sky, which a golden spike of lightning occasionally polished into gleaming brilliance.

Samarra shivered in the damp chill as she poured herself a cup of tea. Three sips later, guilt reared its head. No matter how angry she was with the man upstairs, she couldn't enjoy a cup of hot tea while he lay shivering.

"I hope you don't mind taking yours without

114

cream," she announced coolly as she entered his room, carrying a tray. "I don't make tea here very often, and there's nowhere to keep fresh cream." All the while she talked, she busied herself with crossing the room, setting the tray down on the table, and pouring the tea. Not once did she look directly at the bed. "There is honey, though—and some cold apple fritters. I'm sure Nanna will see that you receive some proper food when it stops raining. Enjoy your tea."

She had turned to leave when she felt his hand grasp her lower arm. They had played this scene before. Although he held her lightly this time, she felt as entrapped as a little gray mouse cornered by Clementine, her heart beating erratically in the certain knowledge that the patient victor watched and waited for her ultimate submission.

Well, it won't happen again! I won't let it happen!

"Where are you going?" he whispered, yet his voice sounded like a thunderclap in her ears.

"Downstairs. I have work to do."

"But it's so dark. How can you see? Aren't you afraid?"

She knew he meant "afraid of the storm." She assured herself she harbored little fear, yet her heart pounded heavily in her chest as she acknowledged her fear—of him! And of her own physical response to his voice, to his nearness.

"No," she whispered back.

"Can't it wait?"

"Can't what wait?"

"Your work."

"Oh!" she gasped lightly, her face suffusing with color as she fully realized the track her mind was taking. "No, it can't. Not really. I *do* have deadlines to meet, you know."

He released her arm then, and she thought she heard

a sigh behind her. "I suppose I shall just have to withstand my own fear alone."

In total incredulity, she turned toward the bed. "*You!* Afraid of the storm?"

"And why not? Is it written somewhere that fear of the elements is limited to children and little old ladies?"

"Are you calling me a little old lady?"

Suddenly the fire on the hearth caught and blazed, lending a soft yellow glow to the bedchamber and illuminating the fire burning in the hazel depths of Clint's marvelous eyes. A mischievous grin plucked at the corners of his wide mouth, and the cleft in his chin trembled with his mirth. "I wouldn't dare."

"But you thought I should be afraid of the storm."

"Since I am neither child nor little old lady, yet I fear it, why shouldn't you?"

"Well, I don't," she vehemently denied, "nor do I honestly believe you do." But with equal vehemence she squealed and threw herself across his lap when a vicious peal of thunder resounded in the room, rattling the windowpanes and the procelain lid of the teapot. Without conscious thought, she clutched the quilt which lay upon Clint's broad chest and hid her face in its folds.

His warm chuckle brought her to her senses, but when she would have extricated herself, his left arm surrounded her waistline and held her close.

"I thought you weren't afraid."

"I lied."

"So . . . why don't you pull up that chair over there and we'll keep each other company until the storm abates. Maybe you can think of some more lies to tell me." When she made no effort to move, he squeezed her midriff and suggested, "Or better yet, why don't you just stay right where you are and we won't talk at all."

His words were like a splash of ice-cold water on her senses. In a flash as quick as the lightning which popped without, she rose and bolted halfway across the room.

Hearty laughter erupted from the bed.

"How dare you laugh at my fear, you—you despoiler of women!"

"My, my, Samarra," he clucked. "Did you lie awake at night thinking up that particular accusation? How would you know how many women I might have despoiled? Who coined that word anyway? *Despoil* . . . sounds like something one might say of rotting food. 'Hey, Mac, there's green stuff on this bread. That mean it's despoiled?' If it worked like that, despoiled women would sport moldy growths. Make 'em easy to recognize, so that 'despoilers of women' would know which ones not to bother to waste their time on, because they're already despoiled."

If Clint had expected his teasing to soften her anger, he was disappointed. She stood in the same spot, her legs shaking underneath her skirt, her breathing labored. "Must you turn everything into a joke?" she snapped. "Must you forever make light of me and what I say?"

"Oh—then it's perfectly all right for *you* to do your damnedest to tarnish my reputation in front of others, while I sit calmly by and take not only your vicious words but your physical violence as well? But *I,* on the other hand, must never utter one word in retaliation. And that makes you a lady—and me a despoiler of women."

His accusation met its target, and she felt her body go limp in shame and degradation. "I—I'm sorry about the other night."

"As well you should be."

His complacent rejoinder got her dander up again.

"That's no proper way to respond to an apology."

He quirked a russet eyebrow in amusement. "Just how does one respond *properly,* Samarra, to an apology for a totally *improper,* completely unprovoked action?"

She watched the toe of her slipper as she scuffed it on the floor. "You could say you forgive me—and that you will forget about the incident, which *was* provoked."

"You're forgiven and I'll forget. How's that?"

Samarra's head snapped up at the complete lack of sincerity in his voice, but his smile disarmed her and she forgot what tidbit she had ready to hurl at him.

"Come on, Samarra. Think about it . . . moldy patches to identify despoiled women. Don't you like the idea?"

Her mouth twisted in the barest hint of a smile. "Then what happens to married women? Do they mold, too?"

"No, Samarra," he explained as though he were talking to a child. "They're not *despoiled,* they're *despotted.*"

"Despotted?"

"Have you ever known a wife who was not a despot?"

"Clint, that's bad. That's—really—bad." Her last three words were punctuated with snickers, followed by her laughter—and his. Their glee turned into hysterics, resounding pleasantly and cleansing the air in much the same way the thunder resounded and the rain cleansed without.

In resignation, she crossed the room and dragged the straight chair to his bedside. "All right," she sighed, no longer able to keep up any pretense, "if you promise to be civil, I'll keep you company. But when I leave this chair, I'm going downstairs," she warned, her message clear.

"That's all right by me." Clint leaned forward and plumped the pillows at his back. When he had resettled his torso, he retrieved his teacup and saucer from the tray. "It's a shame you brought only one cup." He waved it at her. "Would you like to share mine?"

The thought of such intimacy brought a hot stain rising to her cheeks. "No-no, thank you. Is the tea hot enough? Are you warm now?"

The thought of such intimacy brought heat to his loins. "Yes, I'm quite warm now, thank you."

"And . . . what would you like to talk about?"

He shrugged, the action pulling the quilt off his shoulders, his bare skin stretched over bulging muscles reminding her of his probable nakedness beneath the cover . . . reminding her that a lady had no business sitting alone like this with any man, especially a naked one. Especially one who made her blood run hot and cold, the way Clint Holbrooke did. Her head told her to get away now, while she still could. But her heart bade her stay.

"I really did enjoy dinner the other night. I'm sorry if I embarrassed you."

His gentle apology bespoke his sincerity this time and renewed her shame. She hung her head and spoke to her lap. "'Twas not your fault. I goaded you and behaved in a most unseemly manner. It is I who should be repenting—sincerely repenting for baiting you as I did."

"All is forgiven then. Perhaps we can start afresh."

She lifted her gaze and met squarely the sincere warmth of his. "Perhaps."

"The McLairds are nice folks. Are they still your houseguests?"

"Yes."

"Good. I was hoping I might get to see them again before they return to the frontier."

"Are you fishing for another dinner invitation, Mr. Holbrooke?"

"Would one be forthcoming if I were?"

"No."

For a moment she enjoyed watching the play of emotion on his features as he digested the possible unspoken meanings of that single negative word.

"I was that boorish?"

"Well—yes and no. The truth is, Beth and Edwin are going home. They were planning to leave on the morrow, but that was before this storm broke. Since the coach road is virtually impassable after a heavy rain, I expect their departure will be delayed."

"Which means they will be here at least for tonight, and quite probably tomorrow night as well. By my calculations, that leaves us time for a minimum of one dinner together, and possibly two."

Samarra grinned despite herself. "You, Mr. Holbrooke, are incorrigible!"

"So I've been told. Am I invited to dinner tonight or not?"

"No."

"Surely, Samarra, you realize my need to redeem myself in their eyes. Must I beg you?" He watched her face closely, as closely as the dim light allowed him to, looking for some sign of her disapproval of his familiarity with her and seeing none. Her pale complexion glowed in the firelight, and her topaz eyes danced with good humor.

Samarra had not missed his use of her given name, but she found herself unaccountably pleased by the way it rolled off his tongue, her pleasure perhaps intensified by the way she had gained control of this cat-and-mouse game they played. "Beg all you like, sir. In truth, I am not at liberty to invite you to dinner."

Clint's face mirrored his disbelief. "Do you honestly

expect me to believe that the indomitable Miss Samarra Seldon has lost control over her own destiny, even for one day?"

"Believe what you will. Beth and Edwin have invited me to join them for dinner at Christiana Campbell's tonight."

"If that's all there is to it, then I have nothing to worry about. I'll just take my incorrigible self to Mistress Campbell's establishment and meet you there. What time, did you say?"

"You wouldn't dare!"

"Why not? It's a public place, one I've frequented plenty of times—and not once have I gotten myself thrown out!" *But one where you'd be recognized, Holbrooke.* Damn, if he hadn't walked right into her trap, even if she wasn't aware she had set it. Perhaps the best way out was to push a little harder. "What time, did you say?" he repeated, and was rewarded by her bristling reply.

"I didn't."

He looked crestfallen. "You aren't going to invite me, are you?"

She looked contrite. "I can't."

"Maybe tomorrow night?"

"You don't give up, do you?"

"Not without a fight."

"Duly noted. Maybe."

"That's the best you can do?"

"On that particular subject, yes." On that note she rose and crossed to the fireplace, where she added several sticks of wood to the blaze. The roaring fire had succeeded in banishing the chill from the room, but the storm had failed to abate. Its pelt and boom eclipsed her voice, but Clint could plainly see her lips move as she whirled away from the fire, could see the sudden look of distress that claimed her features, and he wondered what thought had prompted her anguish. Without further explanation, she dashed from the bedchamber and, despite the cacophony of the storm, he could hear the quick but heavy thuds of her slippered feet upon the stairs.

With no small degree of concern, he threw back the covers, snatched open a drawer, and retrieved a shirt. Not bothering to close its front or to stuff its tail into the waistband of the breeches he had worn to bed, he followed Samarra downstairs.

She stood near the back door, her arms cuddling a squirming bundle of white fur in her shawl, tears streaming down her cheeks. Clint's long legs swiftly closed the space separating them.

"What is it, Samarra? What happened?"

She turned moisture-laden eyes to his soft gaze. "It's Clem. I f-forgot I had let her out . . . just be-before you got back. She's been s-standing out there on the back s-stoop crying, all this time!"

"She'll be all right," he soothed, his arm instinctively moving around Samarra's shoulders, pulling her slender body into his. "We just have to get her dry and warm. At least we have a fire now. Come on, let's take her upstairs. She seems to prefer my bed to her box."

Clint moved away from Samarra, toward the stairs, then realized she stood rooted to the floor. "I'm so sorry, Clementine," she moaned. "I didn't mean to leave you out there."

Clint felt torn between sympathy for her heartfelt agony and annoyance at her refusal to cope. His annoyance won. "My God, Samarra! Stop your whimpering. The cat's not dead."

Her eyes opened wide, crystal sparks shooting from their golden depths. Her ire eased the tears and hardened her voice. "That's right! Bludgeon me again with your hateful words. This is all your fault, but would you ever see that?"

"My fault? You're blaming me for your forgetfulness?"

"If it hadn't been for your ranting and raving about being wet and cold, I wouldn't have forgotten her. I made my position very clear when you asked to rent the rooms. I told you I wouldn't be your servant, yet you came storming in here today, treating me as though you owned me."

"That was not my intention. If you took it that way, I'm sorry."

"You're sorry! Well, let me tell you something, Mr. Holbrooke. Your being sorry won't help Clementine. She may not be dead, but a severe chill like this could kill her. Cats get colds, too. And this one's going to be a mother soon."

His exasperation was growing apace with hers. "What does that have to do with it?"

Samarra's voice registered her disbelief of his total idiocy. "If Clementine dies," she carefully explained, hugging the cat tighter to her bosom, "so do her babies."

The additional squeeze was more than Clem could bear. Using the strength of her hind legs, she pushed her back claws into Samarra's forearm, the talons piercing the skin through the lightweight wool of Sam's sleeve. Samarra cried out in pain, immediately loosening her hold on the cat. Clementine lunged forward, coming out of the shawl and flipping in midair before she landed on all four paws on the bare wooden floor.

Clementine shook her wet coat and sneezed.

Clint shuddered violently—and sneezed.

And Samarra laughed. Not loudly, not cheerfully, but resignedly. Her laughter carried sweetly on the air, scattering the tautly strung threads of her anxiety and easing the tension that had sparked between her and Clint.

"I don't know what's gotten into me," she said. "I haven't always overreacted to everything. Go on back to bed, Clint. I'll take care of Clementine."

He paused when he reached the stairs, looking back over his shoulder at Samarra, who had bent down to stroke the long, wet fur on Clem's back. "Poor thing!" he heard her intone. "You look like a drowned rat. Be still so I can dry you off, and then we'll go sit by the fire and get warm."

As he ascended the narrow staircase, a vision of Samarra stroking and cuddling and cooing to an unhappy child imprisoned his thoughts.

It was some time later before he realized she had called him Clint—and not once, but twice that afternoon. She was beginning to fall prey to his charms, just as he had intended. The only problem now was that he was falling prey to hers as well.

Chapter Eight

Sometime late in the afternoon, the storm wore itself out. Clint awoke from a deep sleep to the utter silence of his room—and to Clementine's rhythmic purrs from within. The cat lay curled against his rib cage, her fur now completely dry—and her body mercifully warm.

His tongue flickered out to moisten cracked lips as he forced his sleep-laden eyelids to open. Never had they felt quite so heavy, nor his mouth quite so dry, as though someone had stuffed it full of cotton while he slept. He threw back the covers and rose from the bed, shivering in the chill that pervaded the room. The fire burned low on the hearth, and though the rain had stopped, the wind continued to blow in erratic, lunging assaults that threatened to rip the shingles from the roof. Part of his weakened consciousness acknowledged the tea tray that had not been removed from his bedside table as he stumbled to the fireplace and proceeded to lay on more logs. Apparently Samarra had not returned to his room while he slept.

The tea was cold, but he drank it, swishing it around in his mouth before swallowing it, wishing it were hot buttered rum or warm applejack instead. But there were no spirits in his room, none downstairs either—

at least, none that he had knowledge of.

Clint crawled back into bed and pulled his knees up to his chest in an effort to preserve his body heat. It was almost time for supper. *Nanna will bring me some brandy,* his fevered brain assured him, and he repeated the assurance over and over until his body recovered some of its warmth and he drifted off into a troubled sleep.

And as he slept, two different men, in two entirely separate locations and for entirely separate reasons, received harsh reprimands for their respective lack of action during Lieutenant Colonel Clint Holbrooke's visit to the Palace Green that day.

One of those reprimands was taking place a mere hundred-and-twenty-five feet away, in a dimly lit, third-story front room in the boardinghouse across the street.

A tall, slender man paced the room, his footfalls punctuating his even speech. His carefully delivered words belied the anger the lamplight evidenced on his livid face and in the cold, steely depths of his narrowed eyes as he passed in front of the lamp. He clenched his fists tightly against his thighs, and when, from time to time, one of his fists moved slightly away, he brought it slowly back into position.

"He actually left the print shop and walked several blocks each way to the livery, and you did *nothing* about it?"

The only other person in the room watched those fists, knew that his employer ached to hit him—and wondered why he bothered not to. "It couldn't be helped, guv'ner," that one whined. "There was others about, it bein' broad daylight and the Public Times and all."

126

"Yes, yes," the tall man mumbled irritably, not slowing his pacing. "We can't risk exposure—not just yet." He stopped his pacing and turned abruptly on a booted heel, his unswerving gray gaze boring down into the face of the much shorter miscreant before him. "Tell me truthfully—you did, at the very least, follow him, did you not?"

"Aye, guv'ner, that I did." His voice carried more confidence now, although his shuffling stance suggested his skepticism that all would turn out well for him.

"And where did he go?"

The question was too softly, too innocently spoken to quell the smaller man's trepidation. His vast experience as a ne'er-do-well had taught him all about the calm before the storm. "To the Palace Green. Spent a short time in the guv'ner's office there."

"And when he left?"

"He took the gig straightaway to the livery and walked home—ran, I should say, and still got hisself properly soaked." The ruffian giggled inanely.

"You're quite certain there have been no more visits from anyone in the king's army?"

"No one in uniform, guv'ner. I've kep' a close watch on the place, jest like ye tol' me to. Went wi'out sleep meself, I have, tryin' to do this job for ye." The wheedle returned to his voice as he delivered this last declaration.

Wanting to dismiss the man simultaneously from his employ and from the face of the earth, but fully cognizant of the set of problems involved in locating and hiring someone else, the tall man turned away once more. For a moment all was silent. The smaller man suppressed the tremble that threatened to overtake his thin frame as he awaited his fate.

"I'm paying you well to watch him, and if that means

going without some sleep, then so be it." The tall man strode to the door and left the room without another word.

The smaller man breathed a sigh of relief, collapsed on the cot, and grumbled to the closed door, "Payin' me well! Hah! Ye've promised, is all. Them forty hogs is all I've seen from ye. I may not be here nex' time ye come a-callin', guv'ner. Ye done denied ole Guy Archer his ale and his wenches long enough."

The color washed swiftly from Guy's face when the door flew open. "You walk away from this job before it's finished and you won't live long enough to enjoy either a mug of ale or a toss upon the sheets, Guy Archer," the tall man quietly promised, and there was something so sinister about the way he said it that Guy believed him.

Long after the door had closed again and the tall man's steps had faded away, Guy lay trembling on the narrow cot. Slightly over a fortnight had passed since he'd met the tall man in a local tavern, and all that time they'd conducted business without benefit of either knowing the other's name. Guy had clung tightly to his anonymity—but now he had lost even that. The enforced abstinence from life's dual pleasures had served to parch his throat and engorge his male member, and Guy Archer honestly didn't know how much longer he could endure the intense pain and suffering that double abstinence had caused.

"Ye jest wait, guv'ner," he whispered to the ceiling. "I'm gonna kill that feller—kill him deader'n a doornail. I ain't waitin' no longer, neither. They didn't catch me afore, and they ain't likely to this time. 'Specially if I creep in on him in the middle of the night, him bein' alone over there and all. Yessir, ole Guy Archer's mighty tired of waitin'."

*　　　*　　　*

128

Governor Robert Dinwiddie sat behind his massive mahogany desk, the heels of his hands resting upon its leather top, his long fingers clutching a sheath of papers. Usually he gave the charge lieutenant's daily report a cursory glance at best, there being a myriad of other, more important items continuously parading across his mind. Had a single name not claimed his attention, this report would have followed the fate of the many before it, that of being placed in a file drawer and subsequently forgotten.

"Send that young whippersnapper Morris in here immediately!" he barked to the first lieutenant who served as his personal secretary.

Momentarily, Morris stood stiffly before his desk. "You wished to see me, sir?" he asked respectfully, though a bit tremulously. He had heard the governor's voice resounding throughout the small outbuilding, but for the life of him he couldn't figure out what he had done to arouse Dinwiddie's ire. The governor was known as an even-tempered man, and a fair one. Whatever it was, Morris knew it was serious.

Robert Dinwiddie launched directly to the point. "What's this business about Holbrooke coming here today? Why wasn't I informed?"

"I'm sorry, sir. No one told me you wished to see him, and he didn't ask for you." The callow youth paused, pushed his temerity aside long enough to allow Holbrooke's visit to replay itself in his thoughts. "He did ask if there was a message from you, sir, but I was unable to find one."

"That request alone should have given you cause to notify me, young man."

"Yes, sir. I was wrong, sir. Would you like me to find the lieutenant colonel for you, sir?" Morris hoped his admission of guilt coupled with his willingness to rectify the situation would allay a formal reprimand.

"No. I know where he is."

Morris had trouble meeting the governor's icy blue gaze, but he managed, although he was finding it increasingly difficult to breathe.

"In future," Dinwiddie continued, "I am to be informed immediately should *any* of my emissaries return to this office, regardless of the reason, regardless of whether or not they ask to see me. Is that perfectly clear?"

Was this to be the end of it, then? Morris wondered. Clinging desperately to that hope, he mustered his strength and inhaled deeply. "Yes, sir!"

"Go—leave me now. I must think what to do."

"Sweet angels in heaven above us!" Nanna exclaimed when she learned of Clint Holbrooke's fevered state that evening. With brisk efficiency, she retraced her steps to the house next door, returning to the upstairs rooms carrying a large basket laden with an assortment of her homemade remedies, an iron pot—and a large flask of Scotch whiskey.

"Scat, Clementine!" she scolded the stretching and yawning feline, who exhibited her disregard by resettling herself close to Clint's back. "I expect ye'll move soon enough when I roll him over on ye." Nanna laughed softly at the thought, for no love had ever been lost between her and the cat, then felt a twinge of guilt when she remembered Clem's pregnant state. "'Tis high time ye had them kittens anyway," she muttered in some exasperation as she lifted the struggling cat and moved her to a safer spot.

When Nanna began to bathe his face and chest with a cool, wet cloth, a low moan escaped from Clint's lips and he lifted his arms to thrash weakly at her.

"Be still," she gently admonished as she grasped his wrists and lowered his arms to his sides, then waited for a moment to see if he had heard and understood her. As she watched him, his eyes opened slightly, exposing to her view their fevered gloss. "Ye're mighty sick, young mon. I would na have thought 'twould take sae long for infection t' set in."

He winced as he tried to talk, his voice raspy, his words spoken disjointedly. "My . . . throat . . . hurts . . . not . . . my . . . leg."

Of a sudden, Nanna recalled having seen him leave the print shop that morning. She hadn't seen him when he returned. "Did ye perchance, Mr. Holbrooke, get a drenchin' this day?"

Clint nodded.

"I'm going t' take me a look at that leg anyway." She parted the bed coverings and, out of the corner of her eye, saw his chagrin when she began to unfasten his breeches. "Nae need t' trouble yereself, Mr. Holbrooke. 'Tis na my first glimpse of ye in the altogether, and I see nae reason t' ruin another pair of yere breeches."

Her words reminded him of the morning Samarra had walked in on his bath, and he smiled despite his pain. He closed his eyes and conjured a vision of that one whose face haunted his dreams as her servant's fingers pushed against the scabbed slash on his thigh. Lovely, feisty Samarra. Unpredictable Samarra. One minute, she was the epitome of ladyhood; the next, she hurled fiery words at him or staunchly defended her independence. She was unlike any other woman he had ever known, the sweetest combination of gentlewoman and libertine. And last he had seen her, she had called him Clint—twice!

Nanna's words slashed across his self-induced dream state. "Yere wound healed nicely, Mr. Holbrooke. Can ye lift yere hips now sae I can pull yere breeches back up? I'm going t' make ye a hot toddy. It will na taste real good, but it surely will make ye feel good."

A short time later she helped him sit up enough to drink the bittersweet concoction, a combination of whiskey, honey, and some other ingredient Clint could not identify, but which, he was certain, added the bitter flavor. A shudder racked his frame as the hot liquid traced a fiery path to his stomach.

"'Tis easier t' take if ye hold yere nose," Nanna informed him too late. "Ye'll notice a difference soon. I've put some hot coals in yere bed warmer. 'Twill na do t' let yere feet get cold." She helped him ease back under the covers before settling herself in the straight chair and removing a skein of yarn and a partially worked piece of knitting from her basket. Clint went to sleep listening to the soothing, commingling sounds of her soft hum and the clicking of her needles.

From across the street, Guy Archer sat at his darkened window, his eyes pinned to the patch of light illuminating a parcel of grass between the print shop and the Seldon home. A high brick wall connecting the buildings blocked a goodly portion of his view of the backyards of both, but the height of his room had allowed his earlier witness of a bobbing light moving back and forth between their rear entrances. Whoever it was visiting Holbrooke appeared to be staying the night.

"Damn!" Guy whispered harshly several hours later. He kneaded his sore eyes with his fists, took one last regretful look at the patch of light, and went to bed.

The next morning dawned bright and cold. Samarra awoke with a start, pushed herself up on her elbows, and gasped when she breathed deeply of the icy air. There was something different, something out of the ordinary about this morning, something besides the

132

fact that it had turned much colder during the night, but Samarra couldn't quite put her finger on what it was.

Reluctant to relinquish the warmth of her bed, she put the slight misgiving from her mind, snuggled deeper into the soft mattress, and pulled the heavy covers over her head. In a while, though, her cocoon grew overwarm. Bracing herself for the shock, she scurried from under the covers, pulled slippers over her feet and a heavy velvet robe over her shoulders, and quickly added several pieces of wood to the smoldering coals in her fireplace. Shivering, she moved to the window, which, as was her wont, she had left open a few inches. She paused when she opened the curtains and saw Nanna leaving the print shop.

Now why would she have gone over there so early? Samarra wondered, then sniffed the air suspiciously. No telltale odors of coffee brewing or bread baking wafted upon the frigid air. Never could Samarra recall the absence of these early morning smells before.

Quickly, and somewhat apprehensively, she closed the window and hurried downstairs, arriving in the kitchen as Nanna walked through the back door, carrying a large basket and an iron pot from which emanated a bitter odor.

"Good morning, lass—did ye sleep well?" Nanna greeted her, her own countenance bespeaking a definite lack of rest.

"By all appearances, better than you. What happened?"

"'Tis Mr. Holbrooke. Had a bad night, he did," she explained wearily. "Thrashed aboot and mumbled in his sleep, kept talking aboot you and money! I could na make sense of it." All the while she talked, Nanna unburdened herself of the basket and iron pot and set about making coffee. "Zeke must've been the one t'

133

stoke up this fire and bring in fresh water. From the looks of ye, lass, ye have na been up long."

Before Samarra could question Nanna further, Edwin pushed open the back door, his arms loaded with firewood.

"'Tis ye, then, Mr. McLaird, I should be thanking," Nanna said, her voice growing wearier and her shoulders slumping.

"Sit down, Nanna, and let me do that," Samarra quietly insisted. When Nanna frowned and continued loading coffee beans into the grinder, Samarra gently clasped the older woman's shoulders and moved her to the table. "Sit down," she repeated, her voice brooking no argument. "I've watched you do this hundreds of times, and I'm sure you'll tell me if I don't perform a task correctly. I want to know what's wrong with Mr. Holbrooke. He was fine when I left him yesterday."

"Oh, he'll be all right now." Samarra thought the grin that lightened Nanna's jaded features came very close to being wicked. "I poured enough of my fever remedy down him t' make him feel splendid."

Samarra knew well the list of ingredients Nanna used in her fever remedy. "You didn't!" she gasped.

"I did. Drunk as David's sow, he be. Once he gets over the aftereffects, he'll be fit as a fiddle. Ye're turnin' that crank t' hard, lass."

"Let me make the coffee," Edwin offered politely.

He had been so unobtrusive in tending the fire that Samarra had quite forgotten about him. Self-consciously she pulled at the lapels of her robe and ran her fingers through the length of her untethered hair, unaccustomed to being around men, including her father, in less than suitable attire. She murmured her gratitude and hurried upstairs.

*   *   *

It was almost mid-afternoon before Samarra finally got a chance to see Clint Holbrooke.

All through the day she had worried about him and desperately wanted to dash upstairs just long enough to convince herself, in spite of Nanna's assurances, that he still breathed. Her worrying played on her nerves, causing her to make clumsy mistakes as she attempted to catch up on her work in between attending to customers. This day had brought far more of them through her door than she normally saw in a week. In addition, Eliza Garrett had returned with the preliminary artwork for Clint's book of poems and a special messenger from the governor's palace had delivered identical-looking letters for her and Clint.

She had chafed at the delay in opening her letter, for she had been taking an order for playbills from a theater manager when the messenger arrived. When she did break the wax bearing the royal governor's seal, she sat staring for some minutes at the beautifully penned words: "Governor and Mrs. Robert Dinwiddie request the honor of your presence at a fancy-dress ball on All Hallows' Eve . . ."

Whatever had prompted this invitation? She had attended more than a few of the governor's balls over the past few years, but always as a guest of either her father or an escort who had himself been invited. Her heart thudded in her chest as she considered the implications of this personal invitation. Did it signify her acceptance in the business community, or had it merely been addressed to her in light of Randolph's absence from Williamsburg?

What would she wear? She glanced at the invitation again, assuring herself that she had read it correctly. A fancy-dress ball . . . she would need a costume. Who would she be? Visions of herself dressed as Joan of Arc, Juliet, and Mary, Queen of Scots, flitted through her head, but somehow none quite fit her mental image of herself. Catherine de Médicis? She shook her head. Titania? Andromeda? No. Perhaps something closer akin to the occasion. A gorgon or harpy? She shuddered in revulsion at the very thought of the slimy creatures. Her reverie was interrupted by still another customer, and it was some time later, during the first lull she'd had in several hours, before she remembered that Clint had received what she assumed to be an invitation as well.

A quick glance at the clock hastened her action. In a matter of minutes, Tom would arrive, and she harbored no inclination to argue with him over which of them would carry the letter to Clint. Tom made a point of visiting Clint almost every day, and the two had become fast friends. Completely forgetting Eliza's sketches, which would have provided sufficient need for her to see Clint instead of Tom, Samarra locked the front door and put the "Closed" sign in the window.

Clint Holbrooke lay prone upon the bed, a pillow covering his head—and the counterpane mercifully covering his body. Samarra stepped lightly to his bedside and stood stock-still for several minutes, watching his slow, regular breathing. He must have sensed her presence then, for he pulled a corner of the pillow upward and gazed at her briefly with his exposed eye before burying his head beneath the pillow again.

"Go 'way," he groaned. "Come back later."

She reached a hand tentatively under the pillow and rested her palm against his cheek. Despite its stint beneath the feathered cushion, it felt cool to her touch. Satisfied that he would live, she left the letter on his table, tended the fire, and tidied his covers before returning to her work downstairs.

*   *   *

If the fever hadn't killed him, starvation surely would.

At least, that was the way Clint felt a long time before Nanna appeared with his supper.

"Where have you been?" he teased when she bustled in well after dark, his nostrils expanding as he inhaled the delicious odors wafting from the covered tray. He waved her back into the sitting room. "As you can see, I'm much improved, and will be even better when my ravenous appetite has been satisfied."

"Praise be!" she crooned, her wrinkled face wreathed with the pleasure of seeing him not only out of bed, but bathed and clean-shaven as well. "Ye was a bit on the sickly side last even. Had me concerned, ye did."

"Last evening has me befuddled, Nanna. I'm never sick, but I suppose I was last night. I can't seem to recall many details, but I'm certain I owe you my utmost gratitude for my present robust state."

Nanna screwed up her nose and scrutinized his mien. "Ye are na' sufferin' any ill effects from my potion?"

"No, ma'am!" he enthused. "Should I be?"

"Most do." She shook her head in vexation as she placed the tray on the low, square table in the sitting room and picked up a corner of the linen towel. "Ye may na be sae happy when ye see what I brung ye," she warned before removing the towel and exposing a bowl of steaming chicken soup and a thick slice of bread.

His face fell.

"Ye just eat this now, Mr. Holbrooke, while I strip those sour sheets off yere bed. Then I'll gae back and get ye some real food."

Mollified, Clint asked, "What did you cook—besides chicken soup, I mean?"

"I roasted the rest of the bird."

He smacked his lips appreciatively. "D'you bake anything sweet today, Nanna?"

She turned from the bedchamber door and looked at

him sheepishly. "Nay, sir. I—well, I slept most of the day. But there's some leftover brown Betty from yesterday," she quickly added.

He pretended to consider her suggestion for a moment as he struggled to remember the previous night. The sound of knitting needles clicking together penetrated his deliberations. "You stayed up all night with me, didn't you, Nanna?" he asked quietly, almost reverently.

She dropped her eyes and scuffed her toe against the bare floor, and when she answered him, her voice was so low, he had to listen carefully to hear her. "Aye," she admitted.

"I can't recall anyone ever doing that for me before. Oh, I know Tom did, but he slept, and you obviously didn't. Besides, that was arranged in advance. He didn't stay with me just out of the goodness of his heart. Thank you, Nanna." He watched the wide grin slowly spread across her wizened face and felt himself go warm inside.

And then he unintentionally dispelled the warmth he had created and placed Nanna at arm's length once again by offering to pay her, thus showing, to her way of thinking, his misjudgment of her motives, his offer negating the sincere gratitude she had thought she heard.

Clint pondered Nanna's sudden coolness long into the night, finding her attitude unexplainable. She had seemed to him such a simple person, not complex, like most of the women he had known. Certainly not like his mother, who would never have sat up with him all night or made chicken soup especially for him. And certainly not like Samarra, with her mercurial moods and delusions of equality with men. It had seemed so natural to him to offer Nanna extra payment beyond what he normally gave her for doing his laundry, cleaning his quarters, and bringing his meals that he never considered how deeply that offer had hurt her.

Having slept the clock around and finding no great desire to drink himself into oblivion, Clint unwrapped the package Mac Reed had left for him, collected paper, quill, and ink, and set about "translating" the letters.

As he worked, he cursed himself for selecting French as the writer's native language. Whatever had possessed him to do so? He asked himself irritably, knowing in his heart that the decision had been an impulsive one. It had been his way of challenging Samarra's masculine choice of profession. If she could be a printer, he could be a translator of French letters, a profession he considered a dandified preference if ever there was one. Now he must live with the consequences of his decision.

Well-versed in both Greek and Latin, but having been schooled only briefly in French, Clint discovered that he could do little more than maintain sentences and paragraphs of approximately equal length with those in the letters Mac had secured. His lack of comprehension forced him to compose their contents as well, and he realized quickly that creative writing was not his forte, his handicap in that area only increased by the necessity of writing from a woman's point of view. He constantly questioned a turn of phrase, the depth of personal feeling a mother would communicate to her daughter, the particular problems that should be revealed and discussed.

In defense of his ineptitude, Clint occasionally reminded himself of the unlikelihood of anyone's ever reading his "translation." But when Clint Holbrooke undertook a task, he saw it through, exercising great care along the way to give it his all. And so went the way of his writing.

When he had reached the point of hurling his quill against the far wall, it occurred to him that all he had to do was pretend Nanna was the mother and Samarra the daughter. By embodying the fictional French *maman* with Nanna's distinctive matriarchal characteristics, softening them as she did with warmth and a sense of humor, his work began to show promise, and he continued writing long into the night.

Thus, for the second night in succession, Guy Archer's determination to fulfill finally, once and for all, his contract with the anonymous tall, slender man foundered.

No one had ever accused Guy Archer of taking unnecessary chances. And he wasn't about to start now—even if it meant having to wait still another day for a drink and a doxy.

Chapter Nine

From a nearby yard, a rooster crowed. The cock's welcoming of a new day grated on Clint's raw nerves. Wearily he collected the scattered sheets of paper, rose from the overstuffed, ratty chair, and stumbled into the bedchamber. His energies spent, he stuffed the papers into an empty bureau drawer and crawled into bed fully dressed. But as he reached out to snuff the candle flame, his tired eyes fell upon the parchment envelope lying on his bedside table.

The boldness of the hand which had scrawled his name across the creamy paper struck a familiar chord in Clint's memory, but his listless mind could not quite put a name to its owner. In spite of his extreme fatigue, the mystery ignited his curiosity. He turned the envelope over. The sight of the colonial governor's seal precipitated conflicting feelings for him. Even as he shook his head in frustration at Dinwiddie's sending him a message which very well might prompt questions from Samarra, his mouth twisted in a wry grin. Damn, but it felt good to hear from the man!

Solitary assignments had never been the norm for Clint Holbrooke. Not only had he never investigated a woman before; this was also the first time he had ever worked as a spy in Williamsburg, right under the collective noses of the men assigned to the royal governor's office. By nature, he was not a loner. Clint could—and had—spent weeks on end in Norfolk, Richmond, and Fredericksburg without once yearning for word from Williamsburg, but always in the company of other military officers. With this assignment, however, holed up a mere three-quarters of a mile from the Royal Palace, he had begun to feel ignored and neglected.

His lean fingers broke the wax seal and unfolded an engraved invitation. "What the hell!" he hissed, his mind grasping for whatever reasons Robert Dinwiddie, whom he had credited with having more sense, could possibly have for subjecting him to exposure even as he picked up a separate piece of paper which had fallen onto the counterpane.

"In light of the absence of Miss Seldon's father and out of deference to her, I am requesting your escort of her for this occasion," Clint read, noting the governor's initials beneath the message.

Clint groaned, placed the invitation and note which had accompanied it on the table, and extinguished the candle. In the predawn darkness, he threw an arm over his eyes and refused to give Dinwiddie's obvious idiocy any further consideration at the moment. Instead he concentrated on relaxing his tense muscles and trying to fall asleep.

In the big house next door, Samarra sat up in bed and stretched her arms over her head. For some presently unaccountable reason—certainly not from undisturbed rest—a feeling of exhilaration sluiced through her petite frame. With uncharacteristic alacrity, she tossed the heavy cover aside as though it were

142

featherweight and bounced out of bed.

Although the temperature had dipped even lower during the night than it had the night before, Samarra didn't feel its intensity, not even when she splashed the frigid water from the ewer onto her face. She dressed carefully, selecting a gown of brighter color and finer fabric than those she usually wore to work without questioning her motives, and she came very close to giving in to the urge to slide down the banister.

It was not until she entered the kitchen, her lips pursed as she whistled a merry tune, her eyes twinkling brightly, that she sought explanation for her chipper mood. And then, only because Nanna took note of it.

"Land's sakes, Miss Sam!" the Scotswoman exclaimed. "Ye must've slept awful well. I can't remember when ye came downstairs sae happy sae early in the morning."

Samarra grinned widely. "Neither can I, Nanna," she replied in a voice as exuberant as the bounce in her step. Then she remembered what had put that bounce there, abruptly plopped herself in a chair, and set her gaze on the gleaming copper kettle hanging over a roaring fire.

In her mind, the gleam transposed itself into that of hundreds of flaming candles standing tall and proud as they lent their glitter to a crowded ballroom. Costumed dancers whirled around on the polished wood floor, the women holding feather-trimmed masks to their faces. The eye of her mind focused itself on one particular couple and followed their graceful progress among the many dancers. The woman wore a diaphanous gown fashioned in the Greek style; one shoulder gleamed like luminescent pearls where it had been left bare, while the other sported a heavy golden brooch atop the many folds of sheer fabric draped there. Above the feathery fringes of her white mask, ropes of pearls entwined themselves among golden, honey-colored tresses. The woman smiled demurely at her partner as he led her through the steps of a courtly promenade.

"What would ye like for breakfast, Miss Sam?"

The tinny clatter of a porcelain teacup against its saucer, coupled with Nanna's softly spoken question, pierced Samarra's daydream, and she lifted misted eyes to the wrinkled face of her beloved servant and blinked incomprehendingly. "I'm sorry, Nanna. I—my mind was elsewhere. What did you say?"

"Will ye be wantin' eggs this morning? Or maybe some oatmeal?"

Samarra shook her head. "Just coffee, thank you. I'm not very hungry." Her stomach rumbled loudly then, belying her words. "Perhaps a slice of bread, Nanna," she amended, her thoughts continuing their foray among costumed dancers and glittering candle-light. Never before had an invitation excited her so. But somehow, she knew this one was different, this ball would be unlike all others. Samarra had the strangest feeling that this fancy-dress ball was somehow tied to her destiny, and she knew with unshakable certainty that the partner of her dream would also be her escort to the ball.

Nanna's uncharacteristic silence during the meal cleared the path of her wandering throughts while the soft hiss and crackling of the fire accompanied them.

Even nature seemed bent on nourishing her reverie. The full face of the sun, just breaking above the horizon, was visible today, the pale blue sky almost completely clear of clouds. The rain had soaked the half-bare tree limbs and the plummeting temperature had frozen the droplets there. The trees stood in shimmering silver splendor against the clear sky, their jeweled limbs and autumn-kissed leaves sparkling in kaleidoscopic array in the sunlight, completely capturing Samarra's attention as she made her way across the backyards to the print shop. Her heart sang with joy, her golden eyes sparkled with good humor, and her feet practically skipped down the frosty path a myriad of footsteps had worn between the two buildings.

Had she not been so absorbed in the beauty of nature's pre-winter face, perhaps she would have paid more heed to the slushy ice patches littering the back step.

But she was absorbed, she paid no heed, and she leapt upon the icy brick slab.

From his bed above her, Clint came fully awake as her scream wrenched the cold, still air. He hurtled from beneath the covers, slid his stockinged feet into a pair of shoes, and, not stopping to buckle them, raced downstairs. From the kitchen next door, Nanna heard the scream as well. The two of them reached a smiling though shaky Samarra almost simultaneously.

She sat upon the icy step, attempting to regain both her composure and her strength as they approached. Her broad smile and the tinge of pink blossoming on her cheeks eased their concern but failed to eradicate it altogether.

"I'm all right—truly I am," she assured them, offering an outstretched hand to each of her rescuers. "Help me up."

As they stood her on her feet, she twisted her head around to survey the damage to her skirts, which sported several damp patches streaked with mud, one large oval one darkening the fabric covering her buttocks. Clint grinned mischievously as his gaze settled on the clinging wet fabric there. His free arm slipped around her shoulders for support.

Despite her assurances that she was uninjured, when she put her weight on her right leg, a sharp pain stabbed

145

her upper thigh and a grimace replaced her smile. Clint felt the sudden tight grip of her hand in his and the dip of her shoulder beneath his arm as she favored her right leg. Without warning, he released her hand and scooped her into his arms.

A gasp erupted from her mouth. Her plea was uttered naturally, without thought, devoid of pretense. "Clint, put me down! I can walk."

A few steps ahead of them, Nanna noted Sam's use of his Christian name and she smiled in satisfaction.

"Perhaps you can," Clint teased, the corners of his lips turned up impishly, "but there's no need for you to try. I expect that hidden somewhere under those voluminous skirts is a rather nasty bruise."

"I think you may be right," Samarra admitted, her arms moving of their own accord around his neck. "That was rather clumsy of me." Her eyes surveyed the near smirk of his grin, the trembling cleft in his chin, then traveled upward to scrutinize heavy-lidded, red-streaked eyes. At small risk—surely Clint wouldn't kiss her here, in broad daylight and with Nanna present—Samarra pulled her head closer to his and sniffed, then wrinkled her nose at the smell of whiskey on his breath. "You don't appear to have slept well, sir," she observed with mild concern, her own grin matching his smirk.

Clint's gaze drifted out to Nanna's back several paces ahead of them and then down again into Samarra's happy face. His own face lowered so that his mouth almost touched her ear. "While you, my sweet Samarra, appear on top of the world this morning," he muttered, his breath tickling the fine hairs on the side of her neck.

Instead of withdrawing immediately, as Samarra expected, his lips nibbled at her earlobe, sending shivers of delight through her. A part of her desperately wanted his attentions to continue—not merely for the

146

moment, but for hours on end, perhaps forever. But the part of her that grasped at sanity, that dictated reason, demanded sobriety. Not daring to protest verbally and thus draw Nanna's attention, Samarra pushed her ear against his chest. Her movement brought his lips across her cheek to the corner of her mouth, startling her with the intensity of their brand on her cold skin. Her eyes sought his, begged his understanding. She could not read the expression in his hazel orbs; it seemed to hover somewhere between passion and contempt.

Not contempt, surely! she corrected herself. Perhaps it was reluctance she saw there. She thought she felt the slightest tremor ripple through his chest as he raised his head from hers and fixed his gaze upon the bobbing movement of Nanna's head as that one mounted the rear steps to the kitchen.

The hinges on the back door creaked as Nanna opened it wide and held it there so Clint could enter with his burden. "Just put her there," Nanna said lightly, nodding toward the table, "while I pour us some coffee. Ye look as if ye could use some, Mr. Holbrooke."

"'Just put her there,'" Samarra mimicked as Clint kicked out a chair and carefully lowered her into it. "I'm not a delivery from the greengrocer, Nanna," she chided gently, the smile that had been her constant companion that morning continuing to play around her mouth.

The look Nanna shot her from the proximity of the fireplace was one of narrow-eyed assessment. Samarra felt suddenly as though she were some prize cow on the auction block. "Nay," Nanna murmured, "I can na say that ye resemble any cabbage head I've ivver seen, 'cept for the mud."

Clint settled himself into a chair across from Samarra and accepted a steaming cup of coffee from

147

Nanna. A feeling of belonging, of utter contentment swept over him. Was this what life was all about, this warmth and good humor among people who had lived together and loved each other for years? He was awarded little time for further analysis or reflection on the matter, for at that moment, Edwin and Beth bustled in. The two stopped short at the sight of Clint Holbrooke sitting in wrinkled clothes and unbuckled shoes at Samarra's kitchen table.

"Top o' the mornin' t' ye," Nanna greeted cheerily. "Sit yereselves down while I whip us up some breakfast. Can na have ye folks leavin' with empty bellies."

"Leaving?" Clint questioned.

Edwin nodded as he held Beth's chair. "Should have been on our way already, but Beth wanted to wait for sunup. It's going to be a cold ride back, I'm afraid."

"Ye ought t' wait a few more days. Let the sun dry up the roads," Nanna suggested as she passed out more hot coffee. "They'll be treacherous now. Miss Sam slipped and fell this mornin'. Lucky she did na break her leg."

Following a brief description of the accident and assurances that Samarra had suffered no long-range ill effects, Beth turned pleading eyes to her husband. "Let's do wait, Edwin. We can't risk a lame horse or a broken axle . . . not in this weather. It's too early in the year for it to last for very long. Besides," she added as she saw his resistance beginning to melt, "I wanted to go to the theater one more time."

His large, work-roughened hand left his cup to cover her soft, white one. "Perhaps you're right, my dear. I'll go right after breakfast and see about getting tickets." His gaze raked Samarra and then Clint. "Shall I get four?" he asked, his meaning obvious.

A dead silence hung over the room as Edwin awaited

an answer. Feeling suddenly very uncomfortable, Samarra chanced a look at Clint and was rewarded with a broad smile that reached upward to crinkle the skin around his hazel eyes. The look of utter fatigue she had witnessed just minutes before seemed to have vanished from his countenance.

"Would you like to go, Miss Seldon?" Clint asked, the formality of his speech at odds with his roguish grin.

"But of course," she responded immediately. "I never refuse an invitation to the theater."

Samarra's lighthearted mood remained with her all that day and the next. As Clint had predicted, her upper thigh bore a large, ugly purple bruise where she had fallen against the edge of the brick steps. But it caused only a slight soreness, which Samarra found it no trouble to overlook.

Her work progressed smoothly, despite periodic bouts of inattentiveness. Clint babbled effusively over Eliza Garrett's artwork, proclaiming that it far surpassed his expectations. A long-overdue shipment of paper and ink arrived from England, and just in the nick of time, since Samarra received two rather large print jobs the day of their theater date. Never had she been quite so busy—or so content.

She ought to have known something would happen to burst her bubble of euphoria, she chastised herself later. But would foreknowledge have been beneficial? she questioned. And answered, Probably not.

Edwin had secured tickets for a performance of "Lethe, or Aesop in the Shade," a satirical comedy, for the night after Samarra's mishap. The thin layer of ice which had covered the ground and the trees that morning had melted away, and the sun had performed its duty in drying up the earth. Edwin had proclaimed conditions safe for travel, and he and Beth planned to leave soon after sunrise the next morning.

At four o'clock, Samarra left the print shop in Tom's capable hands and hurried home to dress for the theater. Nanna had prepared her bath, and Samarra and Beth took turns dressing each other's hair while Georgiana sat and visited with them. Beth and George had struck a close friendship, having spent much time together while Samarra worked in the shop and Edwin conducted necessary business in town. Even in her preoccupation with her soaring emotions, Samarra had noticed a positive difference in her twin's disposition. As a direct result of Beth's almost constant companionship, Georgiana had begun to come out of her shell.

According to their prearranged plan, Edwin had left for the theater near the Palace Green around mid-afternoon, in order to secure and hold choice seats for them in the boxes that curved in a horseshoe around the pit. Samarra had expected Clint to volunteer to go early with Edwin, but when he didn't, no one suggested he do so. Perhaps, she reasoned, Clint had expected an invitation from Edwin. Whatever lack of communication had occurred, it didn't appear to matter to either of the men. Clint would meet the two women promptly at 5:30 and accompany them to the theater.

Dressed in heavy satin gowns and high-heeled slippers, their hair piled high upon their heads, their eyes sparkling in anticipation of the evening's entertainment, Beth and Samarra descended the massive front staircase at 5:25. Through the mullioned glass panels that flanked the front door, they could see the coach Edwin had ordered parked alongside the curb, the liveried driver standing beside the prancing steeds, awaiting them.

150

Clint was nowhere in sight.

"We're early," Beth said by way of excusing him. "Sometimes Edwin takes almost as long to dress as I do. Mr. Holbrooke will be along."

But he had not arrived ten minutes later.

Samarra could not sit still. Beth's mouth twisted in a wry grin as she watched her wiggle and squirm on the edge of her chair and tap her closed fan against her open palm. Finally Sam arose from her chair and started for the door.

"I'm going to send Nanna over to see what's keeping him," she explained, then disappeared down the hall. A few minutes later Samarra returned to the salon, her eyes downcast and her cheeks washed clean of the high color that had tinted them just moments before. "Come, Beth, let's go," was all she said, her voice flat and dull.

"Without Mr. Holbrooke?"

"Without Mr. Holbrooke."

"What's wrong? I thought he wanted to go."

"So did I. He told Nanna he got so involved in his translation, he forgot about the time. He said to try to hold his seat and maybe he would join us later."

"Oh, poohey!" Beth gushed, taking Samarra's elbow with a white-gloved hand and leading her out the door. "Now, isn't that just like a man? We can enjoy the theater without him, Samarra. We *will* enjoy it without him."

Samarra offered her friend a half smile, the best she could muster under the circumstances, all the while thinking about how much she'd like to give a certain man a piece of her mind. If it wouldn't have made them late for the performance, which started precisely at six, she would have, too.

*   *   *

From the advantage of his upstairs window, Clint watched the hired driver assist first Beth and then Samarra into the coach. Meager rays of light from the dying sun turned Samarra's hair to molten gold and set her emerald green satin dress to shimmering. Damn, but Samarra Seldon was one beautiful woman! He would have like nothing better than to escort her to the theater that evening.

But he had known when Edwin had extended the invitation that his attendance was impossible. On the one hand, he could ill afford to risk recognition and thus exposure; on the other, Samarra's absence from the house for an entire evening presented him with an opportunity he could ill afford to waste.

He hadn't wanted to lead her on, but neither could he explain to her—or to the McLairds—why he couldn't go. Allowing them to believe he would accompany them and then backing out at the last minute was his only choice. He had considered playing sick, but that would have aroused Nanna's concern, and quite possibly enticed her company. And the task Clint intended to accomplish this night required both absolute secrecy and solitude.

Clint knew what had to be done. Why, then, did he feel like a schoolboy playing hooky?

Long after the coach had pulled away from the curb and the crunch of its wheels against the cobblestones had died down, Clint stood at his window, gazing out into the ever-darkening sky. No candle burned in his room to obscure his view, and he became one with the encroaching darkness. He watched Nanna cross the backyards and heard her mount the stairs with his supper, but when he didn't answer her timid knock at his door, she retreated. He watched the moon rise in majestic splendor; he watched first one star and then

152

another add its twinkle to the dark blue sky until the heavens were fully adorned with a multitude of tiny, flickering lights.

Occasionally Clint's gaze drifted from the radiance of the October night sky to the warm lamplight emanating from the windows of the house next door. He had spent countless hours watching the house, and by now he knew the relative locations of both Nanna's and Samarra's bedchambers. Nanna slept on the third floor of the main structure, while Samarra's chamber was one floor lower, in the wing, facing the backyard. On several occasions he had witnessed Samarra's silhouette floating behind her drawn curtain, had noted the light filtering from Nanna's room on the third floor, as befitted her station. At times, threads of light were visible on the outside fringes of a pair of heavily draped windows adjoining Samarra's. These, he had concluded, must be the windows in her sitting room.

Old Zeke, the gardener, kept rooms above the stable—and went to bed with the chickens. To the best of Clint's knowledge, this accounted for all the permanent residents of Samarra's house.

Tonight, light from the kitchen windows had spilled into the herb garden for a long time after the sun had set while the rest of the house appeared dark. From his limited vantage point, Clint could not see the front of the big house. Nor could he see into the kitchen, since it was part of the main structure and, therefore, perpendicular to his window. At long last, the kitchen lights were extinguished, and Clint waited in breathless silence for the illumination of Nanna's window.

Instead of going straight to her chamber, though, she went first to Samarra's room. For some time Clint watched shadowy movements there and assumed

Nanna busied herself straightening Sam's things. As he watched her, his imagination created pieces of filmy lingerie and lace-trimmed nightgowns being carefully folded and put away. Finally Samarra's room returned to darkness, and after a while, a thin stream of light appeared in the third-story window. Within minutes, it, too, faded.

Clint pulled the curtains closed, moved away from his window, and lit a candle. His clock showed the time to be almost 9:00. He needed to complete his task and return to his room no later than 11:00. If he could be certain that Samarra and the McLairds would dine after the performance, he would have until midnight, but he dared not risk discovery. Nor did he dare attempt entry now. He must wait until he was certain Nanna had fallen asleep.

He took his candle into the sitting room and ate his now-cold supper, putting his scraps in Clementine's bowl when he had finished. It occurred to him that he had not seen the cat all day, and he wondered if she had been left outside again.

He extinguished the light and reestablished his post at his bedchamber window, smoking his pipe as the minutes dragged by. He waited until almost ten, fretting with every minute that passed. To ensure his safe passage, he went first to the privvy, where he stood in the cold darkness listening, but hearing no human sounds. When he finally made his way through the gate and down the path to the kitchen door, he silently prayed he would find it unlocked, yet he did not want to think Nanna would leave the door open. The release of his pent-up breath hissed in the chill air as the knob turned with well-oiled ease beneath his sweating palm.

A fire burned low on the hearth, partially illuminating the room. Clint eased the door closed, then bent down and removed his shoes, setting them nearby. In his stocking feet, he moved stealthily through the kitchen into the wide hall which occupied the center portion of the main structure and then up the main staircase to the second floor. Nanna had left wall lamps burning in the front hall and at the second-floor landing, but the meager light failed to reach the entrance to the hall leading into the wing. He knew he would probably be perfectly safe taking a candle with him to light his way, but it was a risk he chose not to take.

Clint moved more carefully now, anxious not to overturn an urn or candlestand along the way and thus awaken Nanna. Down the hallway he tiptoed, counting the doors as he touched them, conjuring a mental image of the exterior of the wing. At the fourth door, he paused and took a deep breath before pushing against the heavy oak portal. He felt it swing open easily beneath the flat of his palm and hastily grabbed its edge to prevent its crashing against a wall or some piece of furniture behind it. A fire burned here, too, but failed to illuminate much of the uncommonly large room. With the stealth of a mountain cat, he crossed the room to the windows and opened the curtains wide.

Moonlight flooded the room. Quickly but silently, his movements based on experience and instinct, Clint searched the room. Fortunately, but just as Clint expected, Samarra's furniture had been crafted by masters: all the drawers and doors opened with silent ease. But none yielded contents other than what one would expect to find in a woman's bedchamber: stockings, gloves, petticoats, and chemises filled her drawers; one large chest held blankets, quilts, and bed linens; daygowns hung in one tall, mirrored armoire, and a matching one held more formal gowns and a

155

multitude of hats and slippers.

Atop her dressing table sat a small lacquered box which contained some jewelry, and another, larger one filled with combs and hair ornaments. Clint ran the pads of his fingers over the back of a silver hairbrush, then lifted it and pulled a few strands of golden hair from its bristles. For a moment he stood stock-still, closing his eyes and breathing in the fragrant atmosphere of Samarra's private quarters. For a moment, but only for a moment, he felt guilty about being there without her knowledge, without her permission.

Disgusted with himself, with this suddenly unprofessional attitude, he laid the hairbrush down with more force than he had intended. The heavy brush banged loudly against the polished top of the dressing table, its crash resounding in the stillness of the room.

Almost immediately, the sound of rustling fabric captured his attention. He surveyed the moon-dappled room, caught the movement of sheer curtains against heavy silk draperies, and attributed the movement to a soft night breeze coming through the slightly open windows. He expelled a long breath, calculated the time by the position of the moon, and, deciding he was safe for a few more minutes, moved to the door connecting Samarra's bedchamber with her sitting room.

This door opened as easily as the others in the house. Samarra obviously believed in well-oiled hinges. As he had previously observed, the windows of this room were heavily draped. Silently and with dispatch he opened them wide, admitting the moonlight, then turned on his heels—and froze.

This was not a sitting room, but another bedchamber. An occupied bedchamber.

The slight form of a woman lay beneath the covers.

Golden, honey-colored hair spilled upon the pillow in glorious disarray. Moonlight and shadow danced upon her delicate features as the nearly bare limbs of a tree in the rear garden swayed in the breeze. Although they uttered no sound, Clint's lips formed the name Samarra.

But no, it couldn't be . . . he had watched her leave with Beth and Edwin. Could she have returned while he ate his supper? If so, she had left the theater early, for the performances always lasted at least several hours, and quite often ran longer. And why would she have chosen to sleep in this room when he knew the adjoining one belonged to her? For a long moment he stood in front of the window, mesmerized by the play of light and shadow upon the counterpane and the peaceful face of that one who rested beneath it.

His captivation with the scene proved his undoing. Before he could retreat, the woman stirred and sat up in bed.

"Is that you, Sam?" she said, her voice falling with similar timbre to that one to whom she thought she spoke, her question puzzling Clint.

How could she not know he wasn't Sam? He, Clint Holbrooke, a man who stood more than a head taller and whose breadth almost doubled that of Samarra Seldon. A man who stood in full view of the woman in the bed. A man who could not possibly be mistaken for a woman—any woman.

He knew he should leave, and leave immediately, but something held him still until he realized his bulk obscured much of the silvery light from the moon. Maintaining his stealth, he stepped aside, his movements as light as those of a ballet dancer. Even then she heard him—or felt him move, for her face twisted in fear as the opalescent light fell fully upon it. Clint's heart wrenched at the sight, and though he was able to stifle the words of reassurance he wanted desperately to utter, he did not stop the groan of despair that tore from his throat.

The woman's white-glazed eyes flew wide and her head moved to face the source of the sound.

And then Clint understood.

Chapter Ten

The tall, gray-eyed man had chosen well when he had conned Guy Archer into working for him. Anyone else would have demanded monetary reward long ago for the tiresome task of constantly watching the print shop and house across the street, would have left the man's employ when no payment—no real payment—had been forthcoming. Guy didn't consider a wad of almost worthless colonial currency payment.

But Guy Archer had made no demands . . . not yet, anyway. Although he yearned for both a woman and a drink, Guy had suffered through many a dry spell before. He had also spent more than a few cold, miserable nights curled up in an alley or holed up in a deserted barn. His present arrangement afforded him both a decently comfortable private room and three square meals a day, for which his employer picked up the tab. Oh, Guy loved to grumble and complain, but these whims he indulged in the privacy of his room or in the company of a friend—never in the presence of an employer.

Guy still cringed when he recalled the grumbling his present employer had overhead. Guy might be a coward at heart, but he was a shrewd coward. Had he not been, he wouldn't have lived this long. Guy's first cardinal rule was, "Never let the employer know who you are or much about you." The men who employed him seemed to prefer things that way. Over the years, Guy Archer had lied, cheated, stolen, and murdered for profit, but always following someone else's plan. He didn't possess the mental wherewithal to mastermind even the simplest crime. There wasn't anything he wouldn't agree to do if the coin was right, and there wasn't any job he wouldn't have quit if he had a mind to.

But never before had Guy worked for anyone who seemed to embody evil, and there was something about the tall man with the piercing gray eyes that gave him the willies.

As much as Guy Archer wanted to walk off the job right then and there and flick his middle finger at the bastard who had hired him, deep down he knew that same man would not hesitate to track him down and kill him. Guy didn't intend to spend the rest of his life looking over his shoulder.

He had convinced himself that the sooner he took care of the situation across the street, the better. He would collect his payment and hightail it out of there. Guy's second cardinal rule was "When the job is over, leave town."

Whatever was going on across the street this night had him befuddled. He had watched Miss Seldon's male guest leave just before three that afternoon. Close to six, both Miss Seldon and her female guest had left in a hired coach. Not once had he seen Holbrooke, and yet the window of his apartment had remained dark all evening, as though he were not there. Guy had considered going over to look into the situation, then decided to wait. The night was still young.

Close to nine o'clock, when a narrow beam of light suddenly appeared in Holbrooke's window, Guy knew his decision to stay put had been the right one. Again he was confused when, within minutes, the light disappeared. For a long time Guy sat at his window, chewing his lip as he contemplated the possibilities. The most logical explanation, to his way of thinking, was that Holbrooke had been sleeping, got up to relieve himself, and returned to bed. After all, the man's lamp had burned all night long for two nights in succession. Everyone had to sleep sometime.

Guy Archer waited again, biding his time and watching the traffic on the street. At ten o'clock, he made his move. He put on a heavy workman's coat with patched elbows and ragged hem, knit gloves with most of the fingertips missing, and a floppy suede hat stained dark around the crown. When he entered the street, he hitched up his collar and lowered his head, but his shifty eyes never missed the slightest movement around him.

Cloaking himself in the shadows close to the buildings, he ambled down the street a couple of blocks, taking care to stumble occasionally as though he had imbibed just a mite too much. No one paid him any heed. Indeed, what few pedestrians he passed afforded him wide berth. At a point where the street and sidewalks were completely clear, he crossed the wide thoroughfare and headed back toward the print shop.

Not only did he find the gate unbarred, but the rear door was unlocked as well. Such a minor inconvenience as scaling the one and breaking into the other would not have stopped this felon, but Guy appreciated the time such easy access saved him.

Divesting himself of his cumbersome coat and floppy hat and leaving them in the workroom, Guy furtively made his way up the stairs, pulling a long-bladed knife from his waistband and holding it firmly

161

in his right hand as he used his left to feel his way along the wall. Thrice a warped board squeaked beneath his covert tread, and though he paused each time to listen intently, he heard nothing more than the wind soughing in the trees outside and the occasional pop and crackle of the fire which burned on Holbrooke's sitting room hearth.

Like the thief he was, Guy Archer slinked across the sitting room and into the bedchamber adjoining it. No fire burned on this hearth; only a few red coals nestled among a pile of ashes, their paltry glow insufficient to illuminate the room. Moonlight penetrated the sheer curtains, which had been pulled across the small window, but it fell in a lopsided square on the floor near the foot of the bed.

Guy stood very still, his breathing shallow, as his gaze attempted to discern the position of the furnishings. The bed occupied the center of the small room, halfway between the fireplace and the window, an area which was swathed in deep shadow. He couldn't be certain whether Holbrooke lay beneath the drawn cover or not, but as he listened carefully, a soft whistling sound pierced the quiet.

A wide grin split his face, exposing rotting teeth. So! Holbrooke *was* here, and he *was* asleep.

Holding the knife high, Guy walked swiftly to the bed and struck downward, embedding the knife to its hilt in the moss tick. Supremely irritated, he pulled the knife against the layers of cloth, rending them for several inches before lifting it upward for another strike. Again and again the knife plunged into the mattress; again and again Guy pulled it out, ripping and tearing tick, counterpane, and quilt in his frustration. The feather pillows suffered equal treatment from his blade.

At long last he held the knife at bay, his breathing

now labored from his vain attempts. Where *was* Holbrooke? He had not mistaken the soft whistling sound coming from the vicinity of the bed. Was the man sleeping on the cold floor?

Guy knew he had to consider the possibility. He made his way around the foot of the bed to the other side and found there only a small hooked rug on the bare floor.

"Hellfire and damnation!" he breathed, replacing the knife in his waistband.

At that moment Clementine's paw swiped out from under the bed to nail him solidly on the ankle, her claws tearing slashes in his stockings even as they ripped through his skin.

"Shi—it!" he bellowed, turning and running back across the apartment rooms, knocking over a chair and table along the way, and bolting down the stairs, now unconcerned with the noises the heavy, wooden heels of his wornout shoes made on the uncarpeted stairs. In the workroom he snatched up his coat and hat, and when he let himself out the back gate, he continued running until he reached the outskirts of town. An isolated barn yielded a nag of a horse which Guy nabbed without conscience, and a bare willow yielded a switch which he applied to the poor horse's flanks without remorse.

By morning he had reached Yorktown. The nag bought him passage on a coastal packet, which he boarded as one Samuel Holbrooke. Let the tall man hunt him down, he decided. When he discovered Guy's fiasco, he would want him dead, anyway. At least this way the fiend had to find him first.

All through the evening, Samarra waited for Clint to join them. The opening performance, she assumed, was

163

hilarious . . . Beth and Edwin and the rest of the crowd seemed to think so, anyway. The large, open space of the theater resounded with almost constant laughter; there was so much of it, in fact, that the play lasted almost twice as long as it should have, for the actors were often required to delay the delivery of their lines until the audience quieted down.

Occasionally, when Samarra intercepted confused looks from Beth or Edwin, she would comply with a laugh, but her laughter rang too high and ended too abruptly to sound sincere. Never was she certain about just what she was supposed to have found comical. Her heart and her head were otherwise occupied.

During intermission, when Edwin left their box to purchase food and drink from the vendors outside, Beth turned concerned eyes to Samarra and placed a comforting hand over one of Sam's clenched fists. "Maybe he will come yet, Samarra," she said in an attempt to soothe her. "Why don't you relax and enjoy the performance?"

Samarra compelled her mouth to smile, but her stiff demeanor bore witness to the lie. Her reply, however, was spoken with true candor. "Thanks for caring, Beth. I guess my behavior has spoiled your evening."

"Not at all! Don't even think such a thing," Beth assured her, her fingers coercing Sam's fist open and then gently massaging her palm. "I just wish you were enjoying the evening."

"I'll try," Samarra promised, Beth's concern boosting her spirits somewhat. "What's coming up next?" she asked then, her voice a bit more enthusiastic.

"Let's see . . ." Beth consulted her playbill. "Another comedy in which 'a dour and unforgiving master is outwitted and made to look the fool by his clever and likable servants,'" she read. Samarra knew the words

164

well; she had been the one to typeset them. "Sounds like fun, huh?"

"What sounds like fun?" Edwin asked good-naturedly, returning with an assortment of fruit and cakes.

Though she had little appetite, Samarra accepted a small, maple-flavored cake from Edwin and commanded her wayward thoughts to concentrate on the lighthearted conversation as she nibbled, and then on the play when intermission was over, but her efforts won her little recompense.

Why hadn't Clint joined them at the theater? she asked herself countless times. She had thought he enjoyed her company, and he had made a point of inviting himself to spend an evening with her and the McLairds before they returned to their home on the frontier. Was his work so very important, so absorbing, perhaps, that he could not take time out for an evening's entertainment? Samarra just couldn't make any sense of it.

It was after midnight when the trio returned to the Seldon home, having stopped off for a bite at the Raleigh Tavern following the performance. They all saw the light burning in Clint's window, but no one made mention of it. Still, it served to remind Samarra of her having been left without an escort that evening, a reminder that continued to rankle as she bade Beth and Edwin as warm a goodnight as she could muster. She hugged each of them in turn and promised to see them off early the next morning, then left them at the door to their room and walked wearily down the hall to her chamber. Never could she recall having felt quite so disappointed.

With dragging feet and sagging shoulders she entered her room. Her numb fingers jerkily unhooked

165

the frogs on her cloak and she hurled it viciously at a velvet-covered settee without paying much attention to her actions. When the sofa seemed to gasp its surprise at her abuse, she turned toward it in utter amazement and no small degree of fear.

Simultaneously Samarra saw that someone fought to remove her cloak and realized that her drapes had been opened wide in her absence, admitting enough moonlight to allow her some discernment. For a moment she could not move, and though she opened her mouth to scream, no sound came forth. Her chest pounded with the increased beating of her heart, and she now found the normally simple task of breathing extraordinarily difficult. Her head seemed lighter than air, and the windows wavered in front of her. Had the occupant of her settee not emerged at that moment, she would have collapsed on the floor.

Instead, the recognition that it was Georgiana who struggled with the heavy cloak washed over her in waves of relief. "Goodness, George!" she barked without intending to, then hastened to explain. "You gave me quite a scare. You didn't have to wait up for me."

"I hadn't planned to," Georgiana muttered sleepily, sitting up straight and arranging the cloak over her lap.

"Did you get cold?" Samarra babbled as she lit a candle. "Let me build up the fire."

One of the few things Samarra and Randolph had forbidden Georgiana to attempt by herself was tending a fire. Sam added several pieces of split firewood to her own hearth and closed her drapes, all the while gathering the few tidbits of memory she retained from the evening's performances so that she might satisfy Georgiana's curiosity.

More than anything, Samarra wished she could

confide in her sister, but she feared baring her soul might cause George more than a little worry about her own uncertain future. She couldn't tell her—she couldn't tell anybody that the man who resided over the print shop had weaseled his way into her heart. It was better to pretend everything had been wonderful, to pretend even to herself that Clint Holbrooke meant nothing to her at all. Nothing.

"I'm sorry I wasn't here for you," she apologized as she reentered her chamber, mentally adding, *but never would I leave you for long.* "I'm surprised Nanna didn't stoke your fire before she went to bed."

"Oh, she did," Georgiana hastened to defend the woman. "I—I wasn't cold. That's not why I got up, Sam."

Still much preoccupied with her own thoughts, Samarra missed the slight tremble in Georgiana's voice. She set the candle on her bedside table and began to remove her satin gown. "I had a wonderful time at the theater," she lied. "One play featured two fabulously clever servants, one of whom reminded me so much of Nanna."

That wasn't exactly true, but it sounded good. Her account of the particulars of the performances became muddled when she pulled her chemise over her head and then replaced it with a flannel nightgown, but Georgiana was as immersed in her own thoughts as Samarra was in hers and thus took no notice.

"Could I get into bed with you for a few minutes, Sam?" George tentatively asked. "There's—there's something I need to talk to you about."

"You know you can, George. You can stay with me all night if you like."

Samarra and Georgiana shared that special rapport which often seems to exist between identical twins.

Suddenly Samarra's problems seemed minuscule in light of whatever it was that so deeply troubled her twin.

"Why don't I put the bed warmer beneath the covers, and we'll prop up our feet by the fire while the bed gets toasty," Sam suggested, scurrying to shovel hot coals into the brass pan. When all was ready, she helped Georgiana settle into one of the matching wing chairs in front of the hearth and covered her legs with a knitted afghan. When she herself was settled similarly, she asked, "Now, what is it you want to talk to me about?"

Her voice was neither chatty nor somber, but somewhere in between. It was a voice which said, "I'm here. I'm your friend. You can talk to me without fear of ridicule or reproof."

"I don't quite know how to tell you this," Georgiana hesitantly began. "Promise me you won't panic."

Her words alarmed Samarra. She had honestly expected to hear about some ghastly nightmare, but Georgiana's entreaty quickly dispelled that notion. She forced an evenness into her voice she did not feel, refusing to panic—at least for now. "I promise."

"I wasn't hurt, Samarra. Please know that." She waited for her sister's assuring reply.

Samarra's heart cried, *Tell me. Quickly! Tell me what happened.* But she restrained the impulse to give voice to her heart's plea and said simply, "Yes, Georgiana. I can see that you aren't injured."

"There—someone was here, Samarra. While you were gone."

"Who?"

"I don't know. A man, I think."

"When?"

"I'm not sure. An hour ago. Maybe longer."

Samarra's heart had begun to pound heavily again,

and without conscious thought she placed a hand on her chest and let it absorb the thudding palpitations as her mind attempted to absorb Georgiana's revelation. She had seen no evidence of a break-in, nothing out of the ordinary . . .

The drapes! Suddenly Samarra remembered they'd been open in both rooms when she'd come in. Georgiana's drapes were almost never open, and Sam knew she had left hers closed.

"Did this man do or say anything?" Samarra asked quietly, halfway afraid to hear the answer.

"No. He didn't say anything, but I heard him in your room before he came into mine. I think he went through your things, and he dropped something, your hairbrush, maybe. Whatever it was, it was hard and it didn't break. I thought it was you, even when he walked into my room. Sam, he wasn't wearing shoes. I could hear his stockings swishing on the floor, and he stepped lightly, as if perhaps he wasn't very big."

Samarra wanted desperately to believe that Georgiana's visitor had been Nanna, whom she intended to question once she'd heard George out. Had the drapes not been left open, Sam might have attributed all this to one of her sister's frequent nightmares, regardless of Georgiana's sincere belief in what had happened. "Why do you think it was a man?"

"Because women don't usually smoke a pipe, and this person smelled like pipe smoke. Not a stale odor, but a fresh one, as if he'd just finished."

"And when he came into your room, George, what did he do?"

"He opened my drapes. I thought it strange that you'd be opening my drapes, and when I sat up in bed and called your name, he groaned, a deep, throaty groan, as though he wasn't expecting anyone to be here. And then I knew it wasn't you."

That part didn't sound strange to Samarra . . . anyone could watch her house for days on end and not know Georgiana lived there. "And what did he do then?" she prompted.

"He left."

"Just like that?"

"Just like that. I sat up in bed and he groaned and I smelled pipe smoke. I was afraid, Sam." Her voice broke then, but she swallowed and said, "And then he left."

A shiver ran along Samarra's spine as she considered the implications of her sister's story. Despite her promise to be calm, her voice was filled with panic when next she spoke. "He left this room, or he left the house?"

"He left the house. I heard him close the back door, and then I went downstairs and locked it."

"Oh, my God, Georgiana!" Sam cried, jumping up from her chair and throwing her arms around her sister. "How could you be sure he actually left the house? He could have gone out and come back in before you got to the door. Or he might have let someone else into the house instead of leaving. Anything could have happened to you! He could still be here, Georgiana!"

"No, Sam," her twin soothed, rubbing Samarra's spine with the knuckles of her right hand. "You know how keen my senses are . . . I'd have heard. I think the intruder was just looking for something, something he thought he might find in your room."

Samarra wasn't appeased. "I'm going downstairs, George. Will you be all right for a few minutes?"

"I'll be fine. What are you going to do?"

"Be sure the doors are locked and barred." *And get a pistol,* she mentally added. "Did you wake Nanna?"

"No. And Sam—" Georgiana put a restraining hand

on her twin's arm as Samarra stood up—"I don't think you should, either. Don't frighten her over nothing."

"Nothing? Someone broke into this house, Georgiana. We have no idea what he might have taken or what else he might have done. This isn't *nothing."*

"Nothing happened, Sam. He didn't come near me. And I don't think he took anything. I wouldn't have told you about it except—well, except that he went through everything in your room. I was in that kind of half-dream state and I heard drawers being opened and closed in here, but I thought at the time that you had come home. I just kept thinking later about how awful it would be for some stranger to handle all your things. And I just thought you ought to know. And you promised not to panic!" she reminded her.

Samarra bent over and hugged Georgiana. "Thanks for telling me, Georgie." It was an endearment she hadn't used in years, but one that seemed suddenly appropriate tonight. "But I won't sleep at all if I don't check the doors. I'll be right back."

Clint Holbrooke was mad, partly at himself, and a whole hell of a lot at someone else.

He hadn't known what to think when he had turned from the window and seen the young woman who was the spitting image of Samarra—except for her eyes. In his mind he kept seeing those pitiful, white-glazed eyes.

Was it possible Samarra Seldon had a blind sister? Perhaps even a twin sister?

It seemed the only logical explanation. But when he'd first seen the woman, logic had not been his ally. Clint Holbrooke had done something he never did! He had panicked.

He had panicked and run.

It was some time later when he remembered he

hadn't closed the drapes, and that oversight had made him angry at himself.

But it was his anger at some person or persons unknown which really had his blood boiling.

He had come back to his room to find his mattress and pillows ripped to shreds. A quick yet thorough search of the print shop had yielded neither clue nor foe. He could find nothing out of place downstairs, saw nothing missing. For a long time afterward, he had just sat and stared at the mess that had been his bed, wondering not where he would sleep, but how he would ever explain all this to Samarra.

He recalled how he had mentally accused her of hiring someone to murder him, but that had been days ago, long before he had come to know her, and—he had to admit—trust her. He was convinced now that Samarra Seldon was no more a felon than he. Her fierce independence and her intense privacy were all that separated her from other women.

And no wonder she clung to her privacy! Clint realized now that she, along with Nanna and Tom and probably Randolph, shielded and protected a blind woman from the cruelties of the outside world.

Now he had to convince Robert Dinwiddie of Samarra's innocence, which might not be an easy task. In his heart he knew it was not Samarra who wanted him out of the way; it was someone else, someone who didn't want him to prove Samarra's innocence. To convince the governor, he would have to find the perpetrator who had made two attempts on his life. And when he found him, Clint felt certain he'd find the real counterfeiter as well.

His most immediate problem, however, was his ruined bed. Someone—some madman—wanted him dead. That he could deal with. Whoever had done this had thought him asleep, had gone into a frenzy when he had discovered an empty bed. If Clint had been in it, as he should have been, that madman would be in chains at this moment, for Clint harbored no doubt that he would have survived to catch the fiend. But Clint had not been where he should have at the time, and therein lay the problem.

What plausible story could he offer Samarra for having been absent from his room long enough for this to happen?

Clint didn't want to deceive Samarra again, yet his loyalty to the governor forbade his admitting the truth. He knew that if he told her he had been at her house, in her room, that he was the one who had frightened the blind woman, Samarra would never trust him again. She would probably never speak to him again.

And Clint didn't want to consider what his life would be like without Samarra—any more than he wanted to consider what his life would be like with her forever. He wanted present circumstances to continue just as they were, at least for a while longer . . . at least until he had time to sort out his feelings for her and decide what to do about them.

But time had become his enemy.

Chapter Eleven

When Samarra unlocked the back door of the print shop and walked into the workroom the next morning, Clint was sitting there waiting for her. Neither one had slept at all, and each looked immensely relieved to see the other. They both started talking at once.

"You go first," Samarra offered, but Clint politely declined, wanting to hear her story first, needing to know how much she knew and what she might suspect so he could reshape his story, if necessary. He pulled out a chair for her at the ink-stained worktable where he had been sitting and poured them each a cup of hot tea.

"I hope you don't mind my finding the makings," he said, "but I needed some myself."

"No, not at all. I should have already told you where I keep it all."

Clint grinned sheepishly. "I just opened cabinet doors until I found your stash." And while it was the truth, he made it sound as if he had looked only that morning, when in actuality he had known exactly where to look, having discovered the tin of loose tea, pot, cups, and spirit lamp the first night he had foraged through the print shop.

Samarra sipped her tea and forced herself not to grimace at the bitter brew. Someone needed to teach Clint Holbrooke how to make a pot of tea! Although she had carefully practiced her speech, she couldn't recall how she had planned to begin. Clint's sitting there waiting for her, armed with a pot of tea, had caught her off-guard; and as always, his quirky grin, his sparkling hazel eyes, and the dimple in his chin combined to dazzle her to distraction.

He watched her closely, sensed her discomfort, decided maybe he should begin after all. "Before you say anything, I want to apologize for not going with you to the theater last night. I trust it was an enjoyable evening for you."

Samarra's thoughts were too disjointed for her to notice he'd offered no reason for his failure to join them. "The performance was excellent. I'm glad Beth and Edwin were able to attend before they left."

"Did they go back this morning?"

"Yes, and fortunately without knowing what happened at my house last night while we were gone. I doubt they'd have slept any better than I did, had they known. That's what I need to talk to you about, Clint. I have to tell someone."

He winced inwardly at the wave of distress that washed over her face . . . distress he had caused. It wouldn't happen again, he promised her silently. He was going to see the governor today and tell him everything he knew and felt instinctively to be true. Robert Dinwiddie was a reasonable man . . . wasn't he?

"I'm glad you want to tell me," Clint said, his voice soft and mellow. The hand he used to cover one of hers assured her she was doing the right thing.

When he had held her and kissed her and whispered sweet words in her ear, she had sensed the depth of his passion. The comforting hand he offered now was not that of a lover, but rather that of a friend. Samarra harbored no doubt that she wanted him, needed him as a lover. But at the moment, she wanted—and desperately needed—his friendship. She sighed heavily, grateful that he knew and understood her needs without her having to communicate them verbally.

"I can't tell Nanna," she explained. "Nanna pretends to be strong, but her health has been failing her for years now. I don't know what this might do to her if she knew. If only Papa were home . . ."

"I'm here. Tell me."

I want to tell you, Clint . . . I want to tell you everything. But I can't. Not just yet. Samarra had struggled for hours over what to tell him. In the absence of her father, Clint Holbrooke had become her port in the storm. Her heart wanted to believe that she could trust him, that he was truly her friend, but her head insisted that something was not quite right, that he was not being completely honest with her. The fact that he made her blood run hot and cold when she was near him did not assuage her doubts. If anything, this fact caused her to be even more wary.

Samarra took a deep breath and let it out in a whistle. "Someone came into my house last night, Clint. While we were at the theater. Someone came into my room and went through my things."

"Are you sure? Is anything missing?"

"No. At least, I don't think so. You know how you look at the same things day in and day out, and after a while, you start taking them for granted. You don't know something is gone until you reach for it and it's not there. But I went through my jewelry case, and I know none of my jewelry is missing."

"Did this—uh—person leave a mess?"

"No. Whoever it was is incredibly neat. My clothes

176

were jumbled a bit, and some of the drawers were left slightly open."

"But"—the confusion written on Clint's face was only half sincere—"you said you couldn't tell Nanna, so she obviously doesn't know about this. If nothing is missing and nothing was actually moved, and Nanna hasn't said anything, what makes you think someone was there while you were gone?" *Tell me about your sister, Samarra,* Clint silently willed.

"Whoever it was opened my draperies, and those in the chamber adjoining mine. I left them closed . . . I know I did."

"That's all your evidence, Samarra? You could be mistaken, you know." When he saw her dogged determination to believe it had happened, he asked, "How did this alleged intruder get into your house?"

"I—I'm not certain. Maybe Nanna left the back door unlocked."

"And maybe Nanna opened the drapes; maybe Nanna put some of your clothes away and wasn't neat about closing the drawers. You must ask her, Samarra. And if she did leave the door unlocked, she needs to know she did it so she won't do it again. Don't tell her about the intruder. Just ask her about the drapes and the door."

Could Clint be right? Nanna could have opened the drapes for some reason and forgotten to close them. Georgiana could merely have had a bad dream. Sometimes dreams seemed so real that later it was difficult to distinguish them from reality. Samarra began to feel foolish for ever having spoken to Clint about all this.

Clint was disappointed that she didn't trust him enough to confide in him completely. He had asked all the leading questions he could, but he saw she wasn't going to mention the blind woman. A part of him felt relieved that Samarra had no idea he was the guilty party, but as he held her hand and watched the play of emotions on her delicate features, he realized that she wasn't certain he believed her. If he could do nothing else for her, at the very least he could substantiate her story. He had to tell her what had happened in his apartment, anyway.

"Your suspicions would never stand up in a court of law, Samarra, but I think you may be right. Come upstairs with me. There's something I have to show you."

The feeling of horror Samarra had experienced just seven hours before flooded through her again when she saw the havoc that had been wreaked upon Clint's bed. She stood rooted to the floor just inside the doorway, one hand clutching at her throat in an effort to keep the bile from rising any farther.

"Obviously, someone would prefer me dead," Clint mused aloud.

"The man who threw the knife at you?"

"Possibly."

"Good Lord, Clint! This is . . . awful! Where did you sleep?"

"I didn't."

"I mean, where were you when this happened?"

"I was outside looking for Clementine. Come. There's something else you have to see."

Clint led her to the bed, where he squatted and lifted the tail of the slashed counterpane. Clementine lay upon an old woolen laprobe which she had dragged off the natty chair in the sitting room, and four tiny, fuzzy kittens lay there too, each of them suckling hungrily.

"Oh, Clem!" Samarra crooned, momentarily dismissing her worries. "You finally had your babies.

178

How does it feel to be a mother again?" She sat down on her knees beside Clint, who regarded her with amusement as she continued to talk to her pet as though the cat were human. "Four of them, Clementine . . . and not one of them white. Let's see, you have a gray one and a black one and two calicos. Yes, I can see how proud you are of your brood. We won't bother you or your little ones."

Sam replaced the counterpane and stood up. "She's not going to like it when we replace this bedding, but it has to be done. Clint, you roll that mattress up with the linen and cover inside, then tie it in a bundle and stand it in a corner somewhere. I'll give it to the ragman the next time he comes by. Meanwhile I'll collect the feathers and sweep up the moss."

Clint burst out laughing. He laughed so hard, he had to hold his sides.

Indignation flared on Samarra's face. "Whatever is so funny?" she demanded.

"You are."

"I am?"

"You're so unpredictable! I sat here all night, looking at this mess and thinking, 'What is Samarra going to say when she sees this?' And you come in here and take it all in stride and act like nothing really happened at all. Damn, Samarra! I could have been killed!" The merriment in his voice diminished the seriousness of this last declaration, but his words hung between them nonetheless.

"I know, Clint." She turned to him then, put her arms around his waist, and hugged him to her. Going to him like that seemed so natural; being in his arms felt so right. "I'm glad you weren't. Maybe you should move. This is the second time there's been an attempt on your life in my print shop. Don't you have any idea

179

who might want you dead?"

"No, not really. But this wouldn't have happened if you treated me as a tenant and not a guest."

"What do you mean?" She pulled back and looked up into his face, her golden eyes seeking the warmth in his hazel gaze and glistening when they found it.

"If I were your tenant, if I paid you rent, then you would have to give me a key to the back door. Then, when I wanted to leave here at night, I could lock the door behind me. I left it open, Sam . . . I had to. Whoever it was walked right in, just as he did at your house."

"But—do you honestly believe the same person came to both our bedchambers?" Samarra shuddered against Clint's hard chest, and he pulled her closer to him. "I just realized that if that is true, then the man who was in my house had a knife."

"This may not have had anything to do with an attempt on my life, Samarra," Clint said reflectively. "You said the man went through your things. That means he must have been looking for something, maybe something that belonged to the old printer who used to live here. Maybe that's why my mattress got ripped up and yours didn't. The intruder thought something was inside it."

"Clint! That makes sense."

He knew it did. He'd spent hours dreaming it up after he had discovered Clementine and her new kittens beneath his bed. Clem had given his absence the perfect excuse. The one witness to his presence in Samarra's house was blind. All he'd had to do then was construct a plausible reason for one man to have visited both places. But right then, Clint's heart rent with the thought of having to deceive her yet again.

"But what is there to keep him from coming back?"

"Nothing, I suppose . . . but now we've been

warned. Neither of us will leave a door unlocked again. Both of us will sleep with one ear tuned to danger. Do you have a gun, Samarra? Besides the horse pistol you keep behind the counter downstairs?"

He felt her nod against his chest.

"And you do know how to use one?"

"Yes."

"Then I will have the one here for protection at night, and you will start sleeping with one under your pillow."

"I wish Papa were home . . ."

Her voice sounded so small, so pitiful, so defeated. Clint tried to imagine how she must feel, saw again her sister's terror-filled, white-glazed eyes. All this was his fault . . . somehow he had to make it better. "Would you like for me to move in with you?" he asked.

She pulled away from him then, and the horror that filled her visage bore no relationship to that the intruder had precipitated. "Good heavens, no! The gossips in this town would have a field day with that. No, thank you—I can take care of myself."

Clint chuckled. "Somehow I think you can." He surveyed his room again. "What will you tell Nanna about this? She's bound to know something happened here."

"We'll tell her Clementine had her kittens *on* your bed instead of under it. And we'd better get this mess cleaned up . . . she'll be over here soon with your breakfast."

What a consummate little liar she was, Clint thought as he rolled up the mattress. But he had to admit, when Samarra fabricated untruths, it was to protect someone else, never herself. His own little inventions and distortions were designed to protect himself; the only honor in them lay in the fact that what he did, he did for the sake of his government.

"I'll send Zeke over with a nice, plump feather tick,

181

one more comfortable than that moss mattress," Samarra babbled as she worked, her speech reflecting her disjointed thoughts. "And then I'll send him to fetch the constable. There's no shortage of linens and quilts. I think I have an extra key in my desk drawer. I'll look for it when I go downstairs."

"Will you allow me to pay you rent?"

"Why not?"

Clint's heart leapt at the lilt in her voice, at the absence of either reservation or resignation. They settled on a reasonable amount and Clint counted out the coins from his purse.

"I owe you three shillings in change," she said. "I'll bring it up later. Do you mind taking colonial currency? I'm not sure I have it in specie."

Though innocently asked, her question served as a stark reminder of his assignment. If he had his way, that would all end today. As soon as they finished here and he had his breakfast, he was going to see the governor. He was going to convince him of Samarra's innocence.

But if he did that, Clint suddenly realized, he would have to leave the print shop. Robert Dinwiddie would give him another assignment . . . and Samarra would inevitably discover what he had been doing all this time. No . . . that couldn't happen. Not yet.

For a short time Clint had forgotten that he was not his own boss.

There was something else Clint had given much careful consideration lately. Someone had wanted the governor to believe in Samarra Seldon's guilt, had meticulously laid out a series of paths which led eventually to her door. If Clint were taken off this case, he would not be there to protect her. The attempts on his life had further convinced him of the potential danger from the true counterfeiter. Perhaps, in an odd,

182

twisted sort of way, he had done her a service the night before. At least now she would be on her guard.

But perhaps the strongest motivator of the moment was Clint's complete unwillingness to return to life at the barracks. As Samarra's guest he had begun to feel a sense of home, of family, and—damn it!—a sense of independence that he had never before known.

"I've never really had a place I could call home," he said in a faraway voice as his eyes raked the small room and its meager contents.

And though Samarra heard him, she wasn't at all sure he had meant for her to.

Clint sat and listened to the printing press until he thought he would go mad.

He couldn't help but admire Samarra. She had experienced a terrible fright, but there she was, calmly running her press as though nothing had happened. The real rub, though, lay in the fact that she had work to do, productive labor, while he was bored to distraction. Samarra had been right in everything she'd said about him to the McLairds. He was no more suited to a profession as a translator than a doxy was suited to a profession as a schoolmarm.

And lately he'd begun to wonder how well suited he was to being a lieutenant colonel in the British Army.

Samarra looked up when he entered her workroom, but she did not seem surprised to see him. "Did Nanna finish in your room?" she asked casually while she changed the paper in her press.

"A long time ago. Did you speak with the constable?"

She nodded without looking up. "Briefly. He was more accusing than helpful, I'm afraid."

"How so?"

183

"He lectured me about locking doors. Said I should have a man living under my roof."

"My offer still stands, Samarra."

She looked up then and smiled wanly at him. "And I appreciate your concern, Clint, but—well, the answer is still no."

A few days before, Clint would have viciously attacked her concern over public opinion. Instead, he said quietly, "People are always going to think the worst, Samarra. In order to maintain peace with oneself, a person has to learn that honor comes from deep within one's soul."

"'To thine own self be true,'" she quoted without real feeling. She returned to her work, mentally listing the reasons she could not allow herself to occupy the same house as Clint Holbrooke, most of which had nothing to do with public opinion, knowing that she would willingly sacrifice her honor if that should happen— and then hate herself for doing so. "I'm trying to be true to myself, Clint. Please try to understand that."

A long moment of silence stretched out between them before Clint broke it. "I—uh—I thought I might go for a walk. Can I bring you anything?"

"No, thanks."

"Would you like to go with me?"

Samarra didn't believe she'd heard him correctly. "What?"

"Why don't you stop for a few minutes? We could get a bite to eat somewhere if you're hungry."

A smile wreathed her face and put sparkling flecks of light in her golden eyes, but she shook her head. "Look at me, Clint." She held out her hands. "I'm all inky. Thanks anyway."

He looked so downcast at her rejection that she added, "But if you want to stay here for a few more minutes, we can eat our lunch together. Nanna should be here with it soon."

"Will you show me how the press works while we wait?"

He couldn't have pleased her more. For the next half hour, Samarra lectured knowledgeably on her favorite subject to a most willing pupil.

"Gutenberg, as you probably know, invented movable type over three hundred years ago," she began, "and adapted a cheese press to make the first printing press. This press is very similar to his. I set the type in a chase and use a wedge to lock it in. If the page I'm printing has an illustration, the engraving has to be locked in as well. The type form slides under this raised platen, and then the type has to be inked." She held up a leather ball stuffed with wool and used it to ink the type then continued to demonstrate as she talked. "The paper goes in the paper holder, which is folded over the type form, and then I move this lever to lower the wood platen, which presses the paper against the type. When I move the lever again, the wood platen raises and I remove the printed page."

"That doesn't sound too terribly complicated. Mind if I try it?"

Samarra waved her hand at the press. "Be my guest," she smirked.

After three vain attempts to produce a clearly printed copy, Clint shrugged. "Maybe this is more difficult that you make it seem," he conceded.

"Oh, if you stuck with it long enough, you'd get a feel for operating a press, but that's not what my job is all about."

"Really? Enlighten me."

"Setting type is no easy feat. Nor is producing high quality copperplate engravings. Both take years of practice."

"And talent?"

"A definite inclination, anyway."

"And you have both?" He retrieved one of her printed pages and eyed it appreciatively.

"I like to think so."

"How many pages can you print in a day?"

"About three hundred, if I stay with it. Tom does most of the printing now, while I do the typesetting."

"And engraving?"

"Some of it. Engraving, as I said, requires both time and talent. Most of my engravings are produced by a free-lancer."

"Like the person you hired to illustrate my book?"

"A different person, but yes, it's the same sort of arrangement."

Clint found himself wondering why he had never asked her about her work before, then remembered the way they had fought tooth and nail until a few days ago. He wasn't sure what had happened to change their relationship, nor was he certain he liked the change. The camaraderie that had developed between them would make their parting all the more difficult. And whether he wanted to acknowledge it or not, its inevitability loomed with a certainty before him.

While they were eating their lunch of thick slices of cold ham and big, hot, crusty rolls, an errand boy from a local tailor's shop delivered a large parcel to Clint, who carefully masked his bewilderment. He managed to field Samarra's seemingly indifferent, teasingly offered remarks—which hinted at a true yearning to know what was in the package—throughout the remainder of their meal, then excused himself to discover in the privacy of his room what lay hidden beneath the brown paper and twine.

Although no note of explanation accompanied the contents, Clint had no doubt who had ordered them. His doubts concerning Robert Dinwiddie's sanity

186

perished as well. No one could possibly guess his identity when he wore this costume to the governor's fancy-dress ball.

"Oh, my God!" he groaned aloud. In the midst of everything else that had occupied his time and his thoughts for the past two days, he had completely forgotten the ball, which was less than a week away—and Dinwiddie's edict that he escort Samarra.

He should have asked her the day he received the invitation. What if someone else already had? What if she refused to go at all? Clint Holbrooke did not relish the thought of having to explain his dereliction of duty to Dinwiddie. But that worry was a fleeting one . . . what really troubled Clint was the thought that she might prefer another man's company to his, and for the first time in his life he experienced true jealousy.

Somehow he would have to convince her to accept his escort, even if it meant she had to renege on a previous commitment.

While Clint was pondering how best to plead his case, Samarra was herself refusing another man's proposal.

She faced her adversary with more strength of character than she would have imagined possible, under the circumstances. *Thank you, Clint,* she silently acknowledged, *for listening to me and offering your friendship this morning when I so desperately needed it.*

"We've had this conversation before," she stated bluntly, her voice brooking no argument, "and I haven't changed my mind. You might as well give up, Mr. O'Quinn. My business is not now, nor has it ever been for sale, to you or anyone else." An inner voice reminded her that she'd made a similar declaration to

Clint Holbrooke about the apartment, but just this morning she had accepted a rent payment from him, the spare key in her apron pocket stark testimony to their agreement.

Sloane O'Quinn's skull face softened somewhat as he spread his hands and shrugged his shoulders. "'Twas not my intention to rile you, Miss Seldon. Did I not believe in your determination to hold on to this print shop, I would have returned before now."

"And what, pray tell, prompted your change of heart today?" Samarra's voice was rife with irritation.

"Words—stories I've been hearing in the dram shops and on the streets. Stories that, how shall I say it—" He dropped his eyes from her stony gaze and sighed deeply. "Stories that are meant to malign your character, Miss Seldon."

"Oh? Is that all?" she asked with disinterest. "The gossips in this town do enjoy wagging their tongues, don't they? Whatever have they conjured up against me now?"

"'Tis said you have allowed that drifter, that fellow who was hurt the last time I was here, to move into these premises."

"And what if I have? There's no law against letting empty rooms." Her hands clenched into fists; her golden eyes sparked with indignation.

"That fact in itself might not be so bad, but add to that a visit from a detachment of redcoats and a multitude of suspicions from your neighbors, and you have a mess, Miss Seldon."

"What suspicions? What are you talking about?" A tiny seed of fear clutched at her heart.

O'Quinn's demeanor subtly changed from one of concern to one of triumph. He had gained the advantage in this particular conversation, and he knew it. "Take the tavernkeeper across the street. Says he

188

had some miscreant staying there who insisted on a streetside private room, which he seldom left. Says this rascal watched your house and your print shop all the time. Even took his meals in his room. The wenches who cleaned his room and brought his meals attested to his interest in your business, said he did naught but sit at the window and stare out across the street."

Samarra snorted in derision. "That means nothing, and you know it, Mr. O'Quinn. The world is full of demented men who—"

He held up a restraining hand. "True, but this scoundrel's bills were paid by a tall, well-groomed gentleman of some means. Paid the rascal a visit now and then, he did, too. Most likely to give him instructions."

"Instructions? What sort of instructions?"

"No one knows."

"It all sounds like speculation to me. Who are these men? Why do you speak of them in the past tense? And how do I know that *you,* Mr. O'Quinn, are not the tall man you speak of?"

"Hold on, Miss Seldon! So many questions at once! If you think I am this gentleman, walk across the street and ask the proprietor. He knows me well. He does not know who these men are, but the scruffy fellow cleared out sometime last night. Left what few possessions he had in his room."

"If his personal things are still there, why would the innkeeper think the man had left for good? None of this makes any sense, Mr. O'Quinn, and you know it. You won't scare me into selling you this shop." Samarra wasn't about to let O'Quinn know how frightened she had been last night, nor how this information distressed her now, for she could not help wondering if the scoundrel who had watched her shop had not been the same one who'd searched her room and demolished

189

Clint's bed. "Even if everything you say is true, my printing business has never been better. If you will excuse me now, I have work to do."

O'Quinn threw up his hands in a mockery of defeat. "All right, Miss Seldon, I'm leaving. But you'll come running to me yet, begging me to buy you out. I'm a patient man. I'll be waiting."

And Samarra had no doubt that he would.

Chapter Twelve

The moment Clint heard the bell signal O'Quinn's departure, he moved quietly back to the seclusion of the staircase. He had not eavesdropped intentionally, had come downstairs to talk to Samarra about the All Hallow's Eve ball. But when he heard raised voices, he had stopped at the connecting door and listened. Although he had not been privy to the entire conversation, Holbrooke had heard enough. Why had he not been informed of this subversive "spy" nest across the street? Was this henchman who had disappeared responsible for the attempts on his life? And who was this tall man O'Quinn had spoken of?

Damn, his costume was hot! He ran a gloved forefinger around the neckline in an attempt to secure some ventilation. If he was to wear this thing for hours, he realized, something would have to be done. When he put on the headpiece, he could hardly breathe.

Clint supposed he should be grateful the costume fit, but then, why shouldn't it? His measurements were part of his permanent record, a convenience in ordering military uniforms, but was this the best idea Dinwiddie could have come up with? He tried to envision how he must look and fleetingly wished there

191

was a mirror close by. Whatever would Samarra think, when she saw him? he wondered. And what sort of costume would she wear to complement his?

He didn't have to wait long to have those two questions answered. Surprisingly, she was whistling when she opened the door to the workroom and went back to her labor at the press. Clint frowned in mild amusement. Samarra was forever catching him unawares with her reactions to life's little mishaps. He supposed that was what having a good sense of humor was all about, seeing the lighter side of things and not letting them get you down. He replaced the headpiece and strolled casually into the workroom.

"Oh, my gosh, Clint!" he heard her gasp. "You almost frightened me out of my wits." She laughed then, her laughter a high, merry tinkle, startling him again. "That costume is—hilarious! Is this what you're planning to wear to the governor's ball?"

The stag's head nodded, sending her into hysterics.

"You should see what happens when you do that!" she shrieked. "The antlers twitter and shake as though they're about to fall off. Isn't that hot? And heavy?"

The stag's head nodded again.

"If you want to talk to me, you're going to have to remove that costume," she tittered.

Obediently, Clint removed the helmet-like headpiece and tried to hold it under one arm, as a medieval knight might have held his basinet, but the stag's head refused to cooperate. The rack would not be still, and when one of the pointed antlers slammed into Clint's jaw, he relinquished his hold and set the headpiece on a chair, his brow beetling at Sam's continued mirth. His sense of humor was no match for hers, not today. He pulled a pair of black leather gloves from his hands, then reached beneath a flat placket that ran the length of the one-piece suit and began to undo the fastenings concealed there.

Her humor fleeing and a look of both astonishment and disbelief replacing it, Sam commanded, "Wait! Forget what I said. I wasn't thinking clearly."

But Clint ignored her.

"You aren't going to disrobe in front of me again," she insisted. "It's not even raining today."

"And what is that supposed to mean?"

Samarra stomped away from the press, untied her apron, and threw it on the floor, the key in its pocket clanking when it hit the bare wood. "I'm going home."

Clint had used the shield of the flap to conceal the lingerie shirt he wore beneath the costume. Baiting Samarra had become one of his favorite pastimes. "Please, don't," he wheedled. "I need your help."

"I'll just bet you do!" she snorted as she snatched open the door.

"Seriously, Sam—look. I'm decent."

Unconvinced, she smugly twisted her head around, her legs poised for flight, a scathing retort about his dishonesty ready on her lips. Clint held closed the torso of the costume, but when his gaze caught hers, he yanked it wide open, then stood grinning at her look of utter incredulity.

"All right," she conceded, coming back inside and closing the door against a cold draft. "You win—this time. What do you need me to do?"

Clint plucked at the deerskin garment. "Help me figure out how to get some air in here."

With lips pursed and eyes narrowed, she walked around him, scrutinizing the well-tailored costume. Her pensive expression cloaked her appreciation of its perfect fit. The hide molded itself like a second skin to his muscular build, leaving nothing to the imagination.

193

Samarra fought back the blush threatening to stain her cheeks as she recalled that other time she'd witnessed every dot and tittle of his well-developed form. When she had completed her tour and stood before him, she felt the hot blush suffuse her face in spite of her determination to hold it at bay.

Clint's eyes followed the path hers had taken and twinkled with amusement when he realized what had caused her embarrassment.

"Down, boy!" he barked, his gaze fixing on the bulge below his waist for a moment before lifting to hers again. Beneath the tight deerskin, his broad shoulders lifted and fell. "I'm sorry, Samarra. I've tried to train him, honestly I have. He just refuses to behave sometimes."

"Oh, you—men!" She stomped her foot. "How can you be so casual . . . so smug about it?"

She turned on her heel and would have taken herself immediately from his odious presence had he not grasped her shoulders and pivoted her back around. He placed a finger beneath her chin and gently lifted her face upward until he had pinned her gaze with his smoldering hazel orbs. Her shoulders trembled beneath his open palms, her lips trembled beneath his hovering mouth, and her knees trembled beneath the sudden weight of desire raging between them.

Clint pulled her against him, against the softness of the deerskin, against the hardness of his manhood. "That's one of the things I love most about you, Samarra," he breathed against one corner of her mouth, his lips nibbling there.

His softly spoken words made her head spin. *One of the things I love most about you . . . I love about you . . . I love you. . . .* Her eyelids suffered from the same trembling weakness as her knees. With a sigh of resignation she surrendered her meager power to hold

194

them open. Clint groaned as his vision caught the fluttering of her long, raw-honey-colored lashes against her crimson cheeks, and his hands slid down the front of her gown before moving around her midriff and downward again to grasp her buttocks and pull her even more tightly into him.

"What's one of those things you love about me?" she whispered.

"You speak your mind."

Her heart wanted to ask him to list the other things he loved about her, but her body demanded she let him tell her with his hands and lips. His kisses said, "I love the shape of your mouth, the tip of your nose, the hollow beneath your ear." His caresses said, "I love the curve of your hips, the slenderness of your waistline, the shape and size of your breasts."

Her own hands and lips answered his, groping, grasping, searching, tasting. She slipped her hands inside the costume and groaned in frustration when they encountered the sweat-dampened fabric of his lightweight shirt. "You might try not wearing anything under here," she suggested.

"You almost walked out on me when you thought I hadn't."

Clint's mouth captured hers then in a searing kiss, his firm, chiseled lips molding themselves to the softness of hers, teasing them in undulating, press-and-release movements which sent wave upon wave of sensation crashing through her. His hands glided up her spine to her shoulder blades, then down again to her waistline and back up, his open palms massaging her back. The action rubbed his inner arms against the sides of her breasts, and Samarra felt them tighten, relished the response of her hardening nipples against the wall of his chest.

As a multitude of sensations sluiced through Clint, a

part of him acknowledged their genuineness. How had he ever thought he could counterfeit his feelings toward Samarra? Everything about her excited him, thrilled him, and his own response to her almost overwhelmed him in its intensity. Simultaneously, he wanted to protect her, to cherish her, to hold her near him always. But more than anything at the moment, he wanted to make love to her.

His arms moved again, this time into position to lift her into his arms and carry her upstairs to his bed. Understanding his intention, she pulled her arms out of his costume and slipped them around his neck, her slight form melting into his much taller, much harder frame. Clint felt her go limp, lifted her with ease, and moved toward the staircase. In spite of his need to mount the steps with all due haste, his mouth couldn't seem to get enough of hers. In response, his feet moved slowly, tentatively seeking a firm stance as they made their way around the work table and across the room.

But when he set one foot upon the bottom tread, the reality of his intentions jarred his senses: as much as he wanted her, an inner voice insisted the time was not right. There had to be a commitment between them before he took this delightful woman—who had come to mean more to him than any other woman before her—to his bed, before he gave her all of himself. The absence of commitment might mean the absence of a lasting, enduring relationship. And suddenly Clint realized that was what he wanted from her . . . not her body by itself, but her heart and her soul as well.

His hesitation at the foot of the stairs brought Samarra to her senses. With all her heart she wanted to believe that something more than passion existed between them. And though her body raged against withdrawal, she knew that was exactly what she had to do. Otherwise she might never know how deeply Clint cared for her, or she for him. His hesitation made the words she had to say easier, and she silently blessed him for that.

With great reluctance she pulled her mouth away from his and dropped her head against his chest, sighing. "I want to do this—" she began.

"I know. So do I," he interrupted.

"But not now, not here, not like this."

"Look at me, Samarra," his soft, mellow voice tenderly commanded.

"I can't."

"Why not?"

"Because I'm afraid I'll lose my sanity again."

"I promise not to let you. Look at me."

Clint's hazel eyes reflected his own conflicting emotions, at once assuring and frightening Samarra. What was this thing that was happening between them, this thing that demanded surcease and yet much, much more than that? his expression asked her. Her golden eyes answered, *I don't know . . . nor do I know if I'm ready to give myself wholly, completely to you.*

He set her down two steps above where he stood, putting their eyes on the same level. "I dressed in this ridiculous costume," he said, "as a way of brooking a petition."

Samarra's heart jumped into her throat. Was he going to ask her to attend the ball with him? What would she do if he didn't? She tried to imagine going without him, watching him shower his attention upon another woman, and knew that was one thing she could not do. The memory of her dream came flooding back, and though she recalled her certainty that Clint would be the one to escort her to the All Hallow's Eve ball, though she recalled the feeling she had had that this ball would shape her destiny, neither of those things seemed quite real to her anymore.

197

He waited for her to say something.

She waited for him to explain.

And then another thought pierced her heart: what if all he wanted was for her to figure out how to ventilate his outfit? His eyes watched her face, gauged her response. Her pride would not allow him to see how desperately she wanted to go with him.

"I'll have to think about it," she said.

"You'll have to think about it?" he roared. "No, no, milady. You must tell me now, before I go crazy with wondering."

"Or swoon from suffocation?" She had intended the question to be light, but it came out sounding petulant.

His brow creased in confusion, then cleared as he comprehended her meaning. "Did you honestly think I referred to the discomfort of this costume? If so, you should reconsider my petition. You cannot know how beautiful and desirable you are, Samarra."

"It's not my fault if you choose to speak in riddles, and doing so does not give you the right to malign my intelligence. So that we may understand each other, tell me what exactly constitutes this petition you speak of. And do not pussyfoot around it again, Clint Holbrooke, if you honestly desire an answer from me."

He laughed, a full-bodied, warm guffaw that melted her irritation. "There you go again, Samarra."

"Doing what? No—don't answer that. You're pussyfooting again, Mr. Holbrooke."

"My apologies, Miss Seldon." His lapse into formality enhanced Clint's romantic intent, which he took one step further by going down on one knee and taking one of her hands in his. "I would be most honored, milady, should you choose to accompany me to Governor Dinwiddie's All Hallow's Eve fancy-dress ball." And then, with an impish grin lighting his eyes, he almost spoiled it by adding, "Is that detailed enough for you, Miss Seldon?"

But it would have taken more than a flippant remark to spoil this moment for Samarra, especially when the tone with which it had been spoken had been more mischievous than condescending. "Yes, Mr. Holbrooke," she beamed, "quite detailed enough. And yes, I would be honored to accompany you to the ball." Her mouth formed a moue then. "There is but one problem."

"And what is that?"

"However shall I dress? What personage should accompany a stag to a masquerade ball?"

He rose to his feet, took both her hands in his, and squeezed them lightly. "I've given that some thought," he mused, "and I think Diana would be the perfect foil for this stag."

"Diana?" Had Clint read her mind? How could he have known that she had daydreamed about this ball, had envisioned herself dressed as a Greek goddess? No matter that Diana was Roman. The dissimilarities were insignificant.

Clint misinterpreted the reason behind her question.

"Goddess of the hunt." *And of the moon, and of childbirth, and of young living things.* Diana also symbolized chastity and purity, and was herself a virgin. That was one thing about Samarra that Clint intended to change.

"Of course. I had momentarily forgotten that particular role," she hastily explained. "If I recall my Roman mythology correctly, Diana was also Apollo's twin sister." *And how appropriate for me, a twin.*

"Should I have ordered an Apollo costume?"

"No-o-o," she quickly objected, much to Clint's relief. Going as Apollo would not conceal his identity.

"I do not think I want to go as your sister. I rather like the idea of Diana and a stag. But you must promise me something."

"And what is that?"

"That you will work a bit harder on training your dog."

"My dog?"

"We wouldn't want his ears perking up at an inopportune time."

She had scooted around him and was halfway across the workroom before she heard his laughter burst forth.

"Now who's dense?" she called back to him. "It took you long enough to figure that out!"

Daylight turned to dusk and dusk to darkness while Clint sat staring at the ten-shilling note Samarra had given him. "Lord, please tell me this isn't counterfeit," he begged aloud, as he had many a time in the past four days.

He had tried to give it back to her, insisting that she owed him three shillings, not ten. Samarra had refused to accept it, smiling innocently. "Now, Clint," she had said, "you know as well as I do that colonial currency has less value than coin. That note probably isn't enough, and it's certainly not too much."

What she had said was true, but that didn't make matters any easier for Clint. He realized that by attempting to return the bill he was ignoring his duty to the British government. But, hell, he reasoned, Samarra was no counterfeiter. Anyone could have given her the note as payment for her printing services, and she had no reason to suspect it. Samarra Seldon was a businesswoman guilty of nothing more than trying her damnedest to succeed in a man's world.

The parchment crackled in Clint's big hand as his fingers closed around it. *All I have to do is wad this thing up and hurl it into the fire. No one need know it was ever in my possession* . . .

But *you* will know, an inner voice admonished him.

Slowly his fingers relaxed and he inspected the note again. Its border was composed of pineapples set in crossed tobacco leaves, combining symbols of brotherhood and prosperity. Virginia did use a border such as this one on its notes, with one major exception: legal tender's border was interrupted at odd intervals by a motif set sideways. On the one Clint held, the pineapples marched in strict formation around the bill. If Samarra wanted to counterfeit Virginia currency, she would notice something so obvious. Clint knew she would.

There were two other reasons Clint was convinced the note was counterfeit.

The first augmented his conviction that Samarra had not printed the bill. When she had discussed printing with him, when she had shown him how to use the press, she had told him how easy it was to have the range and registration off. Samarra was a perfectionist. If the print did not lie flush at the margin or if the alignment was not exact, she would remove the metal tray and readjust the type until it printed perfectly. The currency printed by the authority of the colonial government met Samarra's strict standards. The note he held did not.

The final telltale factor was perhaps the most obvious one, one which did not exonerate Samarra in any way. After the legitimate currency was printed, the bills were hand numbered and signed by three government officials. The printer of this bill could not be deemed worthy as a forger. Clint had noted marked differences in the signatures between those on this bill and those on the legal one he had used for comparison.

The note's only redeeming factor was its ability to prolong Clint's investigation of Samarra. He did not want to believe Dinwiddie would consider it damning evidence, yet the possibility existed. Even then, Clint reminded himself, the governor was a reasonable man . . . surely he would allow Clint a bit more time to prove beyond a shadow of a doubt Samarra Seldon's innocence, to collect something beyond circumstantial evidence.

Whether he liked it or not, he had to turn over the note to the governor. And he might as well do it tonight. Dinwiddie was certain to expect a full report from Holbrooke, and without the counterfeit note, Clint's appeal to remain in Jacob McCauley's old apartment might not carry enough merit.

He had been granted a four-day reprieve already. The day following O'Quinn's visit, Clint had traveled the three-quarters of a mile to the governor's office, intending to apprise Dinwiddie of his latest findings. The same young second lieutenant sat behind the desk, and when he'd recognized Holbrooke, he'd jumped to attention. "The governor told me he wanted to be informed the next time you came," Morris had said. "Please wait here while I tell him."

Clint had known his audience had been denied by the look of utter confusion on young Morris's face when he'd returned. "He said to tell you he is busy, that he will see you at the time he designated earlier." At Clint's frown, he had continued, "You *do* know, sir, what he is referring to?"

Oh, yes, Clint knew . . . but he also strongly suspected that Governor Robert Dinwiddie had conceived a plan which, at that moment, he did not care to divulge to his chief investigator. That speculation had caused Clint additional deliberation as he'd contemplated the evening which lay before him.

Clint sighed heavily, laid the bill on his table, and shuffled over to the fireplace to hang a kettle of water from the hook. The hour had grown late while he had sat on his bed staring at the note and wishing it had never fallen into his possession. Samarra would be expecting him soon, and he still had to bathe and dress himself in the stifling stag costume, which neither of them had ever determined how to ventilate.

In an effort to keep his skin cool and unchafed, a problem which had been amplified by the dense humidity and suddenly much warmer temperature, Clint dusted himself well with cornstarch before he climbed naked into the deerskin. The costume had been designed with casings at the ankles and wrists, and he tied the drawstrings tightly over black boots and black gloves, using his teeth to draw the wrists tight before stuffing the ends of the strings underneath the hide. He decided to carry the headpiece, unwilling to expand his misery just yet.

A quick glance at the clock verified that the hour for departure had arrived. He assured himself that Clementine and her kittens were safe and warm beneath his bed, checked the feline's food and water supply, and added a few chunks of wood to the fire. Finding no other chores to delay the inevitable, he left the print shop, turning his key in the rear door and then pushing against it to ensure it was locked.

Damn, but he wanted this evening to be different! He wanted more than anything else to be the man at Samarra's side, to hold her close and dance with her all evening. He wanted the privilege of being carefree for once.

Instead, he would more than likely spend most of the evening closeted with Dinwiddie. And Samarra would never understand, since he wouldn't be able to explain it to her. Her feelings would be injured, he knew, and with just cause. Life wasn't fair, he railed . . . it just wasn't fair.

With heavy heart he followed the path through the rear yards to Samarra's back door.

The sky was as black as his mood. Dark gray stormclouds scudded across the half moon and obscured the stars. From a distance, a low rumble of thunder intruded upon both the eerie stillness and Clint's vexed spirit.

A vision of Samarra as he had seen her that morning etched itself upon his inner eye. The prospect, the anticipation of this ball had her more excited than he would have thought possible. Part of it, she had unabashedly explained to him, stemmed from his escort of her. But another part, she admitted a bit sheepishly, came from some deep-seated notion she had that this fancy-dress ball was somehow tied to her destiny.

Clint shuddered to think how accurate that notion might be.

Chapter Thirteen

Had he been afforded the privilege of ordering the weather, Clint would have requested a clear, cold night. Such weather would have curbed the discomfort his costume caused, but much more important, it would have provided reason to snuggle up next to Samarra in the confines of the hired barouche. Not that Clint needed a reason—or that Samarra expected him to have one. But this was just not snuggling weather.

Despite the warm, muggy air, Samarra had worn a lightweight hooded cape over her costume, consequently preventing Clint a view of anything other than the bottom of her skirt and the strappy Roman sandals she wore on her tiny feet. The sandals in themselves both shocked him and teased his imagination. A grown woman always covered her feet and ankles. Had she dressed as Diana? And if she had, how had she decided to fashion the costume in keeping with eighteenth-century custom?

Clint very much wanted to ask her, but he sensed her desire to keep the details of her costume a secret until they reached the governor's house. Instead, he merely raised an eyebrow at the cape.

"One never knows in this clime what trend the

weather might decide to take," she explained, the secretive grin playing at the corners of her mouth assuring him this was only part of the truth. "Before the evening is over, Williamsburg could conceivably be held in the grip of icy-cold rain."

"The rain, I'm afraid, my sweet, is inevitable," he conceded with a degree of disinterest. Weather trends were not of utmost importance to him at the moment. Clint was clinging desperately to the hope that he would be allowed to see her safely home, even if Robert Dinwiddie chose to remove him immediately from the investigation. He was dreading his upcoming meeting with the governor. If Samarra was correct in her forecast, then perhaps, he mused in an attempt to adopt a more positive outlook, he might be granted the privilege of snuggling against her yet.

If Clint had been given a second wish, it would have been an increase in the distance from Samarra's house to the Royal Governor's Palace. Although the ride was a short one, the crowded streets did slow the progress of the barouche somewhat, though not nearly enough, to Clint's way of thinking. The minutes flew by, and for all he knew, they might very well be the last he would spend alone with Samarra. He winced inwardly when he felt the coach turn right off Duke of Gloucester Street and start down the two remaining blocks to the palace.

To mask his trepidation, Clint had kept his mouth uncharacteristically busy, chattering away during the entire ride. "Did you know you colonists dubbed the governor's residence 'the palace'?" he asked, scarcely noting Samarra's uncertain nod.

"I seem to recall having heard that before," she responded, feeling her own disquiet at Clint's peculiar mood.

"The building was completed long before you ever

206

moved to Williamsburg—before you were born, actually. Alexander Spotswood, who was governor then, is reputed to have spent a fortune on its construction, the fortune coming from taxes he levied against the colonists. As they became disgruntled at his method of financing his grand plans, they started calling it 'the palace,' and so has it been called ever since."

"For someone who moved to our fair city only recently, you certainly know a great deal about it," she observed, her voice lacking the stigma of cynicism she would have shown—and had shown to him—just a week before.

Clint shrugged. "It's amazing what information one can glean from merely sitting in a tavern enjoying one's supper," he offered as grounds for his knowledge.

Samarra's eyebrows lifted in some disbelief. "I find it difficult to imagine, sir, that occupants of taverns find no more worthy diversion than expounding upon the problems and resentments of their ancestors."

Before he could shape a reply to her astute observation, the barouche slowed to a halt in front of the gate. "Well, here we are!" he exclaimed, suddenly grateful that the ride was over. As much as he enjoyed verbally sparring with Samarra, he wanted this night—possibly his last with her—to be free of argument. He assisted her in putting on her unadorned white domino, marveling at the way the half mask seemed to enhance her beauty rather than detract from it.

As she descended from the coach, Samarra gasped at the display of lights on the wide expanse of lawn and within the crape myrtles bordering it. A myriad of candles burned inside colorful Oriental lanterns in the trees, while flaming baskets called cressets flanked the brick walkway and the steps leading to the front door. More candlelight gleamed from within the three-story,

207

mansard-roofed mansion, whose every window covering had been opened to allow the light to spill out upon the lawn. In deference to the comfort of the guests, those same windows had been raised to permit entry to whatever breezes might choose to blow.

Music spilled out the open windows as well, adding its festivity to that of the decorations on the lawn. A pile of bright orange pumpkins sat on one side of the wide steps; a shock of cornstalks stood on the other. Despite the pall Clint's mood had put upon the evening, Samarra's spirits took flight at the sights and sounds surrounding her. As they joined the flow of other costumed guests on the walkway, her excitement gushed forth.

"Oh, Clint! This is delightful. I expected this ball to be one of the governor's most lavish, but in my wildest imagination I had not expected this." She flung an arm outward to encompass everything within her realm of vision.

When he did not join her in her enthusiasm, she looked at him askance, then laughed aloud when she saw why: in her moment of exultation, she had failed to see him put on his headpiece.

Clint took her elbow in a firm grip and tugged her along, his demeanor daring her to expect any verbal response from him. In rebellion toward his attitude, but with a certain degree of mischief, she plowed ahead anyway. "Don't you agree?" Then, softer, "How are you ever going to enjoy yourself in that outfit? I've thought of little else for days, and, for the life of me, I cannot fathom why you chose a costume so utterly absurd."

His grip tightened and he growled. Although she heard his snarl, the sound came low to her ears, while to him, it rumbled within the confines of the headpiece. If he'd thought it would help, he'd have offered another

208

curse to the continued good health of Virginia's most esteemed governor, whose balls were reputed to be the most elegant social events of British America.

Clint could not recall the Dinwiddies' hosting a fancy-dress ball before, but he supposed, there was a first time for everything. Still and all, couldn't the governor have contrived a better costume for him? He understood the need for secrecy, for it would not do for someone to recognize him and thus reveal his true occupation to Samarra and perhaps others in attendance. Yet, Clint was sure if the choice had been left up to him, he could have devised something more comfortable to wear. Already, perspiration had gathered on his brow and upper lip, and the real rub came from his inability to wipe it away.

Samarra paid little heed to his ill humor. He had done it to himself, after all, she reasoned, when he chose to dress as a stag. Let him suffer the consequences. She intended to have a grand time.

Among the costumes parading in front of them, Samarra recognized a number of Shakespearean and storybook characters, a few monarchs, and, to her surprise, several other animals besides Clint. Why anyone would choose to dress himself from head to toe in some cloying, body-hugging garment she could not understand, but she found herself grateful for Clint's sake that several others had. At least he would not be so conspicuous. She could little hope for the same for herself.

"Let's see," she teased. "I spy a goat and a skunk and a fox and a bear and a—"

His grumbling stopped her.

"What's wrong, Clint? Can't you talk anymore? Please tell me you don't plan to wear that headpiece all night long."

She laughed when another grumble answered her.

Suddenly they were through the door and inside the residence, the press of the crowd growing stronger as they had neared the entrance. Her hand was clasped by their congenial host and hostess, who were dressed as Henry VIII and Anne Boleyn, and who introduced themselves thusly, then requested Samarra's and Clint's costume identities. "For this evening," the governor explained, "everyone will be known only by his or her costume character's name. We welcome you, Diana and Stag. May your hunt prove successful."

Clint was not at all certain he appreciated that remark, which implied his eventual demise, but he scarcely had time to think about it before Samarra twirled the cape from her shoulders and handed it to a waiting servant. Inside the headpiece, his mouth popped open and his eyes bulged at the sight of her standing straight and proud amidst a flood of candlelight.

Samarra was light itself. Light seemed to emanate from her golden hair, her pearly skin, the fabric of her costume, almost as though a halo surrounded her. Her gown had been constructed of white silk, yards and yards of it draped in a most becoming—and seductive—fashion. At both shoulders the shimmering fabric was caught with large, golden, multifaceted medallions set with crystal stones which flashed thousands of tiny pinpoints of light. Her skin, where it had been left bare, gleamed in opalescent splendor. The silk cascaded from the medallions in a multitude of soft folds, forming a V, its vortex nestling in the valley between her breasts. A thin gold chain held the loosely flowing garment at her waist, from which the fabric fell in swirling, undulating ripples of glimmering white. The skirt stopped just short of her trim ankles, exposing the dainty, sandaled feet Clint had witnessed in the coach.

Clint's eyes traveled upward to her face, to the twist of honey-colored hair upon her crown, to the ropes of pearls entwined among the golden strands. He noted the delicate white satin quiver attached to the back of her gown, the gold-tipped arrows it held glistening above one medallioned shoulder. And in her hands she held an equally delicate gold-plated bow.

Never had he seen a vision of loveliness quite so stunning. The rarity of this sight wrenched at his heart and threatened to close off his throat. The vision smiled seductively at him then, her smile reaching the wondrous luster of her golden eyes. Her voice was low and husky, almost gravelly, when she spoke.

"We're blocking the door, Milord Stag. Shall we dance?"

He took her hand in his, knew how soft her skin would feel if he could touch it, and cursed the leather gloves which encased his fingers. Together they moved as one into the hall, both in a trancelike state, but for entirely separate reasons. Their ears noticed the sudden quiet which fell over the throng gathered in the ballroom, heard the loud, almost unanimously uttered gasp which followed it. Their eyes saw the stunned faces, witnessed many a gossip-hungry matron turn snidely to another of her kind. But their hearts heard nothing but their own pounding pulses, saw nothing but each other.

If Clint had been capable of rational thought, he would have been angry at Samarra for wearing such a costume. Too much of her was exposed, and those parts which were not might as well have been, for the fabric molded itself to her luscious curves. But Clint was not capable of rational thought. He was bewitched. When he saw his best friend sit up and take notice, he pulled her against him and onto the dance floor. Clint had never considered himself much of a

211

dancer, but with Samarra in his arms, his feet glided upon the polished floor with a grace he had never known he possessed.

Forgotten was the heavy, suffocating stag's costume. He felt as light as air, as though he and Samarra were mere clouds pushed about by a whimsical breeze.

Her light laughter betrayed her lack of substance, yet served to intensify the soaring, swirling, heady feel of her in his arms. "You were correct, Milord Stag," she crooned. "He does seem to have a mind of his own, doesn't he? 'Twill serve you well to hold me close so that my form might shield his perking ears and thus save you much embarrassment."

Clint rested his deer's cheek against her own, hence putting his mouth as close to her ear—and his own ear as close to her mouth—as he could manage. Although the headpiece had been constructed with holes for eyes, mouth, and ears, the very structure of it prohibited the senses from operating properly. "A blush would serve you well, sweet Diana. 'Tis the way of ladies, you know."

"A certain man has taught me much about such things," she retorted, her voice low so that only he could hear, "and through his teaching I have learned to accept the physical manifestations of two opposite poles. With knowledge comes acceptance, and with acceptance, a serenity of the mind and body. Besides," she giggled, "I am not the one whose manifestation exhibits itself so prominently."

He laughed then, the deep, throaty laugh she loved to hear. "You are not the same woman I met a few weeks ago," he observed when he could speak again.

No, I am not, she silently agreed. *And, you, Clint Holbrooke, are the reason I'm different.* Before Clint had come into her life, she would never have appeared in public dressed as she was, throwing all caution to the wind. Before Clint, she had wasted too much precious time and energy worrying about what her neighbors thought. His coming into her life had changed all that, for his presence, his influence, his caring had taught her that the only honor virtue knows rests within one's own mind and heart. Aloud, she said in purposeful misunderstanding, "No, tonight I am Diana, goddess of the hunt."

The stag's head limited Clint's vision, but he could see well enough to note the stares being hurled at them from almost everyone in the huge room. Clint felt a stir of jealousy grip his heart at the open-mouthed, appreciative gaping of the men, while the women gawking in undisguised envy amused him. It was inappropriate, he knew, for a man to hold a woman so closely in public, yet he dared not leave Samarra's side. Neither did he dare let her go, lest any one of the men in the room pounce on her and twirl her away from him. The stares spoke for themselves. If he ever let her go, she would be lost to him for the remainder of the evening.

What Clint had failed to anticipate was the orchestra's inevitable break. Once the harpsichord and strings were silent, he had no choice but to lead her off the floor.

"Where's the refreshment table?" he asked, moving his head close to hers again.

"Let me guide you," she replied.

They moved into line behind an Elizabethan couple, whose heavy satin and velvet garments occupied more space than was commonly required. Samarra filled crystal plates for both of them and accepted cups of spicy apple-cider punch from a serving girl. Balancing the cups on their plates as they moved with the ebb and flow of the crowd, the Elizabethan couple blocking Samarra's view of possible seating for her and Clint.

Clint had the advantage of having spent many an

hour in this ballroom. His eyes, too, scanned it, looking for an alcove hidden beside one of the long windows. When he spied one, he grasped her bare upper arm gently and pulled her away from the crowd gathered around the heavily laden table.

Samarra could not imagine where he was taking her, but she moved with him toward the long window without protest. As with all the windows, the heavy velvet draperies at this one had been pulled back, their dual widths covering several feet of wall space on either side. The tiny alcove on one side of the window startled Samarra as Clint led her behind the portieres which concealed it.

"My, it's dark in here!" she exclaimed, blinking in an effort to see. "Or is it just that it's so bright out there?"

"Sh-h-h!" Clint hissed from close behind her. "Do you want everyone to know where we disappeared to?"

"With all that noise?" It was true . . . the hall was filled to overflowing with people who were now talking animatedly among themselves; the music had ended. "Shall we just stand here, or is there someplace to sit down?"

In keeping with the romance of the sheltered nook, a rose window had been set high in the outside wall. On a clear night, the leaded glass within the decorative framework refracted the moonlight, scattering it along the draperies and softly illuminating the tiny alcove. But on this moon-shrouded night, almost no light penetrated the curved glass. What light there was came from the lanterns hanging in the trees.

In the near-total darkness, Samarra clutched the plates tighter. "Don't bump into me," she warned, "or I will spill this punch."

"There's a bench set into the corner. Let me put my antlers down and I'll help you."

Momentarily, they were settled upon the L-shaped

bench, the bend of the corner separating them. Clint had begun to question the wisdom of choosing this naturally warm spot, made even warmer by the humidity. Quickly he swallowed his punch, the entire cupful, then immediately wished he had saved some. For some reason an attack of nerves struck him.

Samarra, too, was suddenly uncomfortable finding herself entirely alone with Clint in the close, dark confines of the alcove. No matter that hundreds of the governor's guests swarmed the hall. The heavy curtain effectively closed them off.

"That was good punch," Clint said inanely, knowing he had to do something to pierce the tension sparking between them and grabbing the first thought that entered his head. "I wouldn't mind having some more, except that I don't want to give us away by going after it."

"Poor dear," Samarra punned, "it must be ungodly hot for you in that skin. Here—" She pressed her cup into his hands. "Drink the rest of mine."

"No—No, I couldn't."

"Really. I don't want it. Besides," she added when he hesitated to accept the cup, "my costume is fully ventilated."

Their eyes had become accustomed to the absence of light, and Clint could not resist resting his gaze on her shadowy form. "Yes," he breathed over the rim of the crystal cup, his thoughts flashing back for a split second to a rainy afternoon when Samarra had flatly refused to drink from the same cup as he, "you are ventilated."

Samarra's thoughts traveled the same path as his. Her heart pounded in her chest and she felt her body flush from head to toe. When he'd moved the cups and his plate aside and taken her plate from her lap and set it away from them, she forgot how to breathe. His

215

large hands, now free of the leather gloves, smoothed themselves over her bare upper arms, then traversed the slim column of her neck to caress her flushed cheeks. She felt the flutter of his fingertips against her cheekbones, the compelling press of his thumbs at the corners of her mouth, and willingly swayed toward him. She welcomed the soft touch of his lips against hers, moaned when he seemed bent on teasing her with puckering kisses. Her own hands reached out to touch him, encountered the perk of his manhood, and drew away as quickly as if they'd been scorched.

"No," he murmured, "touch me."

"I can't," she pleaded.

"Yes, you can," he softly insisted. "Serenity of mind, remember?"

With more temerity than conviction, she laid an open palm upon his lap and discovered that she could touch him, could even relish the feel of his throbbing beneath her hand. Suddenly she wanted to strip him of the deerskin separating them. The thought shocked her to her core and she gasped at its intensity.

Clint wanted her more than he had ever wanted a woman before; perhaps someday he would have her. But for tonight, he knew he must settle for what little portion of her the cramped space of the alcove and the threat of discovery from one of the guests allowed. For some moments more he plied his chaste kisses upon her mouth, across her cheek, and down her slender throat. But when she arched her neck and groaned, when her fingers closed around him, his mouth opened of its own accord upon the smooth skin at the curve of her throat and shoulder and suckled there gently.

And Clint was lost.

Lost in the shadowy darkness. Lost in the overwhelming sensation flooding through him. Lost in the arms of this delightfully independent woman who

216

made him feel, for the first time in his life, that he was truly wanted, needed, loved.

A warm, yearning emptiness burned deep in Samarra's belly and spread itself downward to her loins. Her lips parted beneath his when he moved his mouth back to hers; a shiver clutched her when his tongue raked her teeth, coaxing them open so that he might ravish the warm, moist cavern of her mouth. Beneath his large hand she felt her breast tighten, change shape, mold itself to fit his palm. His thumb teased its crest against the slick surface of the silk until Samarra thought she would scream from the exquisite pain he'd caused. Slowly, tenderly, as his mouth worked its wonder upon hers, that same hand pushed against the fabric covering the throbbing peak until he had freed it of all bonds.

Again the pad of his thumb circled the taut nipple, slowly, inexorably massaging the areola and flickering against the hardened pinnacle, then following the feathery movement of his fingers to the base of her breast. She felt the long, hard length of his fingers mold and shape its curve, felt his palm push against the soft flesh, and thought she would faint when his mouth renewed the wonder his thumb had created there.

At first he used only the tip of his tongue to play a sweet arpeggio upon the rigid crest; the music swelled as he laved it with the bumpy-soft surface of his tongue. And when he took her breast into his mouth and suckled it, a feeling like the crash of cymbals resounded through her head. Her fingers wove themselves through the springy hair at his nape and pulled his head even closer to her.

All the while he took succor from her breast, his free hand caressed her, sliding over the silk of her gown, over the tightened muscles of her stomach, roaming down the outside of a thigh, then back up the sensitive inner thigh, finally planting its heel upon the soft

217

mound of her womanhood. Her torso arched against him, her body's response coupled with her soft moans and labored breathing sending further fire to his loins, his own response threatening to burst the crotch seam of his costume.

With a suddenness that both startled and pained her, Samarra felt Clint's head jerk back and his hands quickly move the fabric back over her breast. *How could you do such a thing to me?* her heart wailed. And then she knew how.

"There you are," a deep, vaguely familiar male voice bellowed from the edge of the heavy draperies. "I came to rescue you, Stag."

"I didn't want to be rescued," Clint mumbled, reaching for the deer's head.

"Nevertheless, I am here. Someone of our mutual acquaintance wishes to see you—now. You know where to find him. He says you are not to worry about Diana. I will see to her needs for the time being."

Samarra had turned her head toward the outer wall, away from the portieres, the second she'd realized they were no longer alone, taking the moment to compose herself. Her lips felt bruised, her chest refused to stop heaving, her limbs trembled, and she suffered from acute embarrassment at having been caught in a most compromising position. Fortunately the alcove remained in shadow. Perhaps this unwelcome intruder had seen nothing.

Whether he had or not, she had no intention of going anywhere with this man, whoever he was. Clint would never leave her like this to face the accusing glares of a gutter-minded crowd, a concern which bore graphic witness to the ongoing battle for independence she thought she had won. Given time to collect themselves, they could reenter the ballroom after the orchestra started to play again, could slip in among the dancers and no one need ever be the wiser—with the exception of this interloper.

She twisted her head around then, sought Clint's understanding, and received instead a noncommittal shrug from him. "I'm sorry, Sa—Diana. I have to go." To the trespasser, he barked, "You may dance with her, and you may bring her refreshment. But you are not, under any circumstances, to see to any of her other needs."

Samarra started to rise, but her backside seemed glued to the padded seat. She opened her mouth to utter a plea, but she seemed to have lost her ability to speak. She felt Clint's hand—gloved again—fall briefly upon her bare shoulder, heard him say with some resignation and much regret, "In the event I don't see you again, I thank you for a lovely evening."

She felt as though someone had punched her in the stomach, and she crossed her forearms upon her lap and held her aching belly. She watched him put on the stag's head, watched the antlers teeter and sway, and remembered how they had laughed over his costume, remembered their playful banter as they had stood in her workroom—and later, upon the stairs. She watched him push the curtain aside and walk away from her. She felt her soul depart from her body and walk beside him, leaving her sitting there in the darkened alcove, an empty shell.

The intruder took Clint's place on the bench and waited for her to move, to speak, to show some sign of life. When, after several minutes, she hadn't done any of these, he pried one of her hands loose from her lap and held it tenderly in his own. Her palm was clammy and cold, her fingers stiff. He smoothed her hand between his rough palms, his voice coming low and soothing. "Everything is going to be all right, Miss Seldon. I promise you'll see him again soon."

His tone more than his words penetrated her consciousness. She pulled her hand from his grasp and used it to wipe away the solitary tear that had slipped from her eye. "Did you—" She paused, drew in a deep breath, and let it out in a whistle. "What did you just call me?"

"Miss Seldon."

Her eyes searched the deep shadows that fell across his face. "Mac . . . Captain Reed, is that you?"

"Yes. My apologies, ma'am. I thought you recognized me."

Samarra drew some small comfort from his identity. "Where—where did Clint go? Who wanted to see him?"

"Now, don't worry your pretty little head about Clint Holbrooke. No harm shall befall him this night, although he might think so before it's over," he added cryptically. He stood up then, taking her hands in his. "Come," he coaxed. "The music has started again, and our host intends us to dance for a while."

His hands dropped hers, and Samarra watched him reach for a headcovering similar to Clint's, watched him put it on, felt him grasp her hands again. She followed him on leaden feet, let him guide her through the steps, commanded the barest hint of a smile to touch her lips and hide her thoughts, while her heart cried out for that one who had touched her with such passion and then left her without argument or explanation. How could she have been so wrong about his feelings for her? How could she have allowed herself to be so vulnerable, so foolish?

The orchestra played, the candles blazed, the dancers twirled about the floor, just as they had in her daydream. And from a distance she looked down upon it all, spied the blonde woman from her musings, and witnessed the cold flint of anger as it replaced the pain in her golden brown eyes.

220

Chapter Fourteen

Samarra had no interest in the passage of time. The sweet strains of music deflected off her reeling anger and the candlelight ricocheted off the hard glint in her eyes. Her fascination with the fancy-dress ball had departed with the one with whom she'd arrived.

Where before she had felt beautiful, now she felt conspicuous. Where before she had felt independent, now she felt foolish. Where before her heart had soared, now it lay like a dead weight in her chest.

She had come to the ball feeling more like Cinderella than Diana—and indeed, had she been able to hear the whisperings among the crowd, she would have heard the matrons and many of the men question one another about her identity. The few who recognized her as either the female printer with whom they'd done business or the daughter of one of the city's wealthiest merchants kept this information smugly to themselves.

But there the similarity of the stories ended, for this Cinderella had come to the ball on the arm of her charming prince, and though the sandals on her feet were out of the ordinary, it would do her no good to leave one of them behind. For Samarra, the midnight bell had tolled when Clint had left her side, and no fairy godmother would intervene and restore him to her.

Never before had her pride been so wounded, her temper so enraged, her spirit so deflated.

The astute among the many who watched her noticed the subtle change in her demeanor, recognized her smile as forced, saw the harsh lines which had gathered at the corners of her eyes, and they wondered about and speculated on that which had caused the change. A few of these astute observers had seen this goddess of light and her escort disappear into the alcove, and their speculations naturally centered on some imagined lover's quarrel. Yet the men among them wondered, if that were the case, why she would continue to keep company with the man. Surely she could see their eagerness for an introduction, their willingness to fill the void.

His face completely hidden behind the mask of the stag's head, her escort gave no clues as to what he thought or felt. From all appearances he had not left her side the entire evening. What observers noticed was the way he held her away from himself now, the way they both moved woodenly in each other's arms.

Long before the second intermission, the crowd grew weary with watching and speculating, and they turned their attentions elsewhere.

Samarra, too, had grown bored. When the musicians laid their instruments aside for the second time, Samarra made her appeal to her surrogate escort.

"Captain Reed, would you please take me home?"

Her request took him by surprise, but his costume effectively concealed his astonishment. She heard him mumble something from within the headpiece and could not ascertain whether he'd acquiesced or not. Her gaze raked the room, searching for the governor and his wife.

"First, of course, I want to express my gratitude to

222

our hosts, but I don't see either of them anywhere. And I will need to collect my cape." When he made no move, no indication that he would accompany her, she continued, "If you are unable to leave at present, I shall find someone else to see me safely home."

Not once in the eight years of his military career had Mac Reed disobeyed an order, but it appeared that tonight he would have little choice. Samarra Seldon was determined to leave, and short of causing a scene, Mac honestly didn't think he could convince her to stay. His instructions were to remain by her side until she was summoned, which couldn't very well happen if she was no longer present.

The antlers nodded in what would have been, under other circumstances, a humorous wiggle, and Samarra thought for the first time since Clint had deserted her how odd it was that these two men had dressed alike. The captain took her bare elbow in his gloved hand and led her out of the ballroom and down a hallway to the room where Governor Robert Dinwiddie had closeted himself.

"This is some fine kettle of fish you've gotten me into, Governor," Clint stated without complaint.

"It wouldn't have been if you'd let your head rule your actions. I thought you'd learned that lesson, Clint," Robert Dinwiddie replied, a droll smile plucking at the corners of his mouth.

Clint winced at this reminder. "That was a long time ago. Besides, this is different."

Dinwiddie's bushy, graying eyebrows rose to midforehead. "Is it?"

"You know it is."

"I know that once before in your brilliant career you allowed a beautiful woman to get under your skin, and that time it almost got you killed. From what you've told me about your knifed bedding, I would say this is not so very different." Dinwiddie folded his hands and tucked them under his chin in an effort to hold the ever-threatening smile at bay. He was thoroughly enjoying making Clint Holbrooke squirm.

"The circumstances are not even similar, Governor," Clint insisted. "And you will not convince me that Samarra hired someone to murder me in my bed."

"My, my," Dinwiddie clucked, his eyes twinkling despite his resolve to keep a serious mien. "It's Samarra now, is it? When did familiarity replace formality, Clint? And more important, why? Convince me, Holbrooke, that you are speaking with your head and not your genitals, and perhaps I will change my attitude."

For at least the third time since Clint had settled himself in the comfortable leather chair across from the governor's desk, they were at an impasse again—and both knew it.

A long moment of tense silence passed as Dinwiddie waited patiently for a rebuttal. Then, placing the flat of his hands upon the top of his desk, he pinned Clint with a look that ranged somewhere between "I dare you to defy me" and "You might like this idea." Aloud, he said bluntly, "We are in agreement that this counterfeiting must be stopped. We are also in agreement that Miss Seldon is more than likely not a reasonable suspect."

He waited again, watching Clint's face as understanding dawned there, watching some of the fight leave his favorite officer, but when Clint opened his mouth to speak, Dinwiddie halted him with a raised hand. "Hear me out . . . in recent weeks, while you have been confined to your rooms at Miss Seldon's and unable to uncover even an iota of evidence against her, another investigator has been hot upon the trail of

224

someone who, I think, created an elaborate scheme which led us to believe in Miss Seldon's probable guilt in the beginning, and who is, more than likely, our counterfeiter."

Clint's heart skipped a beat, then pounded against the hard wall of his chest. His spirit soared at the news, his heart beating a tattoo: Samarra is innocent . . . Samarra is innocent . . . That someone else had discovered the proof of this bothered him not a whit. But his spirits plummeted when another thought struck him hard in the gut: if Samarra was no longer a suspect, he, Clint Holbrooke, would be reassigned—exactly as he had feared. From the depths of his despair, he realized Dinwiddie, who had allowed him a moment to digest the news, had resumed his speech.

"Although the successful conclusion of this investigation is of utmost importance to the economy of this colony, my own time and energies have been—and will continue to be, I'm afraid—consumed by the ever-growing threat of all-out war with the French. With that in mind, I have devised a plan which I hope will flush out the counterfeiter."

Clint forced himself to pay attention, and the more he heard of it, the better he liked Dinwiddie's idea. He was shrewd enough to maintain a semblance of resistance, since Dinwiddie seemed to expect it, but by the time Mac Reed knocked on the study door requesting admittance, Clint had resignedly agreed to participate in all aspects of the governor's scheme and found himself eagerly anticipating Samarra's reaction.

She entered the wood-paneled room first, her eyes on the governor as he rose from his chair, her mouth poised to utter the token "Thank you and goodnight." But when she heard the click of the heavy oak panel as it closed behind her, her back went ramrod straight and a look of confusion mixed with a hint of fear washed over her soft features. She whirled around, almost colliding with Mac Reed, who stood with his spine against the portal.

Mac removed the stag's head, shot the governor a look that combined apology and helplessness, then explained to Samarra, "The governor has something he wishes to discuss with you."

When she offered neither physical nor verbal response, Dinwiddie said to her rigid back, "Come, Miss Seldon, sit down. A friend of yours is here, as well. We've been discussing a proposition which I would now like to discuss with you."

A friend? Who could he possibly mean? Her fervent hold on her social privacy had disallowed the luxury of many friends. When she needed a friend, she turned to her father, or to George and Nanna . . . and, recently, to Clint.

Her eyes found him, sitting on his spine in a brown leather wing chair, his long legs stretched out in front of him, his knees slightly flexed, his ankles crossed. The stag costume lay discarded on the floor beside his chair, a heap of soft brown deerskin topped with the full-nosed, floppy-antlered headpiece. In its place, he had donned a casual shirt and breeches. He wore neither cravat nor waistcoat. His demeanor told her quite plainly that he knew the governor well enough to be completely at ease in his company.

So *this* was where Clint had disappeared to . . . Samarra had searched her memory, recalled the captain's words when he'd discovered her and Clint in the alcove: "Someone of our mutual acquaintance wants to see you . . . you know where to find him." That Clint had known the exact meaning of Mac's cryptic message had been as obvious then as now; it was to Samarra that that meaning suddenly became abundantly clear.

She dragged her thoughts back to the present as she moved somewhat stiffly toward the proffered chair beside Clint.

"That will be all for the moment, Captain Reed," Dinwiddie said, his mouth quirking as he nodded a dismissal. "And by the by, captain, excellent timing," he added just before the door closed, his sparkling irises focusing on some indistinct point over the doorway for a moment before settling first on Samarra, then on Clint, and finally attempting to encompass them both as he began to lay out his proposal. He sat down and leaned back in his chair, resting his elbows against his hipbones and forming a steeple with his hands.

Unable to look at Clint—she was still piqued, despite her recent understanding of his immediate departure—Samarra precipitated her gaze upon the governor's hands, watched the steeple of his fingers as he moved the tips back and forth against each other. Behind the steeple, she watched his chest expand as he filled his lungs with air. When it contracted, he dropped his hands to his lap.

She breathed deeply then, too, but held her breath as she awaited his discourse. An errant memory nibbled at her heart . . . the feeling she'd had one bright, icy morning that somehow this fancy-dress ball was tied to her destiny. The feeling made her head spin. She felt her face go hot and cold, felt a clamminess seeping into her tightly clasped palms, felt her blood pulsing erratically in her temples. She closed her eyes, expelled the held breath, and took another deep one, willing her involuntary reflexes to behave themselves as she consciously forced air into and out of her lungs in a deep, regular pattern.

"I didn't mean to frighten you, young lady," the governor soothed. "Let me put your mind at ease. I

227

summoned you here tonight strictly on your own behalf. I understand your father is in London, on business, and will be absent from this fair city for several more months yet."

He paused. She nodded, then remembered this man was the royal governor. A man of his station would expect a more formal response. She cleared her throat and answered in the affirmative.

"Mr. Holbrooke tells me you have reason to believe someone broke into your house and rifled through some drawers in your bedchamber. He also tells me that the same night, someone broke into his apartment and ruined his bedding. I would like to post a guard around the clock at both your residence and your place of business."

A few weeks before, visions of her neighbors twittering among themselves over the constant presence of a uniformed guard would have dismayed Samarra. But that was before she'd had met Clint . . . before she had dared break with custom and show her ankles, toes, and bare arms to Williamsburg society. It was not what her neighbors would think or even the likelihood of losing customers which prompted her immediate protest, but rather the probability of having her freedom curtailed, her independence limited. "I appreciate your concern, sir," she proclaimed firmly, "but I do not think such extreme measures necessary."

"I was fully prepared to hear you say just that, Miss Seldon," the governor continued, "and I remind you that I said I would *like* to post a guard, not that I proposed to do so. With the current political unrest in the Ohio Valley, I'm afraid that I cannot spare a man."

Samarra frowned in some confusion, then cut her eyes to Clint, who seemed preoccupied with a set of botanical prints on the wall beside him. There would be no help for her from that quarter. Robert Dinwiddie seemed bent on shilly-shallying, and somehow she had to stop him, had to make him tell her his proposition. If ever she had need to put the effectiveness of her feminine charms to the test, now was the time—and she knew it. Samarra batted her dark gold eyelashes at the governor and smiled her sweetest, most demure smile. "I mean no disrespect, sir, but I would appreciate your hastening to set my mind at ease."

"And that is precisely my intention, Miss Seldon. Your mind has not been at ease for almost a week, I'm sure—since the night of the break-in. I expect you lie awake every night, wondering if the felon will return, your heart hammering in your chest at the very thought of a strange man entering your bedchamber, more especially with you there. You must wonder if he would do you bodily harm—and you must feel quite alone, quite unprotected with your father gone. And that brings us to my proposal."

Dinwiddie sat forward in his chair, making the springs pop. He rested his lower arms on the top of his desk and folded his fingers together. His glittering irises sought hers, arrested her absolute attention. "Mr. Holbrooke tells me that the two of you have become . . . friends. He is as concerned about your welfare as I am, perhaps more so. He and I have already discussed my idea, and we are in complete agreement."

Samarra thought she would certainly fall out of her chair from apoplexy before the governor made his point. How could anyone in his position ever get any business conducted in this roundabout fashion? She willed him to say it and be done with it. Without conscious direction, she voiced her frustration. "And what, pray tell, is your idea?"

If she offended him, Robert Dinwiddie gave no sign. Instead, he smiled gently at her, his kind eyes begging her understanding and acquiescence. "My idea, Miss Seldon, is that you marry Mr. Holbrooke posthaste."

He gave her a moment for it to sink in. When it did, she gasped loudly, and her right hand flew to the area of her heart, where it splayed itself against her chest. "Ma-Ma-*marry?*" she sputtered.

"Yes, Miss Seldon. Marry."

"But—why?"

"As I explained . . . for your protection. We couldn't have Mr. Holbrooke just move in with you, now, could we?" His twinkling eyes surveyed her upper torso appreciatively. "That would surely set the tongues wagging. And current conditions prohibit my placing a guard at your house. I must do something, Miss Seldon. Your father would expect it. He would never forgive me if I didn't take some action to protect you, and, Miss Seldon"—he shrugged expansively—"this is the best plan I could come up with."

This was not the way marriage was supposed to be proposed! It should happen some starry night, Samarra seated in a moonlit garden with the heady scent of gardenias wafting on an evening breeze. Clint should be on one knee before her, his long, lean fingers softly enfolding her small hands, his mouth uttering sweet endearments and his eyes smoldering a dark, mossy green from his passion. She should fall into his arms, feel the contrast of his hard chest against the softness of her bosom, turn her face up to his, and let his mouth steal her breath away while she mumbled "Yes, yes." They should declare their love for each other and pledge their undying devotion and sit upon the bench holding hands and planning their future together. They should discuss children and careers and servants and a house and a garden, what pets they would have and where they would travel, and what they would do with every day of the rest of their lives.

What manner of woman did he and Dinwiddie think she was, to agree to such a proposal? Did they think her incapable of securing a mate for life? Did they find her femininity, her desirability inadequate?

More than anything, Samarra wanted to turn her head and look at Clint, but she was afraid of what he might misread in her visage if she did. She felt the evidence of her consummate embarrassment stain her cheeks, felt the evidence of her self-contempt harden her mouth, felt the evidence of her supreme defiance at this proposal glint from her narrowed eyes. And she knew Clint would see those things and think her revulsion was directed at him.

And, damn it, so it should be! The governor said he and Clint had already discussed this proposal, and Clint had agreed. What manner of man was *he* to allow his future to be so directed, to allow someone else to propose marriage in his stead, and with him sitting right there beside her? He had yet to utter a word, either in resigned agreement or in caring compassion. He had yet to so much as extend his hand and touch her in reassurance.

Well, let him see her scorn, her utter contempt at being treated so—so meanly! Let him see the full flower of her anger. She would be no pawn in their game. Samarra bolted from her chair, then quickly reached back to grasp one of its arms as her watery knees refused to support her slight weight.

Clint caught her movement out of the corner of his eye and snapped his head around. His gaze raked over the stark whiteness of the knuckles of her right hand as it gripped the chair, then traveled upward to rest upon the livid countenance of her face. He had known she would be defiant, perhaps even angry. And he knew what he had to do about it.

His left hand covered her right one, the pad of his

231

thumb rubbing gently against the taut flesh of the back of her wrist. "May we please have a moment alone?" he asked Dinwiddie.

The governor nodded and left the room.

Samarra's pulse pounded in her ears, and she stiffened her back in renewed rebellion. But when Clint's lean fingers closed around the bare skin of her upper arms, when he turned her to face him, she felt her spirit slowly dying in shaded degrees of obeisance despite her attempts to keep it alive. She would not allow herself to look upon his face, but Clint knew how to persuade her with his hands, with his lips, with softly spoken words, and these he used to ply her into submission.

His hands glided upward, sliding across her collarbone and encasing her neck, his thumbs massaging the hollow at the base of her throat. When, despite her resolve, she shivered beneath the gentle caresses of his hands and lifted her head to meet his searing gaze, the evidence of his ardor manifested itself more explicitly. Clint's mouth sought hers, branding her lips and then her tongue with the heat of his passion as his hands continued their wandering journey over her bare arms and throat, rekindling the same flames within her that he'd had ignited in the alcove. Samarra felt herself succumbing to the blaze and knew, with that tiny bit of rational thought as yet unaffected, that she must put an end to it all.

"No, Clint," she whispered into his open mouth, but when her weak plea garnered her nothing, she placed her hands on his chest and pushed against him, wrenching her mouth from his. Still, his lips sought hers in teasing, plucking kisses. She opened her eyes wide and saw the drooping lids of his own, saw the near torment of her withdrawal tighten the flesh at their outside corners, and she pushed against him again with more earnest.

But he had her in a firm hold and refused to let go.

"This isn't fair," she pleaded, the torture in her voice begging him to stop.

"'All's fair in love . . .'" came his hoarse reply, but he backed off, allowing her some space to assimilate the governor's proposition.

Did Clint's words mean he loved her? she wondered, her heart remembering another testimony, remembering Clint saying, "That's one of the things I love about you." He had come all around declaring his love for her without ever actually saying the words.

Samarra had ceased trying to deny the special magic that existed between them, but she had not as yet clearly defined that magic. That they both longed to harvest the passion raging between them she had no doubt. The prospect of that harvest no longer frightened her. What did bother her—and it bothered her immensely—was the question of whether or not that harvest would be followed by the cultivation of another, and another, and another. . . .

The concept of spending the remainder of her life in abject misery with one who felt nothing more than lust for her rankled. She envisioned the bonds of matrimony as the shackles of a lifetime. Were she to sentence herself to those chains, she needed to hear unswerving assurance from Clint that he would indeed love, honor, and cherish her for the rest of their natural lives, and she wanted him to voluntarily offer that assurance. She needed to know, too, that what she was feeling for him encompassed more than lust.

She needed time. They needed time.

But time was not on their side. The governor had said "posthaste." Although he'd expressed his wish that she marry Clint as a proposition for her consideration, she knew that Dinwiddie was, for all practical purposes, not allowing her decision on the matter. He was the royal governor, a hunter with musket loaded and primed, his subjects mere rabbits and foxes and squirrels. He'd killed the stag, and then he'd belatedly asked the goddess of the hunt to bless the kill. Whether or not she chose to comply was of no consequence.

Her wandering thoughts had prompted her feet to wander as well. She had crossed the room several times in her pacing, and now she stood before a floor-to-ceiling bookcase, one forefinger absently reaching up to trace the narrow spine of a volume of poetry. Clint's soft caress at her shoulder startled her, and she snapped at him, "Don't touch me!"

"Do you find the expectation of marrying me so very distasteful, Samarra, that you are unwilling to discuss it?" he murmured in her ear, his open palm moving upon her shoulder and down her arm despite her cry.

"Distasteful? 'Tis not that I find the thought of marriage to you distasteful, Clint. 'Tis the manner in which the proposal was offered which troubles me." In extreme vexation—at herself, at Clint, at Governor Dinwiddie, at the present set of circumstances—she felt tears well up in her eyes and a lump form in her throat. She wanted to tell him to go away and leave her alone, but her throat refused passage to the words.

Tenderly he turned her around, but this time he held her at arm's length, his eyes searching her face, demanding that she look at him. When a tear slipped from her eye and trickled down her cheek, he rubbed it away with his thumb.

"Samarra, look at me," he insisted, his voice evidencing his emotion. "We have so little time to discuss this, and there is so much I want to tell you. Please," he begged, "look at me."

She lifted her head then, blinking in an effort to focus through the dampness swimming across her vision.

"You know we have no choice in this matter. The

governor will see us married before we leave his house this night. Whether or not we can understand or agree with his reasoning is unimportant. What *is* important is that you know that, given time, I would have eventually proposed marriage to you myself. I have already reconciled myself to being married to a woman with a career. I would not ask you to abandon that which gives you so much pleasure. Please understand that I will allow you whatever time you need to reconcile yourself to this marriage. I must warn you, though, that I will press my suit in the interim, and I cannot promise you that my patience will not wear thin."

She sniffled, and he reached for a handkerchief, then realized he wore no waistcoat. He snatched a small embroidered scarf off a nearby table and held it to her nose.

Shaking her head with such force Clint feared she would dislodge the ropes of pearls entwined in her hair, she muttered, "No, Clint, I can't," meaning she could not agree to marriage. Not tonight.

"Of course you can," he assured her. "The scarf will wash clean, and you must compose yourself. In a moment the governor and his wife will accompany a minister to this room. Show them your spunk, Samarra, not your defeat."

She blew her nose on the scratchy fabric, then used her fingertips to press the tears from her eyes. And she wondered if she and Clint would forever misinterpret each other. She wondered if they would forever regret having attended a fancy-dress ball at the governor's palace as two lighthearted people just beginning to know each other, and having left it as husband and wife.

Chapter Fifteen

Unlike most young women, Samarra had not often indulged in wedding fantasies. When she had, she had imagined her father beside her, escorting her down the aisle of Bruton Parish Church. Not once in those sporadic flights of fancy had she envisioned her betrothed as anything more than a shadowy figure awaiting her at the altar. Never had she imagined herself dressed as she was now; never had she even remotely considered being married anywhere other than the church or without the support of her family standing nearby.

At the thought of her family, particularly of Georgiana, she gasped, raising her free hand quickly to cover her gaping mouth. The minister, a short, beady-eyed man replete with ceremonial robe and powdered periwig, paused briefly in his admonition of the virtues of marriage to bestow upon her a narrow look.

As though she had been stung, she dropped her hand, but her thoughts continued along the same self-incriminating path. Her ears pounded and her head ached with her folly. How had she allowed herself to become so entangled in her own problems that she would forget Georgiana? How was she going to explain this to her sister? More important, how was Georgiana going to receive this news? Samarra knew she wouldn't be able to hide either Clint or Georgiana from the other—not for long, anyway.

Plans raced through her head, and she tossed each one aside after the briefest consideration. The minister's voice droned on through the quiet of the study, but Samarra paid the words little heed until Clint nudged her and she realized the four other occupants of the room awaited her responses with bated breath.

For an instant she considered refusing to say "I do." After all, what could Dinwiddie do to her if she rebelled? Lock her in a dungeon? She didn't think so. She had committed no crime—was, in fact, a victim of circumstance. The fact offered her little security, however. Samarra had heard horror stories of innocent people who were locked away for life or even executed at the whim of a tyrant. Close down her business? Yes, he could do that; all business licenses were cleared through his office. Put her and Georgiana and Nanna and Ezekiel out on the street? Yes, he had the power to take her home away and confiscate her possessions.

How, then, would she care for a blind woman and two defenseless elderly people, all of whom depended upon her, in Randolph's absence, for shelter and sustenance?

Although she had no knowledge of any tyrannical acts perpetrated by the present royal governor of Virginia, she knew he had the authority to do all these things and more, and Clint had said they had no choice. That didn't make what they were doing settle any easier.

She heard the minister repeat the traditional question—and she heard herself respond unenthusiastically, "I do." In minutes it was over. Clint planted a chaste kiss upon her tight lips. Governor and Mrs.

Dinwiddie hugged her in turn, placing their warm cheeks against her cold one, the rustling of their heavy satin costumes reverberating weirdly in the dead silence.

Their hostess poured them all glasses of sherry, and toasts were offered all around while the minister sat at the governor's massive desk and wrote out the marriage documents. Samarra's hand quivered when the quill was passed to her and she frowned at the squiggly lines she had produced. Clint suffered from no such malady, and she watched in some fascination as his long, lean fingers confidently pushed the inked quill against the parchment.

And then she was whisked away out a rear entrance, through a pelting rain, down a brick walk, and into an alley, where the barouche Clint had hired stood waiting for them.

Her cape had protected her from the rain, but Clint was soaked to the skin, his wet shirt sticking to his chest, causing them both to recall another time when he had been caught in a rainstorm. In their haste to get out of the rain, they bustled into the warm, dark cavern of the coach and fell upon the leather seat. Almost immediately the driver slapped the reins, hieing to the horses to skedaddle. The sudden jolt threw Clint against Samarra, sandwiching her between him and a side wall.

Before he could extricate himself, she burst into tears.

With utmost tenderness, Clint pulled her into the comfort of his arms, his hands smoothing her hair while his voice soothed her spirit. "Everything's going to be all right, Samarra," he crooned. "You'll see. Please, don't cry."

He felt as though his own heart was breaking along with hers, and the acknowledgment shocked him. It was his first experience with compassion and empathy, perhaps the first absolutely selfless emotion he had ever felt. He swallowed with difficulty, his throat tightening as his lips brushed the shell of her ear and the fine strands of hair above it.

With a suddenness that shocked him, Samarra pushed against him and barked, "Let go of me, you big ox!"

Relieved that she had broken the tension but irritated at the manner in which she had chosen to do so, Clint attempted a laugh, but it came out a snort. "Oh, so now I'm an ox. I think I preferred being a stag."

"Oh, Clint!" she moaned, turning her head away from him to stare at the runnels of rain coursing down the window glass. "Please don't make light of something so serious. What are we going to do?"

"Do, my sweet? Live with it, I suppose. In time, perhaps, we'll be glad it happened."

"Not in time, Clint, *now*. What are we going to do now—tonight?"

"Go home and go to bed. We're both tired. After a good night's rest, you'll see things differently."

That was exactly what Samarra had feared he would say. Somehow she had to prevent their sleeping together, at least until she had time to talk to Georgiana, until she had time to reconcile herself to this marriage . . . until she heard the words she needed to hear, until she was convinced that something more than lust existed between them. Clint had promised her that time, and she used his words against him.

"Not tonight, Clint. We won't sleep together tonight. I—you promised me time to grow accustomed to the idea."

And that was exactly what Clint had expected her to say, and he had prepared his speech accordingly. "I know, Samarra, but I am under Dinwiddie's orders to

239

sleep in your house from now on. Perhaps I could sleep in a guest chamber for the time being."

"Yes." Samarra thought quickly. The one Beth and Edwin had used was fresh, and, more important, far enough removed from the wing housing her own and Georgiana's chambers to allow the twins this one night for a long, private conversation.

The remaining few minutes of their hurtling ride they spent sitting on opposite sides of the coach, each clutching the edge of the leather seat to prevent being pitched forward in the bouncing barouche, each clinging to silence, to his or her own private emotional battle. They both knew she was stalling—and that she wouldn't, couldn't hold out forever. The physical pull between them was too strong.

"Whew!"

Robert Dinwiddie breathed a sigh of relief as he collapsed into the wing chair Clint had recently vacated. "Pour me a short scotch, will you, sweetheart?"

"Are you sure, Robby?" The governor winced at the solicitous tone in his wife's voice. They seldom quarreled, but when they did, it was usually over his health. "The doctor says—"

"I don't care, Winkie." His use of this pet name generally won him obeisance from her. "You know I don't set much store by his directives—or his methods. I ought to outlaw the use of that grisly little box studded with razor blades. Damn, woman! You'd change your tune if he ever snapped those blades down on your arm or leg. Hurts aplenty, it does! Whatever happened to good old leeches?"

"Progress, Robby, progress. 'Bleeding is essential to the balancing of your humors, while whiskey upsets that balance,'" she quoted even as she uncapped a crystal decanter and splashed the requested liquor into a glass.

"Damn Dr. Hargrove, and damn your excellent memory! Give me that drink, Winkie. I deserve it."

She had, over the years, come to accept his occasional swearing, for her reproof had earned her nothing in that realm. Robert Dinwiddie was going to do what Robert Dinwiddie wanted to do. Fortunately, he was a man of honor. "Yes, dear, you deserve this one drink. I wasn't sure you could pull it off, but you did."

He smiled against the rim of the glass, looking rather pleased with himself. "Yes, I did, didn't I? I have you to thank, though, for suggesting the fancy-dress ball. Turned out to be an excellent cover-up." He took a sip of the scotch. "We make a matchless team."

His compliment conjured memories of other schemes the two had concocted and brought to successful fruition. She smiled broadly as she settled herself into the other wing chair. "We always have. I do hope those two are as happy in their marriage as we've been in ours."

"I thought the girl was going to give me a more difficult time of it than she did, but she fell right into our little trap."

"'Twas the lieutenant colonel I had pegged to be the difficult one."

"Oh, Clint's never given me any problems. He's always done the job, whatever it required."

"But you never asked him to marry anyone before."

"He never wanted to before. Truth is, I was beginning to think he never would. Clint's had some unhappy experiences with women, but Samarra Seldon is different, and he knows it. My concern now is that he'll get so caught up in marital bliss he'll decide to resign his commission."

241

Winkie's eyebrows shot upward and her mouth formed itself into a moue. "Do you really think so, Robby? However would you manage without him?"

"I'd manage. Holbrooke has trained MacKenzie Reed well."

Her frown disappeared and she patted his hand. "Then all is well. Finish your drink, dear. Our guests must wonder what happened to us, and we can't afford too many questions."

Behind his domino, Jarvis Whitfield's steel-gray eyes scanned the perimeter of the candlelit ballroom, searching for the governor or his wife. They had both disappeared, Dinwiddie before his missus, some time ago, as had Samarra Seldon and her escort, and Whitfield had the uncanny feeling something had gone awry, something that might adversely affect the successful culmination of his plans.

Although he had discreetly asked around, no one seemed to know the identity of Samarra Seldon's escort, but Whitfield strongly suspected him to be the military man Dinwiddie had unwittingly planted in the print shop. That one had not remained absent from the ballroom long—not long enough to accompany Miss Seldon home, nor did he seem the least bit dejected over her lingering absence. The man in the stag costume wended his way among the guests, in turn dancing with many of the women and joining various groups of men immersed in conversation.

Whitfield had thought his man, Guy Archer, had done him a service by merely wounding Holbrooke, but he had begun to wonder about the sagacity of this action. Granted, the deed had bought him valuable time, throwing the governor's investigation off course for a while, but Dinwiddie had surprised him by setting

242

another investigator to work on a different angle—an angle that would ultimately lead to him, Jarvis Whitfield. Dinwiddie's man had unraveled his way through the counterfeiting scheme almost to its source before Whitfield had realized what was going on.

Through the influence of one of his wealthy acquaintances, Whitfield had secured an invitation to this fancy-dress ball in the hopes of unraveling some information of his own. He had come alone, oiling his way among the throng of guests, eavesdropping on a number of exclusively male conversations, but he had garnered no new facts pertaining to his own private scheme. The talk centered around the trouble with the French and the imminent threat of war. Those few who might possibly be aware that a counterfeiting scheme was afloat in colonial Virginia found the topic of war more interesting, Whitfield supposed. The waste of the evening rankled, but not quite so strongly as Whitfield's resentment that his own machinations were receiving so little attention.

His inability to find a suitable replacement for Guy Archer rankled as well. Whitfield winced inwardly at the thought of Archer's cowardice and bumbling inefficiency. He had, in his own intimidating way, promised the scoundrel instant death should Archer double-cross him, and Whitfield always made good his promises—almost always, anyway. The fulfillment of this particular promise shouldn't prove too difficult. Whitfield smiled as he considered the absurdity of Archer's thinking he could hide himself for very long. The man should have selected a less obvious alias than Samuel Holbrooke, should have taken more care in covering his tracks.

Jarvis Whitfield was a master of duplicity and chicanery. The British had thought they had him a year ago, but, like the snake he was, he had struck when they'd least expected it and then slithered away. During the entire ocean voyage from Yorktown to England, Whitfield had sat shackled in the stinking hold of the merchant vessel hired to transport him, planning both his escape and his revenge.

He had learned enough about the colonial economy during his stint in Virginia to know that an influx of counterfeit currency would strike a hard blow. Already Parliament had taken steps to keep the colonial notes from becoming worthless by prohibiting four of the colonies from printing any more paper money. Whitfield intended to add Virginia—which, for the most part, was financially stable—to their ranks. He was inordinately proud of this scheme, which could, if it were successful, cripple the colony. Always before, Whitfield's master plan had been fragmented, a collated effort of taking down individuals one at a time, but that method required an inordinate amount of patience and planning. This way, he could impoverish an entire population in one fell swoop. It mattered little to him that the vast majority of that population had done him no injustice, either imagined or otherwise.

At long last, the Dinwiddies returned to the ballroom and began to mingle with their guests again. Whitfield watched and waited until only a few guests remained before he left himself, without ever discovering what had happened to Samarra Seldon that evening. Had he learned that she and Holbrooke had exchanged marriage vows in Dinwiddie's study, he would have altered his plans dramatically.

The harsh, untenable truth of the matter was that in a few days, everyone would know that Samarra Seldon had this night become Mrs. Clinton Holbrooke.

*　　*　　*

Georgiana accepted the news better than Samarra had thought she would. In point of fact, she seemed immensely relieved at having a man added to the household. She had not wanted to trouble Samarra by telling her how she had lain awake at night, shivering in her bed, feeling more vulnerable than her blindness had ever made her feel. Neither had she told her twin how often she imagined she smelled the pungency of the pipe tobacco which had clung to their intruder. Nor did she apprise Samarra of those things now.

Instead, she hugged Samarra tightly and asked shyly, "Do you love this man, Sam?"

Samarra had wanted to gloss over the unexpected event of her marriage, to shine and polish it for her sister until it glowed with the romantic brilliance a wedding deserved. But she could not do that. She had glossed over too many things already, had purposely withheld information from her sister that she had thought might upset her, and in so doing had reinforced Georgiana's reclusive behavior, had contributed significantly to her failure to grow and blossom into social and psychological maturity. There would be no more mincing of words between them.

Besides, Samarra would not be able to prevent Georgiana from meeting Clint and spending time in his company. She would not be able to hide the present instability of their relationship. Better to lay it all out up front than to resort to explanations that didn't ring true later.

"Yes, George, I think I do. The problem is, I'm not at all sure that he loves me."

"How could anyone not love you, Sam? You're so strong and independent and sure of yourself."

Samarra laughed hollowly. "Oh, George! How little you know of men. Most men find those qualities in women quite intimidating. I've tried, George, but I won't ever be sweet and unselfish and gentle, as you are."

"I expect that if Mr. Holbrooke had wanted to marry someone sweet and unselfish and gentle, he would have."

"And I expect that had he been given the choice, that is exactly what he would have done."

Georgiana deftly changed the subject. "When do I get to meet him, Sam?" she asked with much enthusiasm. When Samarra didn't answer immediately, George gushed, "Just think! I have a brother now. Tell me what he's like. Tell me everything about him so that when I meet him at breakfast I'll be able to carry on some sort of intelligent conversation with him."

Samarra was caught off-guard. She had not planned for Georgiana to meet Clint for another day or two, but she realized now that such a separation would be impossible to maintain. Like it or not, before the sun rose this day she would have to prepare Clint to meet Georgiana.

She put it off as long as she could, answering her sister's questions with what little knowledge she possessed of her new husband, and then puttering around in her room, telling herself she was allowing Clint to rest as long as possible, stalling the inevitable until her nerves were stretched to the limit. Finally, as the first pink rays of daylight sifted through her sheer white curtains, she tightened the sash of her robe, extinguished her candle, and made her way down the long, dark hall of the wing and into the center structure of the house to Clint's door.

Even there she hesitated, Georgiana's words returning to haunt her: "You're so strong . . . so sure of yourself." Samarra didn't feel strong, didn't feel so

246

sure of herself now. Was her strength no more than a facade, something she habitually put on each day as a defense mechanism, the same way she put on her chemise and stockings—not because she necessarily wanted to wear them, but because it was expected of her?

But there was no time to debate the issue, no time for acute introspection. Time had become her enemy.

Samarra reached deep into her gut, then, found her strength and drew it upward until it surged through her being, and she knew without a doubt that George's estimation of her character was correct. She knocked lightly on the panel, heard a grumble from within, and pushed the door slightly ajar.

Pale pink shards of early morning light softly illuminated his chamber, their gossamer fibers falling upon the rumpled bedding. The light allowed her to watch his frown transform itself into a devilish grin as his sleep-laden eyes pinned hers, drew her into the room.

"Come in, come in, my sweet wife," he crooned. "What a surprise this is—a most welcome one, I should add. I had not thought your reservation would dissipate so quickly, but you have restored my faith in my own physical attributes."

Samarra forced a sweetness into her voice she didn't feel, subduing the edge of her tension but not eliminating it altogether. "The power you wield in that realm, Milord Stag, is indisputable, as is the stubborn streak which runs through my being. My reservation has not cracked, despite your sexual prowess. 'Tis another matter entirely which brings me here at this early hour."

The door clicked softly behind her and Clint watched, mesmerized, as the silky, ivory-colored fabric of her robe molded itself to her lush curves as she crossed the room and moved a chair closer to his bedside. The bashful light grew bolder, playing upon the golden strands of her hair, which fell in glorious splendor to her hips, and upon her creamy complexion, bathing her in a pale raspberry tint. Just looking at her stirred a deep, abiding passion within his belly; knowing that she was now his wife and he her husband only served to quicken him more. Clint stifled a groan, smothering it in the action of sitting up in bed.

"When did it stop raining?" he asked, thus admitting that he had slept through the night.

Samarra mentally chastised herself for both her envy and her resentment of that fact—envy because she was seriously beginning to feel the effects of her self-enforced sleeplessness; resentment because some strange, new emotion budding within her had wanted to believe that Clint would lie awake longing for her to join him. Obviously, that had not been the case. At least his question had given her another moment to pull herself together, and for that she was grateful.

"About an hour ago, I suppose."

"You've been up all night?"

She nodded, dropped her gaze to her lap for a moment, then took a deep breath and forced herself to look at Clint. Looking at him, at his bare chest with its whorls of russet hair, made this more difficult than she had imagined it would be. Her eyes locked on the hard brown nib of his left breast peeking out at her just above the folded edge of the blanket, and she felt her face color a darker pink.

Clint watched her close her eyes and shake her head as though to erase the vision. He knew he had a similar effect on her as she on him. Why then, damn it, didn't she just give in, just crawl into bed with him and be done with it? She had come to him, not he to her, and he was not about to apologize for the state in which she

248

had found him.

When she opened her eyes, she carefully placed her gaze upon his face. "I—this isn't going to be easy for me, Clint, so please bear with me." Samarra cleared her throat and started again. "I haven't been completely honest with you, and there's something I must tell you, explain to you now, before it's too late."

Clint's heart wrenched. Was it possible, then, that both he and Dinwiddie had been wrong? That Samarra was, indeed, the counterfeiter? If that were true, what was he going to do about it, now that he was her husband? Clint had come to feel a loyalty to Samarra that was almost as strong—nay, he admitted, stronger—than the loyalty he felt to England. Whatever this matter was, he would hear her out impartially, and he would stand by her now, be her helpmeet, as he'd vowed just hours earlier. He moved his arm from his side, reaching out to her, covering her folded hands in her lap with his hand.

She gathered strength from his comforting gesture. "Clint, I have a sister. A twin sister . . ."

This revelation opened up whole new avenues of conjecture, but before he could comment, she rushed on.

". . . who is blind."

Of course! He felt like a dolt. How could he have forgotten the blind woman in the chamber adjoining Samarra's, when just last evening he had reported her existence to Robert Dinwiddie? He laid the blame on the fact that he had not been fully awake, that the very essence of Samarra sent his thoughts and emotions spinning off into a veritable whirlwind of irrationality. His reaction, however, came off looking to Samarra like one of complete surprise, which she was expecting, and not one of total relief, which she very well might have questioned.

"Her name is Georgiana, and she lives here, in this house. And, Clint, she works for me."

The last comment honestly surprised him. "She works for you? Doing what?"

"Georgiana is a master engraver."

"How?" His voice carried his skepticism.

"Just wait until you get to know her, and you won't have to ask. George is amazing."

"But why didn't I know before now? I realize this is a big house, but does she never venture outside? And why did you wait so long to tell me?"

"When it comes to doing things, creating things with her hands, Georgiana's spirit knows no bounds. But something happened when she started to go blind that wounded her deeply and made her afraid of people. She has become a recluse of sorts. I didn't tell you about her before because, well, because I got in the habit of not discussing her with anyone outside the family."

"I still don't understand, Sam, as close as we've become, why you didn't tell me."

"Because, well, because I am as guilty as she is of hiding from the world. I've worked so hard, Clint, at building my business, at proving to a largely masculine clientele that I can ply my trade as well as any man, maybe better than most. It hasn't been easy. I was afraid that if my customers knew most of my engravings were created by a blind person—a blind *woman*—no one would do business with me anymore. Georgiana needs the work, not from a financial standpoint, but because she derives so very much pleasure from it. I can't stand the thought of taking that pleasure from her—or of her believing she was the cause for the demise of my business."

"But that still doesn't explain why you didn't tell *me*," Clint argued. "My book does not require engravings, and, I think, I became more than just a customer to you a long time ago."

Samarra sighed. "This is all so very complicated. Remember when I told you a few minutes ago that there was an incident that had wounded her deeply?"

Clint nodded.

"First, let me explain that she was born sighted. When we were in our early teens, not long after we moved to Williamsburg, Georgiana fell prey to a disease called white eye, which almost always leads to complete blindness. Each case is different. Sometimes it happens almost overnight; sometimes it takes years. In Georgiana's case, blindness set in gradually. Toward the end, two years or so after the onset of the disease, a do-gooder from the Ladies' Aid Society, a Mrs. Robinson, I believe her name was, came to visit one afternoon on the pretext of offering her sympathy."

Samarra paused, her eyes misting as she recalled the details of Mrs. Robinson's visit. She swallowed convulsively, cleared her throat, and continued. "Anyway, this Mrs. Robinson planted her wide hips upon the most delicate chair in the salon and offered no apology when one of the leg braces popped under her weight. She curled her thin lips into a semblance of a smile and bestowed upon Georgiana a look which clearly bespoke her revulsion. I'll never forget her spiteful words, which were directed at my father but clearly heard by us all, including Georgiana. 'How can you stomach the sight of those white-glazed, staring eyes?' she choked out, holding a gloved hand to her throat. 'Why, if she were mine, I would have to send her away.'"

"Oh, my God!" Clint groaned. "No wonder your sister hides herself in this house. What did your father say to the witch?"

"We all three sat dumbly, in shock. Nanna was the one who reacted." A tiny hint of a smile touched Samarra's lips then as the memory flooded in. "She had been in the process of serving tea and promptly dropped the laden tray into Mrs. Robinson's lap."

Clint howled. "She didn't!"

"Yes, she did. Then she had the gall to stand back and grin about it."

"What did the witch do?"

"At first, she just looked at her lap and gasped. The tea had splashed upward, onto her protruding stomach and sagging bosom. Then she abruptly stood up, spilling the tray and its contents upon the Oriental carpet and wiping her gloved hands over her torso. And then, she turned on Nanna. 'You—you insolent woman!' she railed. 'You did this on purpose. I came here with the best of intentions and you dared to treat me so meanly! Everyone in the Society will hear of this. *Everyone!*'"

"I hope she left then."

"She did . . . in quite a huff. But she left behind the stench of her kind, and none of us, least of all Georgiana, has ever forgotten it. We've all made sure nothing like that ever happened again."

Clint's voice was softly accusing. "And did you honestly think I was one of her kind?"

"No, not really . . . as I explained, protecting Georgiana became habitual."

"How did you manage to hide her for the week Beth and Edwin were here?"

"I didn't. I wrote them a long letter about Georgiana, and they didn't disappoint me."

Clint's hand squeezed hers. "I won't either, Samarra. Is there anything else you need to tell me?"

Although it was an open-ended question, Samarra assumed he meant about Georgiana. "Yes. Don't ever

252

mention her blindness. Don't offer to help her with anything, no matter how badly you want to sometimes—except with tending a fire. We won't let her do that. She's been coping for years, Clint, she can cope now. Talk to her. Listen to her. But, please, Clint, try to ignore her handicap."

"I will, Samarra. Have you told her about us?"

"Yes."

"And what did she say?"

"That she's happy for me. That she wants me to be happy."

"And are you, Samarra?"

"I—I don't know, Clint." Her voice broke. "This—this was so—so sudden." She wrenched her hands from his and used them to cover her eyes.

Clint leaned forward, ignoring the blanket when it fell to his waist, and grasped her upper arms in a gentle but firm grip. "Come here, Samarra," he murmured. "We've spent most of our time together with you sitting in a chair while I lay in the bed. And that, my dear, is about to change."

When he pulled her onto his lap and moved his hands to rub her back, she uttered no protest. His heart ached with hers as she sobbed softly against the hard wall of his chest. And when her own arms snaked around his bare rib cage and she clasped her hands behind his back, he pulled her closer against him, his hands and voice soothing, tenderly soothing away her pain.

Chapter Sixteen

It was not his sexual prowess which cracked her reserve, but rather the tender persuasion of his hands upon her back and his lips murmuring soothing platitudes against her ear.

Samarra felt herself melting against him, into him. Suddenly, she felt very tired—and realized in that moment that a great deal of her fatigue came from bearing a burden too heavy for her narrow shoulders. She was tired of dealing daily with life's trivial problems which collectively had added their ounces to the weight until it set like a yoke upon her.

She was tired, too, of opposing the way her heart would go, if she would but allow it.

For a long time he just held her—and she him, drawing from his strength. For a long time, she heard his whispered words without listening to them, until, finally, the combination of soft touch and soft voice calmed her overwrought nerves. The platitudes became promises and began to penetrate her consciousness.

"I'm here, Samarra . . . now that I've found you, the object of my heart's quest, I'm not going anywhere . . . today and tomorrow and a thousand tomorrows from now, I'll still be here . . . let me help

254

you . . . let me be here for you . . . open the door of your heart, Samarra . . . let me in . . . let me love you."

Clint was as surpised to hear himself say those words as Samarra was. Commitment was no stranger to either of them, but neither had ever committed to romantic love before. Clint had come close once, years before, with Judith, had actually given her his heart without ever uttering the words, and she'd betrayed him. She had proved to him that she was no different than his self-centered mother, who had never been able either to show or tell her only child that she loved him.

He had told himself over and over that he had put his emotional disillusionments behind him, that he didn't need a woman for anything other than an occasional toss. But since he had met Samarra, he had begun to realize that he never truly had forgotten Judith or forgiven his mother, that his heart had never even begun to heal until Samarra had come into his life, that he would never be truly whole without this wonderful woman he held in his arms. The reality, the stark, bare truth of this acknowledgment hit him hard, physically jolting him.

Samarra felt him jerk against her and was momentarily frightened by Clint's reaction to his promises, frightened that they held no substance. But when he clutched her tighter, when a sound very close to a whimper bubbled against her throat, her fear took flight. In its stead, her mothering instincts took over, and she found herself comforting Clint in much the same way he'd comforted her. Never had she imagined that Clint might be vulnerable, that he could ever need her in any way other than in the physical sense. Never had she imagined that romantic love encompassed so many varied emotions, emotions which were bombarding her heart, demanding entrance.

A line from the marriage ceremony echoed through

255

her soul: "And the two shall become one." She had never understood what those six simple words meant until now. Becoming one with Clint entailed far more than giving him her body and taking his in return. Becoming one meant that their souls melded, that every thought and word and deed sprang from their mutual love and consideration for each other. Becoming one meant that for the rest of their lives they had each other to lean on.

And she understood, too, what becoming one didn't mean. It didn't mean that she had to sacrifice her identity, to give up her independence, as she'd thought it would. There would be no loss, only gain. If she had learned anything about Clint, it was that he was not a tyrant.

She didn't fool herself by thinking their lives would always run smoothly. Adjustment would take time and effort from both of them. The proverbial bed of roses was full of thorns. But thorns never seriously wounded; their pricks hurt, but they didn't leave permanent scars.

"Yes, Clint," she breathed against his bowed head. "I think you've always had my heart; now I give you the rest of me as well."

His open palms moved tentatively upon her back again, stroking, caressing, eliciting shivers of bittersweet ecstasy from her. "Oh, Samarra," he breathed.

The full realization of what she had just said struck her full force. The path her thoughts took had veered away from the physical aspect of love, but Clint had again misinterpreted her intent, assuming she offered the gift of her body along with that of her heart and soul.

His questing lips soon quelled her trepidation. Their soft firmness moved upon the slender column of her throat, hovering near the base of her ear before fluttering along her jawline and then upward, bypassing her mouth to rain their tender ministrations upon her closed eyelids and smooth forehead. She felt her body go lax, felt her mouth drop open and her head fall back, felt a warm glow ignite somewhere in the very depths of her soul and spread slowly outward until it had encompassed her entire being.

Although a chill pervaded the room, its icy fingers touched neither occupant. Clint's fevered lips seared a fiery trail upon her face; his hands forged a heated path upon her torso, burning through the thin fabric of her robe. Samarra's body answered with its own self-consuming flame, writhing and twisting in a primitive ceremonial dance as old as the dawn of time.

Just when Samarra thought she could stand the heat no longer, Clint's lips found hers. Their mouths came together in mutual need, in mutual longing, in mutual love. The press of Clint's lips was hard at first, his mouth slanting across hers, almost punishing her in his dire urgency for fulfillment. But gradually his lips softened, shaping themselves to her own, plucking and teasing until she moaned in exquisite agony.

Clint responded in kind, his own moan deep and guttural against her mouth, paradoxically eliciting goosebumps upon her fevered flesh. His tongue traced the outline of her lips, and when it sought entrance to the warm cavern of her mouth, she gladly granted it, her lips parting, her teeth shivering as his tongue graced them before delving deeper. For a moment, she basked in the sensation of the roughness of his tongue upon her smooth gums before her tongue offered itself as partner to this dance.

A part of her felt his frenzied fingers plying the knot of the sash at her waistline, felt it slip open, felt his callused palms smooth the fabric from her shoulders, down the sleeves of her nightgown, and over her wrists and hands. Those same frenzied fingers worked loose the tiny buttons marching down the front of her gown, the placket ending in the valley between her aching breasts. Each touch of a fingertip slipping through the placket singed like a firebrand upon her taut flesh. All the while, his mouth worked its wonder upon hers.

When at last the front of her gown lay open, she waited for his hands to slip inside, for his palms to cup her breasts and the pads of his thumbs to tease her nipples as they had the evening before in the darkness of the alcove. Instead, as the beckoning light of early morn washed through the long windows, Clint tore his mouth from hers and leaned back. His passion-darkened eyes scalded a path from her own heavy-lidded orbs downward, pausing momentarily to rest upon her slightly swollen parted lips before continuing their blazing path ever downward, finally fixing themselves upon the last tiny button at the base of the placket. His left hand moved upward, his fingers closing over the placket and gently pulling the fabric aside, just as he had done with her costume in the alcove, until the globular perfection and its dark pink bud were fully exposed to his appreciative view.

Clint had managed to accomplish this feat without his fingers ever touching her skin. He released the placket, held stationary now by the soft mound of her breast, and for a long time did nothing more than stare at its firm roundness, at its rosy areole and its darker pink, quickly hardening crest. The slackness of his jaw and the hooded canopy of his eyelids bespoke his appreciation far more than mere words ever could.

Slowly, inexorably, his head lowered to her chest, but in the same vein of unhurried tenderness, nothing touched her but his breath, his ragged, heated breath. Samarra found herself disbelieving the wealth of sensation his eyes and his breath were causing, found herself wondering how much harder her heart could pound, how much faster her blood could pulse through her arteries, how much more of this studied assault on her senses she could stand before she verbally begged for fulfillment.

Already her body begged. Clint had to see it, had to feel it, had to know that she yearned to surrender wholly, completely to him.

He did feel her response, felt his own urgent need to hurry, but his heart ruled his body this time, and his heart compelled him to cool his ardor, to extend this first time until Samarra had reached a pinnacle of need she had never imagined possible.

His hands, resting lightly upon her shoulders, pushed her back, gently back, upon the counterpane. The movement was so slow that she felt each one of her vertebrae independently touch the nubby, hand-loomed spread until finally her head lay close to the footboard and the wide expanse of the green velvet tester loomed over her head. Her left leg hung over the side of the mattress, her knee cupping its edge, while her right leg stretched itself out upon the soft, feather-filled tick.

Her exposed breast continued to throb, continued to beg for the certain surcease his mouth would bring, but Clint ignored it, his hands gliding from her shoulders downward along her arms and her rib cage, along the sides of her thighs and calves until they reached her feet. He removed first one satin slipper and then the other, tossing them upon the Oriental carpet beside the bed. She heard them fall with soft thuds, knew with a certainty born of her passion that their removal marked the point of no return. She was helpless to stop him—and she relished that feeling of helplessness, welcomed the physical dependency that filled her being.

His hands grasped her right foot, kneading and

massaging it, then releasing it to allow his forefinger to etch a course from her heel to the space between her big toe and the one beside it. The pad of his finger rested there for a short time, then resumed its course by outlining her big toe and then trailing down the edge of her foot to the inside of her arch, where it drew incessant circles around and around until Samarra thought she would surely scream from the delicate pain he caused. And when his tongue replaced his finger, she did cry out, not loud enough to be heard past the closed door, but the appeal of her wail resounded in her ears.

"Sh-h-h, my lovely," Clint whispered against the tender skin of her high arch. "Enjoy it, languish in it, let me love you as I've wanted to love you for a long time."

"You haven't known me for a long time, Clint," she argued softly, her voice fraught with her anguish.

"I've known you forever, Samarra. I just recently found you," he countered.

"Yes," she breathed. "I think I've always known you, too. In the very depths of my heart and soul, I've always known you."

His tongue followed the path his forefinger had traced, resting in the hollow beside her big toe for a moment before taking that selfsame toe in his mouth and suckling it. Never had Samarra given much consideration to those parts of her body which contributed to her arousal, much less had she considered her feet and toes among those parts, but Clint's mouth had easily convinced her of their sensitivity. Desire rushed upward through her calf and knee and thigh, and through her lower abdomen to settle as a throbbing, pulsing pain that manifested itself in a warm dampness between her legs.

His hands pushed the tail of her nightgown upward, letting it glide across her tingling calves and knees and thighs but stopping just short of her buttocks. In reaction, she raised her hips off the bed and sighed when he cupped her bare buttocks with his palms. His head inched under the hem of her nightgown then, his beard-roughened chin raking her taut stomach before the very tip of his tongue found her navel and plunged in and out of it, in and out, in and out, until Samarra thought she could stand no more.

Her hips matched the rhythm his tongue had created, her back arching to meet its plunging, then relaxing with its withdrawals.

Clint's hands moved again, pushing the soft fabric of the nightgown upward, over her hips, over her ribs, over her breasts, leaving it rolled and bunched beneath her armpits. When Samarra raised her shoulders off the bed to allow the gown's total removal, Clint whispered, "No . . . not yet."

His mouth and tongue and hands caressed her torso, setting her skin on fire, but still he avoided touching her breasts. At last, his tongue moved around their perimeters, first one and then the other, and just when she thought he would take one of the hardened peaks between his lips, his tongue moved again . . . back down the valley between her breasts, across her waistline, across her right hipbone, and down to the hollow where her thigh joined her hip.

Her groan at his continued delay tactics won her nothing, nor did her husky plea, "Clint, enough is enough." No longer able to constrain herself, Samarra took his head between her palms and tugged gently, pulling him upward and setting his mouth upon a pulsating breast. He rewarded her efforts by sucking it gently, then taking the throbbing nipple between his teeth and biting it lightly. His tongue trailed across to the opposite peak and resumed its ministrations there, but when he would have raised his head, she held it firmly to her breast for a while longer.

261

Clint had arched his body over hers, not allowing any part of him other than his hands or his face to touch her, but now his torso slowly lowered to meet hers and she felt the warm, hard evidence of his full arousal graze the tender skin of her inner thighs. Of its own volition, her body jerked in retaliation.

"Oh, God, Samarra," he groaned then, arching his back, lifting his face ceilingward, and squeezing his eyes tightly closed. "I don't want to hurt you."

How could anything which had brought her so much physical pleasure culminate in pain? she wondered, her confusion written in the liquid depths of her topaz eyes. Her open hand reached upward and placed itself upon his cheek, softly commanding his attention. "Talk to me, Clint," she whispered. "Tell me why this will hurt."

His head dropped then, and his eyes opened to reveal his own pain, his own vulnerability, but his elbows remained locked, his palms supporting the weight of his torso. For a long moment, his dark green gaze searched her face as though memorizing every minute detail. Then his lips slowly lowered to hers, touching her briefly before he lay fully upon her, his mouth close to her ear. "Only the first time, my love, and then only for a moment. I promise."

He raised himself up slightly and moved against her, reinaugurating the rhythm he had orchestrated upon her navel even as his hands pulled her nightgown higher until he had slithered it over her head. Samarra raised her arms to accommodate his efforts, but when the thin fabric of her gown had cleared her hands and the realization of her absolute nakedness dawned upon her, she turned her head aside in acute embarrassment.

"Samarra, look at me," he softly commanded.

She shook her head in negation, closing her eyes against the threat of tears gathering there. She felt his

262

work-roughened palm slide up her cheek, felt his long, lean fingers embed themselves in her hair, felt the butterfly softness of his lips graze the corner of her exposed eye.

"Samarra, look at me." His voice was even lower, but more compelling in its intensity, and this time she obeyed him. "You have no reason to be shy, my love. Your body is luscious and beautiful." His roving hand sought to prove his words as its callused roughness touched her throat, her arm, her side, her breast.

That part of her which acknowledged her total lack of expertise in the art of loving—and Clint's obviously wide realm of experience in that field—wondered how many other women's bodies he had similarly appreciated. It was that which made her timid and shy, which made her feel inadequate. Clint sensed the source of her sudden and uncharacteristic bashfulness and sought to allay her doubts.

"This is new to me, too, my love."

Her head twisted around then and her eyes opened wide at his admission, and she tried to read the sincerity of it in his smoldering eyes. "How so?" she asked in some wonder.

"Because I've never made love before."

When she continued to regard him with a combination of amazement and disbelief, he explained, "Oh, I've taken a number of women to my bed—and had an equal number take me to theirs, most of whom were paid well to do so. But that's not making love."

"And you want to make love to me?"

"No. I want to make love *with* you."

He kissed her then, tenderly at first, his mouth taking succor from hers even as it gave her succor, even as it assured her that this time for him was different. Gradually his kiss became more heated, more passionate, and she answered the demands of his lips and his tongue with equal fervor. His fingertips combed her body, eliciting tiny shivers of delight from her. When that selfsame hand came to rest upon the downy mound of her womanhood, when a finger trailed down to touch her where no one else ever had before, her body jerked in a spasm of heightened desire such as Samarra had never dreamed possible.

His hands slipped beneath her buttocks, gently lifted them upward and slid her nightgown beneath them before lowering her to the bed again. For the briefest of moments, Samarra wondered why he had done that, but she quickly forgot everything, completely lost her reason when she felt Clint's hand caress her intimately again. Her eyes closed of their own accord and a soft moan escaped her parted lips—and then she felt the soft-hard tip of his manhood touch her where his hand had just been, felt a slight penetration, and she arched against him.

"Slow, Samarra," he cautioned. "Take it slow and easy, sweetheart. This is going to hurt a bit."

But she felt no pain, only intense pleasure as he moved shallowly in and out. Her hands clutched his shoulder blades; her nails dug into his back; her legs spread themselves wide, opening to him, inviting him in. She accepted his kiss, marveled in the multitude of sensations he was causing . . . then gasped into his open mouth when the searing, blinding pain he had promised shot through her. A warm tear trickled out of one eye and puddled in the shell of her ear.

Mercifully, the pain was short-lived. Clint moved slowly, his thrusts penetrating deeper and deeper, drawing out the pain, replacing it with wondrous rapture. Her own movements encouraged him, and she matched his rhythm, her legs entwining around his. She clutched him tighter. His tongue duplicated the movements of his lower body, and she relished its soft roughness against her own. She felt her mind and heart and body meld, felt herself pulled into a reeling vortex that tugged at her, drowning her inhibitions.

Deeper and deeper into the unrelenting vortex she fell until every tiny bit of her seemed joined to this man . . . until finally the vortex had pulled her to its innermost depths and spasm upon spasm of pleasure overtook her.

"Oh, Samarra, I love you," Clint gasped hoarsely a hairsbreadth before he shuddered against her and she felt his seed, warm and vibrant, propel itself into her. Until that instant, she had not considered the possible outcome of this act of love. But the thought of having Clint's child warmed her, delighted her, thrilled and fulfilled her very being as nothing else ever had before.

"And I love you," she averred.

Clint's arms surrounded her. He pulled them together over onto their sides without dislodging himself from her. For a long time his hands caressed her back while his lips kissed her closed eyelids, the tip of her nose, the crest of her cheek.

"Was that as wonderful for you as it was for me?" he asked at long last.

"I don't know," she teased. "It was pretty wonderful for me, but then I have no other experience with which to compare it."

"I'll give you comparisons. As many as you can handle."

"Is that a threat or a promise?"

"A promise, my love. For now. For always."

"For now?" Samarra moved against him, regaled in the tremor that racked his frame, in the power she wielded over him. "You'll provide me with another comparison now?"

His lips quirked upward and tiny gold flecks sparkled in his hazel eyes. "Are you sure, Samarra?"

"Yes, Clint, I'm sure. I've never been quite so sure of anything before. But first, there's something I want to do, something I've wanted to do since the first day we met."

Her sudden and unexpected seriousness took Clint by surprise, but when she laid her finger in the cleft of his chin, his grin widened. "That's it?"

She nodded.

"Why did it take you so long?"

"I don't know. Maybe because it seemed such an intimate gesture to me."

"You know what they say about such malformations of the chin?"

"No. Tell me."

"'A dimple in the chin means a devil within.'"

Her eyes opened wide. "And is it true?"

"What do you think?"

"I think that whoever they are, they don't know everything." She laughed softly, then replaced her finger with her tongue, flickering it in and out of the cleft even as she rocked against him again. "Milord Stag has need of a shave."

"Later," he moaned. "Later."

The sun had reached its zenith before Samarra and Clint emerged from his room, she to collect suitable attire from her chamber, he to collect water for their bath.

Miraculously, no one had disturbed their loveplay, which had been interspersed with catnaps. Finally, their energies temporarily spent and their stomachs grumbling, the two had reluctantly agreed to postpone further affirmations of their love until their basic needs had been fulfilled.

Samarra was certain that Nanna sat at the kitchen

table pulling at her chin, wondering how long the marathon would last. Georgiana had surely informed the servant of Samarra's marriage to Clint. This certainty allayed any worry on Sam's part that Nanna would become concerned about her disappearance from her own bedchamber. If her musings were accurate, Nanna would be sitting there waiting when Clint crossed the kitchen to gain access to the back door and thus the well. Samarra retraced her steps to Clint's bedchamber, whistling in glee as she considered how the two would react to each other under the present circumstances.

When she bounced into Clint's room with her garments casually tossed over one arm, her whistle froze on her lips. Nanna sat staunchly straight in the chair Sam had placed by the bed, her arms crossed beneath her bosom, her brow narrowed in accusation, Samarra's bloodstained nightgown upon her lap.

"It's not what you th—" Samarra began.

"I know what it is," Nanna interrupted. "Georgiana told me. What I want t' know is why."

"Because, well, because we honestly didn't have a choice, but, Nanna, I don't mind. And I don't think Clint does either."

"That does na answer my question, Miss Sam, and ye know it. I've been thinking ye and Mr. Holbrooke were right for each other almost ivver since that first day he came t' yere shop. I've been thinking ye would nivver see it for yereself, and for that, I am most grateful. If any woman ivver needed a mon, ye did."

Samarra raised her raw-honey-colored eyebrows at that declaration, but before she had opportunity to question it, Nanna resumed her speech.

"What I do na understand, what I want ye t' explain t' me is why ye had t' do it sae sudden-like, why ye could na have waited till yere papa came home, why ye could

267

na have been married in the church with yere family there, like ye should've done, why ye say ye had nae choice." She plucked at the nightgown in her lap. "This proves ye was a virgin till this morn, so do na try t' tell me ye are with babe. I want ye t' tell me why, and I want ye t' tell me now. I've been like a mother t' ye these many years. I have a right t' know."

Nanna had risen from the chair on the second "why," and her voice had risen with each subsequent "why" which had followed. She bore down upon Samarra with the vengeance of a wounded grizzly.

"I'm sorry, Nanna, truly I am," Samarra began a bit timorously. "I never meant for you to be hurt, and I think Papa will understand."

"Right now, *I* want t' understand."

Neither of them had heard Clint enter the room. "Let me tell her, Samarra," he said quietly as he set a large, brass hipbath in a corner. "Why don't we all go down to the kitchen and discuss this over lunch? I, for one, am famished."

Chapter Seventeen

Anticipating a long, tiring evening of dancing accompanied by little sleep, Samarra had planned to close the print shop on Friday, the day following the fancy-dress ball. And never did she open to customers over the weekend, although she oftentimes worked at her press with Tom on Saturdays. Thus, she had previously allowed herself a three-day holiday—almost, she thought, as though she'd known she would need it.

Clint had managed to pacify Nanna. Samarra considered herself blessed to have him take this task in hand. There appeared no way around informing the grizzled servant that some danger existed, but in deference to her health, Clint had told her only about the intruder in his apartment, concluding with the same theory he'd used with Samarra.

"I can na imagine what that old mon could possibly have owned that anyone would want t' steal," she had argued, not blinded by love, and therefore not as easily convinced as Samarra had been.

"Where did he keep his money?" Clint had asked her.

"In a strongbox upstairs, but Mr. Randolph put that in the bank for Miss Sam and Miss George when Jacob died."

"Maybe someone thinks it's still in the attic rooms," Samarra, eager to defend her husband's theory, observed.

Nanna had shrugged, but her voice still carried her skepticism. "Maybe. And maybe not. What I want t' know is why anyone would wait seven years t' try t' steal it. Do na take me wrong, Mr. Holbrooke . . . I like ye just fine. But ye tell me why someone threw a knife at ye when nothing like that ivver happened before. And now ye expect me t' believe that ye were na the object of that same mon's vengeance when yere bed was slashed. Ye best protect Miss Sam, if ye know what's good for ye. I will na have her com t' nae harm, nor will her father. Ye do na want t' answer t' Randolph Seldon."

Clint had assured Nanna that she had nothing to worry about, but she had stomped out of the room grumbling, nevertheless. And she had maintained an obvious aloofness around them ever since. Clint and Samarra just smiled secretly to themselves, for they were too happy to allow one old woman's cynicism to spoil their elation.

During those three days of bliss, Clint and Georgiana had become acquainted. Despite Clint's promise to treat Georgiana as a whole person, Samarra could not help being relieved when he had neither reacted negatively to George's blindness nor attempted to assist her twin. The two took an immediate liking to each other. When they were together, Georgiana visibly relaxed more than she had since the night of the intruder; she seemed to be, again, at ease with herself and her dark world. Yet on occasion Samarra noticed her sister withdraw into her shell. At those times she would become inattentive, a look of pensiveness washing over her features. Sporadic moodiness was not unusual for Georgiana, however, and Samarra gave it little thought.

Sunday night, when Sam and Clint were preparing for bed, he had surprised her by saying he had an idea that he thought would get Georgiana out of the house and into society, but he refused to elaborate. "I'm not sure it will work," he said, "and I don't want you to set yourself up only to be disappointed."

Since the consummation of their marriage, Samarra had become determined to move the two of them into the master suite, which her father, a widower when he'd bought the house, had never used. However, the paint and wall coverings had become dull through years of disuse and were not pleasing to Samarra anyway. Nor were the furnishings, which she thought too heavy and dark. She and Clint spent hours combing the attic and guest chambers, selecting pieces which blended their tastes in an eclectic mix.

Among the paintings swathed in yards of heavy canvas stored in the attic, Clint found one of the goddess Diana leading a hunt, an arrow poised in her bow, pointed at a fleeing stag. He had bellowed so loudly the rafters shook. *"This,"* he declared, "is going over the mantel."

Samarra pulled her face into a petulant frown, but her voice carried a teasing lilt when she said, "I would have thought you wanted a portrait of me hanging there."

"That, my love, belongs in the grand salon, where everyone can see it. I will have the real you, which is far better than any portrait, to feast my eyes upon every evening." And the look he gave her then assured her more than his words that no two-dimensional likeness could ever replace her physical presence for him.

"First thing Monday morning," Samarra said, "you can go out and hire some workmen. I have a list of reputable carpenters, stencilers, and painters in my desk."

"Married two days," Clint moaned, "and you're

271

already giving me orders! Didn't I tell you wives were despots?"

"Then where are my spots?" she quipped.

"Invisible."

"Well, I'll take my invisible spots to the seamstress and order new draperies and bed hangings while you're securing the workmen. Or," she grinned mischievously, "if you'd rather, you can go to the seamstress while I hire the workmen. It matters not to me."

"No!" he quickly objected. "Your original plan is fine."

The master suite consisted of two bedchambers, a sitting room, and a dressing room. By late Sunday afternoon, Clint and Samarra had made most of the necessary decisions concerning colors, furnishings, and accessories. With great enthusiasm, they enlightened Nanna and Georgiana about these decisions over tea.

"It's going to seem so strange," Georgiana remarked to Sam, "not having you next door."

Samarra's face fell. In her utter joy over the recent turn of events in her life, she had neglected to consider her sister's perspective. She tried to imagine how lonely and frightening it must be for Georgiana all alone in that wing at night—all alone in a room some strange man had entered just eight days ago. "We could move your things, Georgiana, into one of the rooms in the main wing, if you like. That way you'd be closer to us."

When Georgiana made no comment, Clint offered another suggestion. "I have a better idea. Nanna, why don't you move into Samarra's old bedchamber? It must be a great deal larger and more comfortable than your room on the third floor."

At first, Nanna had objected, but Georgiana's entreaty persuaded her otherwise.

Thus, on Monday morning Samarra faced the new week, the first week of her new life, with a feeling of greater exuberance than she had ever experienced. She and Clint parted at the breakfast table, he bestowing upon her a chaste kiss since Nanna and Georgiana were present. She hummed a merry tune and practically skipped across the backyards to the rear door of the print shop, her heart remembering the long hours she had spent in Clint's arms.

Her husband—it still seemed strange to think of herself as married—had preceded her to the print shop earlier that morning and started the fires, for the mercurial autumn weather had turned cold again. The warmth which greeted her increased her good humor, and she bounced upstairs to check on Clementine and her brood. Clint had told her at breakfast that the kittens had opened their eyes, and she wanted to see them before she started work.

When she turned to leave Clint's old room, however, she decided to stay for a while longer and pack some of his possessions. He had collected only the bare necessities on Friday, and they had been too pre-occupied with other, more important things to return for the remainder of his clothes since then. Since he had used his carpetbag on Friday, she removed a couple of pillowcases from the linen press; into these she placed shirts, trousers, stockings, and cravats she found in his bureau drawers. Never had she expected a man to be so neat, but each drawer had been carefully organized according to the type of garment stored within, each garment folded to meticulous precision.

While she packed, Samarra talked to Clementine. "You're going to miss Clint, aren't you, old girl? But he didn't go far, just next door. You'll still get to see him often. Maybe one day I'll become a mother, too, and I'll be a good one, just as you are."

She paused in her one-sided conversation, attempting to visualize herself holding and nursing an infant,

273

Clint's baby. Never before had she given any serious consideration to motherhood, but suddenly she found the prospect quite agreeable. Perhaps they could turn the second bedchamber of the master suite into a nursery. Her daydream continued to spin itself so intricately while she packed Clint's clothes that soon she was paying little attention to the task at all.

Until her hand closed over a sheath of papers stuffed unceremoniously into a lower drawer.

"Whatever do we have here, Clem?" she mused aloud, resuming her conversation with the cat. Her absentminded gaze raked over the top sheet, mentally recording the language as French without actually absorbing any of the content. Beneath the papers lay a leather portfolio, which she held open with one hand while she slid the papers in with the other. "Clint's translation, I suppose. He hasn't mentioned his work in a long time. Perhaps he operates as a freelancer, without anything other than a self-imposed deadline. Did he ever talk to you about it, Clem?"

She shrugged nonchalantly and laid the packet on the bed beside the stuffed pillowcases, then bent down to rub Clementine's soft fur one more time before going downstairs. "You take good care of those kittens," she admonished, and was awarded with a deep, satisfied purr from the feline.

The leather packet drew her attention once more as she stood up and shook out her skirts. For a long moment she did nothing more than stare at the minute creases worn into the soft brown calfskin and think about what a fine, expensive case it was. She reached out with the intention of stroking it, merely because it belonged to Clint, then, on impulse, picked it up and carried it with her downstairs.

* * *

On Friday, Jarvis Whitfield had moved into the tavern across the street from Samarra's print shop. He had watched Clint leave the Seldon home and enter the shop, then retrace his steps minutes later, a large satchel swinging by his side. From time to time over the next two days, Jarvis had spied the lieutenant colonel in the Seldon's garden. No light had burned from the shop's upstairs window since Whitfield had moved in, nor had he seen his quarry return to his apartment over the print shop.

From all appearances, Holbrooke had moved into the Seldon home, a fact which tickled Whitfield's fancy. So, the Seldon bitch had the hots for the man who had been spying on her! Whitfield considered marching himself over to her house and telling her all he knew about her paramour, but in order to convince her, he would have to expose his own nefarious operation.

No, there were better ways to skin a cat.

On Monday morning, Whitfield watched Holbrooke leave the house and walk toward Nicholson Street. Some time later, he watched Samarra part the curtains in the front windows of her shop and turn her sign around to "Open." Restless, and unconvinced that his continued watching of the house and print shop would gain him any usable information, Jarvis Whitfield left the tavern around mid-morning with the intention of taking a brisk walk. His stroll took him past the post office, where he stopped to collect any mail which might have arrived marked *General Delivery* for Jake White.

There was a letter for him, a letter which Whitfield hoped would provide the missing link he needed to proceed with his plans.

While Whitfield was sitting in his room across the street, reading his letter and smiling evilly, Samarra was sitting at her desk reading the French letters and laughing. She had imagined that they would be stiff and formal; instead they were filled with warmth and good humor. This French noblewoman—Samarra could not find her name among any of the papers—had been able to look at life with a freshness and wholesomeness which took Samarra completely by surprise. She had written candidly about her obese husband's many affairs, most of them with friends and acquaintances, drawing verbal pictures of him rolling in bed with wart-nosed, middle-aged women, slobbering on their flabby breasts, then panting heavily as he attempted to prove his virility to them.

The more Samarra read, the bawdier the letters became. Was it possible for a mother to write such things to her daughter, who was also the daughter of the man she so wittily maligned? she wondered. More importantly, why would she want to?

No small wonder Clint enjoyed translating such letters! In the very recent past, the letters would have flustered her. Now that she fully understood the dark secrets of womanhood, they amused her. Reading them untangled much for Samarra. Her husband had led her to believe they were of some literary value, but she could not imagine their being read in proper homes. Why, they were almost smutty! She began to see Clint's work in a new light, one which she regarded as somewhat complimentary. She recalled the night she had attacked his profession, implying that it seemed a feminine thing to do. No woman she knew would ever translate such letters! Not for a living.

Curious as to how Clint had managed some of the trickier French phrases which did not translate well to English, she sifted through the papers written in his handwriting, attempting to place them with their French counterparts. But she could not find one which even remotely resembled those letters she had just read. In some confusion, she sorted them by date, then one by one compared the original with Clint's translation of it.

By the time she had finished, her heart was thudding heavily in her chest and her breath was coming in short pants.

Beguiled. That's what she had been. Beguiled.

The word stuck like a jagged piece of glass in her throat.

"What am I going to do when she discovers who I really am . . . what I was doing all this time?"

Clint paced Dinwiddie's office, the one he kept in the small outbuilding on the Palace Green. A nervous tick pumped in his temples, and his hands alternately splayed open and then closed themselves into tight fists on the sides of his heavily muscled thighs.

"Relax," Dinwiddie offered succinctly. "Relax, my good man."

"That's easy for you to say!" Clint snapped. "You're not the one wholly immersed in this fine kettle of fish—just the one who put me there."

"From what you've told me, I see no reason to presume your wife suspects anything out of the ordinary yet. Go out and hire the workmen today, act the part of loving, devoted husband. Take her a new bonnet or a pair of gloves or some other little gift."

Clint whirled around on his heels, his voice and his features saddened by his employer's lack of perception. "It's not a part I have to feign, Governor. In all these years, you haven't really come to know me at all, have you? Did you honestly think I would marry a woman I did not love? Even for you, or for the good of Mother England? There is some honor in me yet, though I have recently begun to wonder how much of it has been eroded during my service to my country."

"There is but one honor, and that is to oneself," the governor philosophized. "Perhaps you need to re-examine your priorities, Clint."

"Perhaps I do," Clint responded cryptically—and excused himself from Robert Dinwiddie's presence without offering further explanation.

For the remainder of the day, Clint immersed himself in the trappings of busywork. He located, interviewed, and contracted skilled craftsmen to execute the redecorating and remodeling he and Samarra had agreed upon for the master suite. He visited an apothecary who recommended a maker of eyeglasses who, in turn, assured Clint he could produce the darkened lenses Clint required. He collected his mother's ring from the bank's vault, took it to a goldsmith for cleaning, and ordered a band for himself while he was there. He spent an hour at the barbershop getting a shave and a haircut, needing the latter but ordering the shave as well as a method of filling up the time. He had himself measured for a new suit of clothes at the tailor's, had the tobacconist mix a bag of his favorite pipe tobacco, a special and unusual blend, and stopped off at a dramshop for a short glass of whiskey on his way home.

Home.

The word resounded in his heart. Never before had Clint Holbrooke known a place he could honestly call home. Born the only child of a sea captain whose ship was lost at sea when his son was but a toddler, and an aristocratically born though indigent mother, Clint had spent his childhood being dragged from one relative's house to another. Throughout her life, which was mercifully cut short by acute pneumonia, Millicent Holbrooke had whined and complained incessantly about the cruel twists of fate which had conspired to ruin her existence. Not once had she shown her son any affection. Not once had she considered his feelings. His care had been left in the hands of servants who were employed by his mother's relatives.

Clint had spent a solitary childhood, more often than not left to his own devices. He had learned to read, write, and cipher at an early age, having been allowed to sit in on his various cousins' tutoring sessions. A stableboy had taught him to ride; a gamekeeper had taught him to shoot; a scullery maid had schooled him in the art of lovemaking.

What would Samarra think, he wondered as his leaden legs brought him closer and closer to home, if she knew these things about him? The only way she would ever know would be if he told her, for always had he kept these facts private. Not even Robert Dinwiddie knew what devils from Clint's past besieged him. No, he would never tell Samarra . . . the last thing he wanted from her was her pity.

She was in rare form when he encountered her in the dining room, where two places had been set at one end of the long, stately table.

"What's this?" he teased, attempting to banish the unpleasantness his mind had dragged up and enjoy his wife's company.

"Dinner, I hope," came her rejoinder, and he thought he detected a flippancy in her manner but could find no readily apparent reason for such an attitude.

"But why so formal?"

"Why not? We have been married for three days now, but not once have we dined alone during that time."

Except in the privacy of our bedchamber, Clint mentally added, recalling the picnic lunch he and

Samarra had spread in front of the cold hearth on Friday. After they had satisfied Nanna's inquisitiveness and then spent the better part of an hour luxuriating in a warm bath from which neither had wanted to emerge, Clint had collected a basketful of apples, spice cakes, cold meats, and thick slices of brown bread from the kitchen. They had taken turns feeding each other morsels of food, not really tasting anything, each feasting instead on the physical presence of the other. And Clint recalled, too, where that picnic had led them—back to the soft mattress of the bed and the wonders it held for them.

But if Samarra chose to ignore that memory, then so be it. At least she had not sat them at opposite ends of the long table.

Clint held her chair for her, and when she was seated, he lowered his chin and let it rest for a moment on top of her head before sliding his chin downward to her nape and burying his face in the fragrant mass of her hair, which she wore, in consideration of his preference, in a cascade of curls down her back. He pulled the skein aside, exposing the tender skin beneath her hairline and caressing it with soft nibbles. A shiver of delight, which Samarra was hard-pressed to subdue, coursed down her spine. Clint turned his head sideways to secure a better view of her chest, which had begun to heave. His hazel irises darkened at the sight of her milky white skin quivering above the daring décolletage of the ice-blue gown she wore. All he had to do was slip one hand down her neck, over her collarbone, and down over a soft mound to the barely hidden treasure beneath the silk.

Without conscious thought, he did just that, his fingertips encountering the quickly hardening bud even as his lips trailed forward to the sensitive skin below the delicate shell of her ear. He heard her gasp, felt her stiffen, then pulled abruptly away when she began to spout effusively in French.

Whatever had brought this on? he wondered, moving slowly to his own chair at the head of the table, which put Samarra at his right hand. That one continued her monologue in French, while Clint, utterly confused but trying not to show it, bestowed his attention upon the tureen of steaming fish chowder, removing the lid and ladling first Samarra's serving and then his own into their soup bowls.

Oh, my God! he mentally groaned as he spread creamery butter on a thick slice of sourdough bread, the stark memory of his lie flooding through him. The flow of French halted, then, and he chanced a peek at her face, knowing by her tone that she had asked a question for which she awaited an answer.

"Yes, I had a very productive day, thank you," he winged, silently praying he had hit somewhere close to the expected mark, and wishing he had never pretended to be fluent in French. But then, he hadn't—not really. Although he could read Latin and Greek, he could not speak them. On the other hand, many people were fluent in languages they could neither read nor write. Why, then, could he not read French without knowing how to speak it?

He tried to read her expression, but she'd kept it bland. When she offered no comment, he grinned charmingly and said, "How about you?"

Her voice was as bland as her face. "Extremely productive. But that is not what I asked you."

He shrugged noncommittally and sipped his soup, quickly deciding honesty—or at least part of it—was the best policy. "I have no earthly idea what you were talking about, Samarra."

Her raw-honey-colored eyebrows lifted themselves to midforehead. "A translator of French does not

281

understand the language?"

"Not verbally, no."

"But you can read it?"

"I thought we had been through this before, Samarra. I told you I was translating some French letters into English. If you doubted my ability in that realm, why did you wait so long to confront me with your skepticism?"

She answered his question with another. "Will you let me read them sometime?"

He shrugged again. "If you want to. I suppose you read French as well as you seem to speak it?"

"Almost." She was quiet for a moment, stirring her soup pensively. Clint had let down his guard a bit, but her next observation, though quietly and innocently spoken, confirmed that she was not finished with her inquisition. "I've been trying to figure out why a sedentary translator would have hard, callused hands and such a well-developed frame."

"Can you honestly imagine me being sedentary? I am a man given to long walks, and even longer rides on horseback. My injury, coupled with the foul weather of late, has grossly curtailed such activity." Though guilty of no legitimate prevarication, Clint winced inwardly. It seemed he had lately become rather adroit at telling half-truths.

For a short while she ate her soup before resuming her interrogation, this time masking her questions in the guise of statements. "You never said specifically who would be publishing the translation. You are now married to a printer and binder. Perhaps I could publish it for you."

"Perhaps." Clint bought himself a few seconds by chewing and swallowing a large bite of the crusty bread, then following it with a sip of water and the touch of his napkin upon his mouth. When he had resettled the cloth in his lap, he picked up the stemmed goblet again, gesturing with it as he talked. "I will first have to write to my publisher in London and receive his approval."

"You are under some sort of contract, then?"

"Only a verbal one."

Samarra paused to consider his words. "Funny. I thought you had been in Williamsburg for some time now."

Clint nodded. "Yes, I have. About two years." It had actually been closer to a decade. Although much of that time had been spent in other parts of the colony of Virginia, Williamsburg had always been his base of operations.

"So it was two years ago that you spoke with this London publisher? He has, in all likelihood, forgotten about you in that length of time."

Suddenly, Clint thought he understood what she was trying to do. He had wounded her pride by not asking her to print his translation, but she didn't know how to tell him. "I'm sorry, Samarra." He laid a comforting hand on her bare shoulder. "Of course, you may print and bind my translation—as soon as it is finished. I'll write to the man in London tomorrow and tell him our deal is off."

And, Lord, he silently breathed, *please get me through this without hurting her again.*

Chapter Eighteen

Samarra had never felt so miserable.

And, by the end of the week, the misery of her heart
had become a misery of the body as well.

Her head resounded with questions for which her
heart knew no answers. Why had Clint lied to her
about his knowledge of French? Why would a
translator have calluses on his hands or a hard,
muscular body? If he was not a translator, then what
was he? How did he know the governor so well? Why
did he never mention his mother, or any other family,
friends, or acquaintances? Why did he always avoid
answering her questions or answer them with additional untruths? Why did he not trust her?

That he had lied to her Samarra was certain, but she
not only wanted the truth from him, she wanted an
explanation as well. She desperately wanted him to
smooth everything over, to persuade her that good,
sound reason existed, continued to exist for his
perjury . . . although what reason there could be she
had no clue.

Each night he made love to her, his hands and his lips
and his voice tender and gentle and loving, persuading
her body to succumb to his lovemaking even if her

heart could not. Each day she promised herself that she would pin him down, force him to provide specific answers, to tell her the truth. But in the face of her planned confrontations, sitting beside him at dinner or lying beside him in the bed, she lost her resolve.

A part of her clung to hope. *This is all going to work itself out* had become her heart's chant. Nevertheless, her vanity insisted that she do something in the interim, something that would hurt Clint as much as his lies had hurt her.

Had Nanna not moved into Samarra's old bedchamber, she might have moved back into it herself, using Georgiana's fear as an excuse, but her pride prohibited her from any such action. There were numerous other bedchambers in the large house into which she could have moved her clothes, but to do so would have been tantamount to admitting that her marriage to Clint was a mistake. She resigned herself to the fact that she would have to stay put until the master suite was complete. Without discussing her plans with Clint, she had instructed the workmen to move additional bedroom furniture into the second bedchamber, which they'd intended to leave empty for the time being. She would just have to bide her time until the suite was complete.

The incessant battle of heart against vanity twisted her insides, threatening to make her physically ill. With each passing day she became testier, her temper flaring without cause, her tongue becoming waspish. When she was with Clint, she forced herself to be docile, her heart begging him to trust her implicitly, as she was trying to trust him. But when he wasn't around, when she was working side-by-side with Tom or consulting with the workmen, her tongue sharpened and her patience waned. Even when she was with Nanna or Georgiana, she lost her temper over complete trivialities.

On Friday morning, a week following Samarra's wedding, Nanna appeared at the print shop with the cup of coffee she brought to Samarra daily.

"Ye gads!" Samarra gasped, almost choking on the hot liquid. "This is awful! Wherever did you buy this coffee, Nanna?"

"'Tis the same coffee ye've been drinkin' for years, Miss Sam."

"It can't be! This doesn't even taste like coffee. It's so bitter. Here—" She pushed the cup into Nanna's hands. "You taste it."

"I already did. Had me a cup out of the same pot, Miss Sam. Tastes like it always does t' me. Are ye well?"

"Of course I am." She regarded the cup itself for a moment. "Maybe this cup wasn't clean. Bring me another one, and make sure you rinse the cup out with hot water first."

But while that one tasted equally as bad, her reaction to it was worse. Samarra took one swallow, grabbed her midsection with her crossed forearms, and doubled over in pain. Her face, bleached of all color, contorted into a grimace, and before Nanna could do anything more than take a tentative step toward her, Samarra bolted. Nanna found her retching violently just outside the door.

Placing a comforting arm around the young woman's bent shoulders, Nanna crooned, "Ye are na well, Miss Sam. Come back home with me, where ye can lie down and rest."

"No!" Samarra shook her head, then lifted the skirt of her apron and used it to wipe her mouth. "I have too much to do. I'll be all right. The coffee just didn't settle well this morning."

"Nor will it tomorrow, Miss Sam, if what I'm thinking be true."

Samarra turned cynical eyes to her servant. "And

just what are you thinking, Nanna?"

"That ye be with child."

"No!" she staunchly denied. "That's not possible."

"And why not? All that blood on yere nightgown proves it is."

"No!" she continued to deny. "I can't have a baby now. Not yet."

Nanna clucked her tongue. "Ye should have thought of that sooner, Miss Sam. Now come on home with me, and let me take care of ye, as I've always done."

But Samarra resisted Nanna's pleas, willing her stomach to behave, and then ensuring its cooperation by eating nothing and drinking only water. By the time Tom arrived that afternoon, her temples were throbbing and her shoulders ached. He noted her wan face and drooping eyes and inquired about her health.

"Not you, too!" she snapped. "Here, finish this print run. I'm going upstairs to lie down for a while."

Tom shook his head at her slowly retreating back and wondered, as he had every afternoon that week, what had gotten into Miss Samarra. He had thought Mr. Holbrooke would be good for her, but that didn't appear to hold true.

Later, when darkness was settling itself upon the earth, Tom locked and barred the front door and went home. Another hour passed before Clint and Nanna realized Samarra had never come home.

Clint found her asleep upon his old bed, her right hand clutching the counterfeit ten-shilling note she'd given him as change, the pillow upon which her head lay damp with her tears. He slipped his feet out of his shoes and tiptoed around the room as he covered her with a blanket and built a fire upon the hearth. His feet beat a hasty path next door to assure Nanna that Samarra was all right, then back again he came to the print shop and up the stairs to stretch out beside his wife and pull her into the comfort and security of his arms.

Samarra stirred against him, murmuring his name. "I'm here, sweetheart," he whispered into her hair, his heart gladdened at hearing her call his name.

Something was wrong. Something had been wrong since dinner Monday evening, when she'd greeted him in French. Had she just been playing a game with him, or was she testing him? Had she perhaps found his "translation" and recognized it for the fraudulent piece of work it was? He had collected the remainder of his clothes from this room that very evening, finding them neatly packed in pillowcases—and finding, too, the French letters and his translation in the bureau drawer where he had left them. They'd appeared undisturbed. Clint had removed the sheets in his handwriting and burned them in the fireplace; then he had returned the portfolio to the bureau drawer.

But something had disturbed Samarra . . . and if not the letters, then what? He remembered the ten-shilling note she clutched in her hand, remembered he had stuffed it inside the pillowcase upon which her head now rested. Why had she gone to sleep with it in her hand? Did she realize now that it was counterfeit? Why would she not confide in him? he wondered, his heart squelching the answer he knew to be true. In her own way she had been begging him to trust her. Damn it! He had to tell her the truth. And he would, too—just as soon as the real counterfeiter was in custody.

Jarvis Whitfield regarded the woman named Judith with a look akin to derision, yet sweetened with delight. The derision was for her lowly profession, the delight for the story she had just told him.

She regarded him with gray-blue eyes glassy from

having witnessed too much of the nether side of life. She sat before him, sipping brandy from a chipped glass greasy with fingerprints, her cuticles ragged and her nails lined with black grime. Her more than generous breasts threatened with every breath to overflow the revealing décolletage of her faded red satin, black-lace-edged gown. Her strawberry-blonde hair, braided and twisted upon her head and adorned with a black feather, had lost its luster, but Whitfield sensed that at some point it had shone with the same warmth and intensity as the midday sun. There was about her a palpable staleness, both of mind and body. Preparing her to meet Samarra Seldon was going to take some time.

"So, what you're asking me to do is clean up my act, travel with you to Williamsburg, and pretend to be Clint's wife?"

Whitfield nodded. At least the woman's speech had not completely lost its culture. Perhaps when she was dressed properly her former beauty would be restored somewhat.

"And you will pay me to do this? To exact the revenge I've been waiting for all these years?"

Again he nodded.

"When do we leave?"

Clint finally went to sleep holding Samarra in his arms.

For a long time he had just lain there, feeling her heart beat against his chest, relishing the softness and nearness of her slender body against his much longer, much harder frame. From time to time he would kiss her hair or whisper a comforting word. Occasionally she would stir against him, snuggling closer or seeking a more comfortable position, sometimes sighing softly.

289

Her voice woke him, and the near panic in it frightened him.

"Clint . . . where are we?"

"*Sh-h-h,* little one. We're in my old bed, above the shop."

He felt her move her arms, thought that she rubbed her eyes. He heard her sigh . . . a long, whispery sigh that bespoke resignation more than relief.

"What happened?" he asked.

"I—I must have eaten something that disagreed with me."

That was all Nanna would tell him, but Clint could not help wondering if perhaps she was carrying his child. Was it possible that she would feel the effects of his seed so soon? Clint had no experience in this realm, but his heart soared with the thought. Yet an inner voice reminded him that if it were true, he was going to have a hell of a time convincing Samarra to slow down and take care of herself and the child she was carrying.

"Are you hungry?" he asked solicitously.

"No . . . yes."

He smiled to himself, stifling the laugh which had gathered in his throat. "Well, which is it?"

"I feel empty, but I have no appetite."

"Do you think you could drink some broth, maybe eat a slice of bread?"

"Maybe."

Samarra was able to eat a bowl of soup, but because she continued to suffer from extreme lethargy, Clint did not question her, and she offered no comments concerning either her condition or her change of attitude toward him. Later they lay curled against each other in the guest chamber they were using temporarily, Samarra's back curved against Clint's chest, his arms around her midriff. Late into the night he lay wide awake, listening to her slow, even breathing, thinking about how very much he loved her—and the child she might be carrying.

He supposed Samarra had dropped the ten-shilling note on Jacob's bed while she'd slept in his arms next door, for she'd not brought it home. He hadn't told Dinwiddie about the counterfeit note and honestly didn't know why he'd kept it. Tomorrow he would find it . . . and burn it. He mentally chastised himself for not having burned it earlier, just as he knew he ought to have burned the translations before Samarra had a chance to find them.

And he was beginning to think that was exactly what had happened. It was the only reasonable explanation for her French monologue at the dinner table, the only reasonable explanation for the distance she'd placed between them. Early the next morning, when he found a note from her—pinned to her vacant pillow—a note written in French, he *knew*. And the knowledge sank with the weight of a twelve-course meal in his gut.

He knew too that he was not at liberty to divulge pertinent facts to her yet. But by God, he was going to see Dinwiddie first thing Monday morning and persuade the governor to grant him permission to tell her everything.

In the meantime he would do all he could to show her how much he loved her.

Samarra waited all that day and the next for Clint to answer her note. When none was forthcoming, she wanted to sit down and cry.

In the past few days, the urge to cry had come often. Samarra was generally not one given to long, drawn-out sobbing. Nanna had always insisted that "a good cry does ye good," but Samarra had never figured out what good it did *her*— unless one considered blubbery lips, an aching chest, and red-rimmed eyes good, which she didn't. Even the loudest sobs and a virtual torrent of tears had never earned her anything, certainly not sympathy or a yielding to her way. But suddenly everything made her want to cry—long and hard.

She had risen before daylight Saturday morning, penned the note to Clint, attached it to her pillow, and then removed herself to Georgiana's room to bathe and dress so as not to disturb Clint. Her message had been simple, yet her request was out of the ordinary: "If you can read this, show me by wearing your waistcoat turned inside out."

When he'd appeared at breakfast properly dressed, she had battled with herself to hold back the tears. When he'd insisted on going with her to the print shop and assisting her there all day, she'd battled with herself to hold back the tears. When she'd found a nosegay of purple and pink pansies on her desk and read the accompanying note—*"Your beauty far surpasses that of any flower. I love you. Clint"*—she'd battled with herself to hold back the tears. And always, she had been victorious.

Even that night, when he'd done nothing more than hold her close again, when she'd silently begged him to open up to her, to talk to her and tell her everything, when he said nothing, she had remained victorious over her tears.

Even when they'd sat in Bruton Parish Church Sunday morning, Samarra refused to give in to the tears. The November sun seeped in through the stained glass windows, diffusing the pinks and purples and greens and scattering them upon the pearl gray skirt of her gown. Of its own accord, her gaze fixed itself upon the dancing, shimmering splotches of color. In her mind's eye they swirled into a semblance of design and became a nosegay of pansies. She lifted her gaze immediately, willfully blotting out the memory, and saw in its place a wavering image of a bride and groom standing before the altar. The bride turned her head toward the seated congregation and smiled at Samarra, who gasped aloud when she found herself staring into her own golden brown eyes. Clint had taken her hand, then, holding it firmly but gently in his own, his thumb stroking her knuckles, soothing her. She felt the warmth of his gaze upon her, felt his own disquiet join that in her soul—and held back her tears.

A multitude of regrets weighed down her heart. They should have been married in the Church. Nanna and Georgiana and Randolph should have been there. She should have a ring to wear. Clint should be honest with her, should trust her implicitly, as she was trying to trust him.

But did she trust him . . . wholly and completely? If she did, she realized, she would wait patiently for him to explain. She would stop playing games with him. Although she had not known him long, Samarra thought she knew him well. Clint could not be involved in anything illegal. She recalled the day Captain Reed had visited Clint, the day after she'd met him, when he lay wounded upstairs in Jacob McCauley's old bed. That day she'd wondered if perhaps he was guilty of some crime, if he was absent without leave from the military barracks. Surely if either had been true, Captain Reed would have arrested him then and there.

The night they were married, she had realized Clint and Governor Dinwiddie knew each other well. The governor would not consort with a common criminal. No. Whatever it was that Clint was involved in, whatever had caused him to pretend to be a translator of French literature, involved far more than Samarra understood, and perhaps far more than she wanted to know.

She left the church oblivious to anything the minister had said, yet feeling cleansed and whole again. A number of people congratulated her and Clint as they were leaving and wished them well. Samarra smiled and thanked them—and wondered how they knew.

Clint supplied that information for her as they walked home in the brilliant sunshine. "Wasn't it kind of the Reverend Jackson to announce our marriage?"

"Yes, wasn't it?" She answered as though she had heard every word of the public disclosure.

"How would you like to take a picnic lunch somewhere—that is, if you're feeling up to it. We couldn't ask for a more beautiful day."

Samarra smiled up at him and was rewarded by an equally bright smile beaming down at her. "Yes," she said enthusiastically. "I think I would like that."

He took her hand briefly in his and squeezed it lightly. "Good. I'll tell Nanna."

The livery was closed, and they had to settle for the old buckboard for transportation. Zeke hitched the horse, an old dappled mare named Blossom, to the wagon and stood in the stableyard waving good-bye, his wrinkled face wreathed in good cheer. "Papa used to keep a stable full of horses," Samarra explained from her perch beside Clint, "but as Zeke got older and less able to care for them, Papa sold them off. He sold the phaeton, too. Said it was just too much for old Zeke to worry over—and too easy to walk around the corner and rent one. But he kept the buckboard and Blossom for those times when Nanna buys more food than she can cart home herself."

The vision of short, grizzled Nanna carting home food sent Clint into gales of laughter. Samarra joined in his mirth, their laughter resounding through the encroaching woods as Clint led Blossom down the bumpy country lane. So happy were they that they barely took note of the way the buckboard jounced them unmercifully as the big, wire-rimmed wooden wheels rolled into and out of the many holes in the roadbed.

A few miles out of town, Clint pulled off the road and into the barnyard of what had once been a pioneer homestead. All that remained of the house was a mud-daubed chimney standing sentinel in the clearing.

"What do you think happened here?" he asked Samarra as he helped her down, then reached in the back for their picnic basket.

She pirouetted beside the buckboard, her wondrous gaze absorbing the quiet dignity of what had once been someone's home. "A family lived here," she mused, her voice thick with awe. "A father who farmed and a mother who tended an herb garden. Children romped in the barnyard, chasing the chickens and tormenting the cat." Her musings abruptly stopped and her eyes misted when her roving gaze came to rest upon a series of primitive wooden crosses set side-by-side under the spreading arms of a mighty oak.

"A family died here," Clint finished for her.

"Who do you think buried them?"

"Perhaps a neighbor, perhaps a passer-by who arrived too late to be of any other use."

"Indians?"

"Possibly." His hazel eyes searched her face, read her discomfort. "Would you like to picnic somewhere else?"

Her eyes tore themselves away from the half-dozen graves and roamed the countryside. She pointed, into the sun and away from the lane, her eyes squinting until she shaded them with her free hand. "There . . . there's a pasture."

Clint started to put the basket back into the wagon, but she stopped him. "No, Clint . . . let's walk."

"Are you sure?"

"I'm not an invalid," she said, more sharply than she had intended. "I feel great today—wonderful, in fact."

And she looked wonderful, too, Clint thought, with the sun turning her hair into spun gold. A healthy glow had replaced the pastiness her skin had worn on Friday. Her smile and her laughter flowed spontaneously, warming his heart.

The dry pasture grasses whipped at their legs, depositing burrs and beggar's lice upon the fabric of their garments, but they paid them little heed, noting instead the dazzling display nature had provided for their pleasure. Warm, golden sunlight frolicked upon the silvery grasses; songbirds twittered and warbled from the widely scattered trees in the pasture, and from the thick groves of willows, oaks, and beeches surrounding the meadow, the trees enclosing it from the eyes of the world to create a private lovers' haven. Occasionally, the deep *gr-r-umph* of a bullfrog or the high whine of a drove of dragonflies added their harmony to that of the birds. A few big, puffy clouds adorned the robin's-egg-blue sky. The tantalizing, earthy smells of grass and decaying leaves and the soil itself wafted upon a gentle breeze.

Succumbing completely to nature's wiles, they spread their blanket in the mottled shade of a nearly bare walnut tree, then picked it up again, laughing, when Samarra plopped down on a walnut. "Yipes!" she gasped in mock injury, her palm dramatically rubbing her backside even as her laughter resounded in the rural stillness, the sound flushing a covey of quail from the vicinity of the willows. She untied the strings of her bonnet, which she had allowed to hang down her back, and used it as a receptacle for the walnuts she and Clint picked up. "Maybe we can talk Nanna into making us a nut cake with these," she said.

296

"Is there anything that woman can't cook?" Clint asked as he unpacked the basket.

"No, I don't think so. She's a treasure."

"How long has she been with you, Samarra?"

"Since Mama died—no, before that, I think." She chewed a bite of roasted chicken breast, trying to remember. "I was so young, Clint, not quite three when Mama died."

"What happened to her?"

"Some strange fever, I think. Papa doesn't talk about it. I think he's never quite gotten over it."

"I know . . . my mother was like that." The words were out of his mouth before he realized that he had spoken his thoughts.

"Your mother?" Samarra prompted, wanting him to talk about his own childhood, his own family.

"Yes."

"But she doesn't grieve anymore?"

"No."

"I don't suppose Papa actually grieves now. But he still misses Mama terribly. I think that's why he left England and moved us here—to try to put the past behind him. You implied once that he might have been on the lam when we came here, and I suppose he was, in a way."

"Samarra, I've said a lot of things to you I regret. I hope you will forgive me."

"We agreed to start afresh, remember?" Her easy smile assured him she had overcome whatever misgivings had been troubling her.

How far they had come in the month since they had met, Clint reflected, leaning back against the rough bark of the tree trunk and letting his eyelids slide shut. He listened to Samarra gathering up the remainder of their lunch, packing it away. He listened to the birds twittering in the warm stillness of the afternoon, felt the

297

warm sun penetrating his shirt sleeves, felt a warmth, too, a damp warmth on the top of his head—and bolted upright, knocking the picnic basket over as his mouth emitted a stronger curse than he would normally have used in Samarra's presence.

"What's wrong, Clint?"

"Damn bird!" His fingers raked the crown of his head, and he cursed again at the sight of the dark, oozing glob on his fingers.

Samarra laughed heartily at his expense. "There was some water left in the jug, if you didn't spill it just then. Stand still while I soak a napkin and I'll see what I can do for you."

"Any soap in there, too?"

"No."

"It's going to take more than water to get this nasty mess out, Samarra."

"Sit down, Clint! You're acting like a child—but you're much taller than one. I can't reach you."

Clint complied, albeit reluctantly. "There's something very degrading about having a bird choose your head upon which to deposit his mess," he complained, "and then having to let someone else remove it."

"I wouldn't know," she snorted between giggles. "It never happened to me. Awg!" she choked. "This is awful!"

"There's bound to be a stream around here somewhere. Let's find it."

"You won't hear an argument from me!"

They raced across the pasture to a grove of willows, which grew along the banks of a narrow stream. For a moment they stood still, each bent over with palms resting upon thighs, panting.

"All these weeks of inactivity have ruined me," Clint observed—and Samarra thought again about his callused hands and muscular frame, and wondered

298

about his normal—his genuine occupation. Clint watched her catch her breath, remembering that she might be pregnant and worrying about her running like that. He'd have to be more careful with her, more watchful of her condition if she was.

He fell down on his knees, immersing his head in the cool water and running his long, lean fingers through his hair until he had to come up for air. Over and over, he rinsed his head, until, finally, he decided it was as clean as it was going to get without soap. When he stood up, his entire head was soaking wet, water streaming down his face and neck in thick, cold runnels. He shuddered.

Samarra tugged on his arm. "Come on . . . back to the sun," she coaxed.

But when she tried to run again, Clint slowed her down, using his own physical sluggishness as an excuse. They dragged the blanket away from the tree, used a corner of it to dry his face and his hair, then stretched out upon it to let the sun finish absorbing the moisture.

They lay on their sides, facing each other. Clint reached out tentatively, placing his open palm upon her cheek and letting the pad of his thumb trace the length of her nose. "A while ago, you called me a child."

"I'm sorry."

"Don't apologize, Samarra. With you, I feel like a child sometimes, like the little boy I wanted to be but never was. With you, I feel young and alive and free. Don't ever apologize for making me feel so good."

Slowly he inched closer to her until only a hairsbreadth separated their parted lips. Their breaths mingled, their heartbeats melded, their bodies quivered in mutual desire. When he took her mouth with his, she gave it readily. Gone was her reticence. Gone were her misgivings.

A breeze rustled the few dry leaves clinging to the branches of the walnut tree and sent a flurry of leaves sailing around them, but neither Clint nor Samarra took note. She sighed into his heated mouth; he moaned into the dark, velvety cavern of hers. Their tongues came together in a dance fraught with longing, with need, with insatiable hunger for one another.

The first time he took her quickly, ignoring her needs, and yet she reached a pinnacle of emotion—if not of body—as strong as she ever had before.

The second time he teased and toyed with her, dragging out the erotic play until she begged him for surcease.

And afterward, while their pulses slowed and their breathing returned to normal, they lay comfortably in each other's arms, sharing a peace unlike any other.

It was a peace which was to prove short-lived.

Chapter Nineteen

The favorable weather held on Monday, allowing Clint an opportunity to scurry around town and thus dispense with his errands by noon.

He ticked off the list in his mind, visiting first the livery, where he ordered a carriage built and rigged to his specifications. Next, he visited the eyeglasses maker, then moved on to the office of the *Virginia Gazette* to place an advertisement for a stableboy in that week's paper. At the goldsmith's, he collected his wedding band. By the time he stopped by Dinwiddie's office, the errand which he'd dreaded and purposely put off till last, he fought to maintain the good mood he was in.

Lieutenant Morris snapped to attention when Clint strolled through the door, and, forgoing the customary announcement, showed Clint directly into the governor's office.

Dinwiddie growled when he saw Clint. "Where have you been, young man? I was about to send out a search party." His mouth twisted into a half smile then. "I'd wager they wouldn't have had much trouble finding you, either, though you and that little wife of yours might not have appreciated the disturbance."

"It's a good thing you didn't place any bets this morning, sir. Your search party would have followed a trail all over town, I'm afraid," Clint said dryly.

Dinwiddie nodded, waving a hand at a chair, but his twinkling eyes expressed his disbelief. "Sit down. Sit down. We have much to discuss."

Clint's heart skipped a beat. Had they arrested the counterfeiter? Could he, at last, tell Samarra? Dinwiddie's next words quashed his soaring spirits.

"The counterfeiter has skipped town, and we have yet to pick up his trail. Good thing I sent those dispatches to the other colonial governors, asking them to watch for the counterfeit currency. Maybe our man will drop some, and then we'll know where he is—or, at least, where's he's been. But that's not what I wanted to tell you."

Clint's eyebrows rose to mid-forehead.

The governor pushed a newspaper across his desk and under Clint's nose. "Someone wants to know about you, about your past."

Clint's eyes were drawn to a circled advertisement. *"Will pay for information concerning one Lt. Col. Clinton Holbrooke. Reply to Jake White, General Delivery, Williamsburg."* A quick glance at the top of the folded newspaper revealed it to be a recent copy of the *Boston News-Letter*. In an instant Clint was on his feet and headed out the door.

Dinwiddie's bellow stopped him. "Where do you think you're going?"

"Excuse me, sir. May I be dismissed?"

"No. Sit down." His voice brooked no argument. "Now, where were you going?"

"To the Williamsburg Post Office, then to Boston."

The governor nodded. "That's what I *thought* you would do." He opened a desk drawer and retrieved a stack of newspapers, his forefinger rifling their edges.

302

"All of these contain the same advertisement, Clint. The *American Mercury* from Philadelphia, the *New York Gazette,* newspapers from Annapolis, Charleston, Newport. And Mac's already been to the post office. Jake White, whoever he is—and we think the name is an alias—picked up a letter last week. Several more have arrived for him since, but he hasn't been back to get them."

From the same drawer Dinwiddie removed a bundle of letters tied together with twine. These he pitched across the desk. "Look at those and tell me if you know any of the writers."

One by one Clint unfolded the letters and read them, but he shook his head when he'd finished. "They're all written by charlatans. Most of these places I've never even been to."

"Just as I thought. We cannot discount the writer of the letter this Jake White picked up, but we can hope that person was also a fraud."

"Does the postmaster recall anything about that letter—or this Jake White?"

"Not about the letter, and only that the man who collected it was tall and well groomed."

Clint whistled softly. "Doesn't give us much to go on."

"It wouldn't, no—except that we've learned that a man matching the general description and using the name Jake White rented a room in the tavern across the street from Miss Seldon's—pardon me, your wife's print shop the day after your wedding."

"Where is he now?"

"We don't know."

"Why don't you?" Clint barked, his voice a loaded cannon of exasperation.

Dinwiddie held up a restraining hand. "Calm down, Clint—you know what investigative work is like. Just when you think you've got your man, he slips away from you. But there's another thing you need to know. This man Jake White fits the same description as the man we think is the counterfeiter. And they disappeared at the same time."

"That's logical. He attempts to implicate Samarra, then he goes after me when that doesn't work."

They sat for a moment in tense silence, which Dinwiddie broke with what seemed to be a change of subject. "When did you last hear from Judith?"

Clint shrugged. "I don't remember. Years ago, I guess."

"She wrote to you?"

"Yes."

"Was she still bitter?"

"Yes, but—" Clint's eyes narrowed and his teeth clenched as the governor's train of thought became clear to him. "You don't think—"

"It's a possibility. Where was she living when last she wrote you?"

"Philadelphia."

Dinwiddie scratched his chin. "Could be where our man Jake White went. I'm dispatching a letter to the governor of Pennsylvania this afternoon. Think I'll send Mac Reed with it, have him do a bit of sleuthing while he's there."

"Let me go with him, Governor."

"Not on your life. Could be we're wrong, and I promised your wife you'd be there to protect her."

Clint had been waiting for an opening. "Don't you think it's time we—*I* told Samarra what's going on?"

"Is she asking questions?"

"Not really, but she's suspicious. She knows I have no real knowledge of French. And I'm not comfortable with the deceit."

304

"You know it's better this way, Clint—for her own protection, if not for that of our operation. She'll understand. When this is all over . . ."

The phrase replayed itself in Clint's mind the rest of the day, which he spent laboring with the hired workmen in the master suite. *"When this is all over . . ."* It became for him a stimulus of hope, of encouragement; it bolstered his spirits again, gave him the willpower to continue the deception for a while longer.

Samarra took advantage of Clint's absence during the morning hours to visit Dr. Hargrove. She had mentally calculated the number of days since her last monthly time and realized her susceptibility.

"It's entirely too early to make a conclusive diagnosis, Samarra," he said when she'd finished listing her symptoms, "but you may very well be with child. Some women suffer discomfort almost from the first day, others never do, and there's a whole realm in between. You'll know for yourself in another month or so. For the time being, I want you to take it easy, just in case."

"Does that mean I can't work in the print shop?" she asked uneasily, wondering how she would manage to fill her days without her work.

"No. But I do want you to take time out each day to rest. Maybe you should consider hiring someone full-time. I know you have Tom in the afternoons, but you're going to need someone during the day if you're carrying a baby."

"Are there other precautions I should take?"

"Just use good, common sense. Eat well and rest often. Don't push yourself. Don't lift anything heavier

305

than a half-stone. The Indians say a tea made from black currants or brown cedar berries provides some relief for female troubles. If the signs of childbearing hold true, come back to see me in, say, two months. Sooner, of course, if you have problems."

She was almost out the door when he called her back. "Have you mentioned this to your husband?"

"No, and I will appreciate your not saying anything about this visit. I want to be the one to tell him—and I want to be sure first."

He nodded. "I understand."

Telling Dr. Hargrove had been easy; writing to her father was not. Each day she'd intended to write to him, but each day she'd found something more pressing to occupy her time. Not once in the twelve days since she had married Clint had she written to her father. It was a task which, she knew, must be undertaken without further delay. She sat at her desk, penning him one letter after another, wadding each one into a tight ball and hurling it at the fireplace. Finally she gave up trying to find the softest words and told her father quite bluntly about the wedding and the series of events leading up to it, but carefully omitted anything relating to Clint's professed occupation and to the possibility of pregnancy. She saw no purpose in upsetting him on the one hand or in thrilling him on the other with suspicions based solely on circumstantial evidence.

"Holy moly, Miss Samarra!" Tom exclaimed when he spied the mound of paper balls scattered among the ashes. Samarra was never wasteful and insisted Tom save the occasional sheets of paper ruined in the press to be used for notes.

"Don't swear, Tom," she admonished, her voice fraught with irritation. "Here." She handed him a letter and some coins. "Take this to the post office for me. And hurry back!"

306

"Yes, ma'am!" he hollered just before the door banged shut.

She was squatting in front of the fireplace making a tidy mound of the wadded paper when Sloane O'Quinn walked in.

"Afternoon, Miss Seldon," he greeted her in his dry, raspy voice.

"Good-bye, Mr. O'Quinn," she snapped, her fingers fumbling with the tinderbox.

"Pardon?"

"You heard me correctly. Unless you wish to make a purchase or place an order, we have no business to conduct."

"But, Miss Seldon—"

The spark caught, and Samarra blew gently upon the tiny flame until the paper blazed. "It's Mistress Holbrooke now, thank you." She stood slowly and faced him squarely, her eyes blazing with an intensity as great as that of the fire she had just started. He looked at her in some confusion, but she gave him no quarter. "Since you're still here, I assume you have legitimate business. What can I print for you?"

His mouth dropped open and his watery blue eyes bulged in his skull face. "Why, Mistress Seldon— Holbrooke!" He sounded distressed. "I just came to tell you that you're being watched again."

Her hands formed themselves into tight fists which she set upon her slender hips. "Do you know what you are, Mr. O'Quinn? You're nothing more than a measly little spider, spinning webs and lying in wait for unsuspecting victims to get caught in them. You didn't have the gall to approach me as long as my father was in town, but as soon as he left for London, you came in here thinking you could intimidate me into selling you this business. Well, your little scheme didn't work this time, Mr. O'Quinn. I won't be one of your victims."

307

She thought he would surely die of apoplexy before he gathered his wits about him and stalked out the door. For a long time afterward she sat at her desk and shook. Never before had she talked so to anyone, and while she felt relieved that she had rid herself of this one particular thorn in her side, she also ached from the memory of the pain on his face as he had turned to leave. Had she been unjust in her accusations? Was there some truth to his warning? Perhaps his intentions had been honorable.

The thought plagued her for the next hour, and she carried it with her when she left the print shop for the day and went home for tea. Georgiana and Clint awaited her in the petite salon. She gave them but a cursory glance before plopping into a plush wing chair on the opposite side of the room and letting her eyelids slide closed. Noting the violet half-moons beneath his wife's eyes and the paleness in her cheeks, Clint covered one of Georgiana's hands with his and softly shushed her when she would have spoken. Moving then to Samarra's chair, Clint placed an open palm on her forehead and breathed easier when he felt no fever there.

"May I get you something, Samarra? A glass of water, perhaps, or a dram of sherry?"

The pink tip of her tongue emerged to wet her lips. "Water sounds good. Thanks." She accepted the glass from him and took several sips before sighing heavily. "I'm just so tired! I think I'll go up to bed."

It must have been about the same time Friday, Clint thought, when the last vestiges of his wife's energy had deserted her. He wished he'd considered that before he made his plans. "Why don't you have a cup of tea first?" he asked, attempting to sound more courteous than eager. "Nanna made Sally Lunn."

It was the prospect of this treat which decided the

308

issue. No one made Sally Lunn teacake as light, as mouthwatering as Nanna's.

At the merest hint of a smile and the barest nodding of her head, Clint's eagerness burst forth, but she was too exhausted, too outdone with herself to notice. "Sit right here, Samarra. I'll move the tea table, and Georgiana and I will come sit with you."

Quietly, Clint turned a chair to face Samarra's and sat her sister upon it. When all was ready and Nanna had deposited the tea tray, Samarra opened her eyes—and found herself staring straight ahead at a new Georgiana.

"Good heavens, George! Where did you get those?" Her voice carried the evidence of her surprise, which Georgiana had expected, but without even the tiniest hint of her approval.

"Do you like them?" Georgiana asked shyly, almost reluctantly. A tentative hand reached up to touch the thin wire rim of one of the cobalt-blue lenses, which effectively hid the glassy whiteness of her irises.

"Like them? I love them!" Samarra's sudden and overwhelmingly natural enthusiasm served to erase both her fatigue and her sister's apprehension.

"Clint gave them to me."

"Clint?" Samarra turned awestruck yet grateful eyes upon her husband. *I have an idea which may bring Georgiana out of her shell and into public,* he had said over a week ago, but she had forgotten it. And what a wonderful idea it had been! He could not have given her a gift which would have meant as much to her as the dark glasses did both to her and to Georgiana. "But, how . . . ?"

"I just went to the proper craftsman and ordered them."

"Why didn't I think of dark glasses?"

"Perhaps you were too close to the problem."

309

Samarra returned her attention to her sister. "And do *you* like them, Georgiana?"

"Oh, yes! Do they look all right, Samarra? I mean, do you think people will stare at me if I decide to go to church with you sometime?"

Samarra shot her husband a *rescue me!* look.

"If anyone stares, Georgiana," Clint avowed, "it will be because you are a beautiful young woman!"

"I am?"

"Of course you are! You're your sister's identical twin, are you not? Do you think I would have married her if she were not beautiful?"

Both women laughed at his teasing, yet they knew he found them both very attractive.

"And you, Clint, are you beautiful, too?" Georgiana asked wistfully.

"You'll have to ask your sister that."

"Yes, George, he's beautiful, too, and in many ways."

"I can see the beauty of your heart, Clint. Will you allow me to see the beauty of your face as well?" She sat very still, awaiting his response.

Clint slid his chair closer to hers, then lifted her hand and placed it upon his face. "You have a cleft in your chin," George marveled. "And a tiny scar near the corner of your mouth."

"From a fistfight when I was a child."

Her fingers continued their exploration of his face. "Prominent cheekbones, wide-set eyes. What color are your eyes, Clint, and your hair?"

"He's the color of autumn," Samarra supplied, her voice thick with pride. "Russet hair, eyes that change from green to gold, like the leaves, and a complexion that's the palest copper."

"He sounds beautiful."

"You girls had better stop calling me beautiful!"

Clint chided in mock offense. "Men are supposed to be handsome, not beautiful."

"Ah, but we have you outnumbered."

The hot tea, together with Clint's gift, the delicate Sally Lunn, and the warmth and good humor permeating the room, revived Samarra's spirits. Her vitality received a further boost when she went upstairs to bathe and dress for dinner.

Soft light coming from both the late afternoon sun and the fire upon the hearth bathed the bedchamber in varying shades of orange, ranging from the palest peach to a deep, rich pumpkin. A huge copper hipbath, which Samarra had never seen before, sat before the hearth, simultaneously casting its own orange glow while reflecting that of the light. Wisps of steam rose from the surface of the water and wafted across the room, precipitating its foggy breath upon the window glass and mirrors. And drifting among it all, the fresh, pungent scents of rosemary, mint, and thyme teased and welcomed and promised relaxation.

From behind the dressing screen emerged a tall, thin young woman dressed in white mobcap and apron. Bright hair the color of pomegranates framed a square-jawed, pug-nosed face peppered with light brown freckles. Samarra gasped when she saw her.

"Pardon me, mum. I did not mean to frighten you."

"Who are you? Where did you come from?" Samarra asked with a mixture of amazement and confusion playing upon her delicate features.

"Jennie Craxton, mum. I come from Liverpool."

"No . . . I mean, I'm pleased to meet you, Jennie, but what are you doing in my bedchamber?"

"She's your new lady's maid."

Samarra jumped at the sound of Clint's voice from behind her.

"I'm sorry, Samarra. I thought to come up with you,

311

but Georgiana detained me for a moment to thank me again for the glasses."

"I—gosh, Clint, I don't know what to say. Glasses for Georgiana, a new maid for me."

His hands fell gently upon her shoulders and he turned her around. "You don't have to say anything, except that you love me."

Her arms moved around his waist and she squeezed him tightly against her slender form. "You know I do."

"Thank you, Jennie. Miss Georgiana is expecting you now in her chamber."

"Yes, sir," the maid mumbled, taking her leave of them.

"I hope you won't mind sharing her with Georgiana, at least for the time being."

"Good heavens, no, I don't mind. Neither of us has ever had anyone to tend to our needs, other than Nanna—and each other. It's not that Papa can't afford to hire a lady's maid, it's just, well, we never asked—and he never thought of it, I suppose. Papa has never allowed ways of spending money to occupy his mind, rather ways of accumulating it. Oh, I don't mean to imply that he isn't generous, because he is—to a fault. It's just that—"

"You don't have to explain, Samarra."

"I just don't want you to think badly of Papa."

Clint's hands snaked down her back to cup her buttocks and pull her tighter against him. She felt the hard ridge of his manhood pressing against her stomach, felt her own body grow warm and liquid with her own passion.

"Come," he whispered hoarsely. "Let's get you into your bath before the water grows cold."

He reached behind his back to close the door and lock it, then took Samarra by the hand and led her over to the hearth. With an appreciative and loving gaze he unfastened her daygown and slipped its fabric from her shoulders, letting it fall into a puddle at her feet. Her chemise and petticoats followed suit, until she stood before him in all her naked splendor. His smoldering green eyes raked her petite body from head to toe, then slowly retraced their journey to rest upon her parted lips. She shivered beneath the boldness of his gaze—and groaned when he placed the flat of his hand upon her belly.

"Has my seed taken root, Samarra?" The words tore from his throat, as though he'd tried unsuccessfully to keep them at bay.

"Would it please you, Milord Stag, if it has?"

"Most assuredly, my love."

She smiled sweetly, almost wistfully, down at his hand. "I cannot say, milord."

"But your stomach has been queasy and you tire so easily."

"Dr. Hargrove says we must wait. Only time will tell."

His eyebrows rose slightly at the mention of the physician's name. "You have discussed this with him?"

"This morning." She shivered again.

"Into the hipbath with you!" he growled, scooping her into his arms and carrying her across the room.

She giggled and her arms clutched him tightly. Reluctantly she released her hold when he set her into the warm, herb-scented water. "Aren't you going to get in with me?" she invited.

"Not at the moment. I'm going to play lady's maid and give you a bath." He was already rolling up his shirt sleeves.

Samarra leaned back and let the water and the long strokes of the soapy cloth work their magic upon her.

"Um-m-m," she sighed, "this is heaven. What other surprises do you have up your sleeve, Clint Holbrooke?" A questing hand eased out of the water and snaked up one of his shirt sleeves in feigned exploration of another "surprise."

He laughed. "I'll never tell."

A pensive, almost sad expression washed over her features. "I had thought to surprise you, too, milord."

He understood her reference and mentally kicked himself for his lack of patience. "You will surprise me, Samarra, for how can I possibly know whether the child you carry is a boy or a girl?"

His rationale appeased her. "'Tis not something which can be long concealed anyway. At least now you will understand my moods. Before this is over you may wish you had never married me."

"Your pain will be my pain, your joy, my joy," he quietly assured her.

"Is this what it means to become 'one'?"

"I suppose. Now, enough philosophy and reflection. Scoot down into the water and wet your hair so I can wash it."

He drove his long, lean fingers into her hair and used his nails to massage her scalp. "I had forgotten how good this feels," she said. "It's been simply years since someone else washed my hair. I think I could sit here all night."

"Well, I couldn't! My knees are giving out."

"Oh, Clint, why didn't you say something? I can finish with my hair."

"They aren't gone yet," he quipped. "Besides, this is fun."

"It would be more fun if you were in here with me!" Catching him off-guard, she pulled him into the hipbath on top of her. Water splashed out of the tub,

314

and Samarra's mirth bubbled forth.

"Damnation, woman! You got me all wet!"

"That was the general idea."

She spread her legs wide to make room for him, and it was some time later before the two were dressed for dinner.

"I have one more surprise for you tonight, dear wife," Clint announced almost sheepishly as he fastened the back of her gown. From the pocket of the frock coat he had worn that day, he removed a small package, his fingers fumbling with the knot in the twine as he spoke. "It seems our lives have been filled with surprises lately. I was as surprised as you at the governor's insistence that we be married the night of the ball, and, therefore, as unprepared." The twine fell away from the box, and with shaking hands he withdrew a tiny gold band studded with diamonds.

Samarra gasped in awe when she saw it, her left hand automatically rising from her side and placing itself in his. "Oh, Clint!" she breathed. "I love it!"

He could not resist sliding the delicate band onto her third finger, then bending his head and placing the softest of kisses upon it. "It's such a small, insignificant ring," he apologized.

"I would not have wanted one any larger," she assured him, "and significance lies in the gesture, not the gift. This one I can wear while I work. But," her face fell, "I don't have one for you."

Clint smiled secretively. "I took care of that, too. I hope you don't mind, but I want the world to know I belong to you."

She watched him remove another ring from the box, a much larger gold band, and she took it from him and placed it upon his finger. Their throats were too full for words.

The evening had been perfect in every way, an indication, Samarra hoped, of what their life would be together.

As well it might have been—had Clint not broken with tradition after dinner and lit his pipe in the presence of the ladies.

Chapter Twenty

The moment he lit the tobacco in the bowl, an unhealthy pallor suffused Georgiana's face. Samarra noticed it immediately, and pondered its cause. Randolph Seldon often smoked in their company, and Georgiana had granted her permission, along with Samarra, when Clint had asked if they minded.

Georgiana wiped her hands nervously on her lap; her mouth opened slightly to permit the tip of her tongue to rake her lips; and her chest heaved as she took a deep breath. Samarra had half risen from her chair to go to her sister when that one jerked the dark blue glasses from her head and almost slammed them down on the table next to her chair. They teetered precariously for a moment, the wire earpieces clattering against the hardwood surface before the glasses finally came to a rest standing upright on the lenses.

"Georgiana!" Samarra's voice came sharply. "Whatever is the matter with you?"

That one's white-glazed eyes fixed their non-seeing though steady scrutiny upon Clint Holbrooke. They were the only part of her, however, that appeared steady. Her body shook and her limbs trembled. Within her a mixture of shocked disbelief and

317

undisputed revelation vied for control. When she spoke, the words came out haltingly, mirroring her uncertainty. "It's ... probably nothing, Sam. I—I must go upstairs now."

It was as much distance as she could put between herself and Clint Holbrooke for the time being. It would have to be enough.

For more than a fortnight, Georgiana had ofttimes imagined in the darkest depths of her soul that she smelled again that peculiar pungency of the tobacco smoke that had clung to the late-night intruder. It was in itself not an unpleasant odor. But each passing recollection had empowered it with an ability to sicken, until each stark memory took the form of a slow, heavy grinding stone, rolling against her insides and gnashing them together, hurling the dross into her throat and gorging her with its vileness.

More often than not, lately, the bile churned in her stomach only when she was around Samarra's new husband. Georgiana had mentally shrugged off the connection, laying the blame upon the novelty of having another man in the house besides her father. She was not going to allow the insignificant fact that Clint smoked a pipe to color her feeling toward the man her sister loved. No, she had assured herself time and time again, the familiar, pungent odor her nostrils breathed was nothing more than a figment of her overactive imagination.

But then the smoke had actually wafted around her head. She had actually *breathed* it. And though the message her brain had received was too stark, too real to attribute to mere imagination, Georgiana fought valiantly against her mind's perception of the truth ... if she could just get away from the smoke, go back to her room and lie upon her bed, the sickness would go away, her head would clear—and she would know that her keen sense of smell had tricked her into believing something that could not possibly be true.

She wended her way a bit shakily from the room and into the front hallway. Samarra frowned at the slump of her sister's shoulders, the shuffle of her feet, the movement of her head from side to side as she left the room.

"I hope she isn't sick," Clint said, his brow puckering into a frown at the blind woman's abrupt, odd behavior.

Samarra wanted to believe some physical illness had befallen her sister, but she could not discount the anger with which George had removed her new glasses nor the way she had looked at Clint, as though she could actually see him. She had never seen her sister act so strangely. For a moment she sat upon the edge of her chair, willing her mind and body to relax, willing her heart to quell its sporadic, heavy beat, willing herself to believe that nothing more than a spell of weakness or a digestive disorder had befallen Georgiana. But that one's look of utter disappointment, of bitter disillusionment preyed upon her mental efforts.

"I'm going with her."

So slowly, so dejectedly had George left the salon that Samarra thought to catch up with her at the landing. Instead, she found her sister near the end of the hallway of the wing, entering her bedchamber door.

"George, wait! I want to talk to you!" she called, starting to run when her sister scurried through the doorway. Samarra's blood ran cold when she heard the key turn in the lock.

Desperate to talk to her sister, to discover what had upset Georgiana so much, she banged her fist upon the door, but her entreaties went unanswered. Refusing to be defeated by something as simple as one door when there was another, Samarra dashed back through her old bedchamber and thus to the door connecting it with Georgiana's, but she found that one locked as well.

"Georgiana!" she cried out. "If you do not open this door immediately, I am going to get an ax and rip it to splinters!"

"Please, Sam, just go away. I want to be alone." Her voice was thick, almost hoarse, as though she were crying—or trying very hard not to.

"Not until you tell me what's wrong." Samarra waited breathlessly, her heart in her throat, but Georgiana said nothing. Though she racked her brain, she could not conceive of anything Clint had done to upset Georgiana, but her twin's actions indicated that Clint had somehow been responsible. If that was true, then the last person Georgiana would want to see right then was Clint.

Samarra changed her tactics accordingly. "All right, George . . . you win. You know I wouldn't ruin a perfectly good door. I'm going back downstairs to get Clint. He can break this door down without damaging anything except the lock."

Fully intending to carry out her threat, if need be, she moved at a snail's pace toward the hallway door, setting each foot down firmly so that George would hear. She had but reached the foot of the bed which Nanna now used before the metallic click of the key turning in the lock halted her progress.

"No, you win, Samarra—you always win."

Georgiana had run the gamut of grief-related emotion when, as an adolescent on the verge of becoming a young woman, she'd learned she was slowly going blind. She had known shock, anger, denial, anguish, and resignation. Somehow, all those emotions melded into one big lump of distress for George as the words fell like leaden weights from her mouth.

Certain that Georgiana was distressed and not ill,

Samarra followed her back into her room, lit a candle, and closed the door. When Georgiana sat down in front of the fire, Sam joined her there. An eerie sense of déjà-vu arrested her hackles, and her entire body shuddered uncontrollably. The adjoining room . . . a pair of matched wing chairs . . . a warm fire . . . Georgiana's consternation over an uninvited guest tiptoeing around, rifling through Samarra's possessions.

Georgiana's words came back to haunt her: *"He smelled like pipe smoke. Not a stale odor, but a fresh one, like he'd just finished."*

No! her heart cried out in pain . . . it couldn't be. God, don't let it be Clint.

She turned heartsick eyes to her sister, saw upon her twin's face the same denial her heart screamed, the same truth her head acknowledged. As though she were still in the salon with the smoke wafting around her, she smelled the pungency of the unique blend, so different from the tobacco their father smoked.

"You don't have to tell me, Georgie. I know what's troubling you."

A solitary tear slipped out of a white-glazed eye and trickled untended down Georgiana's cheek to plop upon the fabric of her bodice. Samarra stared unseeing at the dark, wet slash upon the silk, the fingers of her right hand absently twirling the golden band upon her left.

"Mayhap I am wrong. If only I could see—if only I could have seen that man that night. If only—" George's voice broke and she buried her head in her hands. "I like him so much, Sam," she sobbed into her lap.

Samarra's voice was low, filled with a curious mixture of sorrow and fear. "I know . . . I like him, too."

Was it possible Georgiana was right? Samarra did not want to believe it, but that blinded view offered the easy way out.

A deathly silence hung over them, the hiss and crackle of the fire and Georgiana's soft sobs the only sounds in the room. Across the open space between them their hands reached out to each other. Samarra forced herself to obliterate the sound of her sister's sniffles, forced aside the vertigo threatening to undo her, forced herself to deal with the myriad possibilities vying for attention in her mind.

Each avenue of speculation led her down a cul-de-sac. By his own admission, Clint had been absent from his room for a few hours the night Samarra had gone to the theater with Beth and Edwin—the evening Clementine had given birth. Had Clint slashed his own mattress later as a diversionary tactic? Samarra didn't think so. If Clint had been in her chamber and Georgiana's that night, could he have been so comfortable with either of them afterward? And what possible motive could he have had for sneaking into their rooms?

From all appearances, Clint was as much a victim as were she and Georgiana. After all, someone had thrown a knife at him. Someone had ransacked his bed. And Sloane O'Quinn had insisted that someone had been watching the print shop.

Clint's only real crime had been his lying about his occupation. The more Samarra had thought about that, the more her vanity had gotten in the way. The explanation could simply be that he'd made it all up as an excuse to be close to her, somehow securing the French letters she'd found and then faking the translation in order to create some evidence to substantiate the lie. Or the explanation could be extremely complex, with Clint using her as a cover for some sort of covert operation.

Samarra could make no sense of any of it. But in the depths of her soul, she could not believe her husband to be either a lunatic or a criminal. There was too much evidence to the contrary.

"Where's Nanna?"

"In the kitchen, I suppose." George sniffed loudly.

"Shall I stay with you until she comes to bed?"

"Yes, please."

"May I get you a glass of sherry to calm your nerves?"

"You don't believe me, do you?" Georgiana asked, incredulous.

"I believe that the blend of tobacco Clint smokes is probably the same used by the man who came into your room that night."

"I wish I *knew* Clint was innocent. It's different when you're blind, when you don't have your eyes to corroborate the messages from your other senses. I remember, Sam . . . I remember what it was like to be able to see. I miss it so much!"

Samarra thought her heart would break. So often had she admired her sister's aplomb, her seeming acceptance of her blindness. Apparently George had repressed her anger, her sense of loss far more than any of them had realized. "I would gladly give you my eyes if I could, George."

"I know you would, Sam."

"But you wouldn't see as well then as you do now."

Georgiana raised a puzzled look to her sister. "What a silly thing to say, Sam . . . of course I would!"

"No, you wouldn't, George. Your blindness enables you to see with your heart. You see people for what they are, what they really are—inside. When you see beauty, it is the beauty of the soul. Your blindness knows not the prejudice vision creates."

They sat for a long time, wrapping themselves in a

cocoon of warmth created by their love for each other, reminiscing. By the time Nanna came up to bed, they were laughing over some shared childhood memory and Samarra had successfully—she thought— pushed the reason for Georgiana's odd behavior to the back of her mind.

What she did not take into account was her spiritual exhaustion. Samarra moved down the hall and to her bedchamber in a trance. She found Clint sitting up in bed, reading a book, a lone candle on the bedside table, the fire burning on the hearth was the only other light in the spacious room. He marked his place, laid the book aside, and opened his arms to Samarra, but she stood very still, looking at him as though she'd never seen him before, as though he was a total stranger to her.

Suddenly he *was* a stranger to her, and his presence in her bed, in her house, in her life frightened her to her core.

A log, burned through the middle, crashed in the fireplace, hissing like a tightly coiled snake and dispersing a myriad of sparks. She heard the familiar noise and saw the sparks fly as one who dreaming hears and sees and yet does so from afar. For an instant the fire blazed brightly, its glow beaming out in a shaft which hit Clint full on the face, turning his sun-darkened complexion to an orb of light which emphasized the deep shadow of his cleft chin.

He had told her! Oh, God, he had told her! His words mocked her now, mocked the sweet mystery of their lovemaking.

A dimple in the chin means a devil within.

"Samarra," he called softly, and when she didn't respond, he rose from the bed and went to her.

"Don't touch me, you black-hearted fiend!" she hissed, her golden eyes glazed with terror.

"Samarra! Whatever has gotten into you?" Clint

grasped her upper arms and shook her gently, but she continued to regard him with a hard, blank stare.

"I will hear no more of your silver-tongued lies, Milord Devil."

Oh, my God! Clint vehemently denied the sudden blinding flash of truth. It was simply not possible. Georgiana had not seen him that night, could not possibly know it had been him in her chamber. Yet something had triggered Georgiana's brusque withdrawal from his company, and now Samarra attacked him with cold, deadly aim. Her detached demeanor frightened him more than her hysteria would have, but he treated her as though she were an hysteric, shaking her roughly, then slapping her cheek hard.

She emitted a wail that was more a keening than a scream, and she collapsed against him, her chest convulsing with deep, wordless sobs. With little effort he lifted her into his arms, taking her to their bed and holding her long into the night until she fell into a light, restless sleep.

And though he comforted her, he found no comfort for himself.

Samarra replayed the scene over and over on the stage of her inner eye. Georgiana's sobs . . . her certainty that the tobacco odors matched . . . Samarra's own near-hysteria . . . the cold, detached way she had seen Clint as a stranger . . . the hard words she had spit at him . . . his bringing her to her senses and comforting her.

In the hard light of day, the very conception of Clint as a suspect seemed ludicrous. Not the warm, considerate, affectionate man she knew . . . no, it just wasn't possible.

But while her heart contradicted every speculation,

her subconscious refused to let go of the fact that Clint had deceived her, that he had yet to come clean.

Several days later, when Samarra passed a tobacco shop on her way to see the seamstress who was making the master suite draperies, Samarra doubled back. Once she was inside the small, fragrant shop, she pondered her sanity. Whatever did she think to accomplish? She stood just inside the door, disoriented, then moved swiftly to a display of pipes when she caught the proprietor's eyes upon her.

A middle-aged man with smiling brown eyes and red lips, he watched her peruse his selection of pipes while he measured tobacco into a pouch for a customer. Having a woman in his shop was rare indeed, and this one seemed unusually ill-at-ease as her hands nervously stroked the bowls and stems of his pipes. When he asked what he could do for her, her eyes refused to meet his, her gaze focusing on the stocked shelves behind him.

"As I passed your shop, I thought perhaps to purchase a new pipe for my husband. The bowl of his cracked recently, you see. But I don't see one that looks like his old one."

The tobacconist regarded her with some bewilderment. "Most men would rather choose their own pipes, madam. They must fit the teeth and lips, much as a pair of shoes must fit the feet. Then there are the matters of style, weight, and material to consider. If 'tis a gift you wish to take him, perhaps a new pouch or a bag of his favorite blend would be appropriate."

"Therein lies another problem, I fear. We have only recently wed, and I have no knowledge of which blend he prefers." She half turned to leave, wanting desperately to be out in the fresh air again, to remain blissfully ignorant. But something in her demanded that she stay.

A large, brown-stained palm rose before her, deciding her course. "Ah, but that problem I can solve—that is, if your husband is one of my regulars." The proprietor retrieved a small wooden box from beneath the counter. "His name?"

"Clint Holbrooke," she supplied.

The tobacconist raised questioning eyes to Samarra, his winged brows tilting higher at the ends. *"You?* You are the lieutenant colonel's new wife?"

"Pardon?" Her look of confusion equaled his.

He smiled. "Lieutenant Colonel Holbrooke is one of my best customers." His fingers snapped the box lid closed. "I do not even have to look at his card. Knows his tobaccos well, Clint does, knows what he likes, too. Many don't, you know." He had turned his back to her, his hands searching among the cloth bags of tobacco on the shelves, removing three of them and busying himself with measuring the cured, shredded leaves into a large crock and mixing them with his hands. "I had heard he'd taken a wife. Matter of fact, he was the one told me, when he came in here last week. Funny, he didn't mention needing a new pipe."

A mist had gathered in her eyes as he talked, as she tried to assimilate the information he had so inadvertently given her. Lieutenant Colonel? An officer of the British Army? No . . . it wasn't possible.

"That will be twenty shillings, three pence, Mrs. Holbrooke."

Mechanically she counted out the coins from her reticule, murmured her thanks, and accepted the bag from the tobacconist. As she left the shop, her heart fervently denied that which appeared true. There must be some mistake, another Clint Holbrooke, perhaps. Her feet moving without direction, her head reeling, her hands clutching the bag of tobacco to her chest, she wandered blindly past a group of boys tossing quoits,

327

past a parked buckboard loaded with pale gold butternut squash and bright orange pumpkins, past a knot of old men arguing loudly. Only one of her senses was consciously operable: her sense of smell. The aroma of the blend the tobacconist had prepared exactly matched that Clint smoked.

She had seated herself in the common room of a tavern and ordered tea and crumpets before she realized what she had done. Two words rolled back and forth inside her head: *lieutenant colonel . . . lieutenant colonel.* No small wonder Clint knew Governor Dinwiddie so well! What was their scheme? What kind of political web of deceit had she been caught in? What kind of pawn had she allowed them to make of her? However had she allowed herself to fall so hopelessly in love with a man who would deceive her, use her? What had he thought to do with her once the game was up?

Never had she felt so hurt, so foolish, so angry, but it was the cold, hard edge of her anger which controlled her actions. Clint would answer for this, Clint and the governor both. She would have the truth, and she would have it now.

Leaving the teacup half full and the crumpets untouched, she stalked out of the tavern, her purposeful strides taking her down Duke of Gloucester Street to the Palace Green.

"You must leave immediately for Baltimore, Clint."

"But, Governor—"

"She can manage without you for a few days. The detachment awaits your leadership. I must have that corpse, and who better to collect it than a possible relative? Besides, MacKenzie Reed is in Philadelphia. I need you. You can change into your uniform at the barracks, take whatever you need from general supply."

Clint did not want to leave Williamsburg—not now.

328

His mind sought a valid argument. "But who will protect my wife if I am not there?"

"You were and still are the one in danger, Clint, not Samarra. By leaving town you may very well draw the culprit out of Williamsburg as well, and thus away from your wife."

"What am I to tell Samarra?"

"Nothing. Leave the explanations to me."

A knock sounded at the door, and Morris opened it slightly, his body filling the gap. He motioned to the governor, whispering to him when he had joined the lieutenant at the door. "Excuse me, sir, but Mrs. Holbrooke is in the anteroom. She demands to see you immediately."

"Hold her there for another few minutes."

When the door had closed behind the young officer, Dinwiddie returned his attention to Clint. "Go now, out the rear door. Here are your papers." He handed over a tied packet. "And Clint, be careful!"

"I will, sir. Please—tell Samarra I love her." His voice carried a fatalistic quality.

"You'll be home within a week, Holbrooke."

"And to which home will I be returning, sir?"

Clint had departed before Dinwiddie could respond.

Though they grew shorter, the pre-winter days dragged by for Samarra. She tried to keep her mind occupied with her work, but with the passing of the October Court, her orders slackened and far too often she found her hands idle. At least twice each day she journeyed upstairs to take food and water to Clementine and to check on the progress of the kittens, but she refused to linger in the rooms Clint had so recently inhabited. The memories those rooms evoked hurt too much.

Still, she thought of him far more often than she intended to. She was defenseless against the stark, graphic memories . . . of his kiss, his touch, his mellow voice . . . which caught at her heart and threatened to be her undoing.

Samarra tried to maintain her anger at Clint, but she found her outrage leveled at the governor instead. That one commanded her husband's actions; the responsibility lay in his hands, not Clint's.

Dinwiddie had told her little enough of what was going on. He confirmed that Clint worked for him, but beyond that she knew only that he had been sent on some sort of secret mission and was to be gone for at least a week. Dinwiddie would tell her nothing of any substance, despite her barrage of questions. As she'd left his office, however, he had warned her to be careful. "There are those, as you well know, who would see your husband crippled or dead. We are on the verge of apprehending the prime suspect in the case Clint has been investigating for some time. I wish I could assure you that you are not in any danger from that quarter, but I can't. However, I do not think the danger is as great as it once was."

"Is that why you set Clint up in my house? Is that why he married me? Why was I—am I in danger? I don't understand."

"Clint's initial visit to your shop was part of the investigation. His being injured there and asking you to allow him to stay were none of my doing. Nor was his falling in love with you—and I assure you, my dear, that love you he does. As for your other question . . . please, trust my judgment on this, Mrs. Holbrooke. Ignorance on your part is for the best, at present. Later, when all this is over, Clint will tell you everything."

"But shouldn't I know something more now? How

can I protect myself and my family if you won't give me some idea of what is going on?"

"I don't think you are the target, Mrs. Holbrooke, but I suggest that you not wander around town by yourself, even in the daytime. Do send me word should anything out of the ordinary occur, and I will contact you should I hear anything from your husband."

She found a small measure of comfort in his words.

Bit by bit she pieced together the fabric of Clint's deceptions—the fraudulent occupation, the reason for Mac Reed's visit, Clint's reluctance to discuss his acquaintances, the source of his knowledge of Williamsburg's residents and its history. Now she understood that Clint's injury, the watching of the print shop, the slashing of his bed were all tied to a case he was investigating.

What she didn't understand—and this frightened her—was how she herself was involved in this case. The governor had sent Clint to her shop because he'd thought her to be in danger. How could he be so confident that she no longer was?

Chapter Twenty-One

A week passed, and then another.

Samarra received no word from Clint, and neither did the governor. She tried to stay busy, tried not to think about all the things that could have happened to him. She handled the days fairly well, but the nights were almost unbearable.

The workmen finished the renovations in the master suite and she moved into it, taking an inordinate amount of time over several evenings to transfer clothes and personal possessions, and then carefully place the accessories she and Clint had selected for their suite of rooms. Tears stung her eyes when she hung the picture of Diana over the mantel. "Come back to me, Milord Stag," she had whispered to the painting. Then she had turned away, wiping her dripping eyes with the back of her wrist, setting herself at another task in an effort to suppress the pain.

She thought sleeping in a different room would make things easier, but it didn't seem to matter what bed she slept in. Night after night she lay awake, longing for Clint. One night she succumbed to the tears which she had wanted to shed for so long, giving in to deep, heaving sobs. But crying into her pillow earned her nothing more than what she'd known it would: a sore throat and red, swollen eyes. Despite her discomfort afterward, if she'd thought tears would bring Clint home, she'd have cried every night. Instead she prayed for his safe return and, when she was alone, talked to him aloud, as though he could hear her.

As the days passed she grew listless and more easily fatigued. An abrupt, unfavorable change in the weather made her diminishing spirits spiral into a dark, deep chasm of melancholy.

The crisp, vibrant autumn weather Samarra so relished had given way to virtually constant rain. The cold dampness seeped in around the doors and windows to permeate everything—draperies and bedding and chairs and sofas. Even the books in Randolph's extensive library absorbed the damp. Nanna, Jennie, and Samarra kept fires burning on all the hearths in an attempt to warm the sodden air and prevent mold and mildew from setting in. But there was little enough fuel for a fire for Samarra to build in her heart—none other than hope, and her reserve of that commodity dwindled each day as did the woodpile by the shed in the rear yard.

On the morning of the tenth day of Clint's absence, a twelve-year-old boy appeared at the Seldon home claiming to be the new stablehand. When Samarra questioned him, she learned that he'd answered an advertisement Clint had placed in the *Virginia Gazette* and that Clint had subsequently hired him.

"But we don't need a stableboy!" she'd exclaimed, then winced at her thoughtless words when the youth's face fell. "Did he tell you what your duties would be?" she asked with more diplomacy.

"No, ma'am, no more'n the usual. Just told me to

333

come today, it being Saturday. Said something about two horses being delivered today." He dropped his gaze and scuffed the toe of his worn boot against a chipped brick on the stoop.

Samarra had no knowledge of a delivery, but neither had she of this boy, she reminded herself. What else had Clint arranged for without telling her? she wondered.

"Come with me—"

"Peter," he supplied.

"Come with me, Peter. I'll introduce you to Ezekiel, and he can show you around the stable and tackroom. Are you any good at cleaning tack?"

"Oh, yes, ma'am. And currying horses and cleaning stalls."

She smiled at his enthusiasm. No wonder Clint had hired Peter . . . who could resist his charm?

Just as Peter had predicted, a pair of matched bays arrived that day, along with the necessary harnesses, reins, and other tack. Samarra could only surmise that a new carriage would be forthcoming, but when she suggested this to the men from the livery, they merely smiled and told her she would have to wait and see. Zeke, who was naturally reticent, surprised her by taking Peter under his wing, and by the end of the day, the two seemed to be great friends.

That night, as her fingers unconsciously worried the gold band Clint had given her, she conjured an image of him and spoke to it. "You chose well, Clint, when you hired Peter. And when you hired Jennie. Georgiana and I don't know how we ever managed without her. George is wearing her glasses again, and she went to church with me last Sunday. When you come home, I thought we might invite Captain Reed to dinner, make it a foursome. I don't think George will object."

Her intellect chastised her for partaking in these one-sided conversations, but they warmed her in a way nothing else did—except, perhaps, her ever-increasing awareness of the child growing within her.

Fortunately, the queasiness had disappeared almost as suddenly as it had arrived, and though her appetite returned, her lack of rest at night continued to wear her down. From time to time, lethargy vanquished her strength, but she had learned to stop whatever she was doing, close the shop, and rest when she felt this way. The dullness of the pre-winter season allowed her ample time to keep up with her orders.

Samarra's attitude toward the very real likelihood of becoming a mother amazed her. She was certain now that she would indeed give birth sometime in early August. Even the prospect of delivering in the middle of deep summer failed to squelch her enthusiasm. How she would manage to juggle her duties as wife, mother, and printer she did not know, but months lay ahead during which she could make her plans. Mayhap she would take Dr. Hargrove's advice and hire additional help. If she could just manage through the busy spring season, she would have Tom full-time thereafter. Perhaps—and she held this possibility close to her heart—Clint would take an interest in the business and they could work side-by-side. This prospect she found almost as delightful as that of having a baby who would be as much a part of Clint as of herself.

There was that one question, though, to which she refused to give consideration. Somehow, by holding it deep inside, she thought to make it go away, but it had begun to pervade her consciousness and haunt her dreams.

What will you do, Clint, when you come home?

Would he resign his commission, or would he remain

335

forever a victim to the whims of Governor Dinwiddie, leaving her time and time again? And, Lord, when was he ever going to come home this time?

What should have been a relatively simple mission— one for which Clint had initially doubted the governor's rationale—turned into one of more complex, far-reaching proportions.

For starters, Frederick Calvert, the sixth Lord Baltimore and present Governor of Maryland, had balked at Dinwiddie's request for possession of the corpse of one Samuel Holbrooke, who'd been found lying face-down in the mud on the banks of the Patapsco River, his throat slit and his purse stuffed with counterfeit Virginia currency. After several days spent slicing through bureaucracy, Clint finally gained possession of the corpse, having to resort to claiming kinship before Lord Baltimore would release it.

Samuel Holbrooke/Guy Archer had been dead for over a week before Clint arrived. Had it not been for the counterfeit currency, his body would have been buried in an unmarked grave and his existence subsequently forgotten. As it was, Clint feared the body would decompose beyond all possible recognition before he could get it back to Williamsburg for positive identification—assuming they could find someone who had known the miscreant. For insurance, he located an artist of some talent who prepared a charcoal sketch of the dead man's face as he imagined it must have looked in life.

Clint could not recall having seen the man before, yet this man matched the description O'Quinn had given of the man who had thrown the knife. Clint could easily have attributed that fact to coincidence had two other facts not stared him in the face: if Samuel Holbrooke was, indeed, an alias, then it could be taken as a combination of both Samarra's and Clint's names; and this man carried an inordinate amount of counterfeit Virginia currency for one supposedly living in Maryland.

Perhaps the man had left some clue that would tie him to the counterfeiter. While awaiting a decision from Lord Baltimore, Clint and his men combed the docks and the waterfront taverns, dramshops, and brothels, talking to longshoremen and stevedores, tavern wenches and bartenders. One dockworker swore he'd seen the dead man disembark from a coastal packet a month or so before; a serving girl recalled how agitated he'd seemed; a bartender remembered bits and pieces of a bizarre tale of subterfuge and revenge the dead man had told when he was well into his cups.

It was this last testimony which made Clint's blood run cold. From the fragments of information he constructed a synopsis of the derelict's last few months of life. He'd been under the employ of a man in Williamsburg, a man the henchman feared. The now deceased "Holbrooke" had been running from his employer when he'd arrived in Baltimore, apparently because he had, on two separate occasions, failed to achieve his assigned task. Due to his fear, or perhaps his ignorance, the thug had never mentioned his employer's name, but logic dictated he was the same Dinwiddie wanted for counterfeiting, the man who'd laid the nice, neat trail to Samarra's door.

Clint had blessed the delay caused by Lord Baltimore's cantankerousness, for without it he'd have reboarded the coastal packet which had brought him to Baltimore and never carried the investigation any further. But now that he had, now that he believed this dead man had been the one who'd tried twice to murder him, Clint wanted to go home; he needed desperately to know that Samarra was safe. The real menace, the mastermind behind the counterfeiting scheme, was, in all likelihood, back in Williamsburg.

While Clint was in the process of securing passage on another boat, a violent storm swept up Chesapeake Bay from the Atlantic, and Clint feared he might be marooned in Maryland. For three days, the storm spewed its wrath before moving inland. Clint had been gone a fortnight before the boat he had hired finally left Baltimore for Yorktown.

Before, such delays would merely have irritated Clint—but that was before he had a wife to go home to. His yearning for her increased with each passing day, and he discovered that the yearning, the longing encompassed far more than just desiring her body. With every fiber of his body and every filament of his soul, he needed to see her, to hold her close, to hear her say, "I love you, Clint Holbrooke."

It took almost every penny of Whitfield's legitimate cash reserves to outfit Judith, purchase their passage to Williamsburg, and secure rooms for the two of them at Henry Wetherburn's Tavern. But the lack of legal specie was the least of Jarvis Whitfield's concerns . . . his spare satchel bulged with the last of the counterfeit currency he had hired printed in London, and it would serve him for the present.

The considerable weight of so very much paper had prevented him from traveling with all of it. He had, therefore, brought only three small trunks of it with him when he'd returned to Virginia in late June. He'd arranged for shipment of the rest to arrive in various ports at various times to be claimed by men of various names, all of them aliases for himself.

Distributing it had proved easier than he'd originally

anticipated. Maintaining a low profile, he had traveled the colony extensively, collecting his shipments as they arrived, paying for his coach and packet fares, his meals and lodging, and a vast array of items ranging from periwigs to horseflesh with the illegal paper money. He had resold many of these in other towns for coin, thus exchanging facsimile for authentic money without anyone ever becoming wise to his scheme.

The beauty of it all, in Whitfield's estimation, lay in its novel approach. Anyone who might think he'd return to the colony would expect him to resume his role as murderer. Furthermore, it allowed him to exact his pound of flesh without ever showing his face to those few who would recognize him for the cold-blooded murderer and adroit tactician he was. The intent of his master plan had been to bring the colony to its knees financially, thus hurting in one fell swoop those few residing in Virginia against whom he sought revenge. If his scheme crippled others as well, then so be it.

The names of most of his intended victims he knew well: the Cavanaughs and the Raffertys on the frontier, an army officer named Washington, and Robert Dinwiddie, who, as royal governor, had signed the documents which detailed the results of the evidentiary hearing at which the governor had presided. These documents set forth allegations naming Whitfield as the serial murderer of more than a dozen smugglers, as well as affidavits attesting to his attack on Glynna O'Rourke Rafferty. The papers further suggested that he'd been responsible for the deaths of Glynna's parents. All told, the mountain of evidence against him, though the majority of it could not be substantiated, secured for him an appointment with the hangman at Tyburn Tree. Had he not been clever enough to jump ship just off the coast of Cornwall and then defy the somewhat disorganized—and largely disinterested—efforts of the King's men to find him, Whitfield was certain that appointment would have long since befallen him.

There were those, too—most of them nameless entities, since Whitfield had not been allowed to hear their testimony—who had stood witness at the hearing in Williamsburg and against whom Whitfield sought retaliation.

Setting up a colonial printer to take the fall had not occurred to him until after he'd established himself in Williamsburg, but the more he considered this appendix to his strategy, the better he liked it. His twisted heart required a victim he could name, one he could observe from a distance, one in whose destruction he could take sustenance.

Once the seed of his codicil had taken hold, Whitfield had surveyed the several printers in Willaimsburg, using a request for an insignificant printing order as justification for his visits. Discovering a single woman whose father and male protector was not only out of the country but who was a wealthy merchant as well, a woman who was being hounded to sell her business, proved the definitive device of his machinations. Thus he had launched the postscript to his scheme.

Laying the groundwork had been easy: a carefully placed word in the appropriate ears . . . providing Miss Seldon with a large, bogus printing order for which he paid in counterfeit currency . . . a sizable deposit in kind to Randolph Seldon's account with a Scottish factor.

When the fruit of his design became evident, he posted a henchman, in the form of Guy Archer, to watch the print shop and murder Dinwiddie's investigator, thinking to cast further aspersions upon Miss Seldon while prolonging an investigation which was bound to lead eventually to him. Archer had botched the job—twice. But the bungler had been easy to trail, easier still to exterminate.

Determined to thwart the budding romance and hasty marriage of Samarra Seldon to Clint Holbrooke, Whitfield had sought prior acquaintances of the lieutenant colonel—and found the one who could accomplish the destruction he desired. He gazed upon that one now, sitting across from him at the private table in a dark corner of the common room of Wetherburn's establishment, and hoped her performance would not disappoint him.

"When do we call upon the 'second' Mrs. Holbrooke?" Judith asked, her zeal for revenge almost matching that of her employer.

"*You* call upon her tomorrow. There's a place I must visit first, a confirmation I must make before we drop our cog."

He knew Samarra's habits well. The most precipitous time to implement this part of his plan, Whitfield had decided, was immediately after lunch. The old woman who attended Samarra stayed close to the house then, and the apprentice would not show up until well into the afternoon. Gainsaying the appearance of a legitimate customer, Samarra should be alone for the space of several hours. The only hitch Whitfield feared was the unexpected return of her erstwhile husband.

Samarra considered closing the shop during the early afternoon hours on Friday—and would have done so had Eliza Garrett not shown up just before lunch. The rawboned artist had delivered the pages for Clint's book of poetry, and the two women had looked over them together, Samarra oohing and aahing while

341

Eliza sat basking in delight at her employer's unreserved approval.

"I'm . . . amazed," Samarra gushed when she'd put aside the last of the delicately rendered watercolors. "Clint will be so pleased, and his mother is certain to be overjoyed when she receives this gift from him." Wistful memories of similarly thoughtful and uniquely appropriate presents from the object of her heart's desire flitted through her consciousness, and she wiped at the tears in her eyes.

"Won't he be surprised when I have this all bound and ready for him when he comes home?" she asked as much of herself as of Eliza, realizing she could now gift him in kind. But to do so she must hurry, for Clint would surely come home any day now.

She ate but a few bites of her lunch, her heart soaring too high, her head spinning too fast to allow her much of an appetite. When Nanna had delivered a token lecture, as Samarra knew she would, and departed with the luncheon tray, Sam sat down at her desk and perused the watercolors again, searching for the perfect motif to be tooled into the leather cover. She had looked at no more than a half-dozen pages before a customer walked in.

One glance at the pale, almost tiny young woman sitting at the desk convinced Judith that this task would be as easy as Whitfield had said. Easy—and not without an element of amusement to make the effort worthwhile. It had been a long time since Judith had wielded enough power to make another human being squirm, and she relished the opportunity.

Squelching her irritation and mentally chastising herself for not ensuring a free afternoon by locking the door, Samarra reluctantly dragged her attention from the watercolors and muttered a polite if unenthusiastic greeting to a tall, elegantly attired, ravishingly beautiful woman who held her chin in a patronizing way and regarded Samarra with frosty disdain.

Samarra pondered the woman's flinch and the rapid batting of her thick, dark eyelashes when she introduced herself as Samarra Holbrooke, and though the woman quickly recovered her composure, her nostrils flared and her lips curled in derision as her icy blue gaze bore down upon the much shorter and suddenly much intimidated Samarra.

"I had been told Clint had taken another wife, but I had to see you for myself." The words dripped like slowly melting icicles from the woman's thin lips, falling with distinctive plops upon the muddy puddle of Samarra's brain.

The tip of her tongue raked abruptly dry lips as Sam attempted to fathom the woman's meaning. *"Another* wife?" she questioned, her voice carrying the puzzlement evident in her golden brown eyes. "Whatever do you mean?"

"How like him to deceive, more especially in the commission of a crime." Her haughty laughter crashed hollowly against the cymbals clanging in Samarra's brain. "Bigamy is still a crime, is it not?" the woman goaded.

"Bigamy? Are you calling Clint a *bigamist?"* Samarra's whispery voice bespoke a tenuous hold on her disbelief. Her mind had grasped the word "deceive" and refused to let go. She had caught him in two deceptions already. Of how many more was he guilty?

"That is the term generally applied to a man who has two wives."

Judith stood her imperious ground, watching in smirking satisfaction as Samarra stepped backward, her hands clutching the desk chair, her knuckles standing out in stark white testament to her extreme perturbation. If Clint was a bigamist, what did that make her? she wondered fleetingly. But no, it wasn't true.

The sneer on the tall woman's thin lips froze when the smaller, younger woman visibly shook off her perplexity, when the chin which had so recently trembled firmed itself and rose in equal disdain, when suddenly hard, golden eyes flashed sparks of anger.

"You have made a grievous mistake. 'Tis not my husband of whom you speak," Samarra leveled at this mysterious woman.

The slight slump of her shoulders, the almost wistful smile upon her wide mouth implied the unwelcome visitor's capitulation, but her speech negated that attitude.

"You are technically correct, madam. 'Tis not your husband of whom I speak, but of mine own." She extended her hand in a gesture of mock-friendliness, but Samarra ignored it. "Allow me to introduce myself. I am Judith Holbrooke, Clint's wife."

"That's not possible. *I* am Clint's wife, his only wife," Sam argued, forcing into her voice a strength of surety she didn't feel. Her heart pounded in her chest, sending her pulse racing. Her stomach sank.

"I did not think you would believe me," Judith crooned. "Therefore, I came prepared to convince you." She lifted a black satin parasol from her side, slipped a black-lace-gloved hand between the ribs and the shaft, and removed a ribbon-tied packet of parchment sheets, which she casually—too casually, Samarra thought—passed to her.

Sam stilled her jittery fingers as she pulled the frayed end of the ribbon and unfolded the manuscript. The parchment crackled ominously in the tense silence. As she'd suspected, it was a marriage document. She held little curiosity for the contents of the contract, her hands sifting through the pages until her eyes fell upon the signatures. Clint's jumped out at her, and yet . . . yet there was something not quite right about it . . . something about the way the tail of the C stopped short of Clint's usual flourish. Desperately, she wished she had a sample of his autograph with which to make a comparison, but her own marriage document was locked in the safe next door.

"I don't believe this to be valid," Samarra averred. "Anyone can contrive such a story, falsify the necessary papers. I don't know what you want of me, or of Clint, nor do I honestly care. Leave. Please, leave . . . *now.*"

An exasperated sigh hissed through Judith's tight lips. "If you know your *husband* at all, you must know he displays a master's hand at deception. I would be willing to wager you have already discovered more than one misrepresentation of the truth from him."

The sudden panic rising in Samarra's golden eyes expressed the verity of Judith's speculation far more than words ever could have.

"Just as I thought," Judith declared arrogantly.

"Tell me what you want. I have money—"

"Humph! You wound me, my dear. Did you honestly think me so callous?"

"Then why did you come here with your tales?"

"To warn you. To save you from public embarrassment when the truth comes to light—and it will. It always does."

"Has this happened before?" Samarra asked incredulously.

"Yes, I'm sorry to say. On two other occasions."

The flat of Samarra's hand moved without volition to lie upon her stomach, to rest against the life growing within her womb. Over and over, her heart chanted, *This isn't happening. It's not possible* . . . But an inner voice chipped away at her resolve, plying her with its wisdom. *Yes, it is possible. You knew deep down that*

345

something was wrong. He lied about his knowledge of French. He failed to tell you about his military commission. Could he not just as easily have forgotten to tell you about a wife?

"On two other occasions?" she echoed inanely. "Why?"

"Well, for the obvious reason—money. Clint collects women of substance the way some men collect clay pipes, and he disposes of them just as easily, once he has filled his purse. Didn't he ask too many questions, perhaps seem too interested in your worth? Didn't you suspect at some point that he'd gone through your possessions in order to ascertain the degree of your wealth?"

It was a shot in the dark, a conjecture based loosely on what Whitfield guessed to be true, but it hit its mark. Samarra's face blanched a deathly white, and she could not draw breath into her lungs. Judith's image swayed before her, and her jellied knees refused to support her weight any longer.

As she sank to the floor, she thought she heard Judith laugh, a high, heinous laugh that sent chills down her spine.

And then her world went black.

something was wrong. He had about his knowledge of ... He failed to call now about his military ... out to these twenty-four hours how to retain ...

Chapter Twenty-Two

Samarra awoke to a feeling of complete disorientation.

It was the unpredictable cadence of being jostled from side to side that first penetrated her consciousness, and then the sensation—or, more appropriately, the lack of sensation in her hands which next she comprehended. Like the apostle, she looked through a glass darkly, and when she came face to face with reality, her mind screamed the rebellion her voice could not utter.

She lay in the bottom of a coach, her wrists tied behind her, a kerchief tied around her head to hold the gag in place. Despite the piece of linen stuffed unceremoniously into her mouth, Samarra's whimpers reached Judith's ears.

"There, there, my dear," that one gloated from the comfort of the single leather seat. "Don't make it harder on yourself. Just lie still. We'll be there soon. I'm glad you're awake now. Give me someone to talk to. This ride is so boring!" she rambled on.

"We had to do it this way. We had to flush him out, you see, get him out of town and away from his military cohorts. I really can't understand what Whitfield has against Clint, but that's none of my business. I know what *I* have against him, and that's all that matters to me. You see, he spurned me years ago, and I've been wanting to get him back ever since."

This sudden dual revelation shocked Samarra to her toes. *Whitfield! Oh, God, please, no!* her mind railed as that one's list of heinous crimes flooded through her. Captain Reed had said the felon had escaped. Could he—would he have returned to Williamsburg? But it was the other half of the revelation which Judith addressed.

She smiled vacuously at Samarra's wide-eyed stare. "Yes, my dear, I hoodwinked you. Did anyone ever tell you how gullible you are? For a while there, though, you had me thinking my ploy wouldn't work. But all I had to do was keep talking until something finally hit home. Talking for me ain't hard. It's remembering to use proper grammar that's the chore. I was a lady once, a long time ago. Then my family fell on hard times, and I learned to earn a shilling the way that came most naturally—flat on my back. That's how I met Clint."

Judith paused, pulling aside the leather curtain and gazing out onto the bare landscape, into the graying darkness, attempting to absorb the neutrality as a method of counteracting the pain. When she spoke again, her voice was pewter-dull. "He thought he could reform me, shape me into a lady worthy of being called Mrs. Holbrooke, and I led him to believe he could do just that. Maybe if things had been different I really *would* be Mrs. Clint Holbrooke now, instead of a jaded woman whose clients have diminished as my age has increased."

As though to reassure herself of her lingering desirability, Judith removed a small looking glass from her reticule and peered into it critically, moving her chin from side to side and flicking at imagined wrinkles. "And I *would* be his wife if I hadn't almost gotten him killed," she mused from behind the mirror. "Damn fool noddy set us up, he did. Said he needed Clint out of the way for an evening so he could rock some greenhorn at cards. Clint ever play cards with you? No? He's a damn good player—and he can spot a cheat a mile away. Clint played a lot at cards then. Getting Clint to come to my room early was easy. Keeping him there was easier still."

Her face softened at the memory, and she laid the glass, its purpose now forgotten, upon her lap. But as she resumed her story, her eyes and voice gradually hardened once more.

"I had no idea Rodney wanted Clint dead. I suppose Clint had accused him of cheating, or some such. Anyway, Rod busted into my room, swaggering from an excess of whiskey and self-confidence and waving a horse pistol. Clint's got quick reflexes. He was off of me and out of that bed in a flash, not caring that his pecker dangled in plain sight. They struggled and the gun went off, and I screamed at Rodney that I wouldn't have had no part of his scheme if I'd known he meant to kill Clint. But it wasn't Clint's blood I saw splattered on the wall; it was Rod's. Clint turned the pistol on me, and I expect if he could have gotten off another shot without reloading, I'd a followed Rod to the grave. I tried to tell Clint about the mistake, but he wouldn't listen."

For a while, Judith was silent, the creaking of the coach wheels and the clomp-clomping of the draft horses as they picked their way down the muddy road the only sounds reaching Samarra's ears. Once she thought she heard Judith sniff. Samarra twisted around on the floor, attempting to secure a better view of her captor, but that one held the leather curtain aside again and used it to mask her countenance as she stared out the window.

Somehow, Samarra knew, she had to free herself. Taking advantage of Judith's preoccupation with the landscape, she struggled against the cords cutting into her wrists and felt them give some small measure. Encouraged, she doubled her efforts, but her squirming arrested Judith's attention.

"Freeing your hands will serve no purpose," Judith observed, almost lamentingly. "Though you might overcome me, which is doubtful, you would then have to contend with Whitfield"—she inclined her head toward the front of the coach—"and you would never get away from him—and live to tell about it." The plaintive, anguished cry of a mourning dove pierced the air, and a shudder wracked Judith's buxom frame.

"He didn't tell me it was such a long way to this place," Judith complained. At the questioning lift of one of Samarra's eyebrows, the other woman merely shrugged. "All he told me was that we were taking you someplace isolated, somewhere no one would ever find you. It could be days still before Clint returns, and we can't risk losing our trump card in the meantime."

Samarra could easily believe the place was isolated. Although she had no idea which road Whitfield had taken out of Williamsburg, she knew they'd traveled some distance, and not once since the swaggering coach had roused her to her senses had she heard either horse or wagon pass them.

Judith remained uncharacteristically silent during the last leg of the journey. At long last the coach turned off the road and bounced a short way down a deeply rutted track before the horses were reined to a halt, the sudden stop throwing Sam hard against the front wall of the vehicle. So concerned had she been for her own safety, she had forgotten about that of the child she carried, but the bone-rattling jolt jarred her mother's heart as well as her body, and she gasped behind the gag.

"Don't let on if it hurts," Judith hissed, her blue eyes darting to the door in some trepidation.

The door was jerked open, and Samarra found herself staring up at a tall, slender, handsome man with piercing gray eyes. She pondered the fear this amiable-looking man had instilled in Judith's soul, the fear the mere mention of his name had instilled in her own . . . until his chiseled lips curved upward in a smile that could only be termed sinister. Instead of warming his eyes, the smile chilled them. Her heart wrenched with the slashing memory of the harsh words she'd hurled at Clint, calling him "devil" because he'd planted the idea with his joke about the dimple in his chin—because she had not allowed herself to trust him. If ever she had looked upon the countenance of Satan, she did so now.

"I trust your ride was pleasant," Satan epitomized said, his deep, golden voice hinting at scorn. She watched his nimble fingers work loose the knots at her ankles, and she stifled a sigh when the tether slipped loose. With gentlemanly grace, he grasped her elbow and assisted her from the coach. But when she thought he would remove the bonds from her wrists and the gag from her mouth, he merely pulled her along the muddy track, motioning to Judith to precede them.

"I hope you're up to walking a spell. Damn rain has all but washed out the road. The mill's just a half-mile or so from here." His words and his manner were deceptively solicitous.

The mill . . . was this Ware's Creek Road, then? A tiny seed of apprehension began to grow deep within Samarra. If that was Ware's Creek she'd heard gurgling in the distance, then Whitfield was taking her to the old, deserted mill, a mill that was said to be haunted. No one in his right mind ever visited Ware's Creek Mill on purpose. Judith's words rang in her ears . . . "someplace isolated . . . somewhere no one would ever find you."

Samarra prayed she was wrong.

They left the road and headed down a weed-encroached trail barely wide enough for two people to pass. Rain-soaked pine saplings slapped at her free elbow, showering her left side with cold droplets until her bodice and a good portion of her skirt were drenched. The dampness seeped through her thin slippers, and the hems of her skirt and petticoats were soon waterlogged. *Lord, let this mill be solid and dry,* she prayed, but when they came to a clearing, when she looked up from picking her way down the muddy path and spied the mill, her heart plunged into the nether regions of her abdomen.

Scudding clouds dispersed the feeble rays of the wintery mid-afternoon sun into a silvery pale halo of light which cloistered itself behind the dilapidated wooden structure that had once housed a thriving business. They'd come in from the waterwheel side; the swollen waters of Ware's Creek rushed down the old wooden flume and fell in a crystal plummet onto the cracked and broken paddles of the wheel, forcing it into a creeky, slow-moving spin. Samarra fixed her gaze upon the waterwheel, dragging her eyes away only when they were so close to the board-and-batten-walled building that its corner obscured her view of the millrace and the wheel.

The dusty interior smelled of vermin and fermented grain. Samarra fought the bile rising in her throat as the noxious odors filled her nostrils and pinched her glands. Judith's face had turned a sickly shade of green, and she dug in her reticule for a perfumed handkerchief, which she held delicately to her nose.

"Good heavens above, Whitfield!" that one screeched. "Could you not have found a more suitable hideout?"

"Suitable? You mean more comfortable? Less airish? I never promised you luxury, my dear." His left hand continued to hold Samarra's elbow tightly, but he gestured broadly with his right arm, drawing their attention to the large, open, unadorned space—and to the gaping holes in the roof through which gray light filtered down to illuminate that space. "I cannot imagine a hideout more suitable than this one, more especially since it carries the stigma of housing a ghost."

His laughter, high and shrill, echoed eerily in the three-story structure. Samarra stood stock-still, refusing to let him know how very much she trembled inside. He stood still for a moment, too, his pale gray eyes surveying the corn and wheat mills, the receiving hoppers, and the toll box occupying the ground floor. "Come, Little Miss Printer," he sneered, tugging again at her elbow. "Let me show you to the guest chamber I have prepared for you."

He dragged Samarra to a ladder built into the back wall, then moved around behind her. She breathed easier when she felt the tight cords fall away from her wrists. But when she would have massaged the chafed skin, she felt the point of his knife pricking the skin on the back of her neck.

"Climb, madam!" he barked.

Upward she went, her sodden skirts and mud-slick soles impeding her progress. Whitfield was right behind her, but he could not hold his knife on her and maneuver the widely spaced rungs at the same time. If ever she would have an opportunity to best him, it was now. Pretending to slip, Samarra kicked back with her

353

right heel, landing her jab squarely on target. Her heart thrilled at the deep, guttural sound of his groan, but she'd underestimated Whitfield's stamina.

Instead of crumpling to the floor, as she'd anticipated, he remained on the ladder, preventing her descent. She twisted around, witnessed his pain in the pasty pallor of his complexion and the deep pleats on his brow. His torso was bent almost double, and his right hand clutched his groin, but his left held firmly to the pole supporting the ladder.

She kicked out again . . . one, two, three times, catching his averted jaw with the flat of her foot this time. The final thrust propelled him off the ladder and landed him in a heap upon the planked floor. Quickly she climbed down, leaping from the second rung to alight just on the other side of his bent-kneed form. She landed flat-footed and felt the jolt of her folly ricochet off her bones all the way to her neck. Shifting her weight to the balls of her feet as quickly as her body would allow it, she was poised for flight when Whitfield's long, lean fingers closed around her ankle, and he yanked her to the floor.

"Damn you, bitch!" he ground out through clenched teeth. "You'll pay for this."

Undaunted, Samarra struggled against his steel-like grip, her efforts dragging both of them a few inches before Judith's slippered feet planted themselves at her head.

"Did you forget about little ole me?" she trilled, her toe tapping against the planked floor.

Later, when the silvery dust of moonbeams sifted down through the holes in the roof, Judith no longer trilled; she screeched.

"How can you be so confounded complacent?" she demanded of Samarra.

"What good can come of your screams?" Samarra returned, her own voice low but pierced with a tinge of exasperation.

"Maybe someone will hear me."

"This mill is well off the main road," Samarra, careful to keep her voice even, reminded her co-prisoner. "Even if someone should happen to come by this late, which is doubtful, and even if that someone should happen to hear you, he'd think it was nothing more than the wail of the ghosts which supposedly haunt this mill. Your infernal screeching is preying on my already overwrought nerves and cannot possibly be calming to your own."

The two women sat with their backs against one of the long wooden chutes set into the floor to hang suspended from the ground-level ceiling below them. A length of hemp encompassed their waistlines; additional rope had been employed in similar fashion to secure their wrists on either side of the chute so that they were bound to each other, facing opposite directions, the chute between them.

"Why did he do this to me?" Judith whimpered. "I helped him, damn it! He could never have lured you out of that shop without me. I was the bait."

"And that is the gist of it."

"What are you talking about?" Judith snapped.

"You were the bait. Does a fisherman have further need of a worm once he has caught his fish?"

A short pause ensued, then Judith said matter-of-factly, "He raped me, you know." The implications, both of Whitfield's heinous act and Judith's attitude toward it, were frightening.

Samarra nodded, then realized Judith couldn't see the gesture. "Yes, I know. At least, I thought so," she whispered, her voice catching in her throat as she wiggled her swollen jaw. Whitfield had taken his pleasure with her as well, though blessedly, only with his fists.

"He beat me, and then he raped me, and then he tied me up over here with you. Oh, God!" she moaned. "What are we going to do?"

"I don't know. Invoke the spirits of this place to assist us, perhaps."

"The spirits of this place?" Judith's voice rose hysterically. "Please tell me it's all a hoax. You don't honestly believe it, do you?"

Samarra shrugged. "The story behind it is very sweet."

"Tell me," Judith begged. "Tell me a sweet bedtime story." She sounded like a forlorn child.

"It's just another tale of star-crossed lovers. The miller had a lovely, fair-haired daughter who was in love with her father's apprentice."

"But the father didn't approve," Judith supplied, her voice calmer now.

"Correct. The daughter would wait until her father had gone to sleep, then she would come up here, stand on the balcony over the wheel, and flash a silver coin in the moonlight as a signal to her lover. The young man, waiting on the other side of the stream, would flash a coin in acknowledgment, then cross the stream to the wheel. There were living quarters then that adjoined the mill on the opposite side from the wheel, so if the lover came in through the front door, he risked rousing the father."

"Then how did he get up here?"

"The maid was a clever girl. She wedged a piece of timber between the hub and the mill wall to lock the wheel. Once the nave ceased turning, the lover would climb up the wheel onto the balcony."

"Sounds like Romeo and Juliet," Judith said wistfully. "How can this be a ghost story?"

"Because one night the young man was standing very

356

close to the balcony when the wedge slipped from its place, unlocking the massive wheel. The man's weight caused the wheel to turn very quickly. The maiden, in her terror, leaned over the balcony and reached for her lover. She was pulled over the railing and into the wheel with him, and they were never seen again."

"And it's their ghosts that haunt this place?"

"So the story goes."

"I guess you could say Clint and I were star-crossed lovers." Judith gasped. "Oh, I'm sorry. I forget you're married to him."

"I may be naive, Judith, but not so innocent that I thought him a virgin when I married him." *I just never thought to meet one of his former lovers,* she mentally added. "I admit I don't know him well. We haven't known each other very long, you understand. Tell me what you know about him."

"I've known a lot of men," Judith candidly admitted, "but none quite like Clint Holbrooke. How anyone who had a mother like his could turn out to be so warm and considerate, so generous and thoughtful . . ." She let the statement hang, as though she did not know how to proceed.

"A mother like his?" Samarra said quietly, wanting desperately to know, yet wishing she didn't have to ask. Clint should have told her himself.

"Hasn't he told you? That's right . . . he never talks about her unless he's drunk—very drunk. Clint's father died when he was only knee-high and left his mother nearly destitute. She dragged them all over England, from pillar to post, as they say, sponging off whatever relatives she could find to take them in and support them for a spell. Clint never had a place to call home. If that man ever needed anything, it was a woman to love him—and a real home."

Samarra let her heart digest this bit of information,

357

then asked in as casual a voice as she could manage, "If Clint wanted to put down roots, why did he enlist in the army?"

"Oh, he had no choice . . . not really. Not after his mother died. He was but fourteen, I think, but even then he was a man. Clint's not the kind to mooch off of someone else, and, well, I suppose it came down to a choice between land and sea. His father was a ship's captain, and maybe his being lost at sea soured Clint on that idea. I hope you realize that all those things I said about him in your shop this afternoon were lies, and I'm sorry now I told them. Damnation, it's getting colder by the minute! We'll freeze to death, if we don't starve first."

Samarra ignored Judith's abrupt change of subject. "Why were you so certain I'd believe your lies?"

"Because I know Clint. He's a tight-lipped fellow if ever there was one, clings to his privacy. I wouldn't know the tidbits I do if he hadn't been such good friends with a flask when I knew him. But if he married you, Samarra, he must think you are the woman who can give him what his mother could not. He's a good man at heart. I hope you don't disappoint him."

"I won't—that is, if we get out of here alive."

"Oh, you don't have to worry much about that, not for a while, anyway. *You're* the bait now. *I'm* the one who's dispensable."

"For the moment, we have to concentrate on survival," Samarra said pragmatically. "We can't do anything about food, but I think I've figured out a way to be warmer."

"You have?" Hope swelled in Judith's voice.

"It's going to be tricky, but I have a blind sister who has taught me that anything is possible. Can you see those empty flour sacks near the wall?"

"Not now, but I remember noticing them earlier."

"Good. Your legs are several inches longer than mine. Try to reach them with your foot."

Judith stretched her near leg as far as she could. "I can feel them with my toe, but I can't get my foot under one of them."

"We're going to slide down as far as we can. Ready?"

In unison they inched their spines down the wooden chute, but Samarra stopped when Judith swore softly.

"What's wrong?"

"This damned rope is caught."

"Try again."

Several minutes passed, the quiet punctuated from time to time by Judith's grunts.

"There!" that one exclaimed. "I have one! What should I do with it?"

"Pick it up with your foot and bring it to your lap."

Judith repeated the process several more times until her lap was piled with dusty, smelly, rough-textured flour sacks. "What do I do now?"

"You're going to sit up, but I'm not. Then try to get your fingers on one and pass it to me."

By the time they had managed to divide the sacks between them, their breathing was labored and their wrists were bleeding where the rope had cut them as they'd maneuvered the sacks. Despite their mutual discomfort, smiles of satisfaction touched their lips.

"We did it!"

"Yes, Judith, we did."

"Samarra—" Judith began tentatively, then more firmly, "Can you ever forgive me?"

"I think I can," Samarra responded honestly. "You see, Judith, I have to forgive myself first."

"Forgive yourself?"

"For not trusting Clint. For not trusting in his love. Can you understand that?"

"Yes. If you'd trusted him, you wouldn't have

359

believed me—and we wouldn't be in this pickle. How are we ever going to get out of it?"

"I'll think of something," Samarra said with much more confidence than she felt. "Let's try to get some rest."

At Samarra's instruction, they folded their legs and sat Indian-fashion, using their chins to spread some of the sacks over their bosoms and leaving some on their laps. As makeshift blankets, the sacks were sadly lacking in comfort, but they did provide a measure of warmth. Neither of them knew when she went to sleep, but sleep they did . . .

. . . Until the wailing wind and the pelting rain woke them.

Chapter Twenty-Three

Home!

Clint's heart sang the word over and over again.

The pale gray light shot through with red streaks marked the morning of the seventeenth day since Clint had left Williamsburg. He'd counted every one of them, counted the hours and even the minutes these last three days. A gusty norther had whisked him home, and if that blustery wind begot more foul weather, then so be it . . . Clint wasn't going anywhere again—not for a long time.

The fallow time on the journey home had provided many hours for reflection, and Clint had willingly participated in his soul's bent toward that dominion. By the time he stepped off the packet in Yorktown and mounted his horse, his purpose was as set and unyielding as the thunder bellowing its wrath and the hard, pelting rain the clouds hurled down upon him, as unyielding as the stretch of road which led to home.

And home was where he was going first. His men would deliver both the corpse and Clint's dispatch to the governor, and Clint would see him later in the day. But first, he wanted—nay, *had* to see Samarra. This need he had for her, for her whole person, amazed him still.

It was well past dawn when Clint dismounted and flipped the reins over the hitching post in front of the print shop, expecting to find his wife at work there. When no one answered his knock, he used his key to let himself in. Clementine bounded down the stairs and mewed plaintively as she rubbed against his boot. Absently, Clint picked her up and ruffled the fur behind her ears, his eyes searching the workroom but seeing no evidence that Samarra had been there that morning. And then he remembered that it was Saturday. The cat's meows became louder, demanding his attention.

"All right, little mama. I know you want me to see your babies, but I have to see Sam first. I'll be back," he promised, putting the feline on the floor and hurrying next door.

The house seemed unusually quiet. Clint found the kitchen empty, and there had been no food prepared recently. Even the coffeepot was empty. The fire, burning low on the hearth, further attested to the indisputable fact that something out of the ordinary had happened.

Nanna! It had to be Nanna. Was she sick—or, perhaps . . .

At that moment, the well-loved servant padded into the kitchen from the front hall, her chin pleated in multiple folds, so low did she carry it. Her rheumatism must be bothering her again, he thought, and no wonder, with the weather so cold and damp.

"Nanna!" he almost shouted, relief flooding through him. "Thank God!"

Her chin jerked up and her watery, aged eyes snapped with anger. "It's about time ye came home, Mr. Holbrooke. Or should I call ye Lieutenant Colonel Holbrooke?"

"Nanna, I can explain—"

362

"I can na ken why ye would do such a thing t' Miss Samarra. Lyin' t' her, deceivin' us all. But there be nae time now t' worry about that."

The slump of her shoulders and the dejected edge to her annoyance caught at his heart, but he refused to allow her disappointment in him to deter him from seeing Samarra. Damn, if *Nanna* was this upset—

Long, purposeful strides took him swiftly across the kitchen.

"Ye will na find her in this house."

Her words stopped him cold. "Oh, God, Nanna, she didn't leave me—"

"Nae of her own free will." Tears welled up in her eyes and spilled down her cheeks.

Near panic, Clint recrossed the room, grasped Nanna by the shoulders, and shook her none too gently. "Tell me she's not dead! For God's sake, woman, tell me!"

Nanna's head lolled from side to side, but when she tried to speak, the words came out in a loose-lipped blubber.

"Where is she? What's happened to her?"

"We aren't certain."

Clint dropped his hands and spun around at the sound of the familiar masculine voice. "Mac! What are you doing here?"

Georgiana, who was wearing her dark glasses, stood beside the captain. "Thank God you're home, Clint. We need you to help us find Sam."

"Find her? Tell me what happened!"

MacKenzie Reed regarded his friend with a look that combined kindness and consolation, a look which frightened Clint to his core. "Come, Clint, and sit down. Nanna, do you think you could make us some coffee? I'll tend the fire, and then we'll talk."

His years of military training had taught him self-discipline, but it was all Clint could do to sit still and stay quiet until Mac joined him at the table. Fighting to keep his wits about him, he sat with his elbows on the table, his fingers laced under his chin, his muscles tensed and his nerves taut. He watched Mac bring in water and wood, watched Nanna hang a kettle on the hook dangling in the fireplace, listened to the grating noise the grinder made as Nanna turned the crank, and all the while his heart threatened to explode in his chest.

Mac Reed believed in coming straight to the point. "Samarra disappeared yesterday shortly after noon."

"Disappeared? What do you mean?"

"Be quiet, Clint, and I'll tell you all we know, which isn't much, I'm sorry to say. One of the neighbors, a woman who lives across the street, saw a coach parked in front of the print shop early in the afternoon. After a while the driver dismounted and went into the shop. A short time later the coach pulled away. The neighbor sat at her window all afternoon, knitting. She says no one else came or went until Tom arrived. When he couldn't find Samarra, he came over here looking for her. Nanna hadn't seen her since noon; she sent Tom to the constable's office, and when Jeremiah Woodcock was told who you are, he sent for me."

"You think she was abducted?"

"It looks that way."

"Why didn't this neighbor do something sooner?"

"She had no reason to suspect foul play because the coach had blocked her view of the front door. Woodcock and I have knocked on every door within sight of this place, and she's the only one who saw anything, Clint. It's all a mystery to us. There's been no ransom note, no demands made, nothing. We haven't a clue."

Nanna set steaming cups of coffee in front of them,

then settled herself in a chair by the fireplace.

"I know who has her, but I can't imagine where he took her," Clint said quietly, but the calm timbre of his voice didn't fool Mac Reed. He'd seen that hard, temple-pulsing expression on Clint's face before. Mac waited for Clint to explain and was taken aback by his superior's next words. "And, damn it, it's all my fault! He doesn't want Samarra, he wants me. What did you learn in Philadelphia, Mac? Did you locate Judith?"

"No . . . why do you ask?"

"You talked to no one who'd seen her recently?" Clint prodded.

"She's still working in a bawdy house, if that's what you mean, but she's left Philadelphia."

"When, Mac? When did she leave?" His question bespoke an urgency Mac couldn't comprehend.

"Apparently the same week I arrived there. Why? What does Judith have to do with Samarra's disappearance? You don't think she—"

"Why did she leave?"

"She told one of her friends that some man had offered her a bigger share of the profits, and she supposedly left town with him."

"Did you get a description of him? Tall, well groomed, gentlemanly type?"

Mac nodded uncertainly, then froze as realization struck him head-on. "Jake White? You think he and Judith came back here and kidnapped Samarra? For what motive?"

Clint's shoulders moved slightly, and he mumbled, "I should have killed Judith when I had the chance." He fixed his gaze upon the flickering flames on the hearth while he sipped his coffee. Mac watched his friend closely, watched the invisible cogs turn behind Clint's blank expression.

"Come on, Mac," Clint ordered, standing abruptly

and donning his tricorne. "We have to get that sketch back."

Although Mac had no idea what sketch Clint referred to, he followed him without question. If anyone could solve this puzzle, Clint Holbrooke could.

Mercifully, Whitfield returned to the mill around mid-morning, bearing a loaf of bread, a wedge of cheese, and two blankets. He untied Judith first and followed her outside while she performed her ablutions. When she had eaten half the bread and cheese under his watchful eye, he retied her and repeated the same procedure with Samarra.

With the exception of barking a few orders, he said nothing, so that when he left them tied together again on the second floor, they had no idea of his intentions.

"At least I'm warm now, and my belly's full and my bladder's empty," Judith remarked when they were alone, "but there's no telling how long it'll be before he comes back."

Such crude language would have elicited a reprimand from Samarra a few days before, but now she accepted it the same way she had learned to accept Judith. They might never be friends, but for the time being, they were victimized partners, and as such, they had to pull together in order to survive.

"Do you have a plan yet?" Judith asked after a while.

"No . . . any ideas?"

"You're the smart one."

"Intelligence and experience are different. I have no experience to fall back on."

"And you think I do?" Judith asked testily.

"Don't go sour on me, Judith. Our lives are at stake here."

"I'm sorry. I'm just so damned miserable—and scared."

"So am I."

The temperature was dropping rapidly, and by noon the rain had turned to sleet. When the first tiny shards of ice struck the wood-shingled roof and fell through the gaping holes to hit the floor above them, Judith began to cry.

"Let's try to free our hands again," Samarra suggested, grasping at the only viable plan. "My right hand, your left."

Whitfield had wrapped the hemp cord in a tight figure-eight around their wrists, and it soon became quite clear that they would never get loose. Nonetheless they worked at freeing the opposite hands, but to no avail. With each attempt they drew the knots even tighter.

Judith sobbed louder.

"Please," Samarra begged earnestly, "save your strength. You may need it later. We'll rest for a space, then try again."

By late afternoon their wrists had been chafed to a bloody pulp from their efforts, and they had given up hope of escaping before Whitfield returned.

"Whatever I tell you to do, Judith, just do it . . . don't ask questions."

"What is it you want me to do?" Judith asked meekly.

"I don't know yet. But when he comes back, he'll have to untie us again, and then we'll make our move."

"Are you sure that's smart?"

"He's going to kill us both anyway, right? I, for one, would rather go out fighting."

"*Sh-h-h!* I think I hear something."

Samarra listened intently, but all she could hear were the wailing song of the wind, the metallic melody of the sleet, and the steady thrum of her heart. And then she heard it—a low soughing that came from within the mill itself. A cold draft swooped by her, and she thought she felt the swish of silk upon her cheek, thought she caught a whiff of rosewater upon the air. She blinked in confusion, searched the lead-dark space for some clue, felt Judith's fingers reach back and lace together with hers.

The balcony door flew open, admitting a blast of cold air and exposing the slowly turning waterwheel to Samarra's view. She shivered violently and blamed the sensation on the frigid wind, cursed it for blowing the door open.

Just as swiftly as it had opened, it closed, slamming shut against the jamb, rattling the aged hinges.

"Was that the ghost, do you think?" Judith whispered, her fingers squeezing Samarra's.

"Just the wind, Judith," Samarra answered without conviction, adding for good measure, "coming down through the roof and the shaft. Just nature's way of preserving us for that demon Whitfield."

As though her words had conjured him, Jarvis Whitfield burst through the door downstairs. They could hear him talking, but the moaning wind obliterated the words. Several minutes passed before something large and heavy yet soft plunked against the floor, something that wiggled and squirmed and wimpered. Samarra strained her eyes to see through the thick, dark shadows swathing the second level, to see what menace Whitfield had brought to torment them with.

He came back up the ladder then, holding a candle high above his head. A shaft of pale yellow light fell upon golden hair and glinted off a piece of dark blue glass.

Samarra screamed.

"Shut up, bitch!" he bellowed. "I thought you'd be pleased to have company besides Judith. You can imagine my surprise," he sneered, "when I knocked upon the front door of your house and thought you were the one standing there." He gathered Georgiana's hair at her nape, jerked her to her feet, and pushed her toward Samarra. "I'd be careful where I walked if I were you, blind girl," he taunted. "You might step into nothingness and fall to your death. Go on over there and sit down by your sister, and I'll be back in a while to see to your comforts."

As soon as he had descended the ladder, Samarra hissed, "Georgiana! Over here."

"Oh, Sam! I'm so scared!"

"I was, until you got here. Trust me, Georgiana, and do what I tell you to. You're going to get us out of here, but we have to work quickly and quietly. Are you ready?"

"Yes." The word came out breathily.

"Feel along my arm. My wrist is tied to Judith's."

"Who's Judith?"

"I am."

Samarra almost laughed at the ludicrous response from the woman behind her. "I'll explain later. Don't ask questions. Do you feel the rope?"

"Yes."

"Good. Now, break your glasses."

"Sam!"

"Do it, George. We've pulled these knots so tight you'd never get them untied."

The barest hint of a sniffle accompanied the shattering of the glass, but Samarra refused to allow entrance to the conflicting emotions surging within her. This was a time for logic, for action—not for feeling.

"Now," she instructed quietly but firmly, "use one of

369

the shards to cut through the ropes. Be careful, don't cut yourself."

"What if I cut you?"

"It wouldn't matter. My wrists are raw anyway. Use your instincts, George . . . they've never failed you before."

"If my wishes make a difference, which I doubt," Judith whined, "I'd rather not have my wrists slashed."

"Hush, Judith! Whitfield's liable to come back any minute. Don't you want to escape?"

"Aye, but I want to live through it. How are we going to get past him?"

"I'll think of something. I got us this far, didn't I?"

The rope fell away, and Georgiana scooted around to the opposite side of the chute to cut the remaining hemp. When their hands were free, Samarra and Judith stood up and wiggled out of the rope which had surrounded their midsections. And suddenly Samarra knew what had to be done.

"You aren't going to like this, Judith, but you promised to do as I said." She heard the woman sigh in resignation. "Sit back down against the chute. And, George, you take my place. I'm going to put the rope back around you, but I'll just loop it."

"You're going to make it look to Whitfield like we're still tied up and you are your blind sister?"

"That's the plan."

Judith surprised her by agreeing. "I like it."

"George, keep your head down so he can't see your eyes, and both of you pray he doesn't remember what we were wearing. Now, for a weapon . . ."

Sam dropped to all fours and crawled around in the dark, her hands feeling for something—anything small enough for her to wield, yet sturdy enough to do some damage. Her hand closed over a broken piece of timber, and she winced as a splinter shot into the soft

370

flesh of her palm. Willing herself to ignore something so trivial, she lifted the board and tested its weight, its flexibility, flailing it through the air as though it were a broadsword.

But she dropped it to her side, turning away from the ladder and crouching again when simultaneously she heard Whitfield's far-flung curses and the pounding of horses' hooves upon the muddy track.

Clint! her heart cried, her tense muscles relaxing as the horses whinnied and booted feet hit the ground. And he had been shrewd enough to bring someone with him. She sank closer to the floor, resting her weight upon her forearms, letting her head drop in utter relief.

Her relief proved short-lived.

Whitfield bounded up the ladder and dashed to the chute. Without the benefit of light, he used his knife to cut the looped ropes, not realizing in his haste that they were no longer tied. "If you try anything, Judith, I'll kill her—and then I'll kill you," he promised.

"But that's not—all right."

He paid her words no heed, instead jerking Georgiana up and dragging her with him to the ladder. George protested loudly, kicking and screaming, until he threatened to drop her to the floor below.

Oh, my God! Samarra thought. *What have I done?* The instant he was gone, she felt her way to the opening and peered down into the dimly lit space below. Her heart rammed into her throat at the sight of Whitfield holding Georgiana in front of him, a knife poised at her throat.

"Put the guns down and back off," he sneered, "or I'll cut her throat wide open."

Samarra ached to know the identities of the men who had come to rescue them, but she dared not lower her head through the opening for fear Whitfield would see her. She dared not place Georgiana's life in further

371

jeopardy. She sat watching, her breath coming in short pants, and she compelled her weary brain to offer her some direction.

The wind whistled around the corner of the mill, its force giving the waterwheel a harder turn, making it speak loudly in protest. *Thank you, kind spirits,* she breathed.

"Give it up, White—or is it Whitfield? We have the place surrounded. You may as well come peacefully."

Samarra recognized the voice as belonging to Captain Reed. Where was Clint? Had he not yet returned home? Or was he there too? She was certain she had heard at least two horses.

"I'm not going anywhere with you," Whitfield argued, pulling the knife tighter against Georgiana's throat. "I can assure you that I have no compunction about killing her." He pushed Georgiana closer to the door, closer to the light of the candle so that the men could ascertain her identity.

Sam snatched at the opportunity, lowering her arm through the opening and pointing in the direction of the waterwheel. *Let one of them see me and understand,* she prayed, scurrying to the balcony door and out onto the rickety balcony. Icy shards of sleet slapped at her hands and stung her cheeks as she wedged the broken timber between the mill wall and the hub, and she silently petitioned the Almighty to let it hold. The wheel stopped turning.

Holding her breath, Samarra waited for one of the men to come around the corner. *I have no coin,* she silently wailed, *nor has fate provided any moonlight.* As was her wont when she was agitated, she worried the golden band upon her finger. And at that moment, as though in answer to her entreaty, the wind blew the clouds from the face of the moon and a shaft of silvery light flooded down from the heavens.

The ring had not left her finger since Clint had placed it there, but she removed it then, holding it up and turning it in the moonlight. Its reflected glitter spooked one of the horses, who reared up, slashing his front paws in the air and whinnying loudly as he pulled against the tied-off reins.

A man calmed the horse, a tall, broad-shouldered man in military uniform and black tricorne. The man turned around then, turned into the moonlight, and Samarra's heart skipped a beat. He had come! She flashed the ring again, slipped it back on her finger when his long strides brought him swiftly to the wheel.

"Be careful!" she whispered, the wind catching her words and tossing them thither and yon. "It's rotten."

Ignoring her warning, Clint jumped onto the wheel. His boot went right through a paddle, snapping it in half. The timber slipped against the hub, and Samarra dropped to her knees, wedging it back and holding it in place as Clint employed more care in climbing the waterwheel. She squeezed her eyes shut, praying for his safety even as she heard another paddle give way.

Suddenly he was standing beside her on the balcony, and she fell into his embrace. For a long moment they held each other tightly, each emptying his heart to the other, words unnecessary.

Then he gently removed himself from her arms and stood back, watching the play of moonbeams upon the strands of her golden hair and thinking how he would always remember, as long as he lived, the way she looked standing on the mill balcony, glowing with moonfire, her golden eyes glittering with the magic of her love. His heart rebelled against breaking the spell, but two lives hung in the balance.

"How did you—is that Georgiana with Whitfield?"

"Yes, Clint, and you have to help her."

"Can you help Judith climb down the wheel?"

"Yes—I think I can. What are you going to do?"

"Save Georgiana from that fiend."

"Don't let him hurt her!"

Clint waited on the balcony while Samarra slipped back inside to get Judith, and though he dared not tarry any longer, still he hesitated to leave Samarra.

"We don't weigh much. We'll be fine. Go!" she insisted.

"Stand by the horses and wait for me—both of you! Promise me you won't come back inside the mill, no matter what happens."

And then he was gone.

Samarra instructed Judith to climb down the opposite side Clint had come up, thus avoiding, she hoped, some of the broken paddles. She helped her over the balcony railing and under the flume, cautioning her to take care with her descent. "Some of the paddles are rotten. Test each one before you put your weight on it."

With each passing minute the moonlight grew more feeble and the sleet more intense, the combination diminishing Samarra's ability to see Judith. At last she heard Judith's feet splash into the cold stream. When a string of healthy curses wafted up from that direction, Samarra knew Judith had made it, but she realized, too, that she had failed to take into account the icy water of the stream. Their feet did not wear the protection of heavy boots, as did Clint's, and without something to dry them and keep them warm, they would surely suffer from frostbite.

"Wait for me. I have to get something."

Intending to retrieve the blankets Whitfield had brought that morning, Samarra dashed back inside. But when she heard Clint's pleas and Whitfield's denials, she forgot her purpose, forgot that she had left Judith standing outside in the frigid weather. By

374

coming back for the blankets, she had broken her promise to Clint. Now that she was inside the mill again, she wasn't leaving until she knew Georgiana and Clint were safe.

She moved prudently to the opening, lying on her stomach to secure a better view. What she witnessed chilled her far more than had exposure to the icy, wintry weather outside.

Clint had slipped down the ladder, thus sandwiching Whitfield between himself and Mac, the two of them effectively closing off both avenues of escape.

"Let her go," Clint demanded.

"When hell freezes over." Whitfield's high, piercing laughter reverberated through the mill.

"It's not her you want, it's me. Release her, Whitfield!"

Though only a single candle lent its faint illumination to the large, open space, Whitfield stood close enough to it for Samarra to discern the near panic on his face, the terror blazing from Georgiana's white-glazed eyes. Demon that he was, Whitfield tightened his hold on George's waistline and pushed the knife deeper with the other. A gasp of horror escaped Sam's throat when a thin stream of blood trickled down her sister's neck.

"You will behold your wife's death first, Holbrooke. Watch her die!"

"Your taste for the macabre sickens me, Whitfield, but this time your scheme is foiled. 'Tis not my wife you hold, but her twin. You will have to kill me before you can get to Samarra."

"You lie, Holbrooke!"

"It's the truth," Samarra declared, descending the ladder to the center rung, putting herself in clear view of that one to whom she spoke.

Whitfield released his hold around Georgiana's

waist to grasp her chin and turn her face upward. At the sight of her white-glazed eyes, his own pale gray orbs acknowledged his mistake.

Clint seized the advantage Samarra's surprise appearance had offered him. He lunged at Whitfield, spinning Georgiana away and into the safety of Mac Reed's arms, but failing to wrest the knife from the felon. Whitfield, quickly recovering his poise, slashed out at Clint, who jumped back, but not fast enough. The knife tip sliced his red wool coat open just above the sash.

Out of the corner of his eye Clint saw Mac heading toward him. "Stay back!" he yelled. "Let me take him."

Whitfield grinned evilly at the damage to the garment, taking succor from the minor victory. He swung the knife again and again at his opponent. Clint successfully dodged each thrust, but each evasion cost him ground, until he found himself pinned between Whitfield and one of the receiving hoppers. Clint grabbed for Whitfield's wrist, caught it, and fell back into the hopper.

Although Samarra could not see Clint's face, she envisioned the tendons in his neck bulging as he strained to keep the knife at bay. Closer and closer the blade came to Clint's neck. A part of her desperately wanted to scream at Mac Reed, to beg him to rescue Clint, but she dared not break her husband's concentration. Another part of her knew Mac would never allow Whitfield to kill Clint, that he would intervene if and when it became necessary.

And that time is now! Samarra wanted to scream at Mac.

As he attempted to propel himself out of the hopper, Clint felt the top of his head strike a crank handle. While his left hand continued to hold Whitfield's wrist just short of destruction, his right hand reached and grasped the crank. He pulled hard on the rusty yet sturdy piece of steel, pulled it loose from its decayed moorings, and swung it in as wide and powerful an arc as his position allowed. The shaft of the crank caught Whitfield's head solidly, striking him just above his left ear.

He must surely be the devil's disciple, Samarra thought, watching in horror as Clint's strength wavered, as the point of the knife plummeted downward. The instant she realized that Clint's blow had knocked Whitfield out cold—and that the fiend's dead weight was the force behind the blade's thrust—Mac Reed rushed from his poised position a few feet away. The captain hurtled himself into Whitfield's trunk, catapulting both of them to the planked floor.

Epilogue

In the wee hours of the morning, the rain started, slow and gentle at first, becoming peppery after a while. Shortly before dawn it completed its metamorphosis, maturing into a full-fledged storm, replete with whistling wind and intermittent flashes of bold lightning. A deafening, sleep-obliterating crash of thunder brought Samarra to full alertness, and she reached instinctively for Clint.

"I'm here, sweetheart," he whispered against her hair.

"I know, Clint, I know," she murmured so low that Clint had to strain to hear her over the cacophony of the midsummer storm. "I think I've finally grown accustomed to sharing my bed with someone else again."

Her admission stirred a jealous envy in him which manifested itself in an immediate stiffening of his frame. Samarra giggled at his reaction.

"Did you never sleep with your mother when you were a child?" she teased.

"No." He dragged the word out, effectively muddying any underlying meaning.

"Don't feel bad. I didn't sleep with mine, either. But

I slept with George. You should have had a brother. Georgiana and I have always shared so much, including a bed when we were small. We used to lie awake at night, talking, until Papa would come in and bellow at us to be quiet and go to sleep."

"Your father bellows? Funny, I can't quite imagine his being gruff."

"Only when he's been pushed too far. And George and I became quite adept at irritating him."

"I can't imagine how," he commented drolly.

Chatting pleasantly, sharing bits and pieces of themselves, came so naturally now. Their prattle continued while they snuggled against each other until, when Clint could take Samarra's wiggling no more, he groaned in frustration, muttering something about his own firsthand knowledge of her adeptness at the art of irritation. The bulk of the baby she carried rested between them, and Clint's palm slipped between them to rest upon her swollen abdomen.

"What name shall we give this babe, my love?" he whispered into the delicate shell of her ear.

"If it's a boy, let's name him after your father."

"Jonathan," he mused aloud. "I like that. Mayhap Jonathan Randolph, for both our fathers. And should we have a daughter?"

"I've always been rather partial to Katherine. That was my mother's name."

"It's settled, then." The tip of his nose nuzzled her neck, eliciting a giggle from her. "Now, for more important matters . . ."

They arose for a late breakfast, long after Nanna and Georgiana had partaken of the fresh bread, butter, and corn gruel Nanna had prepared. "Everything's cold," Samarra lamented, turning a forlorn look upon her husband. "And I must warn you. I'm not much of a cook."

379

Clint shot her a devilish grin as he shook the coffeepot. "I didn't marry you for your culinary skills—or lack thereof. Can you make a decent pot of coffee?"

Samarra matched his grin with a devilish one of her own. "Probably better than you make tea," she quipped.

Clint shot her a look of mock offense. "Now, what's wrong with my tea?"

"Oh, nothing much. It's just bitter from over-steeping."

"So I could use some tutoring in the kitchen. Come over here and tutor me, woman. Show me how to make this darned thing work!" Clint fought with the coffee grinder, into which he had put some fresh-roasted coffee beans. Before Samarra could rescue him, the grinder slipped from his hold, spewing beans all over the highly polished floor. She laughed lightly and bounced clumsily toward him, the merry twinkle of her brown eyes pinning his brooding gaze.

And then, suddenly, she wasn't bouncing toward him anymore. The smooth sole of her slipper set itself too lightly on one of the slick beans. With arms flailing and laughter dissipating, Samarra landed on her backside with a resounding *thump*.

Clint dropped the grinder on the worktable and flew to her side, his arm sliding under her shoulders and lifting her torso off the floor. "Oh, my God, Samarra . . . are you all right?"

The pink tip of her tongue flicked out to moisten her lips, and her eyes rolled back in her head. Her chest rose and fell in quick, jerky movements. "I . . . I'm not sure."

He scooped her nearly limp frame into his arms, rose a bit unsteadily, and whisked her out of the kitchen and into the dark hallway, where he encountered Nanna.

"Send for the doctor," he barked, pushing past the servant and taking the stairs two at a time.

All that day and well into the night, Clint sat by Samarra, holding her hand and crooning soothing words, refusing to leave her side even when Dr. Hargrove ordered him from the room. When the pains of her labor moved into the small of her back, he gently turned her to her side and massaged her lower spine. With a cool, damp cloth he washed the perspiration from her face, and his own pain increased apace with hers. Never had he imagined childbirth could cause so very much pain, and he cursed himself for causing Samarra such agony.

Those who sat in the kitchen, waiting and trying not to worry, talked until their tongues were tired, then sat glumly over forgotten cups of tea.

"'Tis nae the first time a baby came early," Nanna observed for the umpteenth time that day. "We should be thankin' the good Lord for letting those two have this child. 'Tis surely a wonder, considering everything that girl has been through these past months."

The three to whom she spoke—Randolph Seldon, Georgiana, and Mac Reed—nodded slowly in agreement, but offered no comment.

His business in London concluded, and eager to meet his new son-by-marriage, Randolph had returned to Williamsburg in mid-April, which was the earliest the weather and his business would permit. His delight at Samarra's pregnancy and his hearty approval of Clint were tempered by his failure to hire another agent in whom he could wholly place his trust. But there were additional unexpected joys awaiting him when he arrived home, not the least of which was the budding relationship between Georgiana and Mac Reed. When Mac had requested Georgiana's hand in marriage, Randolph gladly relinquished his hold on her, making his own proposal to the army captain. They were to be married in early September—and Mac had accepted a position as Randolph's agent.

Clint, too, had resigned his commission, much to the chagrin of Robert Dinwiddie. In recompense, Clint and Samarra had given the governor and his wife, who admitted to being the poet, the book of poems Eliza Garrett had illustrated and Samarra had bound. Clint had become a willing apprentice—a "printer's devil," he preferred to call himself, forever teasing Samarra about the cleft in his chin—and in a few short months had become quite adept at setting type and operating the press.

Judith had gone to Baltimore, with the intention of starting her life anew. Clint and Samarra had received a missive from her in June, a letter bursting with zest and restored purpose. She had secured a position as a seamstress and hinted at a love interest.

Jarvis Whitfield had, this time, been retained in Williamsburg. Clint and Samarra had stood as witnesses at his trial during May Court, and Clint had insisted on attending Whitfield's hanging a few days later.

Samarra had often marveled that Clint had been able to put together all the pieces of the puzzle and find her and Judith and Georgiana as quickly as he had. It only made sense, he assured her, that one man had masterminded the scheme. The sketch of Guy Archer had led him eventually to another ruffian, who had accompanied Archer to the old mill to meet with a man who fit the description of the counterfeiter. Dinwiddie's other investigator had learned enough about the man to believe he was none other than Jarvis Whitfield, the escaped murderer, returned to Virginia to exact further revenge. Playing out a hunch, Clint and Mac had ridden out Ware's Creek Road, frightfully uncertain of what they might find, neither aware that Whitfield had nabbed Georgiana while they'd gone from tavern to tavern searching out an acquaintance of Whitfield's henchman.

Once Samarra had been apprised of all the details surrounding the investigation, she'd closeted herself in the master suite for two days, opening the door only to Nanna when the servant brought food. Clint had paced Randolph's library, drinking himself into oblivion, then reviving to repeat the punishment as he worried that Samarra was forever lost to him.

But she had merely needed that time to sort through the legion of emotions raging through her, to let the anger and the hurt play themselves out so that she could finally begin to heal.

Georgiana's reaction had taken them all by surprise, for she'd immediately experienced a surge of relief at knowing for a fact it had been Clint who'd stood in her room that night, and not some strange man with cruel intent who might one day return. Clint had gifted her with another pair of dark glasses, and they had proved the catalyst he'd hoped they would, removing Georgiana from her defensive shell once and for all.

As the four occupants of the Seldon kitchen sat in frustrated silence, each reliving in part the events to which Nanna had alluded, a piercing scream brought them abruptly back to the reality of the rain-drenched, windswept night. In unison they leapt from the table and started for the staircase, where they met a haggard-faced Clint on the landing.

"It was a breech birth," he announced in a drained voice tinged with joy and relief. "But Samarra's all right."

"Well, tell us, mon—is it a boy or a girl?" Nanna demanded.

"A boy." Clint beamed.

"Clint, get back in here!" Dr. Hargrove bellowed.

The four huddled around the closed master-chamber door, worrying their lower lips or twisting their hands, as applied to their individual wonts, while they waited again in tense silence. The interval was, blessedly, short in duration.

"And a girl!" Clint reported with undisguised glee when he reopened the door moments later.

"Twins?" Randolph asked in some amazement.

"Twins!" Clint averred before dashing back inside to share with Samarra the wonder, the magic of it all.